SONG

OF THE

SEA

MYA ROBERTS

CRANTHORPE
MILLNER

First published by Cranthorpe Millner Publishers (2022)

ISBN 978-1-80378-051-1 (Paperback)

www.cranthorpemillner.com

Cranthorpe Millner Publishers

I'll sing thee a song
A song of the sea
That flows like my love
To bring thee to me.

As I sing that song
That song of the sea
My heart reaches out
Thy heart touches me.

I follow my star
My bright guiding star
That brings me so near
That takes me so far.

Just bide by the shore
And set thy heart free,
Together we'll follow
The song of the sea.

Anon, Eighteenth Century,
Translated from Guernsey Patois

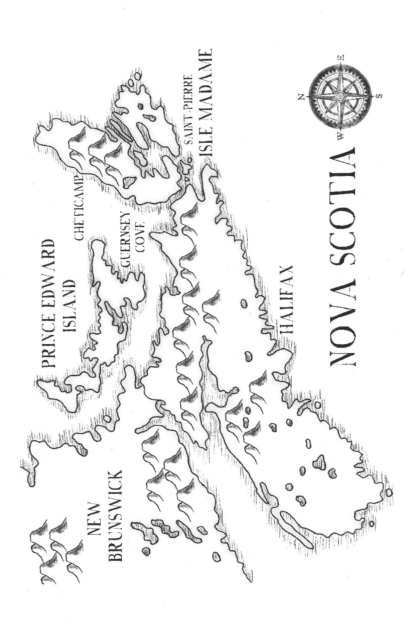

JERSEYMAN ISLAND

ARICHAT

ISLE MADAME

PART ONE

Guernsey

CHAPTER 1

'You're as stubborn as a donkey.'

William's words jolted in time with the motion of the cart as both wheels found every muddy pothole in the narrow lane. He snapped the reins and looked at Elise with all the scorn an older brother can muster. William was an expert at mustering scorn when the mood took him. She supposed that the mood had taken him today for he continued, 'It's madness to cross the ocean in a bouncing wooden tub to be with that husband of yours in the Maritime Provinces. You haven't seen Thomas Galliard for two years, and him a mere fisherman, for goodness sake! Who knows what wolves and savages will eat you when you get there? And why,' he demanded, barely pausing for breath, 'did Thomas have to go all that way to work for those Robin brothers?

1

Jerseymen, to boot. Jerseymen! What's wrong with Guernsey fishing outfits and Channel Island waters? That's what I want to know. And what about Mère and Père? Have you even given a thought to their heartbreak to see you go?'

'Of course I have.' Her face flared at the sting of his words. He was too unkind.

'Your trouble, little sister, is that you're naïve. The rest of the world isn't like small, civilised Guernsey.' His voice softened as though suddenly aware he'd been rather harsh. 'There's a big fierce world out there that you know nothing of, girl.'

Elise opened her mouth, then closed it again. What was the point? William's words prodded at her heart, yet she knew her brother spoke roughly only out of concern for her. Maybe she was too naïve. Should she be staying at home with her family after all? Maybe he was right. Truth be told, she'd had so many misgivings these past weeks that she wasn't sure of her own mind anymore.

The wooden seat bit into her and she clutched at her bonnet and her brother's arm. The clank of metal, the creak of leather and wood, the thump of the horse's hooves – all as one with the bluster of the wind. She gritted her teeth and, as a distraction from her rattling bones, made use of her vantage point above the hedgerows to gaze greedily at the many strips of land neatly laid out. Arable fields lay quiet and ready to produce vegetables, maize, wheat in abundance. A few winter-coated sheep grazed, and some curious cows looked up as the cart trundled past. Here and there stood a thatched cottage with its vegetable plot. As was the custom, some had a fig tree sheltering the tiled pigsty. She loved the taste of figs. Most likely she wouldn't see any of these beloved and familiar things again, and so she tried to imprint the sights, the smells, the tastes of Guernsey, onto her memory. Sadness curled up inside her like a lead ball.

From the tiny hamlet of Le Bellieuse they approached the orchard where Gran'père once grew his cider apples and there, across the field, was Gran'mère's cottage by the stream. A different family lived there now, but in her mind it would always be Gran'mère's cottage. It was there that her grandmother had knitted stockings to sell to Merchant De Sausmarez, and she and Elise would sit beside the furze oven when it was filled with bread or bean-jar. Oh, the smell of that bean-jar and fresh bread.

When at last William reined the horse in by the gate to St Martin's churchyard, he gently straightened his sister's bonnet for her.

'I'll be back after my chores. About half an hour.'

Elise nodded and jumped down onto the pathway. Before waving her brother on his way she promised not to keep him waiting. Heading up the path, she passed lines of granite headstones and wooden crosses to where her grandmother and grandfather lay. Elise had never known her gran'père but dearly loved the grandmother whose given name she bore. She stood before the headstone as she had done so often since dear Gran'mère's death. Tracing her finger over the rough stone she read: *In memory of Helier le Tissier 1690-1741.* Her hand lingered over the newer inscription: *And Elise Rebecca, wife of Helier. Born 1701, left this earth 1774. Together in heaven.*

'Gran'mère,' she said. 'Here I am again.' She swallowed down her tears and added in a bright voice, 'See, I've brought flowers.'

A decorative apothecary jar, originally from her father's shop, stood empty by the headstone. She removed her gloves and filled the jar from the rain butt before kneeling by the grave.

'I've picked some campion and hawk's-beard, then I got this maidenhair by the gate. Isn't it pretty? And look, some celandine, your favourite. And these primroses. I begged William to stop so I could pick them.'

She filled the old jar with the yellows, greens and pinks so loved by her grandmother.

Shivering, she fished her gloves from her pocket and pulled her wool cloak tightly across her chest, glad of the shelter provided by the gorse hedge. The weak March sun had made little effort that day. Although not long after two, the grey surliness of the sky pressed down on her and the rough wind snapped at her cloak.

She took a deep breath. 'You know, don't you Gran'mère, that I sail within the week? And you know I won't be able to visit you anymore?'

She sniffed and wiped the back of her hand across

her nose, then felt shamed by her coarse behaviour. Glancing up she hoped her grandmother hadn't noticed.

Gran'mère had taught her so much. As far back as Elise could remember she had shown her the properties of plants and vraic: seaweed mostly gathered to use as fertiliser. She had learned how and when to pick and harvest them, how to preserve them, and how to prepare them for use in poultices, tinctures and ointments. Gran'mère had possessed a marvellous instinct when it came to healing.

'You have the feel for it too, my child,' she once told her, before whispering, 'but not only in the healing. You have the gift about which we do not speak.'

Gift or curse? Elise shuddered. Gran'mère had been discreet when it came to her talents.

Now Elise knelt by the grave, trying not to pick up grass stains on her grey woollen skirt. Elise told her grandmother not to worry, and she promised to mind all she had taught her, and she would take Gran'mère with her in her heart. How could it be otherwise? 'I'll always try to be as wise as you were and never will tell of our secret,' she whispered.

Nobody shall ever call me witch. This last thought she kept to herself.

Unlike her grandmother, Elise never believed that witches still met at Le Catioroc on Guernsey's west coast. Until the day Gran'mère died she had insisted that rowan twigs be placed above her doorway to protect her against misfortune and evil spirits. And perhaps they had. Yet witchcraft or not, there *had* been witch hunts. One persecution not so very long ago had haunted her grandmother; a woman and her daughters burnt at the stake. One of the daughters gave birth on the pyre and the bailiff (horror of horrors), ordered that the infant be thrown back into the flames to perish with his mother. As a child Elise used to have nightmares in which she and her grandmother faced the searing flames. Elise tried to smother the dark images. It will be good to live in a land free from such wicked things.

She sat back quietly on the tufty grass for a moment, thinking of William's words of censure. 'Gran'mère, do you remember Mère's pet name for me when I was little? She called me "imp". She said it was because I was impatient and impetuous. I'd never make a good marriage, she said, if I didn't learn to be more demure.'

Elise looked up at the grey sky for a few moments. 'She was right, of course. And I did learn to curb my nature. But I kept asking myself if I really wanted to be that sort of lady. Was that such a wicked thing? To be hungry for life? To know what you want and not to falter?'

Her grandmother's kind voice and sweet face seemed so close at that moment. 'Do you recall, Gran'mère,' she whispered, 'when you asked why I'd chosen Thomas, and why I intended to join him across the sea? I said at the time that I wasn't sure, but I've thought long and hard since then. I wouldn't admit this to anyone but you, Gran'mère. I've never considered myself to be courageous, and yet I began to yearn for something beyond these shores – something grander, bigger, more exciting than that which life had waiting for me.

'It was me who persuaded Thomas to try for the New World and it was me who insisted I join him. I want to be a pioneer, an explorer, an adventurer. I want to experience something of this world we live in. Is that wrong of me?

'For better or worse, Thomas has sent for me. I miss him so very much. He's waiting for me to join him, and maybe I'll have a few adventures of my own along the way. There, now I've opened my heart to you. I hope you approve, for I'm not sure I do.'

She got to her feet and adjusted her fur collar then brushed herself down. 'I ought to go,' she said. 'William will be by with the cart and I promised not to keep him waiting. He must get back to town, firstly to the stables then on to his militia training.' She attempted to lighten the mood by adding, 'I know he's my brother and of course I respect and love him, but Gran'mère you should see him with his makeshift rifle as he struts like a turkey-cock to the sergeant's barking.' A giggle escaped her and then became a sob.

Before she left the graveyard she kissed her fingers and touched the gravestone one last time. 'À la perchoine Gran'mère. Goodbye.'

On her way to the gate she stopped for a moment to study the stone menhir figure of La Gran'mère du Chimquière. It had stood on this spot since before history was ever recorded, a pagan goddess, they said. As was the custom she placed a copper coin on the statue's head for luck.

Her thoughts turned to Thomas. Shortly before he'd left for the New World, they'd stood side by side on the shore. She'd linked her arm through his and said, 'Mon chéri, when you hear the song of the sea, you'll know I hear it too. No matter how far away you are, this is something we'll share. This song will be a song of my love for you.'

He'd squeezed her hand and said that he would carry that song in his heart.

***

After William dropped her off in St Peter Port she turned down Rue Berthelot. Her father's shop and their rooms above nudged between the gunsmith's and Mr Tom's house, near the bottom of the hill. The sea, glimpsed from this vantage-point, was a flurry of white tips and she noticed a few ships scurrying for the harbour. The easterly wind whistled up through the gap between the narrow, medieval houses that crowded in on themselves. With the wind came the ordure-laden whiff of the harbour. Today was not as bad as some, especially in the heat of summer; never more so than if the wind was in the north when they emptied the latrine barrels at the Town Hospital. Unconsciously, her nose wrinkled at the memory. *Some things about home I will not miss,* she thought.

Chilled through, she soon arrived at Père's shop. As she had done so many times before, she paused to admire its painted sign: Victor Machon & Son: Apothecary. Her childhood; her security; her known world.

Family legend told of how her paternal grandfather bought this shop with privateer's gold and the profits made from supplying English smugglers with French brandy. Long since gone to his grave, Gran'père Machon was apparently a rogue and, according to Mère, not to be discussed in polite company. But, gentleman or not, he left behind a comfortable pile (along with his tarnished reputation). Elise secretly found the idea of a privateer and smuggler in the family intriguing and rather exiting. Had her own yearning for adventure been inherited from this scapegrace?

The glow from the lamps showed the shop window to its best advantage, as did the display she had been responsible for creating. She looked at the fine specie jars: cobalt blue for poisons, actinic green for syrups. Many were decorated with scrollwork, and painted and gilded. She smiled as memories sweet as lavender flooded her whole being. As a child she had learned to read the pretty labels, such delicious names. Aqua Rosae, Syrupus Rhei, Tinctura Limonis. Who would care for her father's displays after she left? Maybe George, her father's apprentice? George was an immigrant from England with whom she'd been practising her English in exchange for patois lessons. In the gathering dusk the brass bell above the door jingled as Elise stepped into the light No sign of life. She wandered around bidding a silent farewell to her childhood. Closing her eyes she took in the familiar sharp aroma of lamp oil mixed with a subtle blend of spirits and a brew of earthy aromatic fragrances.

Ever since she was a tiny child she had helped, if indeed help was the right word, in this shop. She ran her hand along the polished wooden counter. How proud she was when she turned ten and Père had bade her mother make her a white apron, a smaller version of those worn by his apprentices. After that she was allowed to care for the leech jar and sort and label the new herbs, roots and powders as they arrived from England or France.

And now my whole future spreads out before me; an unknown, unexplored road leading to a huge cavern of fear and adventure, but also love. Her thoughts conjured up images of gigantic forests and howling wolves. With the sound of footsteps, the trees and wolves dissolved. 'Père, you startled me. I didn't hear you come in.'

Her father hugged her. He stood looking at her then rummaged for his handkerchief and noisily blew his nose before saying, 'I've just been writing a few letters. You're quite clear about us spending the night on Jersey before you board Mr Robin's ship for the New World, are you not?'

'Yes. You said we are to stay with the harbourmaster,

I think? I look forward to seeing our sister island, even if for only a few hours.'

'You'll find it not so different from Guernsey, only bigger of course.'

Needful of some time to compose herself, she kissed her father's whiskery cheek then ran upstairs to her room. However, rather than the few moments' seclusion she sought, she bumped straight into her mother.

'There you are,' Mère said. 'I was just putting these in the chest.' She placed two pairs of fine woollen stockings, protected by two linen shifts, on top of the other contents and shut the heavy lid. Then she sat on her daughter's narrow bed and gazed blindly out of the window.

Over the weeks the dowry chest had been filled with essentials. One of her most prized possessions – her grandmother's book of herbal remedies – lay wrapped in fine linen and oiled cloth at the bottom of the chest. Also at the bottom lay a collection of the mundane necessities of her new life as a pioneering woman: lengths of linen and woollen cloth, gloves, skeins of wool, a little soap, some candles and a collection of needles and threads. Many of the dainty items were part of Elise's trousseau and had long lain in a mélange of lavender, dried lemon, sweet woodruff and tansy to protect against moths. Near the top of the chest were the carefully wrapped seeds and dried herbs Elise had collected, and a number of powders her father had given her. Into a small crevice she'd tucked a private indulgence – a tiny piece of home. Wrapped in embroidered handkerchiefs lay a string of pearly ormer shells. People sold the exquisite shells for a few sous to Pengelley, the English clockmaker in High Street. He then sold them on to a furniture maker in England for inlay. Elise had once seen some of this work and it pleased her very much, but only the finest shells were sold. Others were strung up to scare the birds from the vegetable crops.

Mother and daughter sat side by side on Elise's bed. Mère pressed her lips together, a frown etching itself onto her forehead. 'My dear, how will you manage to care for your skin in such a wild land? How will you stop the freckles taking over?'

'I will no doubt make myself a lotion of Calendula and clay as I do now.'

Elise took her mother's hand as they went over the now familiar ritual of "what ifs". Her mother seemed to take a sort of superstitious comfort from this litany of potential hardships and disasters, while it filled Elise with a panic she tried to quell.

Mère smiled and rested her hand on her daughter's cheek for a moment. 'So like your gran'mère.'

Elise, with her strong tall frame and hair the colour of rust, differed from the rest of the family with their typical dark Guernsey looks and stocky physique. 'Thank the Lord for William and John, and gentle Marie, all still at home.'

Tears threatened them both and Elise cleared her

throat. 'Did you see Mr and Mrs Sebire this morning?'

'Yes I did. I'm perfectly content that they will make adequate chaperones for your voyage. You will share a cabin with Mrs Sebire. Mr Sebire will be in with the fishermen. Mr and Mrs Sebire are decent working folk from the Vale. They're going to try for the New World and will meet with you in Jersey. So that's settled. A great weight off your father's mind and mine.'

'Are they young?'

'Both about thirty. Both strong. Both looking forward to their new life.'

'And do they make the whole journey?'

'All but the last few days. They are taking on a trading post at a place called Saint-Pierre. Quite close to your Jerseyman Island, I believe, so you'll be neighbours, more or less.'

Mère patted her lace collar straight. 'I must make haste for I still have to prepare supper.'

Once alone Elise ran a hand over the dowry chest. She gave the contents a cursory inspection and yet again checked the fisherman's jumper she'd finally finished knitting for Thomas. Much to her mother's annoyance, Elise lacked the skill and patience for knitting and the garment had taken her months to complete. The dark blue jumper was windproof and warm; a uniform of pride to the fishermen of Guernsey. She hoped Thomas would not be too fussy about the quality of work and at least slightly impressed by the love she'd poured into the making of it. She replaced it inside the tightly-packed chest.

On her bed sat the leaving gift from her father and mother: a leather valise capacious and strong enough to withstand the rigours of salt and damp during the voyage. A judicious packing of the valise was called for. Within it would be a change of undergarments and outerwear, some tincture of spoonwort (also known as scurvy grass), half a dozen fresh lemons for the same reason, salve of chamomile for headaches and sore muscles, and iodine tincture for wounds. With luck none of these would be called upon. There was also her reticule, her new journal within which she intended to record her new life, a pencil, a small penknife, a beautiful bible from her brothers and sisters, a bar of hard soap and a toothbrush and toothpowder. Finally she added her precious bottle of black horehound extract for the treatment of mal de mer.

Her hands unconsciously stroked the leather-bound bible. She was ready – or so she hoped.

CHAPTER 2

The quayside at St Peter Port was sad witness to many tears and bewailings, to desperate hugs and pettings, to promises and sobs. All of Elise's resolve and thoughts of heroism crumbled. Instead her escapade felt like a death. Surely it could not be happening? Yet it was. Elise, almost suffocating under the weight of her grief, at last tore herself away and she and her father boarded the single-masted sloop with its tiller steering and open hold. Chilled to the bone, they stood side by side as the sloop headed for Jersey. She clutched Père's arm tightly and they got in the way of the sailors, but she ignored their muttering and refused to move. She needed to capture and keep Guernsey to her for as long as possible. Eventually the only home she'd ever known became obscured by distance, and the island of Jersey approached on the horizon.

'That's La Corbière rock,' her father said, pointing to a looming crag. We give that a wide birth so as to avoid the hidden rocks that run like a lace collar around the coast.'

'Corbière – what does that mean?' She was pleased by the distraction.

'I believe it means *a place where crows gather*.'

'I can see why,' she said, now becoming aware of the throaty, evocative calls of the many black crows that circled the rock before landing then circled again.

'When we circumnavigate La Corbière we come to the southern coast of Jersey – the side we never see from home.'

Under a feeble sun, spume surf became glinting darts of light, and streamers of restless vraic played on the ruffled sea. As they entered the port of St Aubin the sight of children sailing up and down in small boats, and gulls following any likely-looking vessel cheered her a little. She clung to her father's arm as they stood beside her travel trunk on the quay and waved farewell to the sloop. She desperately wished she could return with it to Guernsey.

Some things were just like home. As they stood on the quay the bustle of fishermen, sailors and wharfmen were familiar sights in a new setting. Loitering soldiers made ribald remarks to anyone who would listen. She felt their eyes on her and she clutched her father's arm tighter. A number of merchants supervised the offloading of goods and around them lay a plethora of barrels, spars and staves. Net rigging was stretched out to dry and, like the barking dogs, had to be avoided.

Her father's friend Jean Le Boutillier, the kindly harbourmaster with whom they would stay that night, collected them and arranged the loading of her trunk and valise onto his four-wheeled cart. Of the port of St Aubin she gained but a fleeting impression, but felt it to have a friendly ambiance. She saw smoke rising from chimneys, and lamp-lit shops and houses along the bulwarks. When they reached the harbourmaster's house they gave themselves up to the thoughtful care of Mrs Le Boutillier. Elise was surprised at the similarity between Jersey and Guernsey patois and she had no trouble understanding their words.

Little time remained for much else except a visit to the fishermen's tiny chapel. Here she prayed for her family, for a safe crossing and above all for the moment – now only a few weeks away – when God willing, she would be reunited with her husband.

CHAPTER 3

The brig *St Brelade* heaved and strained, juddered and moaned while Elise huddled in a corner of the deck and braced herself as best she could. *A fine trailblazer I turned out to be,* she thought as she clutched her journal and stared at the untouched pages. *So much for recording my adventures. I don't like adventures.* The first terrifying weeks of her pioneering life had dashed such intentions from her befuddled mind and now the empty pages chided her, for the right words had become no more than a jumble of sensations. How to describe the horror of being shut in with rats that scurry back and forth as though they owned the ship? Of being deprived of fresh air and natural light for great stretches of time? Of being pitched about in a tiny dark box of a cabin until the senses become so confused that one cannot tell between the rising and falling of the ship? Of clinging hour after hour for all one was worth to the sides of a narrow coffin-bed? And all the time the timbers creaking as though they would part. Longing for your mother's comfort and wondering if you would live or die. It was insufferable to be in the bowels of the ship where, once the hatches were battened, no daylight filtered and where wicks and oil were limited. The agony of being forced to behave so unseemly in the company of a stranger, and likewise she with you, was as bad as the sickness itself. Her courage and dignity were sorely tried, as was her skull for the height between decks rarely exceeded five feet and she was forever forgetting to stoop.

During the worst of it, and barely hours out of Jersey where her journey had begun, she and her chaperone and travel companion, Renee Sebire, refused to stay below.

'We will be trapped in the sinking ship!' Renee had screamed.

Elise shared these fears, and so it was that the two women were secured to a lifeline on deck. They watched the ship's crew hard at their perilous duties alongside Mr Robin's fishermen who were outward bound for the new season. The great wheel took the force of two men as they hauled it this way and that and Mr Sebire, doing his best to help, strained at the pumps. The deck vibrated with a low hum that went through her whole body. Even her teeth rattled – but perhaps that was more to do with fear and cold. The sea drenched everyone and everything. The salt-thick air heaved with the noise of ropes and canvas that beat and cracked, writhed and fidgeted against the masts and spars. The clamour filled her head until she thought she would lose her mind. She wept, not just for herself and Renee, but for the indentured boy who, even above the noise of the screaming hell-bent ship, could be heard groaning and crying for his mother.

Elise remembered William's prediction that this journey would be like a bouncing wooden tub in an endless sea. *Please God, if I survive this, let him at least be wrong about wolves and savages.* Not only that, but she would be forever grateful if God, in His wisdom, would spare them from further storms.

***

At last the worst of the weather abated. The tossing and surging of Mr Robin's ship had modified to an erratic, unpleasant roll and a seaman was assigned to wash their cabin with vinegar and sea water.

'That's all we need,' Renee groaned, as she lay squeezed inside her coffin-like bunk a few feet beneath where Elise lay in hers.

Sure enough, the reek of vinegar now joined the stench of wet canvas, stagnant seawater, tar, rotting wood, lamp-oil, live rats and dead fish. Renee rolled over and pressed a cologne-soaked handkerchief to her nose.

'And atop of all that, the odour of illness,' Elise whimpered to herself, making further use of the cologne bottle and a clean handkerchief.

That same cologne bottle came into its own when, as the less incapacitated of the two of them (but much to the vexation of her rebellious stomach), Elise had taken on the task of emptying their slops over the side. This was a perilous chore demanding good timing and an awareness of wind direction.

'Do you suppose,' Renee had asked, 'that your Thomas's journey was so full of plungings and rollings to the point where it was impossible to stand?'

'He did not say so.'

Elise wondered if she would have boarded the *St Brelade* so willingly if she'd been aware of the horrors of the journey. But then had not the shipmaster, Mr Le Cheminant, told her that many journeys weren't so violent, and that this was a particularly unfortunate crossing?

'Oh come on, Elise,' she muttered to herself, 'what kind of explorer lets a rough sea and a creaking ship put her off?' *What kind doesn't?* she thought.

***

The sky remained pewter but nonetheless four weeks into the voyage the storms passed. The repair of the sails along with the carpenter's maintenance became as never ending as the voyage itself.

Desperate for some clean fresh air, as soon as it was feasible to do so Elise staggered up the steps, through the hatch and out onto the deck. The last time she'd been on deck was during the worst of the storm when, hitched to a lifeline and terrified, through half-closed eyes she'd seen only plunging sea and angry sky. Now, clinging to the rail, her heart gave a great jolt as she stared in all directions towards an endless horizon. Her heart thudded against her ribcage and her mouth went dry. That first shock of perpetual ocean eased a little but never left her entirely.

With Mr Le Cheminant's kind offer of the occasional use of his day cabin, Elise at last began to make some progress with her journal.

Has there ever been, she wrote, *a time when I did not taste salt on my lips morning, noon and night?* Thus she opened her narrative.

If I allow myself to imagine how deep the black sea is beneath my feet my mind freezes with fear, she confessed to the clean white page before adding, *Poor Renee, so plump and jolly at the start of our voyage, now so gaunt. She remains indisposed by le mal de mer despite my Horehound Elixir.*

There was a spell when, to make up for lost time, the ship sailed even on the darkest of nights. How the crew can tell where we are by studying the heavens as though reading a hidden code, is beyond me, she wrote.

At times, once the weather improved, Elise, Renee and Amos dined with the master, Mr Le Cheminant, a Jerseyman, along with the chief mate, Mr Johnson, who hailed from England and whose job it was to navigate, and supervise the steering. There was no shortage of food but it was not always the best quality.

'I will never, ever even look at salted beef again as

long I live,' she'd announced to Renee.

The best times were when Mr Robin's fishermen had luck with their lines. The occasional steak of fresh shark or swordfish was a tasty treat. The cook was an old sea dog and, despite his grumbles, he always had a cheery whistle and a toothless smile. His fish soup was good, but then Elise supposed he had many years to perfect his recipe. Of course there was the inevitable ship's biscuit (or hard tack as the sailors called it – and no wonder). They carried a pig and chickens for fresh produce and these, when the time was deemed right, were most welcome.

I sorely miss my mother's cooking, she wrote after yet another meal of dried, salted beef with an overload of boiled onions.

As for the ship's company, apart from the master and chief mate there was a second mate and eight crew including the cook, the carpenter, and an indentured boy on his way to train as a wheelwright. Below deck eighteen of Mr Robin's fishermen were crammed, plus Elise and the Sebires.

Once past the worst of the sickness and able to join Elise on deck, Renee explained that during market days back home, she and Mr Sebire had heard the fishermen and sailors talk of the fisheries and the fur trade, and the fortunes to be had in these Maritime Provinces.

'But Amos is neither a fisherman nor a trapper,' she said. 'Then by chance we met an agent who told of the success of the main trading post at Saint Pierre and how the secondary post was needing a manager. The man was an Acadian. That's someone of French descent, apparently. He told us that he represented a trading company started by an Irish gentleman called Mr Laurence Kavanagh.'

'This Mr Kavanagh – did you meet him?'

'No. He died an early death so a company runs the business now. They have a manager for the sea-based post. But they needed someone to take on the lease of the smaller trading post on the shores of a great lake nearby. Our whole future is in the hands of this Acadian, of whom we know very little. Rather terrifying, don't you think?'

'I'm sure everything will be fine.' Elise tried to reassure Renee, although her words came more from hope than certainty.

Besides the casks of dried and salted foodstuffs from Jersey, they carried numerous barrels of sun-dried salt, picked up from Cadiz prior to Elise's embarkation. A fisherman informed her that Mr Robin was most particular about the quality of his salt. *Bless me*, she told her journal. *All this sea and they have to bring their own salt! How much I have to learn of my new life.*

The sight of burly sailors doing fancy ropework captivated her and one fellow, with the patience of a brother to a little sister, showed her how to make the knots and how to use clay to keep the work white. Useless as she was with any sort of needle, here was some delicate work she could manage quite well. One of the fishermen, a Jerseyman, had a squeeze-box and they all enjoyed some rousing tunes and sea shanties. The crew and the fishermen knew all the words, and sometimes danced a jig on deck though there was little space. For the sake of decorum she could not join in the dancing, but she clapped her hands to the steps; a distraction that always cheered her.

Some weeks after setting sail, and chafing against her restricted existence, she ventured on deck one night to take the air. Without warning ghostly blue flames leapt into the night and clung to the mastheads, illuminating them like God's candles. Had a holy messenger come to speak to her? To take her to heaven? Or to hell? She cringed with fear. The sailor on watch laughed.

'Don't you fret, missus,' he said. 'That there's the fire of St. Elmo, the patron saint of sailors. Our voyage is blessed.'

She prayed that this saint would do his work well.

Mère and Père would be pleased that I do not neglect my immortal soul, she wrote, *for the master holds a service every Sunday, weather permitting, during the second dogwatch. I find the services most uplifting. As well as plain prayers he reads a bible story or an extract from Pilgrim's Progress, and we end with a hymn. The second mate has a fine voice.*

As the ship sailed ever closer to Elise's future, she found herself swamped with memories of family and home. Making use of the master's day cabin to update her journal, she found herself consumed with

25

homesickness. *Nothing in Gran'mère's book of herbal remedies offers a cure for the cruel affliction that is part of my every waking, and oft-times sleeping, moments,* she wrote. *How is it possible to feel such fear and sorrow, and such longing and happiness, all at the same time?*

CHAPTER 4

Running. For her life. Hounded. Purple-black ravens.
Whirl. Dive. Closer, closer. Ear-splitting screeches: kra
kra kra. Putrefaction. Corruption. Defilement. She trips.
Falls. Beaten. Overpowered. Thomas, save me.

She awoke bathed in perspiration. The dream was so
real, so vivid and shocking. What did it mean? Why did
she have these nightmares? This one made itself known
a few weeks into her journey and it left her drained and
trembling. Had she called out and disturbed Renee?
Thankfully the good lady continued to snore in her bunk
below.

These visions surely stemmed from some
unimaginable evil. She lay in her bunk staring into the
dark, trying to erase the fear.

Gran'mère, you said I'd be able to interpret the
raven's message when I was ready. But, when will that
be? Is it a prophesy? A warning? What?

When no older than twelve she'd experienced the
purple-black raven for the first time. There were nine or
ten of the creatures, each vast and raucous. They gloated

over the death of a healthy neighbour just days before it actually came about. At that time she'd been terrified, and still was to this day every time they came back. Some months after that first visitation they returned to show her a rowing boat capsizing beyond the harbour. The following day two fishermen barely escaped with their lives.

'Don't fret, my child,' Gran'mère had whispered. 'This is our gift. You and I are especially blessed. The ravens come to protect and forewarn us and are the voice of your guardian angel. They bring messages, and you will learn to listen to them when you have the wisdom. But, remember that others will not view them in this light. You must tell no one, for folk will cry *witchcraft*.'

Elise and her grandmother kept their "gift" a secret from the world.

Were they a message, as Gran'mère had suggested? Did the raven bring a warning? If so, it was indecipherable and therefore useless and despised. No matter what her grandmother said, Elise was sure that such visitations as these were not an angel's doing but the work of the devil. An unkindness of ravens, that was what a flock was called. An unkindness.

When her thoughts turned to Gran'mère, and to her dear family already far away she was filled with yearning. The pain of remembrance matched the comfort it offered.

That morning, seeking distraction and solace and needing to concentrate on the future rather than the past,

Elise took herself off to the shipmaster's day cabin and removed a bundle of Thomas's letters from her reticule. To read them was a comfort she had often resorted to at home during her two year wait before Mr Robin had given his permission for her to join Thomas. She opened the most recent letter and gently traced a finger across the heading: *Jerseyman Island, off Isle Madame, Cape Breton, Maritime Provinces of Canada. 15th of October 1774.* Sent five months ago with the last ship before the weather cut him off. How heartbroken she'd been when Thomas didn't come home for winter like the other fishermen, but he'd agreed with her, his winter pay was going to make all the difference to their future and it meant that she now earned the right to join him.

His letters told of how hard he worked, but he'd insisted that this was nothing to a fisherman. He said that the Jerseyman was a tough master, keeping his workers in the company's debt during the season, even for their clothing and essentials of work. The frivolous workers lost out, but Thomas assured her that he was abstemious in all his ways. He had more than once mentioned a new friend, a Matthew Barbet, who'd sounded to her like an immoderate man and a bad influence: one of those frivolous fishermen Thomas referred to. Thomas wrote that this Mr Barbet might well be returning to Jerseyman Island on the same ship she would be travelling in.

She had indeed encountered this Matthew Barbet on board but found herself avoiding his company. She thought him overfamiliar.

Thomas's letters described her future home. She was pleased to learn that a whole community lived in the busy port named Arichat just over the water from Jerseyman Island. These settlers had preceded Mr Robin's fishery and now many worked for him in the summer before going inland during the winter to hunt for furs. Thomas wrote that they spoke a French he could understand well enough, and they had Frenchie names though they were not real Frenchies. There were natives too called Migmar, or some such. He said that they kept to themselves and caused no trouble, but still Elise felt nervous at the thought of them. Would they look like some of the sailors she'd seen in St Peter Port who had skin the colour of pitch and hair like the fleece of a black sheep? She supposed they would be heathens.

There in the comfort of the master's day cabin, she sat at the large oak desk and for the umteenth time tried to imagine her married home on the little island named for the Jerseyman. Thomas had written that in high season about thirty fishermen lived on Jerseyman Island, most of them in one or other of two bunkhouses. At least she and Thomas would have their own cabin. She would be the only woman on the Island, which was a daunting prospect. How would she cope, deprived of female company? Would she find companionship over the water on Arichat? He had written that all the vessels stopped over there because it had the biggest and deepest harbour in the whole of the Americas. How grand that would be. So many comings and goings, so many mountains and forests, so many new experiences and adventures. *Yet so far from home. A world away from my family with a man I haven't seen for two years.* Her resolve faltered.

She again read Thomas's words. He had ended his letter with the old Guernsey saying: *To part is to die a little.* She kissed his closing endearments and his signatures, folded the letters and returned them to her reticule. If to part was to die a little, then her life was about to begin.

CHAPTER 5

Fog shrouded everything. Even the vociferous rigging and the clatter and shouts of the crew were muffled. Apart from the occasional blasts Elise made on the fog-horn, the only notable sound was the ever-present creak of the ship's planking. Fog confused both eye and ear. She was aware that land lay close by because of the disembodied calls from the young sailor stationed in his barrel at the masthead. For hours she had been pumping at the bellows attached to a brass trumpet that served as the horn. The slackened sails and shrouds dripped icy water and, despite the benefit of oiled cape and hat, she was wet through and freezing cold. It was good to be doing something useful for a change, and had been happy to volunteer, but she would be pleased when her task was done.

A becalmed silence had settled over them. Even the planking ceased its complaints. Would the fog never clear? She tried to suppress her impatience and at last felt a rustle of air against her face. The blanket of vapour thinned to a veil that revealed a monochrome of shapes, and her spirits lifted in unison with the fog. Suddenly the ship came to life as sailors bustled, called, whistled. The ship's master took the wheel, a sense of purpose in his stance. Her excitement rose. With borrowed spyglass Elise stood by the ship's rail, marvelling at small inlets and islands that came into hazy view as the master tacked in and headed for Saint-Pierre Bay – their first contact with the New World.

The scenery was not as she'd imagined and it didn't take long for a worm of disappointment to crawl in. She'd anticipated tall cliffs and vast mountains but the tired smudge of sun revealed a flat, rocky shore backed by a tall, dark tangle of trees. She thought Guernsey's south coast more dramatic and more beautiful than the one before her.

Thomas, never one to eulogise about the beauty of nature, had been more inclined to write of his surroundings in terms of fishing productivity, weather and risk.

I must memorise all this for my journal and my letters home, she told herself.

They drifted into Saint-Pierre Bay. Ahead of them a sizable and bustling outpost hugged the shore. Her nervousness mounted. Here they would dock and Renee and Amos would disembark to start their new lives at the trading post, while Elise continued on around the coast to Mr Robin's fishing outfit. A reluctant farewell was looming. Mr Sebire, a dour man whom she'd never heard laugh, discouraged confidences, but Renee Sebire was sweet-natured and warm and had smiles enough for the two of them.

Renee joined Elise at the ship's rail and she, too, gazed at the shore. 'Mr Sebire is below seeing to our trunk,' she said. Her face showed the strain of the journey; her once rosy cheeks were gaunt and pale. 'We're going to make our fortunes. I really do believe that.'

'Me and Thomas too.' Elise spoke with an almost forgotten confidence.

Now, with the end of Renee's voyage imminent and Elise's not far behind, they both gazed shoreward. Elise saw an extensive village of wooden houses crowded close to the shoreline and, set apart, a collection of small cone-shaped structures. She could make no sense of those. There were also bigger buildings – warehouses perhaps? – and a store. In front of these a number of wooden landing-stages pointed outward into the bay.

At that moment Amos Sebire appeared with his wife's hooded cape. 'You left this in your cabin, my dear,' he told her. Before she could respond with more than a smile, he nodded towards Elise and scuttled back below deck.

As Renee wrapped herself in the woollen cape she said to Elise, 'We struggled to make a living at home so to venture half-way across the world wasn't such a strange idea. Not at the time at least.'

Elise put a hand on Renee's arm and in silence they watched the activity both on board and ashore. Their private contemplations were disturbed when Thomas's friend, Matthew Barbet, joined them. A slight man, his regular habit of sniffing and rummaging around in his nostrils with a grubby finger made Elise feel squeamish. She had tried, for her husband's sake, to like this Guernseyman, but instinct led her to mistrust him and she'd successfully avoided him for most of the voyage.

'Them boats coming towards us are canoes,' Matthew Barbet explained, as he hitched up his baggy trousers. 'The natives make 'em from the bark of the birch tree.' He turned to her. 'The savages are primitive, but friendly with us Channel Islanders 'cos we speak French 'n so do they. They get on with the Frenchies. Not too keen on the English though.' He chuckled and patted Elise's arm with a soiled hand. 'Don't let the sight of 'em frighten you. Stay by me, I'll take care of you.'

By now the canoes were close at hand. Calls and shouts and all sorts of noises flew through the air. Despite Mr Barbet's unpleasant habits, both women edged closer to him. On shore, as well as the teeming natives, a group of white men watched and contributed to the hubbub. Tethered cows bellowed and penned pigs squealed. The commotion was overwhelming.

'Are those the Acadians, do you suppose?' Elise asked Renee, pointing at the white men.

Mr Barbet chipped in, 'Yes. You got to watch 'em. Tricky lot.'

Elise glared at the man and squeezed her friend's

hand.

Slowly, skilfully, the master steered the *St Brelade* to the landing-stage. Thick ropes were thrown and made safe by those waiting. A few crew members scrambled over the side to help secure the ship. The world of the *St Brelade* came to a halt.

In this wide bay the swell was considerable and the business of descending the rope ladder and going ashore proved to be a tricky one for Elise, hampered as she was by her long skirt, warm, calf-length cloak and precarious dignity. She negotiated her way along the landing-stage until, weak-kneed, she stood on dry land alongside the Sebires. She felt disorientated and the land swayed.

'Don't worry ladies, it soon wears off. Allow me to save you the embarrassment of falling flat on your faces.' The speaker, who held a manifesto, was ticking off items. He stopped his work long enough to guide them to a nearby rough-hewn bench. 'Sit here and I'll bring you a mug of tea.'

The man had an unfamiliar accent. One of those Acadians, Elise guessed. The women murmured their thanks and he slipped away.

Everything was so strange. Noises, smells, colours, shapes, all so much larger than life. It needed a lot of taking in.

After a while Renee turned to Elise. 'Over there talking to Amos, that nice man who assisted us to this bench and promised us some tea, he's M'sieur de Forêt, the agent we dealt with in Guernsey.'

Elise had hardly noticed the man, but now scrutinised him. 'He *seems* agreeable.'

'As long as he's trustworthy, Elise. That's been my fear. We sold all we had…'

'He's here isn't he? Take no heed of Mr Barbet's words. I'm sure you have nothing to worry about.'

They watched the flurried unloading of supplies for the settlement and loading of goods for the fishery. Elise was mesmerised by so much bustle. She risked discrete glances in the direction of the natives. How frightening and unusual they were. What would William and his alarming talk of savages make of all this?

The Acadian re-appeared with two clay mugs full of tea. 'I suspect you could do with this.' Both women nodded and accepted the hot, sweet infusion with appreciation. 'Mrs Sebire.' The man crouched down in front of the bench. 'I trust you survived your crossing in good health?'

'Just about, thank you. Though it would have been much more difficult without the assistance of my friend Elise Galliard here. Mrs Galliard goes on to Jerseyman Island to join her husband. Elise, may I introduce M'sieur de Forêt, the agent who has been representing mine and my husband's interests?'

'You've come all this way to be with your husband?' A wide brim obscured his face. When he removed the brown felt hat she saw that his eyes glinted like coal in sunshine.

'Thomas is a fisherman, M'sieur. He works for Mr Robin on Jerseyman Island.'

'You're a brave woman and he's a lucky man. Ah, here comes Mr Sebire.'

After nine weeks at sea even the most experienced of the ship's company swayed as they walked. With a groan, Amos lowered himself onto the bench beside Renee, wiping his face with his sleeve before starting to engage Monsieur de Forêt in conversation. Elise took the opportunity to observe the stranger. His melodic voice was subtly accented. His black neat-trimmed beard and moustache highlighted the evenness of his teeth. His nose was sharp and well-defined and, despite his not being above thirty, a crinkle of lines were etched around his eyes. Renee and Amos had put their hopes and dreams into the hands of this man. Was he reliable? He was agreeable enough but did that make this foreigner honest?

Free to follow her own thoughts, Elise fretted over the many questions and fears pounding at her mind. The future, once so clear-cut, was now a black void that crept ever-closer. All the doubts she'd been supressing rose simultaneously. Why was she here in this huge strange place, alone amongst a crowd of strangers?

Because, Elise Galliard, you persuaded Thomas he wanted to work in the New World and that he needed you by his side.

She nodded to herself as she acknowledged the truth of this, then admitted silently and slightly shamefacedly,

38

he wanted you all right but he did not crave the rest of it. Not all this. He'd have been perfectly happy to have stayed at home. You sweet-talked him round. All this was the stake and you were the reward. You should have stayed home and helped Père in his shop and learned better knitting and married a nice, sensible merchant. Thus did she scold herself.

The truth was, she wanted a magical, exciting world full adventures and discoveries yet suddenly her hopes and dreams lacked substance. *I want my home and I want my mother. I want to wake up in my own bed. I hate it here. This world is too big and I'm too small. I am too frightened. Why did I come?* Tears obscured her vision. She faked a cough, took a deep breath, whipped out her dainty hanky and blew her nose, remembering even in her dire straits to do so with decorum.

She tried to straighten out the creases she'd wrung her skirt into as questions jumbled around inside her head. What was her husband really like? Would he still love her? The heat rose in her cheeks. Would he still want her in that same way he had two years before? Would she still want him as she once had done?

She felt restless and needed to walk on good solid ground. Slipping away, she wandered along a narrow track through the vegetation. Beyond the port, the land climbed upwards and a forest of trees rose to an infinity of sky. A rat with red-brown fur caught her attention, but this small mammal had dark stripes on either side of its body and a fluffy, feathery tail. Soon another such creature joined it. They chattered to each other and darted about, paused on their hind legs like statues, then darted off again. She watched, spellbound.

The rustle of a bird overhead caused her to glance round. Behind her stood two men. Two *native* men. Tall, muscular. Armed with rifles. As they advanced towards her, panic punched her stomach. Without rational thought she gasped, turned and fled. Losing all sense of direction she thrashed her way through rough undergrowth and the whipping of low branches. Footsteps trampled the brushwood behind her. Closer, closer they came. Deep threatening voices called out in a strange language. She shrieked as a large bird with bright plumage took flight, emitting sharp angry squawks. Was that the heart-stopping *kra kra* of the raven she heard? Her foot became ensnared in a tree root. She cried out, tripped, staggered, almost fell before re-gaining her balance. An unseen hand pulled at her.

Her head filled with a hot, red noise and she heard herself scream, 'Thomas!' She lashed out with both hands, but to no effect. They would slaughter her, or worse. Her cries were of fear, but of anger too; the cruel shame, to have come so far, to have barely begun her adventures.

Words penetrated her brain. 'Madame, please. We are not your enemy.' The restraining hands released her. 'You must not wander alone, Madame.' He gestured about him. 'Cougar are here. And moose. And swamps. You will lose your way.'

The man's eyes no longer appeared evil, his frown no longer threatening. Relief washed through her, swiftly followed by an overwhelming flood of foolishness that made her blush. She became aware of their oak-brown eyes and broad-nosed, sharp-cheeked faces and dark-honey complexions. They wore tunics, leggings and shoes fashioned from soft skins, and capes of animal fur. The shorter of the two men wore a large pointed hat not unlike a bonnet. The other had a mass of black, oiled hair reaching to below his shoulders and restrained by a strip of leather round his forehead.

'Come,' the taller of the two men said. He picked up her bonnet, shook it free of leaves and dust before handing it to her. He showed no sign that she had insulted or amused him, but gestured for her to follow. Behind her walked the other native. Remembering their talk of cougars and moose, (whatever fierce creatures these might be), she was, after all, reassured to be flanked by these men. As they emerged from the undergrowth and reached the shore, Monsieur de Forêt hurried to meet them, her shipboard companions close on his heels.

'My goodness, Elise.' Renee grabbed her hand. 'We were worried about you.' She nodded meaningfully towards Elise's native escorts and whispered, 'Are you all right, my dear?'

Renee led her to the bench seat and Elise sank on to it. Trying to hide her trembling hands within the folds of her skirt, she managed a shaky smile and muttered something about a short stroll. Monsieur de Forêt strode up to the two men. The three of them talked in low voices and kept glancing in her direction. Seeing the Acadian's amused smile, her face burned with humiliation.

The slighter of the two natives turned to the Acadian and as he took a step backwards and pointed at her she heard him say, 'See, Marcel, the young woman has a halo full of sunset.'

Monsieur De Forêt chuckled softly. 'Such a hue is not uncommon in Europeans, but it's true, her hair does glow delightfully in the sun.'

He seemed unaware or unconcerned that his voice reached and embarrassed her, and her glare had no apparent effect on him. She had the ridiculous desire to stamp her foot. Instead she scrabbled to replace her dishevelled bonnet as best she could as the Acadian took the taller of the two natives by the elbow and guided him towards the newcomers. 'If you are steadier on your feet,' he said to the company, 'allow me introduce Moses.'

Now somewhat recovered and decently bonneted she noticed that this native man was young and handsome, robust and broad-shouldered. His quick smile showed small sharp teeth. She stood. 'M'sieur,' she murmured, unable to meet the native man's eyes. Renee curtsied and Mr Sebire shook the man's hand. Then it struck her. 'Moses?' she queried.

The Acadian chuckled. 'The Mi'kmaq people are

almost all Christian. They've lived here for more generations than can be counted. French Jesuits converted them a hundred years ago.'

'Papist?'

He grinned. 'As Papist as I am. At least, when it suits them.' He turned again to the native called Moses. 'These are our latest arrivals,' he told him, then turned to the second native. 'And this is Nathaniel, a companion of mine.'

Elise began to relax. She could now appreciate Nathaniel's friendly expression and Moses' grin, which was as open and amiable as the rest of his face.

'Come,' Moses said in a voice like treacle. 'While you wait for your ship I will show you some of this place you Europeans call Saint-Pierre.'

They met his shy young wife, and Elise glimpsed a clutter of wide-eyed children peering from the open door-flap of one of the conical-shaped shelters she had noticed earlier. A wikuom, Moses told them – one of twenty or more in the vicinity. The sights, the smells, the sounds, the people. She started to feel the reality and excitement of this new land. It was actually happening, and it was happening right now. She bubbled over with questions. Then Renee stumbled and had to be rescued by her husband.

'You're tired,' the Acadian broke in. 'But don't worry, there will be plenty of time to find out all you need to know.'

As they made their way back to the water's edge

43

Elise turned to Monsieur de Forêt. 'Tell me, sir, what brought you to Guernsey?'

'I was acting for the Jerseyman, Charles Robin and his brother, John; the fellows your husband works for.'

These Robin brothers must be mighty important, she decided. 'But why did that bring you to the Channel Islands?'

'I travelled to Guernsey to negotiate with a couple of shipbuilders. Among my many dubious talents is that of marine insurance agent. My employers are based in London and I'd been visiting them.'

She raised her eyebrows. London? Marine insurance? Shipbuilders? 'That's impressive,' she said.

'I'm a tiny cog, I assure you.'

She studied him for a moment. He didn't give the impression of being rich or learned. His garments had a rough appearance. He sported a homespun cutaway linen jacket with pewter buttons, a shirt tucked into brown fustian breeches, and well-worn boots of leather. His hair was pulled back into a waxed pigtail.

'A tiny cog, M'sieur? I think you are too modest.'

He smiled. 'Not something I'm generally accused of.'

'And you are some sort of agent for Charles and John Robin?'

'In a manner of speaking. It happened that I needed to call on their company in Jersey. John Robin, acting for the Kavanaghs, commissioned me to find a good manager for Saint-Pierre. You'll have heard of Mr

Kavanagh?'

She admitted that apart from Renee's brief mention, she had not.

'When Laurence Kavanagh was lost at sea a few years back his widow took on the company that owns the trading posts here till her son comes of age. The Robin brothers help out as and when they can.'

She studied her surroundings. The settlement seemed well-established and the buildings soundly constructed. 'Has this trading post been here long?'

'Years. Near on one hundred and fifty. That's ancient in this new world.'

'What did you make of the island of my birth?'

'Small. Little more than a small rock in a small sea.'

She felt slightly miffed, although admitted to herself that she supposed, in truth, he was right.

'You'll feel at home with your near neighbour, Isle Madame, as that's pretty small too. And your Jerseyman Island – well that's pint-sized, so you won't get lost on that.'

'I'm pleased to hear it,' she snapped, before adding in a quiet voice, 'This country of yours is bigger than anything I could ever have imagined, which scares me. Maybe daring-do isn't all it's cracked up to be?'

He took her hand. 'My dear Madame Galliard, in order to make a new life you crossed the Atlantic Ocean to this remote British colony. A courageous woman such as yourself has no cause to be afraid.'

She saw sincerity in his face. Lifting her chin slightly

she set her jaw more firmly. His words gave her courage.

Monsieur de Forêt turned to Amos and Renee Sebire. 'And what about you folk? Do you feel able to make your way to your new home?'

'We do,' Amos Sebire nodded. 'Is it far?'

'About half a mile inland across a thin strip of land, on the shores of the Bras d'Or, a lake so vast you'll think it the sea. To get there we have a steep trek uphill then the path drops down again as it approaches the lake. You'll see the natives carrying their canoes and all their goods across the isthmus from one shore to the other. Even small sailing ships are hauled between the two bodies of water.' Monsieur de Forêt chuckled and said, 'There is talk of joining the sea and the lake by a canal such as the Romans constructed in England.'

Mr Sebire frowned, saying such ideas were fanciful. Elise could see his point. It would be an impossible feat and anyway, if a waterway connected the Atlantic to the Sebires' trading post there would be no need for the trading post on the lake at all. As an afterthought, the Guernseyman muttered, 'Besides, we would be overrun by adventurers of all sorts.'

They all agreed that the idea was clearly preposterous.

'Where do they go?' Mr Sebire asked after a moment. 'The boats that cross to and from the lake?'

'On this side they continue on up the coast. From the lake a good few cross to the far shore or pass your way

46

when they venture to the island mission out there in the lake. You'll find they use the route on a regular basis.'

Amos nodded his approval. 'That should make for busy trading.'

'It will.' Monsieur de Forêt rammed his hat tight on his head. 'I think you'll be surprised at how many visitors you have once word gets out.'

'Well, the more the better,' Renee said. She kissed Elise on the cheek. 'So, my dear, our exploits begin.' She and her husband turned to go.

Filled with alarm, Elise stood transfixed. Monsieur de Forêt gave her a nod and a smile of encouragement. She tried to return the smile, then took a deep breath, straightened her shoulders and made her way back to her ship, alone.

CHAPTER 6

When you hear the song of the sea, you'll know that I hear it too. Her farewell words to Thomas hung on the breeze.

The late afternoon sun had a warmth that the day had lacked so far. As the *St Brelade* followed the coastline at a snail's pace Elise leant on the ship's rail and searched the shore for she knew not what. Nine interminable weeks it had taken to cross the inhospitable Atlantic Ocean from Jersey to Jerseyman Island; an island named for the man who had established his fisheries in these Maritime provinces. Now she saw a low cliff and a bleak craggy headland with huge granite boulders. From time to time landing-stages reached out a short way into the sea and groups of people at the shore's edge watched the ship pass. Her heart shuddered so much it seemed to shake her whole body. As she neared her destination she experienced both joy and terror. She, a stranger in a strange land, was about to meet with the husband she hadn't seen for over two years. What would her life have been like if they'd never met? What would she have been doing at this moment? Although missing her family felt like a burning wound, her hands became clammy at the thought of a life without Thomas. The day he came into her father's shop to purchase some medicine for his father changed her life. She had been just eighteen, he twenty. How young that sounded now. She'd sneak out to meet him when the fishing fleet came in. How exciting, how romantic, how disobedient. She had not, by nature, been a disobedient child, but the love she'd felt for Thomas was so rapid and so deep that she was blinded to all else. She'd never known her father so cross or her mother so upset. He a mere fisherman, and not even a boat of his own. Yet Gran'mère liked Thomas. 'He's a good un,' she'd declared, and could tell how much they loved each other. Elise didn't understand how Gran'mère brought her parents round but bring them round she had. 'God bless you Gran'mère,' she whispered now.

'You'll wait two years, though, my lass,' Père had insisted. She knew this was in the hope of her outgrowing her love, which of course she wouldn't. And indeed she hadn't and neither had Thomas. She persuaded Thomas to pursue his fortune in the wider world, and to arrange for her to join him. Now here she was, about to begin the biggest adventure of her life. Soon they would be together again.

So lost was she in her thoughts that it was a while before she became aware of the shantyman leading his watch with a song to chivvy the men along and keep time as they hauled at the rigging.

A hundred years is a very long time, he chanted.

Oh yes, oh, the response came, Elise joining in with full gusto. The shantyman grinned at her with approval. He was a gruff and kindly Guernseyman who knew her father and took it upon himself to keep a friendly eye on her. Her forward behaviour would have horrified Mère, but she couldn't resist the distraction and release that participation gave her. She found these sailors to be kind and respectful men who didn't think the worst of her when she took an interest in their customs and lives.

A hundred years is a very long time, the shantyman called again.

A hundred years ago, the sailors and Elise repeated.

With the solo call and chorused response she could by now differentiate between the dictates of a short pull, long pull, and a strong pull, with the sailors "singing out" at the ropes in hoarse voices.

'That's Rocky Bay.' Matthew Barbet appeared and stood so close she smelled the sourness of his breath. 'Ahead of us, see, over there. Petit-de-Grat on Isle Madame, so we're almost there.'

'You never thought to overwinter, Mr Barbet?'

'Like to head back to the missus. Never know what she'd be up to without me to check on her.' He sniggered and nodded his head in some private reverie of his own making. 'Anyhows, I got to see to the harvest soon as I'm back in the autumn, me. That's not woman's work, eh? Then I do a bit of local fishing and some work about the farm till the spring. That's when I sow the new crops before I leave the missus in charge till I gets back home again. Works well that way.'

His eyes narrowed as he filled his clay pipe with the dried leaves from his oiled baccy pouch. 'It's no picnic here when the weather closes everything down for all them months. You think to stay over with that husband of yours, missus?'

'I do. Thomas will carry on with the winter work as before, and Mr Robin told him he'll be glad to employ me.'

He rolled his eyes to heaven. 'Then you'll find out what the winters are like soon enough.'

She bit back a sharp reply. 'I think the work will not be so daunting. Tidying up at the end of the season, chopping wood for fuel, occupying the base so as to dissuade opportune adventurers and rivals. Then getting everything spick-and-span by spring for when the first ship comes in.'

He raised an eyebrow in scorn. 'You got no idea how hard the work's gonna be, missus.'

'Oh but I have, Mr Barbet. Thomas wrote all about pulling in the landing-stages so they're above the tideline. And storing away the gear to keep it safe from thieves. And stripping the rotten wood from the flakes – that is the right word, isn't it, for the fish drying platforms?' She held his gaze.

'You're well informed,' he mumbled.

'I hope so.' She turned from him, fixing her eyes on

the slow-changing vista.

'That's a lot of work, and in weather you've not even dreamed of.'

'I'm not afraid of hard work, Mr Barbet.'

'I can see that. But I keeps saying, it's Matthew. After all we are friends and neighbours now.' His grin displayed a gap between his two front teeth. His hand moved to rest on the rail next to hers. Its cold roughness reminded her of a dead fish.

People on the shore waved a greeting. Native, Acadian, European? Waving back gave her the opportunity to put some space between herself and Matthew Barbet. He turned his back to the wind and struck flint on metal. A small spark caught the tinder in his box and he drew on his pipe until the tobacco emitted a faint crackle. 'These sailors, they're a superstitious bunch.' He turned to face her again.

'Is that right?'

'You've heard tell of unlucky ships?'

'Those the sailors say are cursed?'

'Aye. Then there's the phantom ships – the ghosts of sunken vessels. They loom out of the fog, real spooky like.'

Born and raised in a busy port, these myths were nothing new to Elise so she remained silent. The pungent smell of pipe tobacco reminded her of Thomas.

'And the seabirds o' course,' Matthew continued. 'The giant albatross, or Mother Carey's Chickens as they calls 'em. The souls of drowned sailors, they are. If one of 'm sets down on the ship it's a sure sign a sailor will be lost. You've gone pale. I'm scaring you!'

She smiled. 'Not at all, why should I fear sailors' superstitions?'

'Maybe because they believe that a ship with a woman aboard is asking for trouble.'

She pulled her woollen shawl tightly about her shoulders. How provocative this man was. She hoped she could avoid him after they landed. 'Is that right? And you? What do you say Mr Barbet?'

'I think all women are trouble, me.' He smiled through cracked lips yet his dull grey eyes remained cold. She turned away and focused on the rocky coves, the inlets and beaches fringed with trees, the circling host of raucous gulls. As they rounded yet another headland there was a long necklace of an island she was later to learn was almost in three parts, each joined to the other by a natural causeway. It guarded the entrance to the Bay of Arichat and the busy port that lay to its east.

The *St Brelade* nudged around to the leeward side of this narrow island and she caught her breath. Jerseyman Island – her new home.

PART TWO

Jerseyman Island

CHAPTER 7

The first things she noticed about the island were the flatness of the landscape and the scrubland lacking any sizable trees. On the landward side she saw a craggy shore lined with rough warehouses, cabins and outbuildings. Great swathes of netting were hung out to dry, barrels were stacked, dories propped, ropes curled and a shingled beach was festooned with all sorts of fishing paraphernalia, pretty much the backdrop of most working harbours. Landing-stages beckoned them in, and, inevitably, in they slipped. A hustle of people went about their business or stood watching the *St Brelade* glide towards them.

Her restless fingers toyed with her hair, her lace-trimmed bonnet and her fresh woollen gown saved for the occasion. There was no going back. This was it – the rest of her life starts here, right now. Had she found the words, she would have prayed, though she's not sure what for. To be home? In his arms? Anywhere but here? Those distant figures on the shore – which one was he? Her heart thundered in her chest, and her head reeled so that surely she could faint.

'No, I'll not allow that,' she muttered. She took long, slow breaths of damp, fish-clogged air.

Time played tricks as it seemed to both race and slow all at once. Her undignified disembarkation was made even more ungainly because her body, mind and soul quaked. *He's a few feet away, watching me; I feel his eyes upon me. Do I disappoint him? I don't like being brave. I don't like adventures anymore.* Her feet found the landing-stage and she stumbled. Someone caught and steadied her. Then she was in his arms. His kiss was salty, his face rough, his smell unfamiliar. Then oh so familiar. Her passion caught her unawares and she became oblivious to decorum. Her arms, with a will of their own, encircled him and held him tight. She breathed him in, caught her breath then forgot to breathe out until he released her and she gazed into the sparkling blue of his eyes. Were her own eyes alive with desire too?

It felt so right, his powerful arms wrapped round her waist as he led her down the landing-stage to the shore. Here they paused as each took in the other. He was so handsome, so broad and strong. She touched his hair – longer than she remembered it but the same soft rabbit-brown. They both broke into inane grins and she wept with wonder and joy. To her surprise tears filled his eyes and fell unhindered down his dear face until she brushed them away with trembling fingers. Later he was to deny such a womanly exhibition of sentiment but at that moment neither of them cared for the world nor its opinions.

He was the first to speak. 'My dear…'

Her voice was as shaky as his. 'Thomas…'

'Oh but you're… you're more beautiful than I remember.' His fingers were a butterfly-touch on her cheeks, her forehead, her chin, her eyelids.

She placed her hand on his and drew it to her lips. 'And look at you! More handsome even than in my dreams.'

All at once the outside world pierced their bubble of emotion. Ribald jeering and salacious banter reached her from the crowd. She became aware of the banging, scraping, cussing, laughing and shouting that surrounded them. Also inescapable was the reek of fish, wood-smoke, wet rope, leather and sweat. They broke apart and a blush scalded her cheeks. She was rescued from further embarrassment by the striding approach of a ruddy-complexioned man of middle height and robust build.

'Welcome, Mrs Galliard.' His voice was kind as he heartily shook her hand. 'John Robin, at your service,' he said. 'Glad you got here safely. We're not used to women on Jerseyman Island, so let me know if you need anything.'

His words were polite but even as he spoke his eyes surveyed and assessed the activity around them. He frowned a warning at a group of fishermen who stood by snorting at the lovers. Nodding at Elise, he marched down the landing-stage towards the *St Brelade's* master.

She looked at Thomas. He returned her gaze and, ignoring the sniggering men, took her hand and led her away.

CHAPTER 8

How shy they were with one another as they stood in his tiny cabin scuffing their feet and staring at the ground until their two years' separation dissolved and they were as before. Elise's body soared to his touch, his smell, his skin, the sounds of his pleasure. Their love had survived the years apart and its rebirth shone as fresh as the day they had wed; more so, for they lacked their earlier ignorance.

Yet life will not remain at bay for long, even for lovers. She was soon taken aback by the want of all but the most basic necessities.

'I'm sorry,' Thomas said. 'It lacks what you're used to, but you can put it right, can't you?'

I can? An image came to her of her mother's home, especially the kitchen at the rear of Père's shop. She saw the bright, whitewashed walls, the scrubbed stone floor, the glazed window - a room sparsely but adequately furnished. The brick fireplace, a furze oven inside which the bean-jar cooked overnight. Mère's copper and brass pots ranged along the wall, each polished to a soft sheen.

Her mother's kitchen was warm, cosy, clean and welcoming. These things she had taken for granted, but now she blinked away this picture and turned to Thomas with a smile of reassurance.

'It's fine, really. And as you say, I'll soon fix all this up for us. Don't fret.'

Indeed, in the first flood of bliss it hardly signified. After a week or so, however, her spirit of adventure became a little dented. Their cabin, like the other buildings, was made of split birch trunks lined up vertically, the wood lashed together with strands of birchbark, the gaps filled with moss and pitch-pine. They had but one room in which to sleep, cook, eat and spend their domestic lives. There was little natural light as the single window was small and the glass thick, but that was just as well for a larger one would have let in more cold. And cold it was, despite it being nearly June. A shared privy was located some way behind the cabin.

They had a rough bed, two chairs and a table – all hewn from wood. The stone fireplace was of an adequate size but bellowed smoke and she had yet to conquer it. There was one cooking-pot and an iron kettle, two pewter plates, some utensils, an ironstone chamber pot and a wooden pail. On their windowsill clever Thomas had carved notches by which, when the sun did break through, they could read the time so that it became a sundial. The well was not far away so she had easy access to fresh water, which was a blessing. Thomas told her that Mr Robin's house and store had good-sized cellars. Their cabin lacked that benefit. Their bedding was rough but Thomas had traded his spare knife for a black bearskin that was heavy and warm albeit moth-eaten. Their mattress of sailcloth packed with straw was a far cry from the linen, wool-stuffed mattress on her bed at home, but she was getting used to the crunch and scratch of it. This port – her new home – was first and last a fishing port and she was becoming accustomed to the stench. She most likely smelled as bad herself by now. In any case, St Peter Port harbour was no rose garden either.

Thomas was exhausted from the demands of his fishing yet tried so hard to please in all things. She was determined to avoid becoming a scold and was more than capable of resolving petty domestic issues. She had determined to be a pioneer, and pioneer she would be. Scrubbing her new home and its sparse contents was a matter of urgency so Thomas borrowed a bristle brush for her, bought some penny cleaning rags from the store and showed her how to make a twig broom. Dead flies and the remains of spiders clotted the place, but a thorough airing and sweeping made a difference. She fashioned a bright linen curtain for the window and hung a buckskin cover across the door. Creating a home from nothing was daunting but not impossible, and had its own reward.

Once her cabin was liveable she had time to explore, not that Jerseyman Island needed much exploration. It was long and narrow, almost in three parts, joined to become one by natural causeways. From the fishing outfit they had a clear view across the water to the much larger Isle Madame that seemed, from where she stood, to be mostly dense forest. Arichat village was a sizable cluster of cabins and wikuoms to the east. It was with nervous pleasure that she anticipated exploring the village and meeting the people who lived there, especially the women. She'd known that she'd be the sole woman on Jerseyman Island, but had underestimated how alone and isolated this would make her feel. She longed to hear a female voice.

With her new home now scrubbed clean, she could sort out her dowry chest.

'Elise! A fisherman's sweater! You made it for me? I love it,' Thomas said, when she presented it to him. 'A real Guernsey fisherman's sweater.'

He did not even fuss about the quality of work and said he was impressed by the love she had poured into the making of it. He spent many minutes admiring the rope pattern she'd chosen, and marvelled at his initials that she'd stitched into the garment. He proudly wore it when he went out on the boats.

'I'm the envy of my fellow fishermen,' he told her later. 'They even call it my Gansey.'

Apart from unpacking her herbs and medicines and her journal, she left her trunk mostly undisturbed. It would be a pity to spoil the pretty things from home so she decided to await a more opportune time to enjoy them.

Picking up her journal one morning after saying goodbye and good fishing to Thomas, she started with a somewhat censored version of her arrival. She added a description of her attempts at domesticity and her early work on creating a herb patch. *The ground is unforgiving and stony,* she wrote, *but I am optimistic that the seeds I brought with me will have a chance. Meanwhile I hope to find all sorts of herbs such as agrimony and dill, maybe borage and more, across the water.*

There would be plants she was unfamiliar with, so when she felt more confident she would seek the advice of the Indian and Acadian people. Firstly she must get there. To that end she had been teaching herself the local custom of sculling – a skill that didn't come easily.

'You be careful,' Thomas cautioned, after he'd negotiated the loan of a little skiff from the store. 'Follow the line of the shore before you venture out,' he insisted.

It wasn't until he was convinced she was proficient that he allowed her to venture across the water to Arichat. When she heard the fishermen talk of a war between American rebels and the British she had second thoughts, becoming worried about crossing alone to Arichat.

'Don't you fret about that,' Thomas reassured her, as they sat toasting their shins by the flickering firelight. 'It won't affect us 'cos it's all down Boston way, and Boston's in America, hundreds of miles to the South.'

'But what's it about?'

'Some sort of hoo-hah about taxes. Such spats have been on and off for years and years with no more than a few skirmishes to show for 'em,' he said. 'The Americans have to be taxed, so's the British government can cover the costs of protecting the colony.'

'That makes sense,' she agreed, grateful to have her mind put at rest. She set aside her darning and made safe the fire. Grasping his hands she dragged him to his feet. 'If I'm not mistaken Thomas Galliard, the tide is such that your day, and therefore my own, must start before dawn, and the bearskin beckons.'

His eyes lit up with anticipation.

CHAPTER 9

Elise watched the sun slip down a darkening sky. If it were not for the mosquitoes it could almost have been a summer's evening in Guernsey; a Guernsey that seemed more and more remote as the days then the weeks went by. Though she was busy, the ache in her heart was as ever-present as those darned mosquito bites. The homesickness did not ease, but she was determined to learn to live with it. She had made her new home comfortable enough. There was a well-scrubbed trestle table and two benches, hooks on the wall for clothing and pans, and sacking on the floor. She had a husband who was kind and loving, they both enjoyed good health, and she'd started to prepare for her future as a herbalist.

Still in awe of her role as the wife of a fisherman in this strange and remote place, she knew she had much to learn, but everything was manageable. Everything except mosquitoes. Now, in mid-June, they were bad enough during the day, but once dusk settled the wretched things got everywhere, even under her cap to attack her scalp. She liked to sew in the evenings by the light of the slow-dipping sun while Thomas mended his nets, but the constant buzzing was difficult to ignore.

'Why don't the natives suffer?' she asked as she slapped at her neck and wiped the resultant squashed mess on the grass.

He shrugged, shook his head and carried on repairing his net. 'They cover themselves in some sort of rancid fat. There, that's ready for the morning.'

Could she exchange her excruciating bites for the stink of animal fat? There were days, and especially nights, when she felt she could, though what her husband would make of that she dared not think. Finding a way of keeping the insects at bay, or at least alleviating the swelling and fierce itching was going to be difficult, but she intended to experiment with various plants until she found the answer. Then she could focus on the elusive "no-see-ums" – those almost invisible midges that got everywhere and bit like the very devil. Something had to work, didn't it? She was, after all, a budding herbalist and pioneer now – brave and resourceful.

In the gathering dusk Thomas stretched his back and she followed his upward gaze to the pale underbellies and long sweeping tails of the swallows as they swooped their hectic dance overhead.

'Anyhows, the birds are having a feast,' he said. 'Oh, I got something for you.' He took her hand and led her indoors. From amongst his tools and fishing paraphernalia, he produced a bulky object wrapped in canvas. 'Here it is.' He cleared his throat. 'It's for you.' He was unsure of what to do next so thrust the package at her.

She took it and viewed him in wonder. 'A gift?'

'As I'm never going to cure you of all your potion-making I thought you'd better have it.'

She removed the sacking to reveal a fine basket made from woven rushes and birchbark bound to wooden splints. It was a good size, sturdy, lightweight and decorated exquisitely.

'It's for your collecting. You have to put the herbs and such in something, so there you are.'

She knew her remedies and night visions made him uneasy. A deep-rooted part of him was etched with the Guernsey fear of witchcraft, or even the whisper of witchcraft. Yet despite his personal doubts, here was this lovely gift to aid her foraging.

'It's wonderful. Where did it come from?'

He was both pleased and embarrassed. 'The Mi'kmaq make them.' He pointed to the intricate, russet-coloured pattern. 'See, that's porcupine quills. They use them a lot for making things fancy.'

She put the basket down and threw her arms around his neck. 'Thank you. Thank you so much. It'll be really useful and I'll keep it forever.'

He cleared his throat. 'It's getting late,' he said.

The following evening turned cool and Thomas put logs on the fire. Elise loved such evenings. She curled up on the old bear-skin and enjoyed the intimacy of the spluttering flames. As she cuddled up she asked what the Jerseyman, John Robin, was like to work for.

'He's all right. Mind, what he thinks of you after you made a public disgrace of yourself and were all over me when you came ashore, I don't know.'

Having nothing handy to throw at him she made do with tickling the spot at his waist where he felt it most. She did not cease her torture until his pleas for mercy were heartfelt enough to satisfy her.

'I've seen him about of course, and met him briefly,' she said, 'after you stopped molesting me and I could make myself decent again. He seems a strict sort of man. Not one you'd cross.'

'That's true enough. He brooks no argument. But he did welcome you in person.'

'He did. But I got the impression that he wasn't happy with me coming out here to be with you.'

'It's against company policy. Wintering over's not the custom, even for a fisherman. But he made an exception because of my mother,' Thomas said. 'And I make myself useful, so he can't complain.'

She knew it had been a favour to Thomas's mother after she took in a cousin of Mr Robin's at one time. It was written into Thomas's contract that his wife could join him after two years, so Mr Robin couldn't very well renege on the promise. She watched Thomas add a log to the tired embers and she stretched languidly. Joining her, he wrapped his hands around her waist.

'The voyage didn't suit you, that's for sure. We must put some weight back on your skinny bones.'

'I'm a bag of fish bones am I? You can blame my journey. I did better than most, but I never expected such seas. Renee Sebire suggested you could have kept that little snippet of information to yourself for fear that I might not have undertaken the voyage at all.'

His face, full of injured feelings, did not convince, and she added, 'Thomas Galliard, I do believe she may have been right,' before attacking him once again on his ticklish ribcage.

Gathering her hands into his, he said, 'You must agree that I'm worth a few weeks' discomfort.'

'Maybe... we'll see.' She smiled and snuggled closer. 'What about Mr Robin's brother? Is he as quiet spoken? I've heard tell of him but haven't seen him around.'

'Mr Charles? He's away on his half-decked boat a deal of time. He oversees his other fisheries, and trades with settlers and Indians, but he comes here a lot too, especially in winter. They say he likes to keep a close eye on all his stations. As for quiet spoken, I should say not – not one bit.'

Thomas stroked her unloosed hair and told her that she'd meet Mr Charles in good time. He kissed her forehead; little butterfly kisses where the blue and green bruises, evidence of rough seas and low ceilings, had at last faded. He gazed into her eyes.

'When I look at you I still can't believe my luck.

You're so beautiful.' Her breathing deepened as he ran his hand down her willing body. 'And lusty,' he growled softly.

She laughed.

'Let's to bed, Mrs Galliard.'

***

Tall. As a tree. Purple-black raven. In the night. Glowing ember eyes. Fish-hook talons. Dagger jaws to rip her apart. Kra kra kra. Swoops. Gouges. Foul-breathed. Death.

Run! Escape! Get away!

A roar punches the pit of her stomach.

Make it go away, Thomas. Make it go away.

***

The nights shortened and soon the summer solstice came round. The longest day. The sun, like a balm, shone in earnest, trees were in leaf, flowers blossomed, and, despite all precautions, Elise's freckles thrived.

The forest became a fusion of greens. She marvelled at how the first heat of the sun brought out the crimson clusters of the maple trees and fluffy blossom of the wild Indian pear. Everything was immense. So many vibrant colours, so much wondrous fauna, all alive with beauty. Best of all were her sightings of eagles. Black all over but for a startling white head and tail. Such an

69

astounding bird with its great hooked beak, talons like scythes, and a wing-span greater than the height of a Guernseyman.

At last she felt a sense of belonging, and today she was excited for she had plans. Loading her new basket with small samples of her remedies – salve of chamomile, iodine tincture, scurvy-grass, feverfew, powdered pennyroyal and wormwood – she sculled her borrowed skiff along the island's coast by way of the inlets and rocks before crossing to Arichat. With growing confidence, she had already made several trips across the bay. Under a fretwork of clouds, she secured the little boat and strode into the bustling town. In the summer months over two hundred Acadians and Mi'kmaq lived in this settlement. The Acadians came to fish in the spring, mostly for Robins' outfit. Then in the winter, like the Mi'kmaq, they went inland to hunt for food and animal skins. Now, in full summer, she saw children running naked and carefree. She grinned when a small chubby boy with a runny nose approached, touched her skirt, then, unnerved by his own boldness, scampered away squealing.

The locals were getting used to her, and accepted her when she strolled about and smiled, nodded timidly, stopped to ask simple questions and then moved on to search for fresh herbs. Today, as usual, her visit took her by the small chapel. Here Mr Robin and his Channel Islanders – Protestants amongst a community of Roman Catholics – held a simple service every Sunday morning. As ever, she was impressed by this thriving community. She passed the rope-maker busy at work, and the small forge, quiet for the moment, then various log-made cabins, and later some Mi'kmaq wikuoms, stopping now and then to speak with people she'd become acquainted with. The native women were shy, as indeed she was shy of them, but today she found the courage to approach a small group who sat weaving and basket-making while their children ran and played.

'May I join you?' she asked in Guernsey patois.

The women hesitated, exchanged glances, then opened a space to let her in. She placed her basket in the centre of the group.

'We see you go into the woods with your basket.' This observation came from an older woman, perhaps the grandmother of the little child who sat close by and peered at Elise.

'You make remedies?' one woman asked. Elise nodded. 'Is this usual in your country? For women to make remedies?'

'Not so much these days. Would you like to see what I make? What I brought from my home far away?'

She let them sample a little of the tinctures and ointments and they asked how she prepared them. She described the properties and recipes for the items in her basket, and the women, in turn, told her of their favourite curatives. Soon they were laughing and chatting together like long-established friends. She was especially interested in their extensive knowledge of medicinal infusions.

When Thomas came home late that afternoon he found her using her wooden mortar and pestle with great energy. 'Rosehips,' she explained. 'I'm going to make a tea to treat colds.'

He said nothing but she didn't let his lack of enthusiasm dampen her spirits, for she was determined to gain as much understanding of the native curatives as she could. After all, their knowledge, like her own, evolved from their ancient traditions and with such as nature provided.

I don't know what the future holds, she determined, *but wherever we are, I intend to be the best herbalist I can be, and my family will be proud of me. Maybe one day Thomas and I will return home wealthy and successful, and with a family of our own.*

***

It wasn't long before her trips to Arichat became part of her routine and she regularly took the skiff across the water. The Mi'kmaq women had stopped staring at her and started returning her greetings. She hoped to make friends with these local people, and it was good to talk to other women now and again. On one of her scavenging trips, with the sun warming her back, she wandered towards the wikuoms whilst daydreaming and enjoying the port's usual flurry of activity. She recognised a young Mi'kmaq woman minding a small boy near the opening to her wikuom.

'Good morning, Laurel,' Elise called out. Laurel had shown a great interest in Elise's tales of her family and her home in Guernsey. Elise never tired of talking of these things, so the young Mi'kmaq woman and the young Guernsey woman had begun to enjoy each other's company.

Laurel's face lit up as she returned Elise's wave. The boy, Laurel explained, was Aran, her young brother. 'Where are you going?' Laurel asked.

'Firstly I shall pick some yarrow then I'm going along the coast to Robin Cove and into the forest to search for some juniper and anything else I find interesting. Perhaps you can tell me the names and properties of those I don't know?'

'It will give me pleasure.'

Elise admired the unusual circle of willow that Laurel worked on. She was decorating it with beads, tiny stones, feathers and intricate thread-work webbing. A catcher of dreams, the young woman told her. She held it up for Elise's inspection. 'The dreamcatcher has a special purpose,' she explained. 'All dreams, good and bad, float on the night air in search of their destination. We hang one of these above our sleeping place so that it can catch our dreams before they enter us.'

Elise touched the beautiful object with the tip of her finger. Images of a purple-black raven clung to her mind and she nervously asked if the Mi'kmaq believed that dreams held messages.

'Many say they have seen and dreamed things that later happen, although I have not experienced this.'

'But what if these visions are really the devil aiming to deceive?' Elise's mouth turned dry and her heart beat a little faster. 'In my land we're fearful to speak of these things. We talk of dark powers and phantoms endangering our souls. We fear witches who talk with the devil.'

Laurel smiled. 'The Mi'kmaq are taught to listen to their dreams from their earliest days. We dream of what is long past, we dream of that which is to come. Sometimes our dreams simply express our hidden fears. But your people have no wisdom. They do not listen to their dreams.'

'You've given me a lot to think about.'

'When I have finished this dreamcatcher I will make a gift of it to you. You can hang it above your bed where it will watch over your dreams.'

'That would be wonderful, I'd like that.' Elise picked up her basket and smiled at Aran who sat playing with some white and grey feathers.

Elise gathered a good bunch of yarrow then returned to her skiff. She sculled through foam-topped breakers until she reached Robin Cove, thinking what a fine thing it must be to name coves and islands and bays after yourself. This particular cove was deep and pretty. From here she hoped to find the juniper bushes she sought. After securing the skiff she made for the dappled sunlight of the forest and a spot where she had been told she would find them in abundance. Sure enough she soon filled her basket with clippings. She added an interesting dark green, rhubarb-like leaf – one for Laurel to identify later.

The forest was vast and full of evergreen and deciduous trees, many of which she couldn't yet name, and plants both familiar and strange. The air smelled rich and verdant. Birdsong, like the sunlight, was muffled by the tall density of the trees. She could identify the plaintive coo of the dove, the cute little chickadee and the startlingly colourful blue jay, and she was spellbound by the tiny darting hummingbirds. As she walked, her foot disturbed a mound of pale, fresh dust heaped against a fallen tree. When she peered closer she saw the furious activity of ants. A flow of them, black and fat, emerged from the dried resin tubes of the pine in their twos and threes, their fours and fives, each carrying a single crumb of freshly excavated wood. They dumped crumbs onto the ever-growing, and now overflowing heap on the forest floor. Each insect then disappeared back inside what must have been a fast-emptying shell of pine. Clearly the good of the colony was the be all and end all of each individual ant. Was this so in the human world? She thought not. Fascinated, she stood watching for ten minutes or more wondering at the intricacies of nature in this new land of hers.

She stretched her back then spotted some white cedar fronds on a nearby tree and remembered the point of her mission. These fronds were used by the Mi'kmaq. They steeped them in boiling water and the preserved infusion was useful in the winter as a remedy for scurvy. She harvested a quantity, feeling pleased with her success. A rustle caught her attention. She stopped. Nothing. She walked on. The hairs on the nape of her neck rose, her skin prickled. Someone watched her. When she saw it she knew it to be a bear. She cried out before clamping her hand to her mouth and freezing. Her heart jumped loudly but the creature took no notice of her. It capered about and scratched at a fallen tree trunk. It stood no bigger than a large dog, except that this was a most sturdy animal. Where its thick fur caught the sunlight it resonated with an auburn that shone like silk, a far cry from the mangy old skin that covered her bed. Elise crept forward, entranced. She was surprised to hear a *purr* reminiscent of her cat at home. At the sight of her the bear's hackles rose and it made a loud bawling sound as it backed away. *Why, this creature is no harm at all,* Elise realised then. Deciding not to disturb it further she turned back the way she'd come.

Then she saw it. A solid bulk of muscle and dark brown shaggy fur. It stared at her with black primeval eyes. A mother bear ready to defend its young. Elise, trapped by her own paralysis, watched the beast close in. A cold sweat beaded her forehead. Her breath, when it came, was little more than laboured gasps. A mist of terror filled her head. Through that mist she heard a low grumble that came from deep within the beast's chest. A succession of grunts and moans. Loud frantic blowing sounds. Strands of foul-smelling saliva dripped from its jaw. Its yellow teeth were knives fit to disembowel. She heard the distant *kra kra* of the purple-black raven. The bear reared, solid huge broad as a barn. Massive paws hovered before her face, claws ready to slice her to the bone. Her nightmare incarnate.

All she could think was, *not like this, dear God, not like this*. Her gaze was held captive as she backed away step by step. Her legs trembled with fear and weakness. She had no strength to turn and nowhere to run.

From mossy tendrils, from the forest floor, from the tall trees a piercing scream echoed. It rained from the sky. It rose from the depths. It ricocheted both inside her and outside her. Her death scream. It seemed to go on forever.

Her heel caught on a root and she pitched backwards. Her head cracked into the knotted roots of a tree as the world exploded behind her once, and then again, and the air filled with the sound of fire and hell and light and dark. Black night fell.

***

So I am dead. She opened her eyes. A vaguely familiar face came into focus through the red mist of her mind. Wasn't that the handsome Acadian agent from Saint-Pierre? He'd been such a nice man. Was this an illusion, or was he perhaps dead too?

'Are you hurt?' he said. At least she guessed that's

what he said, but the thunder of noise in her ears made it hard to tell. A sharp pain drew her hand to the back of her head where a significant lump already formed. She winced.

'Here, sit up slowly. It's quite safe. There, see. It's dead.'

Sure enough a heap of dark fur lay close by. The stench of it made her reel. The illusion, which was not an illusion after all but a living, breathing man, helped her up. He led her a few yards off and sat her beneath the shelter of a tree. Kneeling, he held her trembling hands until all at once the impact of her experience hit her. When her tears and sobs abated he loosened her desperate grasp and handed her the red linen handkerchief from around his neck.

'Sorry, not too clean, but it serves the purpose. You feeling a little better now? When you get your breath back I'll help you home. Good job I was close by and heard the commotion.'

She remembered his name – Monsieur de Forêt. 'You shot it?'

'Most certainly did. Twice, to be on the safe side.'

'The little one?'

'Ran off. It won't survive.'

'Oh. M'sieur, I don't know how to thank you.'

'No thanks needed, except to the Almighty for sending me this way in search of game. I heard some geese and followed the noise until it was drowned out by a scream fit to wake the dead and I almost stumbled on you doing your war dance with bruin here. No, sorry, don't cry again,' he said. 'I have no more handkerchiefs and would, being a gentleman, have to offer my shirt, of which I have but few. There that's better, a twitch of a smile.'

'You saved my life. How can I repay such bravery, M'sieur de Forêt?'

'Not brave to point my rifle and squeeze the trigger. Though I admit I risked hitting you instead. But there, luck sat on our shoulders. If you want to do me one small favour, my name is Marcel.'

'I'm not sure I...'

'The Indians believe if you save a person's life you're forever responsible for that person. How can we not use Christian names when I must be responsible for you as though we were brother and sister?'

Proprieties had little weight in this wild land so after a moment's hesitation she said, 'Then you shall be my brother. Since I left my own brothers and sisters in Guernsey I have felt the lack.'

'Since my only sister died of the smallpox, I have wished for another. So we're both better for the deal, are we not, Elise?'

'Yes Marcel, I think we are.'

CHAPTER 10

As was their custom after the Sunday Service, Elise and Thomas lingered at Arichat harbour enjoying the bustle. She stood close to Thomas amongst great swathes of netting hung out to dry, stacked barrels, propped dories and curled ropes; a beach festooned with all manner of fishing paraphernalia. This confusion of equipment was so familiar that she barely noticed it except as obstacles to be avoided. Today there were ships freshly arrived from England and with them came the chance of letters; precious letters from family. Today they were in luck. A package was waiting for them and they hurried home in order to open it and exchange news before the tide called Thomas back to work.

They sat soaking up their respective news. Thomas looked up from his letter. 'My sister writes that there's a terrible barley shortage at the moment.'

'I hope it's over soon. Here it's wheat that's always in short supply, and that drives me... oh, Thomas!'

'What's wrong, love?'

She waved her letter at him. 'Mère writes that Marie

is betrothed at last, and a wedding planned for next spring! How excited they must all be. I so long to be there.' The reality of being so far from home and family fell over her like a shadow. Then her world brightened. 'But I will be so in my thoughts. I wish I could send a proper gift. I'll have to think of something.'

She folded the letter with great care and put it with the small collection she kept safe and dry in the valise she'd brought from home. *You'll wear those letters out*, Thomas sometimes teased when he caught her re-reading each one time and again.

Later she proudly showed him how she'd made a pretty collage of some pressed white flowers and green fronds. He nodded his approval. 'That'll make a nice wedding gift.' He kissed her cheek. 'My clever girl.'

'There are masses of plants and trees I can't recognise yet. Lots are only now coming into blossom, but these little white starflowers grow aplenty and they're so delicate and pretty.'

She set to and packed the gift ready for the next ship out. As she did so her mind wandered from ships coming and going, to the mystery of Marcel de Forêt. She'd tried to speculate with Thomas about him, but since he had little or no curiosity of his own, he was unable to satisfy hers.

'Did you know that he lodges with Mr Robin when he's in Arichat?' she probed one night, as they settled down to sleep. No response was forthcoming. Undaunted, she continued, 'Yet, clearly Marcel is no fisherman. I never can pin down exactly what he does, who he works for or where he goes when he leaves here. What is an agent, in any case? It's exasperating.' She nudged her husband in the ribs. 'Does he ever speak to you of marine insurance?' The only response she got was a snore.

They'd befriended Marcel following the incident with the bear, and when he was in the area Thomas invited him to their table. Elise would not have described Marcel as a garrulous man but he did favour them with yarns of his adventures in the great backwoods. 'Trees so tall their tops disappear into the clouds. And where, as you my dear Elise know full well, bruin can run as fast as a horse and climb a tree easy as a squirrel.'

She busied herself with topping up their spruce beer but could not hide the blush rising in her cheeks. 'How was I to know that bears could swim?'

'You do now.' Marcel grinned infuriatingly.

Thomas enjoyed the joke so much that he almost choked on his beer. Marcel helpfully thumped Thomas's back, then said, 'In fairness, a bear is a rare thing to bump into on Isle Madame.'

She insisted that there'd be no more talk of bears and in an effort at diversion asked him about moose. 'I know the Mi'kmaq trap them,' she said, 'but I've never spotted one.'

'We've seen a few hides, though,' Thomas said. 'Good quality, they are.'

The evening passed enjoyably as Marcel regaled them with tales of his encounters with the slow-witted moose. 'Pea-sized brains, they've got. They have a habit of charging at you for reasons known only to themselves.'

Marcel told them that he'd not long returned from Halifax. This, she knew, was the major port on mainland Nova Scotia. When she asked him what he did there, he was his usual evasive self. It was no good pressing him; she had learned that much. Determined not to let him see how his caginess exasperated her, she made a show of stoking the fire until, unprompted, he said, 'I have a cousin in Halifax.'

This was a rare snippet of personal information and she kept her back to him for fear he'd notice her grin of satisfaction. Sure enough, he continued unbidden. 'I worry about my cousin, Sylvie, sometimes. Halifax thrived once but has degenerated into a lawless naval base full of immigrants.'

Elise sat back and studied the two men in the fire's glow. How different they were. Her gaze went from Thomas – fair and brawny – to Marcel who was dark and wiry. Thomas had a gentle, ready smile, and an equally ready frown. Marcel was more reserved, yet when he did smile his face became animated and his black eyes shone. Thomas was an open book while Marcel was unfathomable. Thomas was well acquainted with his small patch of sea and land whereas Marcel belonged to no one or nowhere. Yet they enjoyed each other's company and this pleased her, for she had become fond of the Acadian and he was good to have around.

Each day there was something new to learn - an animal, some herb or bark, a new way to prepare and serve fish, fish and more fish. Was it only she who began to hate the sight and smell of fish in her pan day after day?

Her enthusiasm for fish may have waned but she was excited to begin work for Mr John Robin in the store. This was not onerous work, but work it was, and in many ways was reminiscent of the work she did for her father. She kept the place tidy, checked the stock and made lists of requirements for the next shipment, mostly under the supervision of the clerk, Daniel Bisson. Mr Bisson was a mild man, deferential to John Robin and polite to her, and she found him to be most particular as regards tidiness, keeping the store spick and span at all times. This was a welcome trait amongst a gaggle of fishermen who cared little for such niceties. The unfortunate clerk, however, spent much of his time coughing; something that elicited scowls from Mr Robin, and a great deal of concern and a selection of curatives from her.

'Mr Robin's as cold as the fish that make his fortune,' she soon complained to Thomas.

'You haven't got to know him. He's a good man under all that plain-speaking. But do you dislike the work?'

'On the contrary, I love it. I appear to have a talent for all that bookwork and stocktaking. And it makes me feel useful. I'm helping to build our fortune.'

Daniel Bisson was responsible for making entries in the company's great leather-bound ledgers, although he often delegated this task to Elise whose handwriting, he said, was better than his own. These ledgers made interesting reading. The amount of credit each employee took out concerned her. Mr Bisson explained that this was what Charles Robin and Company called a "Truck System". A means, according to Mr Bisson, of credit that provided the company with long-term stability in exports.

'Cash is rarely used,' the clerk explained. 'Rather, Mr Robin credits the year's catch against each man's keep and any equipment, merchandise, provisions and salt used by them. The balance is paid to them when they get home.'

This bothered her, and that evening she wrote in her journal: *As I see it, this Truck System keeps the whole workforce under Mr Robin's control. Once hooked by credit, the fishermen find it virtually impossible to escape their indebtedness, even when they return home for the winter, so Mr Robin is guaranteed a dependant labour force. Many a man ends the season seeming to owe his soul to the company store.*

'Are we in debt?' she now asked Thomas. 'I can't find many entries for us in the ledgers.'

'We're luckier than most. For a start the two of us

live on little more than it takes for one, and there's your credit for your work in the store. We're both frugal and I don't touch drink, 'cepting for the spruce beer I make. I don't gamble our money away, neither. We do well enough between us.'

One chill evening Marcel re-appeared. He gave her and Thomas each a pair of Mi'kmaq shoes that would enable them to walk on top of the snow when it came. There was a fair amount of revelry as he showed them how to handle the odd-looking shoes. He also showed them how to make moccasins from moose hide, a soft and supple skin which, once greased, became waterproof. He was a good friend, but that didn't stop her trying to niggle away at what Thomas said was Marcel's business, and what she saw as his secrets.

'Marcel,' she asked one meal time as she passed him a plate of fish and sage pie, her latest experiment in trying to make fish into something else. 'Do you consider yourself French?'

He was emphatic. 'No more than you consider yourself English.'

'Only Mr Robin always talks about this or that Frenchman when he means the Acadians.'

'That's his way. John simplifies things.'

'Don't you mind?'

'What's the point of minding? He's the boss.'

'Is he?'

'Maybe… sometimes.'

His enigmatic smile made her want to hit him.

Instead she smiled back and kept her counsel. *I'll find out your secrets one of these days, Marcel de Forêt.*

Throughout the season Matthew Barbet's drinking made him increasingly crass. She'd glance up and find him staring at her, his gaze over-intimate, making her flesh crawl. He'd sidle into the store breathing his fish-and-rum breath over her. If no one else was about he'd make lewd remarks about his willingness to put a light in her eyes that was clearly beyond Thomas's ability. He relished making her feel uncomfortable but she hesitated to unsettle things by complaining to Thomas or Mr Robin. The peak of the cod started to decline by August once the capelin and herring bait became scarcer. After that there'd only be minimal fishing and by October Matthew, along with the others, would head home to tend to their wives and harvests. With the exception of Matthew, Elise would be sorry to see the fishermen go. Matthew, she would not miss. His wife was welcome to him!

On the eve of his departure Matthew came into the store to settle his account. While he delved into the inner reaches of his nose with a forefinger, she studiously avoided looking at him. On consulting the ledger she told him what money he had remaining from his season's work. He stared at her.

'I'm sorry, Matthew, but it's all down here.' She turned the ledger so that he could confirm for himself how little his spending in the company store had left him.

'You know I can't read them numbers.' He shoved the ledger back across the counter. She cried out as it slammed into her stomach.

She glanced around but there was nobody else in sight. 'Calm down, Matthew, I don't invent the accounts. It's not my doing. You need to take this up with Mr Robin.'

He paid no heed to her words. 'You do all these columns.' He jabbed at the open page with a grimy finger. 'You take some for yourself, don't you?'

'Of course I don't! How dare you! I think you'd better get out. Come back when you're sober.'

His mouth twisted but to her relief he turned towards the door. Then before she knew what was happening he had swung back and darted around to her side of the counter. 'You *bougre de chienne*. You bitch from hell.' He grabbed her hair, forced her through the stockroom door and slammed it behind him. 'Don't think I don't know what you are, you cock tease,' he snarled. 'Think you're better than the rest of us 'cos you can do numbers and letters. Steal my money and think you can get away with it, would you? It ain't possible that I've worked all season to earn only sixteen pounds, eight shillings and sixpence. I'm not so stupid as you think.'

Fear immobilised her. 'Please, Matthew…'

'Please, Matthew,' he mocked. His face, already suffering from the rigours of weather and drink, turned purple. The knife he produced was short, the tip honed to a fine point. Still clutching her hair, he leaned forward

88

and spat in her face. She tried to hide her revulsion as she wiped the spittle from her cheek with the back of her hand. The man was drunk, he was angry, but he wouldn't hurt her, not really. It was all bravado. Yet his face was twisted, ready for a fight. He broke into an ugly, cracked laugh.

'You should see your face, girl,' he snorted. 'Talk about shit yourself! Never showed me no respect, did you? Always nose-in-the-air. Don't think I haven't noticed. I'll have some respect now, though.' He gave her hair a vicious tug. Tears of pain came to her eyes. 'I said, I'll have some respect, bitch,' he roared.

The storeroom door flew open. 'What's going on? Mrs Galliard? What in God's name are you doing, Barbet?' Daniel Bisson looked from Elise to her assailant. His eyes fell on the knife in Matthew's hand and the blood drained from his face. The three of them froze in an unlikely tableau. Matthew reacted first. He shoved her to one side and lunged at the clerk. Daniel Bisson, sweat breaking out on his ashen face, took a step backwards. Elise, fuelled by rage, grabbed the first thing that came to hand – a one pound brass weight – and threw it at Matthew Barbet with all her strength. The weight cracked into his wrist. He screamed, dropped the knife, grasped his wrist and fell to his knees with a roar. Daniel Bisson gingerly retrieved the knife from the floor.

'You broke my wrist. You gone and broke my wrist, you bitch,' Matthew sobbed, as he sank down and curled up into a pathetic ball.

'Are you all right, Mrs Galliard?' Bisson asked. With shaking hands he extracted a clean handkerchief from his pocket and wiped his spectacles.

'Thanks to you. But what are we to do with this villain?'

'He must be taken home in irons and prosecuted. Mr Robin brooks no such behaviour.'

'No!' Mathew cried. 'My wife, my family. Please. Please, Elise. It was the drink talking, not me. I'm sorry. Please.'

Still angry, she knelt down, not too gently taking the injured wrist in her hands. The man went ashen and let out a sharp moan, but said nothing. 'I think perhaps this man should go home to his wife and children. His wrist is indeed broken and he's no more use to us here.'

Daniel Bisson shook his head. 'Fair enough, though I think he would have used that knife on either one of us without a moment's hesitation. He must never return for he won't get a second chance.'

It was said that Matthew Barbet had a nasty accident whilst fishing alone along the shore. After his wrist had been wrapped and splinted by Elise, he was dispatched on the first ship home, complete with a supply of knitbone infusion.

CHAPTER 11

That October, the *Seaflower* was the last ship to leave for home. Standing together on the shore, Elise and Thomas watched as the brig's anchor was raised to the beat of the shantyman and her sails caught the sharp breeze as the ship left the harbour. With her borrowed spyglass trained out to sea, Elise could make out John Robin on *Seaflower's* deck. A convoy with its navy guard ship awaited him beyond the harbour.

A grey mantle of sky crushed down heavy and low. Herring gulls shrieked as they shadowed the ship, cormorants surfaced in its wake. The first snows had peppered the hard soil though the sea was yet to grow its fringe of ice. According to Thomas, from November to April deep snow would cover the burnt-sienna landscape, lingering in gullies as late as June. It was hard to imagine, for snow in Guernsey was a rare event. Soon, here on Jerseyman Island there would only be herself, Thomas, Mr Charles and, when he's not in Arichat, foreman Rhiné Therriau. Right now in Arichat the Mi'kmaq were preparing to travel inland to their winter campgrounds and the dark evenings echoed with their rhythmic drumming and mesmeric chanting; evocative sounds that both attracted and chilled her. Most of the Acadians were getting ready to leave as well. Elise's sense of loss was heavy. Having already said farewell to many of the friends she'd made that summer, she would shortly have to say goodbye to the remainder. Laurel, who had talked of remedies and herbs with her and was prepared to listen to her endless tales of Guernsey, Bethel, an old and gentle Mi'kmaq who showed her the art of water divination, Fabrice, Laurel's older brother who taught her how to split logs with one stroke of the axe, and the eccentric Acadian, Pierre, who gave her his recipe for clam chowder and who tried to persuade her to make his formula for crushed crayfish eyes. A most excellent remedy, he assured her, for the treatment of inflamed sores; a remedy she was prepared to forgo.

Early next March, with the snow still thick in places and the sea not yet free from ice, the Acadians would begin returning from their winter camps and would join those few folk in Arichat who had overwintered. Their job would be to help prepare for the arrival of the first ship of 1776 and an early start to the new season. It was a matter of pride to beat one's competitors. The earlier the start the greater the profit.

Now, as she watched the *Seaflower* disappear round the headland, an overwhelming sense of isolation tinged with fear crept into her heart. She glanced at Thomas's jaw-set profile. For a moment she was overwhelmed by the feeling that she had been abandoned here with a stranger. Then he grasped her hand and she felt the roughness of his: the saltwater boils, the calluses and raw fissures, the burns from line and rope. She raised his hand to her lips, aware that nowadays her own hands were near rough as his.

'No regrets?' he said.

'None.'

'And has it been as you'd hoped?'

'I expected it would be hard, and I'm sure the coming winter will be even harder.'

'I didn't lie to you.'

'No, you didn't lie. And yes, I could have wed my father's apprentice and helped run the shop. Or maybe, like my sister Marie, I could have chosen one of my brother's counting-house friends. But I didn't – I married you, for richer, for poorer.'

'So you're saying you'd rather live here in the wilds of the New World than be an apothecary's wife like your mother? At least an apothecary's wife wouldn't be out in the snow chopping firewood.'

'Remember the song of the sea? That song brought us together and I'll tell you this, Thomas Galliard, I'd rather be here with you than anywhere else in the world without you. And it's not so bad. I take care of our home and you, I have the work I do for Mr Robin in the store, I tend my herb and kitchen garden, I make my remedies.'

'Your remedies.' He gave a mock sigh. 'I saw you bedding your herbs down for winter. And everywhere I turn there's another pile of lotions or potions, to mention nothing of all those twigs of shrivelling greenery hung by the fire.'

She laughed and gave him a prod in the ribs.

His face took on a grave aspect. 'We won't have much company through the winter,' he said. 'Not many comings and goings. No letters home. Just some Therriaus over in Arichat, and us and Mr Charles here on the island. A few folk from hereabouts visit Mr Charles, he visits them, but we don't see much of them.'

Foreman Rhiné Therriau stayed in Arichat with his family; a family so large that people gave up trying to distinguish one grandchild from another. These numerous little Therriaus were collectively known as *les petit crapauds* – the little toads.

Thomas frowned. 'I hope my company will be enough till spring.' His voice was low and hoarse. Again she kissed his dear sore hand. He, in turn, gently squeezed hers. 'Not many customers for your potions and curatives either. Mind, I don't think we'll get to be well-to-do on those. You're a poor sort of merchant, Mrs Galliard.'

'I take a small payment from the company men and others pay as they can. A measure of wool, some thread, a few chicken's eggs, a dish of honey, or a rabbit for the pot. It was you who ate all that honey without complaint last time, if you remember. And there's the credit at the

94

store I earn from Mr Robin.'

She contemplated the empty grey sea for a while then smiled at Thomas. 'And don't forget, the Mi'kmaq and Acadians swap knowledge with me, so I learn as much from them as they do from me. Did you know that bark from the hackmatack tree can be boiled in water and used as a laxative?'

He laughed. 'I didn't, but I do now.' Maybe he was feeling less superstitious about her ability with the remedies these days?

In the growing gloom of that late October afternoon, with the fishing season at an end and work finished for the day, and with John Robin and the *Seaflower* out of sight, she and Thomas made their way back to their cabin.

'It is hard work,' she said, as Thomas put his strong arm round her shoulder, 'but I'm living a remarkable adventure, just like I wanted.'

'If you call being chased by a bear an adventure! If Marcel hadn't happened along…'

'Yes, that wasn't a good start, was it? But it didn't chase me, it sort of reared up.'

'Reared up, you say? Reared up? I bet you didn't write "reared up" in your letter home.'

'I didn't put it quite like that.'

'At least I get you all to myself now,' he said roughly. She felt a forceful tap on her backside as they went through their door. When she turned around in protest she found herself crushed in her husband's arms.

The eastern sky had barely begun to lighten when Thomas headed off the next morning to check over the shallops where they'd been hauled up far above the high-tide line. Thomas had assured her that these twenty-foot vessels were as sound and seaworthy as you could hope for.

After she'd waved him off she walked to the company store to meet with Mr Charles, the younger Robin brother. How would it be, working alongside him? She'd got used to the older one, now she had to get used to this one. He'd arrived a few weeks earlier from some other fishery far to the north, but she knew little about him except that he resembled his older brother in appearance, though Mr Charles's smile was rather colder. Appropriately, both men had fish-eyes – ice blue, sparse-fringed with colourless lashes. Mr Charles's face was rounder, his nose rather larger, sharper than his brother's. His wispy hair and heavy eyebrows were too pale to be thought red yet too sandy to be described as fair. A little shorter and sturdier than his brother, his complexion however was as ruddy, his stride as purposeful.

Oh well, a change is as good as a rest, she thought. *Here goes.*

The storeroom door was open and Charles Robin stood at the counter, a sheaf of papers grasped in his hand. Deep in concentration, he chewed on his lower lip, frowning and muttering. She coughed and he glanced up in annoyance, seemingly startled to see her.

It took a moment or two before the light of recognition broke through.

'Ah yes, Mrs, er, Galliard. You are well, I trust? As you see, I prefer to overwinter, let my brother return to his wife. I myself am a confirmed bachelor.'

'Yes sir.'

'It appears that things have got into a fine state. Mr Bisson got sick and rather neglected his duties this past month or two. Come, I'll show you what needs doing.'

'Yes sir.'

'My brother tells me you're efficient. Let's see, shall we?'

'Thank you, sir. I do my best.'

'That husband of yours…'

'Thomas.'

'Thomas. Yes. Sound fellow – for a Guernseyman.' He laughed mirthlessly. 'I remember now, I let Thomas overwinter against my better judgement, didn't I? His mother begged the favour. She thought it would give him a chance to make something of himself. Maybe it will.'

'Yes sir, thank you sir.'

'Anyway, it's worked out well enough and now we have you to help us, Mrs Galliard.' He gave her a long hard stare then bellowed, 'My brother's decision, but a sound one, I'm sure.' She was soon to learn that due to deafness in his right ear, he bellowed quite a lot, but without rancour.

She opened her mouth but no sensible response came

to her, so she closed it again. He was a strange one. She didn't know what to make of him but she got along well enough with most folk, and he'd not find her work-shy.

He studied her once more, as he might assess the quality of a codfish or fox pelt, then picked up a great ledger and strode to the stockroom at the back of the store. He turned and glanced back at her. 'Let's not spend our time gossiping, shall we?'

***

That November she exchanged six embroidered handkerchiefs for an old flintlock musket. What need, after all, had she for fancy handkerchiefs? The Mi'kmaq she traded with had earned a new rifle with his animal furs. Looking to impress a young girl with the delicate hankies, he was pleased to barter away his old musket. She presented the musket to Thomas with pride. 'He even showed me how to care for it. And he gave me a bag of lead balls, a horn and a wrap of priming-powder.' She produced these as further evidence of her trading skills.

Thomas looked askance. 'I'm a fisherman. I don't know about guns.'

'But dearest, you can learn, then hunt for our pot.' She tried to keep the disappointment from her voice.

'Put it away. Better still, sell it. You'll find a buyer easy enough. I'll stick to snares, me.' He turned and walked away.

Why was he being so stubborn? She was annoyed with him and she did not put it away. With this musket she could prove her worth even if Thomas was being stuffy. He was grumpy over her defiance so she practiced only when he was from home. She knew he'd be pleased in the end, but it was harder to fire than she'd imagined. Eventually, much to her astonishment, having missed a wild turkey by a whisper, in early December she bagged a large male muskrat. It had been attracted to her depleted vegetable plot and was picking its tentative way through the smattered snow. She'd tiptoed to the fireplace where, to Thomas's annoyance, she kept the weapon. She'd quietly primed it and crept back to the open door. She'd raised the weapon, rested it against her shoulder and eased the trigger towards herself. Half deafened and choked, she dashed outside where, to her astonishment, the dead creature lay.

'Got you, got you, got you!' she sung, lifting her catch by its ratty tail and dancing round in circles, hardly noticing her sore shoulder. Now let Thomas tell her to sell her gun! It was a whopper – about two foot in length and weighing maybe four pounds. She made a stew.

'Delicious,' Mr Charles pronounced the next day, returning the plate she'd taken round the previous evening. 'Most generous of you Mrs Galliard. Just how I like my muskrat . Gamey, fine grained.'

'Thank you, Mr Charles.' Elise flushed. He rarely gave a compliment.

'And you really shot it yourself? I'm impressed. Tell

99

me, what was that sauce?'

'Foxberry.'

'A triumph. And your own-grown turnips, I'll be bound.'

'And the potatoes.'

'Your husband will be proud of you,' he hollered with an approving nod. He left a small pouch of musket balls for her.

Thomas ate his stew in silence, never mentioning the furry pelt she eventually nailed to the cabin wall. She got to keep the musket, telling him that next time she'd bag a deer. He seemed not to hear her.

***

The days shortened. Early one afternoon she watched a regimented V of geese arrow southward across the bay, honking for all they were worth. How good it would be to head towards the sun. For one moment she was up there amongst the birds, heading home. The sun warmed her back, the wind rustled her hair. Then the moment was gone. Did she really want to leave Thomas and all this behind? To head back to her familiar, safe world? Sometimes she did – just sometimes – then she recalled her hopes and dreams.

She noted in her journal: *I have come to admire Charles Robin's energy and drive. The man is here, there and everywhere as weather allows, repairing his house and the warehouse alongside Thomas, writing his*

many notes and memos in preparation for next season,
supervising the felling of trees on Isle Madame,
checking his ledgers. He is tireless.

One wind-dashed morning she was collecting
firewood from the stack by her cabin door when a
familiar voice startled her. 'Good day, Elise. Are you
well?'

'Marcel! You're a welcome visitor. We're fed-up
with our own company here. Will you eat with us
tonight?'

'Love to, but my business with Charles includes him
providing me with a good wine and some of his fresh-
caught lobster.'

'Business, you say? Is that fishing business?'

'Not exactly. Well, maybe a little.'

She dropped her logs and, hands on hips, looked him
in the eye. 'You drive me crazy, you're so evasive,
Marcel de Forêt.'

He laughed, helped her retrieve her firewood and
gathered up a bundle of kindling for her. Once indoors
he smiled and drawled, 'Oh come, Elise, not evasive,
just boring.'

The following day she picked up her mirror, a small
chipped one given to her by Mr John earlier that year.
Useful for tidying her hair and for Thomas to use when
he shaved. This grey winter's morning she stared at her
reflection, something she'd avoided doing for weeks. A
pinch-faced, red-nosed, smudge-eyed woman stared
back at her. A tired woman with sad greasy hair best

hidden from view. She flung the mirror on the table. 'Hateful cruel thing,' she muttered. Yet she felt compelled to pick it up once more, to stare at the travesty of the fresh, innocent-faced girl who'd left her home but nine months past. *So, that's what Marcel sees when he looks at me. No wonder he prefers to dine with Mr Charles.* She glared at Thomas, who was frowning in concentration as he measured wood. 'All this,' she gestured about her, 'this way of living. It suits you,' she accused him crossly. 'You never were happier than now when we're both trapped here in this frozen purgatory. You're so ruddy and healthy and I've become an old woman.' Tears hovered and threatened to spill down her cheeks.

He glanced up from his repair of the bedpost. 'You exaggerate. You're as lovely as ever. And it's what *I* think that counts. Not what the likes of Marcel de Forêt or Mr Charles or any other man might think.' Picking up his hammer he applied it vigorously. Was that meant to reassure? Or was it just that he took her for granted? She chose to be reassured.

***

The winter growled fierce and dark, frightening yet dull in its monotony.

'Marcel's snowshoes,' Thomas said. 'The ones he gave us. Let's try them out.'

A new distraction – how exciting! She booted herself

up then fiddled until the hide webbing was in place as Marcel had demonstrated. Walking was easier said than done. She staggered like a clumsy bear towards the door. By the time they'd bundled themselves up against the cold, they were laughing so much they could barely stand, snowshoes or no snowshoes. How good it felt to laugh. They danced patterns in the snow. Once conquered, Marcel's gift proved invaluable.

Before long they needed to dig themselves out of their home through snow that reached to the roof, then they had to cut a path through the drifts. A strange acoustic quality reigned. Nearby sounds were muted, yet distant sounds came as clear and sharp as slivers of ice. If the sun broke through it revealed a hard white world so dazzling you had to shield your eyes against it. Tree branches cracked like musket fire. She carried out a stocktake at the store and made sure she tidied everything away from the worst of the damp. She chopped firewood, gathered frozen kelp and dug around for the few surviving vegetables and edible green plants. She continued to experiment with and prepare remedies from such bark and plants that she could gather in the snow and hoar frost, as well as using those she had dried and set aside in earthenware pots by the fireside. Soon there remained little more for her to do in the store until the first ship came laden with fresh supplies, but to give him his due Charles Robin did not reduce her pay.

Then came the real bite of winter.

CHAPTER 12

Before the snows came Elise had dug up a quantity of turfs to fix against the walls of their cabin in an attempt to keep the northwest winds at bay. Better than nothing, she supposed. Despite her best efforts her few chickens did not survive. Thomas had warned her not to name each of them. He had been right and she wouldn't do so again. She hoped they'd be able to afford to buy more next spring. As enjoyable as the stews and broth from those hens had been, she missed their eggs, their clucking and their silly feathery company.

She was disconcerted to find that the spruce beer froze even though stored by the chimney, and their black bread had to sit by the fire for near on an hour before it was soft enough to eat.

On good days Elise remembered to stop and look beyond the cold, the stinging rain, the brutal wind, her raw hands and face, her sore runny nose and her shivering misery. Today was such a day. Although only mid-afternoon, the dark was ever-present. Yet when she bundled up and made the necessary trip outside to empty the slops bucket and collect snow to melt by the fire, she was confronted by a world of extreme beauty. Breathtaking crystal drops hung like diamonds from every tree and the day had a magical quality. For a short time the great weight of cloud lifted. As she crunched on the clean unspoilt snow she marvelled at its rainbow iridescence. The large flakes that cascaded from the heavens and swirled silently made her think, whimsically, of angels – pure, white angels. Her frostbound face broke into a smile at this thought. She would remember to tell Thomas, and maybe he would smile too. These days neither of them smiled much.

She turned and headed back into the wind and its sudden icy force froze the breath in her lungs. In panic she reached frantically for the door but it was almost impossible to see. The tears were drawn from her eyes and by the time she staggered breathlessly into the cabin her lashes had frozen and the skin was starting to peel from her cheeks. Thoughts of shared smiles, crystal drops and white angels were forgotten.

During the peak of the cold little could be done outside apart from wood chopping, though this activity could ruin a good axe against frozen trunks.

That autumn Elise had tidied and cleaned the cellar under the store. Mr Charles, pleased with the extra space she'd created, had told her she could use some of it to store her own produce. She'd aired and dried her stock of potatoes and turnips and stacked them with great care. When she went to fetch some turnips early in the new year she saw a trail of rat droppings. Barrels had been eaten through, twine-secured canvas wraps gnawed away, at least a bushel of precious goods spoilt or eaten. She learned, too late, that rats could eat through everything. When she found a half dozen of the creatures drowned in a barrel of pickled pork and another dozen trapped and starved to death in a hogshead of what had been greens, she gave way to her revulsion and anger.

'The pork, the greens, my dried fish all but gone!' she cried, and shuddered into Thomas's shoulder. 'A keg of oil eaten through and leaked all over the place. A moose skin chewed and useless. And that smell!'

'There, there,' he soothed, 'it can't be helped. We'll figure a way to keep them out.'

'They've invaded everything and driven me to distraction.'

He patted her shoulder. 'They drive us all to distraction. It's like trying to hold back the tide.'

She hated those rats more than anything else in this world.

It was not all work and rats, though. One winter diversion was skating. Thomas showed her how to attach blades to her boots and launch herself onto the ice-topped sea.

'The ice will crack. We'll drown,' she squealed.

He laughed. 'That ice is two foot deep. You couldn't drown even if you wanted to.'

Thomas, being fearless and foolhardy, fared better

than Elise, but when she got the hang of it they skidded and laughed until exhausted. They tried their hand at ice-boating too, mounting a small boat on skids and rigging a sail. The brisk wind sent them along at a rare pace and she shrieked with excitement. For a short while the roses bloomed on her cheeks, laughter filled the frozen air and this icy land was where she belonged.

***

The cold remained tangible. She could breathe it, taste it, smell it. It hit her lungs like a blow. It hung from roof and tree – daggers of ice threatening to pierce her skull. Her world filled with a heavy, white silence, a stillness of sound that swallowed everything around her. During those long winter evenings her mind drifted to her father's warm shop, her pretty bedroom shared with Marie, her brothers' teasing, her father's gruff love, her mother's gentle smile.

Although the simple Sunday sermons had ceased for the winter she prayed each night for more courage and less self-indulgence.

The shortest day came and went and winter was at its worst, which meant the weather would be less severe in a month or so. She had abundant furs including a moose-hide coat and beaver mittens and hat. Much to her shame (and comfort) she also wore full-length breeches of buckskin. She was so bundled that she waddled. Her feet were never warm or dry and she suffered much from chilblains. She had used the last of her lavender oil long ago though nettle juice, such as was left, worked to some extent. She determined to get in a plentiful supply before next winter. Their fire provided some comfort but its flickering glow gave out little light. Neither did their fish-oil lanterns which were always smoky. They'd covered their only window with sacking to reduce the cold. In any case, it was often obscured by drift-snow or ice. She tried to sew, or write in her journal but it was difficult in such a gloomy smudge of light. Her thoughts, too, were gloomy and dark. Could she really cope with all these hardships with resilience and courage? And now she faced the biggest fear of all. Her flow had not shown for two months and her breasts were swollen.

How could she dare bring a child into this damp, dark world? How would Thomas feel when she told him? She would be such a burden to him. How could she give birth with no midwife or mother to care for her, for her baby? She would surely die for want of her family and her Guernsey home. She would die all alone in childbirth.

I want my mother, she whimpered into the black night.

CHAPTER 13

Poor Thomas could do nothing right. Elise knew she was behaving irrationally yet was unable to control her tears and tantrums. It was a badly smoking fire that brought things to a head one ice-gripped evening in March. 'This miserable excuse of a fire is driving me to fury. How am I supposed to live like this?' She threw a log against the wall, shocking them both, then burst into sobs.

Thomas leapt to his feet. 'Elise, dearest. Why so angry? What have I done wrong?'

She hesitated and swallowed. It was time to tell him. 'I have some news.' He frowned and opened his mouth but she rested her finger against his lips and whispered, 'You are to be a father, Thomas. I am going to have our child.'

His face was a picture of shock, then disbelief and finally alarm, as though the possibility never occurred to him. He paced the room then all at once came to a halt and stared at her. Was he angry? Then he grinned like a child about to go on a Sunday-school treat. 'A father? I'm to be a father? Oh dear God. When? Are you sure? Are you well? Will you be all right?'

She waited until he had calmed down then told him that she was most likely three months gone so they would have a September baby.

September when the sun and earth and sky glowed. September when the world shone bronze and red ochre. September, when the last ships were preparing to go home, the Acadians and Mi'kmaq were readying for their winter grounds, and another winter would begin to close in on them.

She pushed this last thought aside and, looking at him, felt so much love that nothing else mattered.

He clasped her hands and kissed them gently. 'But you are well?'

'Apart from mad outbursts about smoking chimneys, you mean? Yes, Thomas, I am well.'

'September, you say?' He drew her to him, held her softly and lay a gentle hand on her still-flat stomach.

'I'm fit, strong and well.' She put her arms around him. 'Think how easily all those Therriaus breed. Anything a Jersey woman can do, I can do better. And Mi'kmaq women manage to produce healthy infants. Once my Indian friends arrive for the season I'll seek their advice. Don't worry. I'm confident all will be well.' She crossed her fingers behind her back, and in reassuring Thomas, she reassured herself also.

As always, the weather dominated everything and a sharp eye was kept on the volatile sky. With spring approaching, Thomas spent more time outdoors. She was proud of how much he knew about the demands of their new life. He even used logs to make her some built-up herb beds and then helped her fill them with soil mixed with sand to lighten the consistency. The foreman Rhiné Therriau and his sons, each one as burly as their father, worked alongside Thomas and Charles Robin helping to prepare the fishery. With the advancing season the Acadians and Indians returned from who knew where, except that they called it winter camp. Wherever it was, it provided good hunting and was a rich source of furs. Jerseyman Island woke up as the pre-season routines began in earnest. Cringing at the reek of tar and the wear and tear on her hands, Elise set to with a willing heart and helped to caulk the sturdy shallops with fresh oakum.

Each morning the greedy call of crows barked the arrival of an unenthusiastic daybreak and each day heavy-bruised clouds raced their restless race. The promise of spring and the incoming drift of neighbours softened her jaded temper and as her nausea abated she became more like her old self. The days, if not yet warm, were now less bitterly cold. Snowmelt drooled from all but the deepest crevices and more sheltered areas of the forest. The sea was no longer a frozen plane stretching to the far shore. Drift-ice floated by, driven along the coast of Cape Breton by the currents from the north. Thomas said this accounted for the long winter-gripped springs.

That April she ran her fingers through the cold, unforgiving soil as she planted out the first herb and vegetable seeds and cuttings of the year. The smell of the damp earth was so good and the weak sun on her face felt so hopeful.

Later that month she examined the tiny shoots that would eventually be early potatoes. No more cooked acorns or smoked and boiled root-tubers. It would be heavenly. As she got to her feet her hands embraced her now gently rounded stomach.

When the first ship arrived early in May on a favourable wind, she rushed down to the landing-stages. Sailors and fishermen were soon dashing hither and thither, cussing, calling and singing. The air filled with new life and her isolation dissolved like the winter snow. What news of home? What exciting packages? What gossip? On board was Mr John. Did this mean that Mr Charles would soon be heading north to open up his fisheries in that place with the unlikely name of Gaspé? On the whole she found Mr John more approachable and less inclined to shout and snap – perhaps because he had a wife and young daughter in Jersey to welcome him home whereas Mr Charles remained a bachelor and, by his own assertion, was likely to stay that way. Mr John, in mellow moments, talked a little of his family and once or twice made some slight joke with her in his awkward unbending way. Besides, he gave a better Sunday service than his younger brother.

As anticipated, with the fishermen came a package of

letters from home, and a parcel from her mother. When, later, she opened the much anticipated bundle, she squealed with delight as she unwrapped woollen cloth for warm clothing, boots of the stoutest leather, seeds of all sorts, and soap – wonderful soap. She spent a deal of time holding the parcel and imagining her parents in their faraway parlour packing it with care. It smelt of home and lavender. Precious letters described Marie's wedding and contained news of her sister Sarah's impending first baby and her brother William's betrothal. Each letter brought bittersweet emotions and floods of longing.

As new stock filled the store she was run to distraction. She would make known her pregnancy soon but for now it remained concealed beneath her many layers of clothing. Meanwhile she unpacked the barrels and checked them against Mr Robin's inventory. All available space in the store was soon filled and the shelves Thomas had put up creaked in satisfied protest. She snatched covetous glances at these goods but mostly resisted their pull. She only ever bought what she could pay for. The company store would never own *her* soul.

CHAPTER 14

Her fifth month of pregnancy. The shadow-world of Ravens gather. *She's cold. Trapped. Rank stygian blackness. Swirling. Helpless. Voiceless. Raven's cry. In the vortex. With her. Claws. Beak. Peck. Tear. Her skirt now a greedy shroud. Drags her down. Down to her death. Death and tears.*

She awoke fighting for air, heart pounding. The devil had returned to fill her nights with evil threats. Some misty truth floated into her view but melted in the shadows before she could grasp it. In the dull blush of the fire's quiet embers her eyes were drawn to the dreamcatcher, a slow-twirling circle of willow. Is this the raven's warning? Is it about my life here? But what? Her hands cradled her stomach as she tried to make a mental connection with her child. Is it my baby, suffocating within me? No, I will not dwell on such dark things. She feared the raven, despite her grandmother's talk of guardian angels. 'Gran'mère,' she whispered into the night, 'I so miss your wisdom. You'd know what this means. You'd tell me what to do.'

She longed to share her thoughts and fears with Thomas but if she nudged him awake he'd give her that look he used when she displayed any sign of what he called her "daftness". Then he would pat her gently, caution her to keep these ideas to herself, turn over and go back to sleep.

The morning light, unfettered by mist, shone bright and sharp, and Elise's gloom dissipated. The air was thick with the thrill of the new season and, pending baby or no, she was soon embroiled in the general excitement. An old hand now, she embraced the tasks ahead of her. That first ship of the year now continued onward, taking Mr Charles to his fishing outfit in the north. On Jerseyman Island, folk were in good humour. The shallops had made an early start.

A fishing community takes the weather for granted at its peril. May turned into June, followed by a July reluctant to let go of winter. Rain fell in cold, quicksilver torrents before it kicked back from the mud-thick, waterlogged earth. A banshee wind whipped off the sea causing it to boil and rage. A strange aqueous light tinted their world. The fishing remained good, if difficult, but nevertheless people muttered about bad omens.

***

Elise had promised to take an infusion of chamomile, fennel and rum to Madame Therriau in Arichat. It was a rash promise, but one of the *petit crapauds* was suffering cruelly from teething pains. There was a lull in the rain so she dragged on her oiled cape and helmet. Seven months into her pregnancy, under the cape her coat stretched tight across the mound of her stomach. The coat should have been stored for summer by now. As she neared the shore of Isle Madame the wind picked up again and sculling was becoming near impossible. She arrived sodden and exhausted.

Bent double, she struggled along until a sound caught her attention. At first she thought it was the wind, then a dog, or maybe someone calling her name. She couldn't locate the source above the howling wind. Then to her horror she saw a small figure clinging to some driftwood and thrashing about in the sea beyond one of the landing-stages. She looked around, shielding her eyes from the wall of rain. No one in sight. She called out then screamed with all her might. Her voice was whipped away. Still shouting, yet aware of the futility of doing so, she stumbled out along the slimy wooden planks. She couldn't reach the child – the drowning child. After another desperate glimpse behind she did the only thing open to her. Tugging off her outer garments she jumped in. Icy water drove the breath from her. Her skirts engulfed her, a winding-sheet to weigh her down. She felt the sharp stab of the raven's beak as it dragged her under. Kicking to free herself she tried to cry out. Salt water filled her mouth. She thrashed and struggled until she felt the inevitability of surrender engulf her. *Thomas, I'm so sorry. Baby of mine, forgive me.* She became aware of the small child drowning in the water beside her. She would not let this happen. Somehow she summoned the willpower to keep afloat. She caught hold of the child and, gasping her last shred of strength, dragged him to the shore. She punched his chest until water escaped from his choking mouth.

Pain knifed through her and dark plunged.

CHAPTER 15

Fever vied with birth pangs and her body shook as if to tear her apart. Then came visions full of ravens so real and so terrible, so strange and distorted. Had there ever been a time without pain?

Before the delirium set in, Elise named her baby after his father. When her senses returned she learned that Thomas would have nobody but himself wash his son and wrap him in fine linen. And it was Thomas who made the tiny coffin and placed the infant in the cold, bitter earth. He erected a little wooden cross marking his son's only home in this world. Possessed by grief and fever, she was unaware of such rituals. It was later that Thomas told her these things as he sat at her bedside and held her hot damp hand.

'We all wept,' he whispered, fighting to keep his composure. 'We covered the tiny mound in great masses of wildflowers and garlands. The Mi'kmaq painted their faces white and chanted, calling to their ancient gods. The Acadian's joined us Protestants in prayer. Mr John led the praying.'

Thomas's words floated inside her head. She managed to open her eyes for a brief moment, but the weight of her eyelids dragged them closed.

'Then we all went back to work,' he added bleakly.

After a while, maybe minutes maybe days, he said, 'The natives told me it takes some while to cross over to the spirit realm. That's to give us time to mourn the loss of our earthly life, as those we leave behind must mourn us. Do you think that little Thomas, who had no time to experience earthly life, would feel that way too? I do. I think that until he's ready to enter heaven, he'll miss the mother who carried him all those months and who loved him as much as any mother can love a child.' He hesitated then added hoarsely, 'Maybe he'll even miss the father he never knew.'

His tears fell on her hand and she saw the sorrow in his face. It was her fault; this was unbearable.

'The Mi'kmaq believe that we need to re-learn what it is to be a spirit. But little Thomas never was much more than a spirit himself, was he?' he persisted. 'I hope he'll find the peace to cross soon.' He took a shuddering breath. 'The natives held a Death Feast in his honour. It was beautiful.'

Thomas had rarely said so much at any one time, nor come so close to accepting a belief outside his Protestant faith. She was deeply moved. She even conjured a wan smile for him. He knelt by the bedside and held her rigid body in his arms. Still she had no words for him, but she did not pull away. Dead in her soul, she nevertheless loved him for what he said.

When she was more in her right mind and more able in her body he took her to the tiny grave on the edge of the forest. Wordlessly she knelt down at the fresh-dug patch of soil and placed purple lupins there. She never got to hold him, see his face, touch him, kiss him goodnight. The pain weighed her down beyond grief and anchored her to a great black void.

***

She found no comfort. For weeks she drowned in the depths of her own misery as surely as if she had drowned in the black sea that killed her baby. The pains of stillbirth were nothing compared to the pains that tortured her heart. Day and night the flames of hell engulfed her and she burned.

Folk were kind, especially the Therriaus, whose grandson she had pulled death-like from the sea. Thomas told her that an Indian, Joseph, found her passed out and bleeding beside the sobbing child. She could not bear the sight of young Guérin Therriau, though she was glad he had recovered. Not his fault. And yet. If he hadn't wandered off... if the *petit crapaud* had not suffered so with his poorly teeth... if she had not sculled across the water... Oh what use such thoughts? And did she detect blame in Thomas's eyes? Her actions killed his child and he did well to blame her. He could not blame her as much as she blamed herself.

Her little boy was torn from this world, so went into the next without benefit of his mother's kisses and without baptism. She was overwhelmed with the fear that he would be trapped in limbo. Her milk flowed and taunted her. She ineffectually cursed the ravens. She cursed herself and her inability to understand their message. A great weight bore down. It was hard to breathe, as though she still fought the icy sea. In her worst moments, God forgive her, she wished she had not woken.

CHAPTER 16

Elise knew that a part of her would always belong to Baby Thomas. Her grief was ever-present, a great weight of sorrow. She sought distraction in her work at the store, and solace in tending and drying her herbs and preparing her remedies. But her heart was not in any of it and her body was leaden. Tears sprung to her eyes at no prompting. She could barely drag herself from her bed of a morning. She would avoid her reflection in the old mirror, hating the sorrow and guilt that looked back. She was ashamed of her lack of mettle. Had not her own mother lost three infants and survived the grief with fortitude?

By September she had tamed her sorrow sufficiently to lock it away. Outwardly at least, she was more like her old self. *It's what women do*, she told herself.

The air became infused with an energy it was hard to ignore. The fishing had been exceptional and the men were in fine spirits. John Robin, along with Mr Charles who'd joined them, was all smiles as they got stuck into the last weeks of the season. Mr Charles, so much in contrast to her own inner bleakness, was disconcertingly and annoyingly genial. However, genial or not he never lost sight of his drive for success and profit. Aside from the quality of their cured fish and their traded furs, the brothers' system of credit made them rich. It allowed them to obtain cod at a price barely above the amount the fishermen needed to live on. Thus some of the men tended to be forever striving to overcome their borderline debt to the company. This season looked to be the one to see them all go home as heroes.

A soft golden sun warmed the air. Swallows, anxious to head south, performed their seasonal acrobatics. The days were full of activity and expectation. Nights and early mornings were chilled by breezes that signified the coming change of season. The fresh dawn air was pungent with damp earth. Shimmering nets of cobwebs threaded and adorned branch and frond.

Before too long the last ship would leave for home, the Acadians and Mi'kmaq would head for their winter campgrounds, and she would close the store – another winter to face. No. She wouldn't think of that. Instead she allowed herself be seduced by the autumnal excitement and bustle on both Jerseyman Island and the village of Arichat across the water. With the torment of mosquitoes abated and the freshness of the sea breezes to stir her blood, she felt a small revival of her former courage. Letters from home consoled her. From Saint-Pierre her former travel-companion, Renee Sebire, wrote offering kind words.

Then the shadowy ravens invaded her nights yet again. *Vaporous. Fetid. Unyielding. Proliferating. Rage. Flail. Jagged wings thrash. Beaks jab at her mouth. Face. Eyes. Everywhere the cries of the damned. But being damned herself, there is no escape. Thomas, help me. Gran'mère, what do they want of me?*

In the cool dawn the ravens were gone but her skin still crawled with their sharp kisses.

Despite her nightmares and enduring grief, her autumn days were full and satisfying enough. She and Thomas continued to enjoy Marcel's friendship and they welcomed him to their table when he was in the area. Thomas even made a three-legged stool especially for Marcel's use. The Acadian managed to distract her, to make her laugh, to feel like the person she wanted to be.

'Cook Bichard produces fine enough fare, but bland,' Marcel announced while tucking into his heaped plate one evening. 'But this venison stew has to be tasted to be believed. Elise, you excel in your use of aromatic plants. You've got the garlic exactly right. And these herby potato dumplings!'

'Thank you.' She beamed. 'The wild garlic works most satisfactorily. It's best if fresh but does well enough when preserved in oil.'

'Steady on,' Thomas said. 'You'll spoil my wife with too much praise.' He laughed, but there was an edge to his laughter. He was still vexed about her disobedience over the musket.

Marcel sat back. 'Thomas tells me you shot the deer yourself.'

She nodded, casting a quick glance in Thomas's direction.

'Amazing,' Marcel added. 'No, don't blush. This is the best meal I've had since I enjoyed your hospitality last time. You are a fortunate man, Thomas Galliard.'

'Thomas doesn't approve of my musket.'

'That's not so. I know I'm a lucky man.' He spooned some meat into his mouth and chewed with vigour.

She changed the subject. 'And where have you been this time, Marcel?'

'Oh, here and there. You know, company business,' he said in his usual elusive way. It had become a game between them. He went about his business, while she tried to fathom what exactly that might be.

'What company?' she now persisted.

'I think if Marcel wanted us to know his dealings, he'd tell us.'

'No secrets here – simply boring business that doesn't make good table talk.'

She accepted defeat with a smile. 'Then tell me this,' she said. 'There's talk of the American rebels. That they're closing in on us and causing great problems up and down the coast.'

For a moment or two he frowned and did not reply. 'You're right to be concerned,' he said eventually. 'But I've not seen any sign of rebel ships for all my comings and goings.'

'You're panicking over nothing,' Thomas growled. 'I said before, we're safe as houses, us. Them rebels are rabble-rousers with no arms and no organisation. Mr Charles said so.'

'That's not the impression I got,' she responded. 'Charles Robin said he's ordered the early closure of his fishery to the north because of its isolation. He was cursing the British guard ships, saying they'd be no help because the rebels are keeping them busy off the American coast.'

Her gaze switched from Marcel to Thomas and back to Marcel. These uncertainties frightened her. 'Mr Charles sounded worried. True, he's overwintering himself, but he said the sooner they secured Jerseyman Island, and his ships were on their way, the better.'

'There you are then.' Thomas wiped his mouth and reached for his pipe and baccy pouch. 'The last of the season's catch will head home, we'll clear up here, and our livelihoods will be safe.'

'But will *we* be safe?' She turned to Marcel who was frowning and looked distracted. 'Will we be safe here for the winter?'

'I—'

'Course we will, us,' Thomas put in. 'There'll be nothing to take but our small supplies. Not worth their efforts. And in any case, once the last ship goes we're going to shift what we can across the water and into the forest behind Arichat. There's a deal of equipment and shallops hid there already.'

'Thomas, I want to hear what Marcel says.'

Thomas sat back and smoked his pipe. She scrutinised Marcel. Eventually the Acadian smiled. 'Thomas is right. After all, if Charles is planning to overwinter again, I don't think he'd put your lives and his own at risk, do you?'

Thomas looked at her knowingly and nodded. Marcel's words should have reassured, but her unease persisted as did her nightmares which increased in number and intensity. Vengeful ravens dived and attacked the vessels in the harbour, their bulk and weight sinking each and every ship. Sailors were cast into a blood-churned sea. Time and again she awoke to the cries of drowned men mingled with the chilling *kra kra* of a hundred ravens. Did these nightmares come from her concerns? Or were they a foreshadowing of some tragedy to come?

How can I know? Not for the first time, she soundly cursed the purple-black ravens and their evasive messages.

CHAPTER 17

Charles Robin's Sunday service was brief, almost cursory, on the morning of the twenty second of September. The day had dawned to a dense fog that chilled Elise to her bones. The deterioration in the weather was reflected in the ill humour amongst the fishermen whose earlier good mood had dissipated. The fleet's departure was brought forward at the last minute because, as predicted, the British guard ships were too busy off the American coast dealing with the situation there to offer any protection for the fishing fleet.

'Mrs Galliard,' Mr Charles barked later that morning, as she hurriedly graded, counted and piled up ropes. 'We need to discuss winter arrangements.'

She was startled. Mr Charles never "discussed" anything with her, simply gave polite and firm instructions. She stopped and looked at him. A tic worked away in the corner of his eye and he ground his teeth. He was fidgety.

'Winter arrangements?'

'I spoke to your husband about coming back with us

on the last ship. Did he not say?'

She shook her head. Going home? To Guernsey? She and Thomas?

'The rebels are more of a threat than we first realised. Better armed. Better organised.' Mr Robin's voice had a sharp edge to it. 'I myself am returning to Jersey. I advise you and your husband to leave. I can't be responsible for you if you stay. In any event, there won't be much work to do as things stand. We would of course consider re-employing you once this war is over.'

Images of Guernsey flooded her mind. Père making and weighing pills, Mère stirring her bean jar, her brothers, her sisters, the nephew she'd never seen. Captain, her beloved cat. Her island – her *home*.

'Mrs Galliard?'

'Sorry Mr Charles, I didn't hear what you said.'

'I said, you're flushed. Are you all right?'

She wasn't, but she nodded.

'I must have an answer today.'

Again she nodded, her face set with anger. What was Thomas playing at? She turned back to her stack of rope, the coils rough beneath her hands. It was no good. Abandoning her task, she slipped out of the store and ran to the harbour where she caught sight of him heaving barrels into place on a landing-stage.

'What's this Mr Charles tells me? Are we going home? He said we should be.'

He stopped work, scratched his head and frowned.

'When were you going to discuss this with me?'

'Elise, you can see how it is. We're up to our necks in work here. I need time to think.'

'And I don't?'

He stood chewing on his lower lip.

'Thomas?'

'In my opinion this is all a great fuss over nothing. I don't see that a bunch of rebels is any threat to us here.'

'But Mr Charles said—'

'He probably meant to go home anyways.' He grabbed her arms and stared into her eyes. 'If we go, Elise, how do I know we'll ever come back? Think about it. How's a fisherman, a fisherman who's yet to make his way in the world, going to provide for his family if he goes back with his tail between his legs? I've no hope of a boat of my own, you know that. What about all our dreams? What about our future?'

'What about the American rebels?'

'I can't discuss this now.' He turned away, grabbed a barrel and started to shift it into place on the landing-stage.

'Thomas!'

'Tell you what.' He stopped his work for a moment but kept his eyes averted. 'Let's both think hard. Then we'll decide what's for the best at dinner. I'll see you in the cookhouse at noon.' He returned to his barrels.

Confusion and indecision held her fast. The cocoon of fog had melted enough for her to register that the landward side of the island resembled a disrupted beehive as men dashed about, made inventories and sorted what they could get their hands on. The smaller shallops were already tucked into Robin Cove. Many of the larger ones were being taken across to Arichat to be hidden in the forest. A few remained to act as tenders to the ships being prepared. The harbour was full and in the churning haze she saw the *Endeavour* rigged and loaded at the landing-stage head, ready to set sail. Alongside it sat Mr Charles's favourite ship, the *Seaflower*, which would be next to line against the landing-stage. Further out she could identify the *Hope*, the *Alexander* and the *Betsy*, all queuing to be rigged and loaded. Dried fish – the lifeblood of these fishermen – was stored in barrels branded with the company's distinctive C.R.C. trademark. It was the dry cure, Thomas had previously explained, the combination of salting and drying plus Mr Robin's fussiness over the quality of his salt, which put his cod in so much demand and fetched top prices. These barrels were stacked under birchbark covers ready for the men to load onto wooden stretchers and carry across to the landing-stage head. Between the flakes lay spars, rigging, yards, anchors, all sorted and piled up. Spruce beer for the journey was brewing in kettles on the beach. Now the end was in sight the men had bucked up and they sang as they worked. A bumper year meant bumper profits. The hated Truck System would not eat away their earnings this year. They were going home. Thomas had no right to ignore her wishes or her fears. She made up her mind and a great weight lifted from her. But for now she couldn't stand about daydreaming; she had work to finish in the store as well as in her cabin. She wrapped her cloak tight about her and turned, bumping into the master of the *Endeavour* as she did so.

He doffed his hat. 'Your pardon Mrs Galliard, I was in a rush and didn't notice you.'

'No sir, I beg your pardon. I was admiring your ship.'

'A beauty, is she not? I've sailed down from Newfoundland and, being the last to leave, I had the hold space to take some of Mr Robin's fish along with my own. Now I must be on my way. Good luck to you my dear.' He turned and hastened to board his ship.

She returned to the store and, with renewed energy and growing anticipation, completed her abandoned task of sorting the ropes, then applied herself to gathering blankets before bundling and labelling them. All the while her mind was focused on her journey home. She pushed away her brother William's all too accurate descriptions of a wooden tub in a wild and endless sea, and memories of the all-pervasive mal de mer. She put aside thoughts of herself as a failed adventurer and pioneer. And mother. For the moment one thought, and one thought only, filled her soul: she was going home. As she dragged the heavy bundles to the door there came a great cheer from the direction of the shore. The *Endeavour* was leaving the landing-stage and heading for the mouth of the harbour, Blue Peter aflutter at her mast. Lucky crew, lucky ship. Now it would be the turn of the *Seaflower*.

The ringing of Cook Bichard's noon-time bell caught her unawares. Where and when would their next meal be? There was just enough time to gather some fennel for tonight's cod stew, should it be needed, and then she'd join Thomas in the cookhouse. She hurried along the shoreline to where the fennel was plentiful and in minutes had picked sufficient. The fog had again settled into swirling damp curtains. Picking her way back she marvelled at a muffled world so much in contrast with the earlier commotion. A creaking caught her attention; the *Seaflower* at its landing-stage, she decided. The heavy air played tricks with direction. Was that the sound of footfall? Strange shapes loomed from the direction of the sea. Bears? Her heart juddered. Then unseen hands grabbed at her, spun her round. She was blind with terror as a rough hand clamped her mouth and covered her nose. Disabled by the iron force of it, her lungs struggled for air.

'All right marine, don't kill the slut.'

'Sir.' The hand remained secure on her mouth but eased from her nose and she dragged in air as best she could.

'Ma'am, if you swear not to utter a sound, I'll believe you because I'm a gentleman, and I'll ask this marine to remove his hand from your mouth. You understand?' The speaker bent down, his face a few inches from her own. He loomed tall, wore a black hat, was clean-shaven. The threat in his voice was palpable. She stared at him then nodded once. The man who held her close

133

and whose rasping breath burned hot in her ear, took his hand from her face but didn't loosen his grip on her arm. Her stomach churned at his touch, his smell.

'I am going to ask you where the occupants of this charming little island of yours are,' said the man in the black hat. 'And you will tell me because if you don't I'll make a nasty cut on your pretty little face, which would be a damn shame don't you think?' He held a knife close to her cheek.

Let me wake from this nightmare, she prayed.

'Who are you?' she whispered, knowing even as she spoke that the worst had happened.

The slap to her cheek was not so much vicious as shocking. Tears filled her eyes. 'I ask, you tell.' The man took hold of her chin and jerked her face up towards his. 'They're at their midday meal, yes?'

She hesitated before nodding again. *God help me. Do I have a choice?*

'So let's go.'

She stumbled but nobody reached out to assist her. After a moment's indecision and another glance at the knife, she indicated the direction of the cookhouse. The man in the black hat signalled silently. A disciplined line of men slid past. They jostled her along and it was as though the fog had seeped into her mind, paralysing it. As they neared the cookhouse cheerful laughter and banter seeped from the building. Restrained once more, she didn't see the men smash open the cookhouse door but the sounds were unmistakable. The initial crash, the

134

tramp and scuffle of boots, the startled cries from within. More crashes. Three shots fired. The mist in her head exploded, releasing her mind from its icy paralysis.

'Thomas!'

His response assured her that no bullet had taken him. There were more scuffles, then someone thrust her into the eating space of the cookhouse. Benches and tables lay upended, the fishermen backed against the walls. The invaders faced them, pistols in hand. Other privateers had swords or knives drawn. Bile rose in her throat. Were they going to die? She saw that most of the invaders wore ordinary seamen's clothes. Some, presumably officers, had uniforms of dark blue coats and breeches, white shirts and red waistcoats. Under their black three-cornered hats they wore their hair tied back.

'Elise!' Thomas called out. She saw him at once and ran to his side. His strong arms enclosed her as he put himself between her and the enemy. For a moment, a brief moment, she felt safe. All became a silent tableau until Charles Robin, followed by his brother, stepped forward. With great dignity, she felt, Mr John introduced his brother then himself. The sharp-faced man who'd threatened to cut her face took one pace towards the brothers.

'I am Lieutenant Grinnell of the newly created American Continental Navy. You and your men are now prisoners of my marines.'

Prisoners. They were all prisoners. She clung tighter

to Thomas.

The lieutenant turned to the rigid, storm-faced fishermen. 'All of you, put your weapons down on the ground in front of you.' There was more scowling, some muttering and a chorus of foot-shuffling. The men, glancing at each other, did as they were told. At a nod from their leader half a dozen marines scooted forward and collected the surrendered knives.

'Excellent.' Grinnell's voice was slow. Measured. Cruel. He fixed his eyes on the Robin brothers. 'Now you two, we'll go to your cabin. Meanwhile my men have need of food and drink and your men will see they get it. The woman,' he turned his cold gaze on Elise. With a whimper she sank further into her husband's arms. 'She'll come with me and serve us with food.'

'She will not!' Thomas's shout brought a burly marine to his side. Before she knew what had happened the snarling man yanked her from Thomas and punched him to the floor then aimed a vicious kicking at his prone body.

She screamed and a shot split the air. Everyone froze. Lieutenant Grinnell's pistol was pointing to the ceiling. 'Enough, goddamn it! We are men of honour and don't make war on women.'

Her recent experiences told otherwise but she was more concerned about Thomas than with quibbling over the man's idea of honour. The lieutenant turned to Thomas, who'd scrambled to his feet and was being restrained by Rhiné Therriau. 'I apologise for my man's roughness. You have my word that your wife will not be harmed in any way so long as you all do as you're told.'

So, she was to be a hostage to their good behaviour. She had little option but to obey. In the Robins' cabin she trembled so much that she had difficulty serving the cold meat, potatoes and spruce beer she found in the storeroom to the rear. The lieutenant attacked the food with uncouth relish but spat out the beer. 'What piss is this? Trying to poison me? Bring wine,' he demanded. She flinched but at a nod from John Robin fetched a bottle. Mr John and Mr Charles toyed with their food and only sipped the beer. Grinnell emptied his beer onto the floor and indicated that Elise fill his glass from the wine bottle. No one spoke. The overwhelming reality of their situation was drummed home by the presence of an armed marine – an awkward lantern-jawed youth who stood guard at the door. Another such brute stood outside.

'Perhaps you'll tell us your plans?' Mr Charles growled eventually. He stared at his plate as he spoke, making patterns with the crumbled pork.

'My commanding officer, the renowned and brave Captain John Paul Jones, will be in charge here.' He sat back, his booted feet resting on the table.

Mr Charles narrowed his eyes and glared at the lieutenant. 'Renowned? Brave? That's not what I've been told,' he bellowed. 'Sailed with a slaver, I heard tell. A captain of dishonour who flogged one man to death and ran another through with a sword. A man who changed his name to avoid justice.'

Elise recoiled when the rebel American jumped up and stabbed his knife into the table-top barely an inch from Charles Robin's hand. 'Bollocks! Filthy goddamned rumours put out by your British navy in their pathetic effort to discredit him.'

'Where is he now, this great warrior of yours?' Mr John asked.

Resuming his seat Grinnell took a slow mouthful of wine. In a drawling voice he said, 'I'm glad you asked. He's dealing with a place up the coast a short ways before he comes here to deal likewise with you.'

Charles Robin flung aside his fork. 'Deal with?'

Lieutenant Grinnell smirked. 'It was like this: we'd had a damned satisfying time of it but needed water and firewood so we went to Canso Harbour.' The brothers exchanged glances. The American was clearly enjoying himself. 'Luck was on our side,' he continued. 'That and your piss-lazy British navy. We helped ourselves to a ship and all the booty we wanted. Fish, furs, a whole bundle of goods. We burned the other two vessels.' He rubbed his hands together. 'A gift.'

Was this to be their fate, she wondered. She jumped as he barked, 'Slut, more bread.'

When she returned from the storeroom the American was saying, 'Our intelligence told us of maybe nine or more brigs and schooners in Petit-de-Grat and here at Narrowshook – or as you so arrogantly call it, Jerseyman Island. Captain Jones is taking on Petit-de-

Grat, and I'm here to sort out you lot.'

'So your brave captain is using his great might to raid tiny, defenceless Petit-de-Grat and destroy the livelihood of a few helpless souls,' rumbled Mr Charles.

'You spoke of intelligence. What intelligence?' John Robin demanded of the lieutenant.

Grinnell raised his eyebrows. 'Now that would be telling.' Again, that same cruelty in his voice. This man, she decided, had no scruples.

She retreated to the far wall wishing she could pass through it and go to Thomas. Was he much hurt? She was sure there'd been blood on his face. The palms of her hands were damp with sweat, alarm gnawed at her stomach. Someone betrayed them. Who could have done such a dreadful thing? Whoever it was, may they rot in hell! This ruthless Captain must be a monster, and these despicable rebels intended to take all that the fisherman had spent the summer working for.

Grinnell mopped his plate with a chunk of bread and examined her for a moment, a sneer on his face. 'Take the slut back to the cookhouse.'

She fought back the desire to spit in Grinnell's face as the lout on guard-duty gripped her arm and marshalled her through the door. The fog had thinned and she could make out some ships resting along the landing-stage head: phantom outlines of a number of vessels hovered on both sides of the harbour. The sound of muffled oars floated in from the sea, muted voices and the smell of tobacco drifted to her from all directions. She heard the clank of chains, an isolated laugh, a sharp command.

She was pushed in through the cookhouse door. Thomas ran to her side and she calmed a little as he held her tight. 'Elise,' he murmured against her neck. 'Thank God.' They clung to each other and the warmth of his body thawed some of the chill that gripped her heart.

The long night was filled with whispers and few slept. She sought comfort in Thomas's arms. He, thank the Lord, had no more than cuts, bruises and sore ribs.

'I'm so sorry, Elise,' Thomas whispered, as he stroked her hair. 'I got it wrong about these ruffians. Say you forgive me for not saving you from all this.'

She hugged him. 'It didn't matter in the long run,' she said. 'They were here before I had the chance to drug you and have you carried on board.'

'Hey you!' a guard shouted. 'If you don't keep the noise down, I'll separate you.'

'Sorry, Ethan,' Thomas said before whispering to her, 'He's not so bad, that one. At any rate he doesn't get nasty like some do. We try to keep him sweet.'

In the morning she was again ordered to serve food at the cabin. Neither brother said much; both were haggard and unshaven. The whole island held its breath.

Once more the guard returned her to the cookhouse. On the way he turned to her and stuttered, 'Don't worry m-m-miss. I'll look after you.'

She stopped and stared at him. She felt tempted to say that he wasn't doing a good job so far, but she refrained. He was young, clearly not too bright and built like the side of a barn, so she smiled into his acne-scarred face. 'That's nice.'

'I'm Jack,' he said with slightly more confidence, as they continued back along the path.

'And I'm Mrs Galliard.'

'You're pretty. Like m-m-my sister Abigail.'

'And what are you doing here frightening people when you have a pretty sister called Abigail at home? Shouldn't you be there taking care of her?'

He jutted out his large jaw. 'I'm the m-m-man of the house. I support m-m-my m-m-mother and sister.'

'Jack, what would your mother and your pretty sister Abigail think of what you're doing here?'

He bristled. 'I'm serving m-m-my country. They're m-m-mighty proud of me.'

'See here Jack, I'm sure you're a fine son and brother and that you love your mother full well, but—'

'Indeed I do.' They had reached the cookhouse and the boy-marine-rebel paused with his hand on the door. 'M-m-mother bakes the finest pies in Kentucky. Apple, blueberry, pumpkin. But apple's m-m-my favourite. Gee, I m-m-miss those pies.'

Poor lad. He was an ordinary, uneducated country boy who loved his mother and had been caught up in a situation not of his making or comprehension.

'Never mind,' she told him. 'I'm sure you'll taste those apple pies again soon.'

He nodded with little conviction before ushering her

inside where she quickly sought out the comfort of Thomas's arms. At midday Jack fetched her once again. He smiled shyly at her as he accompanied her to the cabin. It seemed they were now old friends. This time, no sooner had she put bread and dried fish on the table than the door crashed open and a short man in an officer's uniform stormed in.

'At ease, Grinnell. Petit-de-Grat has crumbled,' he squawked excitedly. 'A great success if I say so myself. What panic! Took them by surprise and they yielded like women. A ball-less victory.' His shoulders shuddered in silent amusement. Then he took in the scene before him. 'So we have the island and the Robins all cosily buttoned. Well done, lieutenant. Now which is which?'

'Captain John Paul Jones I presume? I am John, this is my brother Charles.' The handshakes were cursory.

'What baggage have we here?' The man's stare was bold.

Mr John stepped forward protectively. 'Mrs Galliard is married to one of my men. She's been serving our food at the insistence of your lieutenant.'

Jones removed his hat with a flourish and performed a mocking bow. She glanced at Mr John then stared at the floor. John Robin's face was like granite. Elise could almost feel the captain's gaze crawling over her body.

'Excellent idea,' the captain said. He crossed the room, standing close enough for her to smell the onion on his breath. 'The presence of such beauty gives me an appetite I can't ignore.' He took her face in his hand.

She fought down the rising bile.

'Nice,' he said before releasing her. 'Now, be a good girl and fetch me some bread and cheese. And wine. Two bottles. Good ones.' He sneered at the dried cod on their plates and his upper lip curled. 'Then cook me some meat. My lieutenant and I will dine like men tonight.'

As she turned he gave her a slap on her bottom. In the storeroom she took deep breaths and, still feeling the defiling imprint of his hand upon her, tried to stop shaking. When she returned, Captain Jones had joined his fellow American and the Robin brothers at the table and was picking at his grubby fingernails with a fork. 'So, my dear John and Charles,' he drawled, 'you get the picture? I am here to relieve you of your charming vessels and rich stock. And no tricky business from you. Eighty-three armed men wait outside, each of whom would welcome a bit of target practice.' He glanced up at her. 'Amongst other things,' he added.

She felt the colour drain from her face.

'Just the sort of behaviour one would expect from a privateer,' Mr John muttered through clenched teeth.

'I am no privateer,' the captain snapped. 'I am an officer and commander of the New Continental Navy. You underestimate me at your peril.' He tore at the bread with yellowed teeth and ran his hand across his lips. Then he leaned back and demanded a pipe of tobacco, and one for his lieutenant.

'Pour more wine,' he ordered her. She pictured herself smashing the bottle over his ugly head. Barrel-chested and short-legged, the man resembled a fairground pugilist. Yet his features were vulpine in every respect: small dark watchful eyes, nose and cheekbones knife-sharp. A fox out to slaughter chickens. He even smelt like a fox.

Over the next few days she endured being shuttled back and forth to the cabin to cook, serve meals and clean, before again taking refuge with Thomas and the others in the cookhouse. It wasn't a large space: ten bench seats and five long tables, plain birch walls, two small windows, a privy out the back, and Cook Bichard's kitchen area with its table, pans, kettles and wood stove. The captives made the best use they could of what space they had, clearing aside the seating area at night to provide space within which they did their best to sleep.

Such conversations as she overheard told her that the marines were undertaking an inventory of stock and vessels. Her life became a bad dream played out at a snail's pace. The whispered plans she and her fellow captives hatched together kept them going. They would all storm the door and take over a ship. Elise would distract her guard, Jack. Cook Bichard would get them all drunk. Someone would feign a serious illness and escape to Arichat to get help. Eventually they decided that Elise would mix a potion to knock out the captain and his lieutenant. Then the fishermen could stage a rebellion of their own.

'I know where some hemlock grows,' she said, 'but I've never prepared any. I might kill them.'

The few gathered men exchanged glances. 'Sounds good to me,' one said. She agreed to try gathering some leaves.

Some captives passed the time by ribbing those rebels who were, according to Thomas, less harsh. She disapproved of this fraternisation. When the guard returned her to the cookhouse on the fourth evening she saw Thomas and a short wiry Jerseyman called Benjamin in deep conversation with one of the rebels. She was appalled by the comfortable way in which the three men were seated together. Thomas came over to her and laid a hand on her arm. 'It's all right, Elise, that's Ethan. I told you about him. He's been explaining to Benjamin and me about the patriots, what we call the rebels – what they're fighting for.'

'I neither know nor care what these animals are fighting for.' Elise shook away his hand. 'And I'm astounded that you do, Thomas Galliard.' She stormed up to the Jerseyman and the marine. 'And you, Benjamin Picot – I can't believe you have no more sense than to be talking nonsense with our enemies.' Eyeing both Benjamin and Thomas she added, 'I'm ashamed of you both.' She glared at the rebel before turning away to sit alone, fuming on a bench in the corner. She could still feel the cold touch of the Grinnell's knife on her cheek, the rough hands of his marines, the foul insinuations that made her flesh creep. After a moment the conversation between captor and captives continued and she was forced to hear this traitor preach about taxes and tea and "mad King George". The more she heard the more amazed she was by the gullibility of his audience – and angry. After all, the Channel Islanders weren't even English. Not the enemy. Were Thomas and the others really being swayed by this ignorant bully? This pirate?

When some stupid American dolt cried out, 'That's right, Ethan, you tell 'em,' she could stomach no more and jumped to her feet.

'Tell us what?' she demanded. 'Why you came here to ruin us?' The cookhouse fell silent as everyone turned to her. A tingle of fear rose into her throat, but she refused to cower.

'Give me liberty or give me death!' a lone voice cried from the back of the cookhouse. A flutter of laughter broke through the silence.

'And us? What of our liberty? What of our lives?' She ignored Thomas's startled eyes and the warning shake of his head. Tempers grew heated. Several rebels jabbed the air with their rifles and growled for order.

Thomas strode up to her, grasped her elbow and took her to their usual corner. 'Enough,' he murmured. Then, perhaps to distract her, he asked about the hemlock she was supposed to get hold of.

She pulled away from him, but the fire had gone from her and she sighed. 'I'm always watched,' she whispered back. 'I've been unable to get anywhere near a hemlock plant.' In her heart she knew it to be a foolish hope. It would be impossible to overcome these ruffians. Eventually they settled down for another long night.

The following evening upon her return to the cookhouse she saw that the fishermen had congregated in one corner and the rebels were huddled in small groups, with no exchanges between the opposing sides. *Good, we don't need to listen to their rantings.*

'What's going on out there?' Thomas whispered as soon as she settled next to him. Such snatched conversations as she heard were disjointed but she always did her best to satisfy the restless captives' frantic curiosity. 'There was some sort of bargaining,' she told Thomas.

'What for?'

'Mr John and Mr Charles must order us to help the rebels strip everything and load it into the ships. In exchange we'll be left two vessels in which to return home.'

Thomas whistled. 'That's a devil of a bargain to have to make.'

'Captain Jones said our navy has taken to its heels, and our so-called Acadian friends and the savages they live with have retreated to the forest. He could barely stand for laughing. He said his men weren't interested in Arichat. Not worth the effort, he said.'

'Bastards,' someone mumbled.

'Thomas, if we're abandoned, there's no hope, is there?'

Gloom sat heavy upon them that night. A deal must have been struck because the next day the men were taken outside and forced to fit out and rig all the ships apart from the *Hope* and the *Betsy,* which would be left behind for the Channel Islanders' use. The air hung thick with the anger of powerless fishermen. The men dawdled as much as they could get away with, some attracting a shove or clout for their pains. Nevertheless two days later all was pretty near ready. Captain Jones and his lieutenant were elated as they tucked into the rabbit stew Elise had put before them. Jones drained his glass then took a knife from his belt and slowly peeled an apple. He put a slice of the fruit into his mouth, stared at Elise and then turned to Grinnell. 'I might take some hostages, what do you think?'

Charles Robin frowned and his mouth tightened. His brother sat rigid. Elise, as usual, tried to control her trembling and to shrink into the shadowy wall of the cabin. Later that evening, glad to be back with Thomas, she whispered what had been said.

'I'll kill any man who lays a hand on you!' He spoke with such venom that she had no doubt he meant it.

After she served breakfast the next day, Jack, her guard, decided a diversion to the company store would provide him with a fine source of rum. He was aware that she kept a key.

'But the store's practically empty,' she said when he

demanded they go there so she could let him in.

'I'm not a fool. I've seen all sorts in there – food and drink m-m-mostly. I bet there's rum for the taking.'

'That's for your captain. I've got the key so I can prepare his meals. He'll kill me and you if you make me do this.'

Jack glanced round. 'Do it.' He pulled his pistol from its leather holster. 'You think because I'm nice to you that I won't pull this trigger? You think I'm a stupid boy? I'm not. I'm a m-m-man and I want a m-m-man's drink.' His trembling voice belied his words. She shook her head but with her arm gripped tight and the pistol at her breast, she had no option but to comply. The boy was nervous enough to pull that trigger by mistake. Once inside the store they both peered through the dust motes that now appropriated it. She felt a moment's nostalgia for the days when she'd worked hard to make it clean and tidy. As she knew there would be, a number of barrels and boxes were stashed on the counter. The youth's eyes lit up at the sight of three small rum kegs. 'They won't m-m-miss one.' His voice practically squeaked.

'They will. They checked this lot themselves. I told you, they'll kill us both.'

'Shut your m-m-mouth.' He tucked a keg under his arm and waved his pistol at her. 'Now, secure the door. I'll stash this, lock you back in the cookhouse and you'll forget this ever happened.'

As she re-locked the door with hands clumsy from

fright and anger, a voice made her jump. 'Elise? You all right?'

She spun round. 'Cook Bichard, you startled me. What are you doing here?'

'Fetching a bag of barley.' He held up his own key then noticed Jack. 'He bothering you?'

She glanced at the rotund, kindly old cook then at the jittery guard with the wavering pistol. 'No, Cook. All's well, thank you.'

The cook, known for his inability to suffer fools gladly, eyed Jack up and down. 'What's the boy doing?'

Jack lost patience. 'Get out m-m-my way old m-m-man.'

'You been trying it on with our Mrs Galliard, boy?' The older man took a step towards them. Before she knew what was happening the cook had yanked her out of the way and planted himself in front of Jack.

'Please Cook. The boy only wanted rum. Take care, he's armed.'

The old man had a light in his eyes, the young one had alarm in his. The cook grinned while the boy bit his lip. Cook Bichard turned to Elise. 'Get away from here, Mrs Galliard, leave this to me. I been itchin' to get my hands on one, and this stuttering fool will do nicely.'

She watched in horror as he sprang forward and grabbed the marine's wrist. There were grunts, foul curses, grapples, small, tight, up-close movements. The keg was dropped. A knee found its target. The marine's hat skimmed to the ground. A thunderous bang punched her eardrums. She screamed as a man slumped to the ground. The pistol fell. Someone whimpered, backed away then turned and ran.

Elise edged towards the fallen figure and, hand clasped to her mouth, knelt down. Cook Bichard had been shot through the temple. He lay in the dirt, his unseeing eyes fixed on her. 'No. No, Cook! You silly man.' She cradled his head in her lap and her tears joined the crimson blood that stained her skirt. 'You reckless old man. All for a barrel of rum. What will we tell your family?'

Of course, it was not all about a barrel of rum, she thought. *It was about days and nights of humiliation and fear. It was watching your future disappear into the holds of your own ships and knowing you would go home a poor man. Now this poor man would not be going home at all.*

Rough hands dragged her to her feet, causing her to gasp and the cook to be discarded onto the soil like a used sack. Captain Jones glared at her and demanded an explanation. He didn't wait for a reply before shuffling her to the cookhouse and through the door where he shoved her at one of the guards. Silence sliced the tense, tobacco-fugged air. Thomas shouted and ran towards her. Struggling to breathe, she reached out for him, but the guard nudged him to one side and took her to a bench. 'Sit there,' he ordered. The bloody stain on her skirt drew all eyes to her. A groan escaped from Thomas. Marines shunted the fishermen, including the pent-up Thomas and the protesting Robin brothers, into a corner. The rebels stood alert and rifle-ready.

'A man is dead.' The captain's words immobilised the room. 'One of yours.' His eyes narrowed as he looked to where the men were corralled. The door crashed open causing everyone to jump and swivel to face it. Two marines shouldered their way in. They placed, not unkindly, the body of Cook Bichard at their feet. The men surged forward but were forced back.

'You,' the captain barked, pointing at John Robin.

Mr Robin knelt before the shape on the floor. 'Ebenezer Bichard, our cook.' The room filled with the shocked gasps and mutterings of the captives. John Robins tenderly closed the dead man's eyes then stared at Elise's blood-soaked clothing. His voice cracked. 'What happened, Mrs Galliard?'

She told them everything. Jones pulled her to her feet and stared into her eyes. Filled with hate, she somehow resisted spitting in his face, but she refused to flinch. Jones turned to his lieutenant. 'Fetch Jack Hastings to my cabin.'

A number of rebels followed Grinnell outside. Jones turned to the prisoners. 'If she's telling the truth you have my apologies, you can bury this man, and I will have the boy shot. If she's lying I will know. If she's lying, this man's body will be dumped into the sea and we will shoot her husband.'

***

Darkness crept from the east as the fishermen and Elise were herded outside to watch a group of marines drag a snivelling, bruised boy down to the beach, secure him onto a landing-stage and shoot him. They threw his body into the sea. Elise thought of the boy's sister, Abigail, who loved him and would never see him again; of his mother who would never bake him another apple pie. A short time later, the fishermen carefully laid Cook Bichard in a shallow grave overlooking the shore.

**

That night violent equinoctial gales lashed rain against the cookhouse, engulfing them all in a turmoil of noise. Nobody slept. The following day, with the storm eased, the raw-eyed captives were released for work duty. The aftermath of the squall shocked them. The rigged fleet had been obliged to anchor off the island to ride out the storm, but the *Seaflower* had dragged anchor and run aground. Unable to free her, the rebels chose to set her ablaze, turning her into an explosion of dense black smoke. On the shore Elise held Thomas's hand. In shock she numbly watched the conflagration. Thomas's breath came in short angry gasps. Were the tears running down his face caused by sorrow or the bitter smoke of the dying *Seaflower*? Most likely both. A shout caused her to turn. Charles Robin was rushing to the harbour where he watched helplessly as his much-loved ship went to the flames. 'Goddam them,' he cursed. Then a cold smile curled his lips. 'Still, better that than the ignominy of being taken as a prize.'

Jones joined them. 'Damned pity,' he grumbled, his mask of composure strained. 'She would have made a valuable prize. And she was loaded with fish oil. So neither of us will gain from your *Seaflower*, Mr Robin.'

'This isn't the end, you know,' Charles Robin roared. 'I'll return when all this is history and I'll be greater and stronger than ever.'

Both victor and prisoner lacked height as they postured nose to nose, eyes a-bulging and red of face. If it hadn't all been so tragic Elise would have laughed.

By noon Jones decided no more time was to be wasted. They would put to sea that afternoon. But before they did they took everything, every last cup and nail. They raided the tools of the fishermen's trade. They plundered spirits, wine, beer, and firewood, of all things. They took all their food stocks apart from the meagre rations allowed for the *Hope* and the *Betsy*. Even their captives' spare clothing was taken, leaving them with the few things they stood up in. 'Just carrying out my orders to hinder the enemy in any way I can,' the American captain smirked, as the fishermen, firearms aimed at their heads, were forced to load their worldly goods onto the captured ships.

Apart from the two ships promised for the Channel Islanders' escape, they torched most of what they had not stolen. They were like wild men, taking pleasure in burning and destroying what they could. They hollered and danced obscene jigs as most of the outfit went up in flames.

As the madness abated Elise slipped away to check her home for damage from storm and vandalism. What she found made her howl with futile rage. That which had not been stolen had been destroyed. Her dowry chest lay on its side. Gone were the precious contents, the things she'd brought from home and preserved in lavender for her future.

Memories pierced her benumbed brain: the love she'd put into assembling its contents, her mother sitting next to her at home folding fine woollen stockings, her father's gift of herbs and seeds, her precious, albeit slightly less than perfectly embroidered petticoats and her lovingly selected bedlinen. They were her future. The thought of her private treasures in the hands of these monsters caused bile to rise in her throat.

Thomas ran through the doorway as she darted frantically round the cabin trying to salvage something, anything. 'The fiends have taken my bible,' she sobbed. 'And my musket. And the kettle's gone. And our winter furs, the old bear skin, my precious soap, our last few candles.'

She fell to her knees and began the hopeless task of trying to gather up her beloved ormer shells where they lay crushed into the floor. Her dreamcatcher had been torn from the ceiling and smashed against the fireplace. The beautiful basket Thomas had given her was now in pieces. In their frenzy of despoiling they'd uprooted her herbs. Even the bunches of onions and herbs drying by the hearth were scattered for the pleasure of destruction.

'My valise!' she screamed. Scrabbling to uncover it from its hiding place by the fire, she checked her grandmother's almanac, her journal and her package of letters from Guernsey. 'Thank the Lord.' She cradled the bag to her as tears ran down her cheeks.

Thomas gathered what was left of her treasured things and placed them in her battered dowry chest, then he put his arm round her bowed shoulders. 'Please, my dear, don't let go now.' His own eyes were glazed and reddened. 'You've been so brave.'

'But my home, my home.' Fury welled within her. 'It's as well that my musket is not to hand or I would endanger my immortal soul for the pleasure of shooting Captain John Paul Jones.'

She began pacing the floor as she vowed to grab the knife of the first marauder she came across and slit his throat. She would pour boiling oil over ten of them as they tried to stop her. She would laugh as they pleaded for mercy. Her heart lightened at these fantasies. These evil monsters would be sorry they'd ever landed on Jerseyman Island. If Thomas hadn't grabbed her and held her tight against him she would have rushed outside and clawed out the nearest villain's eyes. Instead she moaned in grief and, exhausted, sank against him.

A marine appeared at the door. 'Come on you two. Get a move on. Back to the cookhouse or there'll be trouble.' He gave her a shove. That was the moment Thomas snapped. He leapt forward and grabbed the man, punched him to the ground, wildly kicking at his face and body. Elise, horrified by the intensity and suddenness of his attack, stepped backwards and screamed his name. Then a shot rang out and Thomas was on the ground, his arm shattered to a bloody mess. They held her back. She screamed, forced to watch helplessly as his face took the force of a rifle butt, not once but twice, his right eye beaten to a pulp, his nose smashed flat, his face ripped open to the bone.

They left him for dead.

PART THREE

Saint-Pierre

CHAPTER 18

Elise watched the *Hope* and *Betsy* sail for home and take her broken dreams with them. She wept. Surely there were no more tears left inside her? Guernsey called out to every part of her being. How bitter she felt when the Jerseymen left. Isolated, abandoned and forgotten by her countrymen, she was frightened to her core.

Left for dead, Thomas did not die, even though he begged her to let him die, to help him die. His cries cut her heart in two.

In truth, so near to death was he that he would not have survived the voyage. Her return home was not to be. Before leaving, a few of the men muttered about looking out for Thomas's mother. Some kept their eyes averted, mumbled and stared at the ground. Some left what food they could spare. The Robin brothers pressed a few coins in her hand and expressed regret. Each man, wrapped in his own misery, boarded a ship and sailed away empty handed.

In the ruins of her home, she nursed the ruin of her husband. All they had left in this world, apart from each other, was her valise and its contents, her battered dowry chest and the paltry bits she had salvaged from the marauders. That and a few coins. To these pathetic fragments of their life she added the seeds she'd saved, the remnants of the herbs she'd managed to re-pot, and some of her remedies, flung aside during the raid.

Thomas suffered a poultice of agrimony to be applied to his wounds. It had no noticeable effect. She slipped some tincture from the root of Valerian into his mouth but again, no effect. His wounds were infected and a fever tore at him.

She watched his agony in an agony of her own. From this pit of hell echoed the song of the sea – a dirge of misery and pain.

The days were shortening and the season turning when Nathaniel, Marcel's Mi'kmaq friend from Saint-Pierre, delivered a note. *All is arranged*, Marcel wrote. She and Thomas must go to Renee and Amos's trading post in Saint-Pierre, one of the few places on the coast bypassed by the enemy. Her former travel companions from Guernsey had offered their hospitality and Nathaniel would take them there by canoe. There were rumours, Nathaniel said, that Jones had returned to the area seeking out more of what he took the first time.

John Paul. Jones. That name turned her soul to ice but, as desperate as she was to escape from Jerseyman Island and that pirate, her husband's needs came before all else.

Now she turned to Nathaniel. 'Surely another few days?'

'We must delay no longer, Madame,' Nathaniel said. 'I should be at my winter camp by now and soon ice will make travel impossible. The weather could break any day.'

'He's too sick. He'll die. It's too soon to move him.'

'I have a canoe ready and my friend Jacob will assist us. I'm sorry, Madame Elise. It's tomorrow or not at all. And not at all won't do, you know that. Neither of you would survive to see next spring.'

He was right, of course. She bowed her head in defeat. 'Very well, Nathaniel. Tomorrow then.'

That afternoon she gathered some late-flowering goldenrod and rich brown cattails and walked to the little clearing where a small wooded cross told of her sorrow.

'I have to leave you, Baby Thomas. I'm not sure I can come back so must say goodbye.' Now beyond tears, she knelt beside the tiny grave and placed a kiss on the cold ground. Icy fingers of wind whipped up from the sea.

They set off for Saint-Pierre at daybreak. Nathaniel had a precious tincture of hemlock, belladonna and henbane; highly poisonous, he warned, and only to be used with care. Once diluted it had an almost instant effect on Thomas who, initially restless, soon quietened and drifted in and out of consciousness under the warmth of a thick moose-skin and a length of sailcloth.

Nathaniel and Jacob handled the canoe with ease in the calm sea. As they left her decimated home and her son's grave, Elise could not help but compare this pre-dawn retreat with her arrival eighteen months before. That had been a journey of hope and trepidation. The months that followed it held so much – the hardships and the rough life, the reality of the harsh and beautiful seasons, the flowering of love and passion for her fine young husband, the sweet child growing within her and the agony of his loss. There was also the growth of her skills with curatives and the friendships she'd made through them. She closed her eyes, hearing the gentle slap of sea against the birchbark of the canoe, the barely discernible dip of paddle into water. The breeze was sharp on her face. She adjusted the moose-skin around Thomas before pulling her own warm blanket tight around her shoulders. No birds sang.

With Jacob in front and Nathaniel at the rear they circumnavigated Isle Madame in a clockwise direction heading for the northerly passage that was too narrow for large ships. She saw countless inlets and islands of all sizes. Clouds scudded low in the sky. To starboard, a tall dark horizon of trees crowded to the ocean's edge, and to port a pewter sea stretched as far as Nova Scotia. At noon they rounded the top of Isle Madame and entered the tight passage. Here the current took hold, helping them on their way.

As the canoe cut through the waves her mind drifted to the place that would be her home for the foreseeable future. She turned to Nathaniel and asked what he knew of Saint-Pierre and Cape Breton Island.

There was a pause before he answered. 'You go now to live by the great Bras d'Or Lake, the spiritual centre of my people. We have no written language, as you know, but have a long tradition of storytelling, so I will tell you a story, if I may.'

'Please. I'd love to hear it.' Glad of the distraction, she settled back as Nathanial narrated his tale.

'Have you heard of our great prophet Klu'skap?' he asked.

She admitted that she had not.

'It is told that the great lord Klu'skap, worshiped by my people in after-days, was formed from a bolt of lightning. He lived among Cape Breton's craggy hills, rugged landscapes and swirling mists. He had a brother, Malsumis. Klu'skap was good and wise but Malsumis was evil and full of self. Klu'skap was the chief spirit of my people and he had many lesser spirits to attend him. He created man from the heart of the ash tree. He named all the birds and animals. But the Great Beaver, a cowardly creature, tempted Malsumis to kill Klu'skap and rule the world himself. So Malsumis thought up a sly plot. He bragged loudly that he was invincible, and the only thing that could kill him was the root of the fern plant. Klu'skap guessed his brother's plot and spoke his fears to the wind. 'It is as well that Malsumis does not know that only a flowering rush can kill me,' he said.

'Beaver, hidden among the reeds, overheard these words. He went to Malsumis and told him he knew the secret of his brother's life and he would tell him if Malsumis promised Beaver whatever he should ask. So Beaver told him what he had heard then asked for his reward. 'I envy the flight of birds and wish for wings like a pigeon,' he said.

Malsumis laughed with scorn and said, 'Get thee hence, thou with a tail like a paddle, what need hast thou of wings?'

'Filled with fury, Beaver went to Klu'skap and told what he had done.'

Elise was so absorbed in Nathanial's story that she hardly noticed the passing of time until he halted to take up a flask and quench his thirst. She checked on the sleeping Thomas then waited until Nathaniel was ready to go on.

'Klu'skap knew that he had no choice but to destroy Malsumis in order that good would survive and his creatures continue to live. So in sorrow and in anger he went to a stream and as Malsumis approached, flowering reed in hand, Klu'skap pulled a fern plant out by the roots and flung it at his evil brother who fell to the ground dead. And Klu'skap sang a song over him and lamented. The spirit of Malsumis went underground, and became an evil wolf-spirit that fears the light of day and torments humans and animals. Klu'skap lived like other men, but never fell sick, never grew old and never died.'

'And do your people still honour him?' Elise asked.

Nathaniel looked sad for a moment. 'When the white man came Klu'skap raged at their treachery and left. We wait for his return, for we believe he will come back to us some day. Then the white man and the native man would live as one.'

Thomas, awake now, was calmed by Nathaniel's melodic voice. Elise, for that moment at least, felt at peace as she helped Thomas to a sip of water. 'Thank you, Nathaniel, your story is beautiful and holds much hope.'

He smiled and checked the sky, now a watery blue scattered with pale grey clouds. 'We make good progress and should be at Saint-Pierre quite soon.'

She sat back, her mind full of Nathaniel's story. It said so much about his people's beliefs and understanding of the world. Yet what of her own? She remembered Laurel's explanation of dreams and visions; that they were messages which should be listened to rather than feared. *But I do fear my nightmares. Especially the purple-black raven. And, like my grandmother, I fear the pointing finger of others, the accusations of witchcraft*. Her peace of mind dissolved into confusion. *Sometimes I think I have more Mi'kmaq in me than I have Guernsey*.

As their canoe consumed the miles she gazed at the

passing shoreline and considered the mythology of this land. Of its sacred places and the curative properties of nature. Her affinity with the healing power of herbs was not a bad thing, surely? Her visions and premonitions were not evil, were they? Frightening, yes. Confusing, always. But the product of evil? A sign of the devil within her? Had her dear Gran'mère been touched by evil? No, never. Was she, Elise, like Nathaniel's villain, Malsumis, a destructive force? A bringer of dark forces and black ravens? Or, like the hero, Klu'skap, a force for good, waiting for the right moment?

Saint-Pierre had grown and spread up the hill, but was much as she remembered it from her brief stop a year and a half before, though much quieter now. The November sun was surprisingly warm but the winter trees failed to touch her spirits. The leaves held no hint of their earlier burnished bronze, mellow amber, and fiery reds and yellows. Instead they fell as sodden, blackened remnants of their glorious promise. *Rather like me*. She crossly pushed that thought from her mind.

To her relief an ox and cart waited for them, guarded by Moses, the Mi'kmaq she recalled from her earlier visit. He was the first Indian she'd spoken to. How nervous she'd been and what a fool she'd made of herself. Now he nodded at her and his crooked grin was amiable. Without delay the three men took the stretcher between them and placed Thomas on the open cart. They loaded Elise's possessions and she was helped up to sit beside the gentle Indian. She bade her farewells and thanks to Jacob and Nathaniel and, as Thomas whimpered in pain, the cart rocked and jolted along the worn, frost-hard path. The air smelled of ripened apples and spruce and the salty tang of sea. It was a short steep climb to the brow of the hill, then one as steep down to the lakeshore. The soporific swaying of the cart was beginning to make Elise feel drowsy by the time they pulled up by a collection of buildings which, according to Mosses, comprised Amos and Renee's small trading post and home.

A door opened and there stood Renee, dumpy, cheerful and clearly pregnant. 'My dear, dear child. Come sit by the fire. I have hot coffee on the stove. Here's Amos to take charge of things.' Renee's arms and soothing words comforted Elise as she allowed the older woman to take control. Soon Thomas was tucked under clean sheets and blankets.

'Here, my love, take this tincture,' Elise later crooned to him. 'I must cleanse your wounds. Yes, I know it hurts. Be brave, dearest. No, try not to fight me, let me smear the compress on. I'll be as careful as possible, I promise. Your poor arm. Your poor face. But take comfort, it will not always be so.' *Please God.*

His groans of pain and shaking body were a torment but soon his exhaustion and the somnolent effects of the tincture took effect and he drifted into a troubled sleep.

CHAPTER 19

Renee's baby was born soon after Elise and Thomas's arrival at St Pierre. Amos named him Saul, and the baby soon settled into a routine of sleeping, feeding and gurgling. Each morning, after seeing to Thomas's needs in their own small cabin, Elise attended to the laundry and gave Renee and Amos's cabin a sweep and dust. Renee was grateful for the help. 'But you mustn't spoil me too long. I'll be back at my duties soon.'

'It's my pleasure,' Elise said, and meant it. Not only did it feel good to repay her friends for their kindness, but watching the baby – holding him, hearing his mewling cries, feeling the warmth of his little body – filled her mind with bittersweet thoughts of Baby Thomas. Her breasts ached with her loss. The joys of motherhood had been snatched from her. What would her son have been like today? Would he be bonny? Colicky? Filled with laughter? Would he have inspired Thomas to fight for a future? She'd never know.

After helping Renee, Elise would head across to the trading post where she kept the books, prepared orders, and dealt with the visiting traders – Mi'kmaq, Acadian, Scottish, Irish, some English and a steady stream of American Loyalists. Mostly good people.

Compared to the hardships of Jerseyman Island, life at the trading post was almost a luxury. That first spring she invested in a pig and some chickens, and a nanny goat that she hoped would be robust enough to survive winters in the barn. She worked hard for her keep. And Thomas's. When she ran low on food she traded with the Mi'kmaq, using what was left of her own remedies or the small popular items like mirrors and bright glass beads that Renee and Amos kept in stock.

With nobody to confide in, she took solace in resuming her journal entries. Here she could speak what was in her heart, maybe ease her loneliness. *I think,* she wrote, *I could survive here, prosper even, given the chance. This is not the life I thought to lead, but it is the life God gave me and there is no reason why I cannot make a success of things. When I am more established, my remedies, along with the work I do for the Sebires, will bring me an adequate income. Thomas will get better, I know it. I will heal him. I will be strong enough for both of us until such time as he is his old self. Then he'll be my husband once more, and I will bear him the son he so deserves, the daughter he longs for. I'll work for the two of us until we become one again, then, God willing, three.*

Hugging her hopes and dreams to herself, she toiled to improve her emergent herb garden and vegetable patch. Her father sent various powders and pastes, her mother enclosed seeds and she collected others. By June some seedlings already reached up through the soil.

Infrequent and precious letters arrived full of news and these she shared with Thomas as he sat by the fire. 'William has been invited to join Père in his Freemason lodge,' she read aloud. She looked up and noted that Thomas was listening. Good, she had his interest. 'I'm sure Père must be proud of him, don't you think, Thomas?' His small smile encouraged her to try again. 'Mère writes that there are plans to build a new market with room for an assembly hall where the rectory garden now lies. She thinks that such a structure would be a great asset to the island.'

Her heart lifted when she saw a glint of interest in his eye and when he said, 'With all those bricks being imported from England you'd think someone would have the notion to build a kiln on Guernsey.' Welcoming this lighter mood, she leaned over and squeezed his good arm. She felt the muscles tense but he didn't pull away as he enquired after her father's cough.

'Mère writes that it remains persistent. She's sure it will clear up when summer arrives. It's so testing, is it not, that letters to and from home are hindered by this war?' What she didn't tell him was how Mère pleaded with her to come home.

'Nothing at all from your mother this time, I'm afraid.' Again Thomas smiled wanly before turning his face to the fire.

She longed for someone, a companion, a trusted person rather than a journal, in whom she could confide. Renee was a dear, but how could Elise tell her what was in her heart? Full of shame, she could not speak of how her husband cried out when she changed his dressings or massaged his damaged skin and wasted muscles, or how he cursed her when she tried to encourage him to use his bad arm. She couldn't speak of how he screamed at her to leave him be. How, God forgive him, he wanted to die. How he shook off her comforting arms. How he lurched from her and sought empty solace alone in the damp woods. These were words she could say to no one.

Her fears for the sight of his eye had been justified. It would never recover, though she pretended otherwise. She told him how well the once raw wound that ran from his eyebrow to his chin had healed, how it mattered not that his nose was a little distorted. Even she was aware of the hollowness of her words and the unspoken sorrow in her voice. He was no fool. The trading post had mirrors. There was no denying the red puckered scar so deeply etched or his misshapen nose that left him breathing through his open mouth. Yet worse than that was his shattered arm. That cursed bullet had smashed his elbow. The arm would never recover any real use. It hung helpless and mocking unless secured in a cotton sling.

Even after all this time he turned from her, flinched from any intimate touch, glared at her with hate. She told herself that it wasn't hate for her that she saw in his eyes, but hate for his misfortune. She flattered and cajoled him in a desperate effort to convince him that he was still loved. She tried to revive his interest in her. 'We can still love each other,' she'd whisper into the darkness, as she tried to stroke him, caress him, murmur her feelings for him.

'Don't!' he'd cry, pushing her aside. 'How can you abide to touch me?'

'You're still my husband. If I stopped loving you because of a lost eye and a poor arm, what kind of wife would that make me?'

Nevertheless, each night he turned his back. She tried to ignore the blood pulsing through her veins and deep within her belly, to ignore her despair of ever conceiving another child. She told herself that patience and time were all that was needed, that the Thomas who had loved her would return.

Rather than get dragged into his pit of despair she grasped the good things still left to her. And these were abundant. They had a fine, solid cabin of their own. Renee and Amos were compassionate, and she did her best to make herself useful and justify their keep and the Sebire's kindness. Amos brushed aside her thanks, telling her that there was trade aplenty and the extra help she gave was welcome. There was indeed trade aplenty, thanks, ironically, to that same American navy that had caused all their troubles in the first place. Now it blocked much of the sea-bound trade but Amos and

Renee weren't solely dependent on the sea. These days most of their supplies and visitors came by way of the huge saltwater lake on whose shores they lived and worked. When a British flotilla did break through to reach Saint-Pierre Harbour it brought plentiful supplies for both trading posts, sometimes the joy of packages from home. On top of that, the sailors were good customers for the trading post and for her curatives.

'Not so very long ago,' she said to Thomas as she prepared a porcupine for the cooking-pot, 'I couldn't watch my brothers catch and skin a rabbit without squealing, do you remember?' Thomas smiled his sad smile and looked away. He wasn't the only one to have changed, she reflected. Now she could trap muskrat without so much as a shudder, and squash a mole without a qualm. Was that a good change? Necessity and familiarity were great teachers, she supposed.

Thomas recovered enough to work in the store and take on simple jobs for Amos, but day by day her hopes and dreams shrivelled, and throughout that first year Thomas's pain and despair was central to their daily lives.

She found some small peace by the lake. Marcel had once described it as so big you'd think it the ocean. Peppered with small islands, it filled a huge basin set amongst marble-laced hills of indigo. Although one could not tell from the shore, she learned that the Bras D'Or was more than one lake, and it formed a vast inland sea within Cape Breton Island. She watched the

172

way the sun's rays reflected on the water and she understood why the lake was called the Bras d'Or – the arm of gold. On a good day it took her breath away. So, not everything was bad. In some ways they fared better working for Amos at the trading post than they did working for Charles Robin. She couldn't, of course, say this to Thomas, who railed and cursed his privations. Hanging on to his anger helped him to hang on to his hopes. 'Once this damned Yankee war is over, Mr Robin will come back and I'll be a fisherman again, me.' But the war dragged on and eventually he bitterly acknowledged that, war or no war, nobody would employ a crippled fisherman. That's when he stopped fighting. Elise was at her wit's end. No matter how hard she tried he sat in morose silence eating little, doing and saying less. He didn't bother to wash, his hair hung in rat's tails and a scruffy, uneven beard sprouted on his pitted face. He took to rum and became even more surly – a moody, bitter stranger. Elise's love for him was stretched, not by the effects of his bad arm or his ruined face, but by his absence from her life in any meaningful way. For her part, she was glad to escape to the trading post, her herb garden or any of the myriad other duties that paid for their keep.

In an effort to take him out of himself she once suggested that life was not so bad. He stared at her. Then he leaned across the table and grabbed at the cotton kerchief she wore round her shoulders and pulled her to her feet, his hand around her throat. 'Don't you tell me how lucky I am,' he snarled, his scar flaring lividly, his breath sour on her face. 'Don't you ever tell me how lucky I am!'

Escaping his grip she tried to slow her breath and calm the thumping of her heart. He staggered out, slamming the door fit to crack the wood. Her legs refused to support her and she sank to the floor.

This is not what I left my family and my home for. If this is what it means to have an adventure, I don't want it anymore. What happened to my future? The children I was meant to have?

She had never felt afraid of her husband till then. The thread of loyalty and love that bound her to him, already at breaking point, snapped. Now tears of anger and regret filled her eyes. He was no longer her Thomas.

Something inside her died right there and then.

CHAPTER 20

With the arrival of Renee's second child, Elise's world shifted once again. Little Agnes was sickly. Renee wouldn't let Elise anywhere near the baby and had no time nor patience for her friend anymore. By the arrival of a third baby ten months later, Renee had turned completely in on herself, becoming sour and gaunt. Some great weight of disillusion had settled on her soul. Elise no longer recognised the friendly woman Renee used to be. Now she only spoke to snap orders. Elise took on more and more work at the trading post whilst skirting clear of her one-time friend as much as possible.

Envy stalked Elise as she looked at Renee's children, Saul, Agnes and now Peter. She ached to her core as she remembered her own baby so far away and gone now to dust. Maybe if she and Thomas could have another child all would be well, but there was little chance of that. A longing swamped her empty life as Thomas continued to retreat further into himself.

With Amos, the change was more insidious. Was it only she who noticed how he always hunched his shoulders these days, and how deeply the lines dragging down the corners of his mouth had become etched? Amos had always been stern, but his wife's snarling eventually got under his skin and he, too, started to become mean and irritable. 'Elise, I told you to put those spades away.'

'No Amos, you did not.'

'Elise, you spent too long gossiping to that customer.'

'I was explaining the difference between the three types of nail.'

'Elise, don't just stand there, sweep the floor.'

'I just did that, Amos.'

The atmosphere was taut. Nothing she did for the Sebires was good enough. She was emotionally deserted, directionless, friendless. Yet the years had been profitable. She knew instinctively that she'd need all the money she could save. Despite his faults, Amos paid her well enough for her labours. She was frugal and, with the extra from her curatives, she'd built up a healthy nest-egg. On top of that she benefited from her bartering and got a favourable deal on goods from the trading post.

On the surface, her life was fulfilling and her work, especially the skills she'd learned from her grandmother and those she'd taught herself, were her salvation and raison d'être, but a burden of isolation weighed her down. That burden lightened when she found the friendship she sought in an Acadian woman named

Nancy, wife of Jake Pinet, carpenter and wheelwright. Nancy had a deep infectious laugh and a cheerful, gap-toothed smile. She welcomed Elise's company and showed a keen interest in her remedies. Having a friend eased Elise's loneliness but nevertheless her strength and resilience were reaching their limits. At night, with Thomas turned firmly away, resentment filled her heart and unrequited, unwanted longings filled her body. Her hands often slipped guiltily between her legs in attempted fulfilment, but what she really wanted, needed, was to be held.

***

Elise had been gathering yarrow and sage in the fragile May sunshine before calling it a day and making her way back to her cabin as the afternoon clouded over. So wrapped up in her own thoughts was she that she yelped when Amos's hound lolloped up to her through the trees and rolled onto his back. His nut-brown fur was soft and warm, his ears floppy and huge, his nose damp and cold. The hound's great paws dug at the air as Elise scratched his tummy and laughed. 'Oh Sampson, that's a nice greeting.' She buried her face into his warm flank.

'And that's a nice sight.'

At the familiar voice she turned towards the speaker. 'Marcel! Where did you spring from? I didn't spot any ship. It's been… oh ages.'

He crouched down and the happy dog had double the

attention. 'Yes I know. Before all these damned Loyalists overran the country.'

'These damn Loyalists, as you call them, are valued customers I'll have you know.' She leaned close before muttering, 'But you're right, they are rather damned.' He always made her smile.

He removed his hat and they sat back to look at each other.

'I saw Thomas just now,' he said.

She said nothing.

'I could hardly get a word from him.'

Again she said nothing, instead giving her attentions to the dog.

'He's not doing so well, is he, Elise?'

Her tears smudged Marcel's image. He had always been a good friend to her and Thomas, arranging their passage here and visiting when business brought him to the area. He had seen Thomas hanging onto the edge of life and he'd seen him sinking into the depths of dependency. She took a shuddering breath. 'It's worse now. He's lost hope. Given up on himself. He finds no consolation, even with a bellyful of rum. I shouldn't be telling you this but sometimes I don't think I can manage anymore. I thought to go home to Guernsey but Thomas won't even discuss it. What am I to do?'

'Come now.' He took her hand, squeezed it and smiled at her. 'Courage, Elise. When first we met I remember thinking how brave you were. I recall saying as much at the time. I was certainly surprised to see you.' He sat back and absentmindedly plucked at the long grass.

'I was younger then, so full of hopes and plans.' She tickled Sampson's ears. 'I think I was a bit pretty, too, back then, but this country eats at a woman.' Rising to her feet she brushed down her skirt.

'True, some do age rapidly in this harsh land. But not you, Elise. Goodness, your hair is still the colour of chestnuts. And your eyes are as green as ever they were.'

She laughed and decided to keep the secret of her arnica and mint hair rinses to herself. Sampson's barking intruded on her thoughts. Amos came stomping through the trees and emerged into the clearing. Sampson's tail drummed the ground and his ears pricked to attention, but he remained at her side.

'Amos,' Marcel said, going up to the man and shaking his hand. 'Good to see you. How are things?'

Amos shrugged his broad shoulders. 'Good enough, Marcel. You?' He turned to Elise. 'A native's asking for you. Wants some of your special embrocation for his rheumatics.'

'That'll be my tansy liniment,' she said. 'I'll go find him.'

'He's in the store,' Amos told her. The permanent frown between his close-set eyes deepened. 'You know how I feel about you trading with the Indians. It's even worse when you take cash from the sailors for your remedies. It does your reputation no good and those sailors and fishermen can be a rough lot.'

'On the contrary,' Marcel broke in. 'Elise knows how to deal with these people and her reputation is unsullied. Word of the effectiveness of her remedies goes far and wide. She's a marvel. The sailors value and respect her. And as for the Mi'kmaq, considering they're pretty darned good at producing their own curatives yet still come to her, it shows she's not only good at what she does, but that they honour her for her gifts.'

She gave him a grateful smile.

'Didn't say she wasn't any good.' Amos's face set in a sulk and he crossed his arms. 'Just said it's not right for her to be selling to all and sundry. It's fine, making for family. That's domestic. Working at the post here – that's decent. But it's not respectable to be selling or bartering her wares like a fish-wife.'

'But I am a fish-wife, Amos,' Elise said.

She was pleased when he blushed. Marcel, she noticed, had to turn aside to hide his grin.

'You know what I mean,' Amos muttered. 'I feel a responsibility towards you.'

'I'd better go and barter my wares.' She turned on her heel and made her way back to the post. Really, Amos was more like a bad tempered bear with each passing day. It jangled at her nerves.

Her business with the Indian was soon done. The liniment was ready in its clay pot and he had the honey she'd asked him to bring as the barter price. She used to be easy-going with her bartering, asking little or nothing and she still did help those without means. However, now she squirreled away her profits as best she could. Whatever the future held she would not face it penniless.

CHAPTER 21

The sun was barely up, the sea was calm, the air chill, and heavy with its unique tang. Elise, with Nancy Pinet's help, set up her stall in its usual spot by the ancient remains of the French fortification, next to the sand and pebble seashore where the ships' crews easily located her.

Nancy, a head shorter than Elise, stood on tiptoe, her hand shading her eyes. 'Can you see them yet?' she asked.

'Two, so far,' Elise replied, as she peered out to sea. 'No, three. Another ship's just coming into view. Good. Busy day today.'

Nancy passed the jars, packets and mixtures from the handcart to Elise, who stacked them in readiness to sell. A now familiar tinge of pride filled her heart as she prepared her display. Who would have thought she'd ever have been an independent trader, albeit on so small a scale?

'What are all these?' Nancy held up one of the small wooden pots.

'I wondered when you'd notice. Allow me to present my new Sarnia Pots.'

Nancy raised an eyebrow, but said nothing as she continued to examine the pot in her hand.

'You know how packaging has always been a problem.' Elise said. 'The dried goods, and herbs for tisanes don't present any difficulties because we sell them in wraps.' Here she waved a bunch of herb-filled canvas wraps in the air.

'Right,' agreed Nancy. 'It's the liquids and liniments that are a dilemma. As you always say, clay pots are fragile, and glass pots even worse, and expensive too. You've found an alternative, by the look of things.'

Elise nodded. 'You know me. Not one to be defeated so I finally invented these.' She held up two different sized pots – one square the other barrel-shaped. Nancy inspected them. She smelled one and shook the other, then cautiously held them upside down. She looked quizzically at Elise.

'It was easy in the end. I hollowed out a small square or round from birch wood, lined it with birch leaves or scraped animal hide and filled it with the liquid or unguent and secured the top. I then added a small piece of bark on which I wrote instructions, and sealed the container with wax. Do you see?'

Nancy peered at the pots in her hand, a grin of approval lighting up her face. 'And these marks scratched on each pot? Is that *Sarnia*?'

'Yes. It's the ancient name for my Island of

Guernsey. And the code tells me what the product is.' She beamed. 'See? Sarnia C1. That's comfrey liniment. C2 is calendula cream. Later I'll show you how I make and label the pots then you can help me, if you want the extra work?'

'I'll say!' Nancy beamed back.

'Thomas would have made them,' she stretched the truth, 'but with his bad arm…'

'I can see that.'

'Customers in sight. Our patrons will be here any moment,' called Elise. The wind held a chill and she pulled her woollen cloak closer in readiness for action. She loved these days of banter, challenging problems, amusing complications; of filling her coffers, and Nancy's companionship and humour. Many a time she actually laughed, not something that came to her freely nowadays.

Throughout the morning she sold her remedies and took orders for new ones. The small queue rarely shortened as she advised and sold. Nancy stood beside her taking the money and noting sales in a ledger. Elise enjoyed having Nancy work by her side. The woman brooked no nonsense and was capable of giving the sailors as good as she got. Since Renee turned her back on Elise's friendship, dear Nancy more than filled the void.

Elise's business thrived and, despite a barren home life, so did she. It was fulfilling to make money, produce her curatives and, at the same time, help folk. Who would have imagined that she could have survived all that fate had thrown at her and yet made a success of things? This life, for all its ups and downs, was a fine one and on a good day she knew she had little to complain about. Her remedies were popular with those who came ashore on their own or the king's business, as well as with her neighbours.

By now the three ships had docked. Sailors, merchants, fishermen and naval seamen all teamed around Saint-Pierre going about their business and enjoying a gossip.

'I don't know about you,' Nancy said during a lull, 'but I'm fed up with all this talk of war against the rebel Americans.'

Elise nodded vigorously.

As was the way with wars, its fortunes twisted and shifted at regular intervals. Nevertheless, it did bring trade to the port, and thus to her.

***

The following summer the raven returns. Rips her sleep apart. Plunges at her. Taunts her. There is a man. A man she knows. Yet doesn't. He's sweat-drenched. Shakes with fever. Coughs to tear himself apart. Veil of blood. Blinds her. Drenches the sheets. Kra kra kra, fills her head. Decay fills her nostrils. Greedy talons. Tear at the man. Dying man. Must protect him. Can't. She screams. He reaches out to her. Thomas? Is that you?

She woke with her mouth dust-dry, her heart pounding. What was the loathsome raven trying to tell her with its message that was no message at all? She kept a wary eye on Thomas, but no fever was apparent.

***

As well as trade arriving with the infrequent flotillas during that summer of 1781, there were letters to despatch and the hope of letters to come. Elise paid a captain to take her package to England from where, all being well, it would be sent on to Guernsey. She groaned with disappointment when she learned that no letters waited for her that day. Her correspondence with her family meant so much, but packages took forever. *Mère, Père, I sometimes think I will die for want of being with you.* She gathered her thoughts. She had work to do.

It was October before a small package of letters arrived. She would savour these when she got home. Meanwhile the new flotilla disgorged welcome goods and eager customers, and her money pouch became satisfyingly heavy.

'I'll clear up here,' Nancy offered, as the fragile sun gave way to the grey of late afternoon. 'You be off before it gets dark.'

'I'm in no hurry.' This was true enough. 'I'll give you a hand to take the trestle back first, then walk with you up the hill.' Elise gave Nancy her shillings, stowed the takings and ledger in her valise and helped Nancy load the trestle supports, make-do counter and unsold items onto the handcart, topping the lot with her weighty valise. They wobbled and pushed their way along to where, for a token fee, Elise rented a small redundant storeroom.

'Good job I'm tough as a team of oxen,' Nancy said.

Elise, unlocking the rickety door, said, 'Me too, though I might not look it.'

'You're distracted today.'

'Lack of sleep.'

'Nightmares?'

'Months now.'

Elise had found herself trusting Nancy enough to confide in her. Surprisingly Nancy had been neither scornful nor shocked. 'I knew a girl once had the same thing. Only she called it a gift.'

'Gift from the devil maybe, but not from any divine source. How can it be a gift to be trapped in this echo, this other-world, unable to interpret what it means? To be at the mercy of the raven? Powerless to understand or do anything to prevent the disasters it foretells?'

She'd confided in Nancy and told her how her grandmother had also called it a gift – a gift from her guardian angel. And how Gran'mère had always insisted it be their own secret for fear of them being labelled witches. Elise spoke of her earliest visions and of the purple-black raven with a voice of death. Of the foretelling of her encounter with the bear, the loss of her baby, Thomas's injuries – all events she might have been able to prevent had she known what to do. 'How can it be a gift to be plagued by Lucifer himself?'

Now, tight-jawed, Elise took up the lantern and her tinderbox. With the lamp aglow she unlocked the storeroom door, stowed the trestle and fetched the ledger.

'Iodine tincture, three pots.' Nancy passed these to Elise who made a note before stacking them in the storeroom. 'Comfrey liniment, five,' Nancy added. She picked up the juniper root tincture. 'Perhaps in time you'll learn to read your visions. Or maybe you aren't meant to?'

'Then what is the point of them!' Elise hadn't meant to snap.

Nancy, unable to answer this, touched Elise's arm before they both got on with the task in hand. While Nancy emptied the cart, Elise made notes and stacked goods in the storeroom. 'I must remember to crush some more slippery elm,' Elise muttered.

Elise's Sania pots were proving to be a big success. Nancy passed her the last of these. 'Maybe I can help you with this nightmare if you tell me what it is?'

Elise retrieved her valise and lantern. 'The dream?' She wedged the wheelbarrow inside and locked the door. 'Oh, the usual garbled things.' She explained about the unidentified sick man. 'I'm sure he's going to die but I can't reach him. And he knows I'm there. I know he knows.' She shook her head. 'It's probably nothing. Let's forget it.'

'In my opinion,' Nancy said, as they made their way back through the port, 'if you aren't there, wherever "there" is, you can't help, can you? Could it be that the person who's sick knows your spirit is present and that is a comfort to him? Is that what it's all about?'

Nancy was a good sort and Elise thought about what her friend said while twilight gathered and begun to close in round them. 'Perhaps you're right, Nancy. Maybe that's it.'

'Or maybe…' Nancy paused.

'Yes?'

'I haven't got the proper words, but what I'm trying to say is, maybe you have these dreams not so you can change things, but to help you prepare for what will be.' She scrubbed at her face with a large red hand. 'Would it be right to change the future even if we could? Maybe that particular door was never meant to be opened.'

'I never thought of it that way. Thank you, Nancy. Maybe the nightmares won't disturb me so much now.' She smiled and felt a little lighter of heart, and together they headed up the hill.

After negotiating the wooden bridge across the stream, they picked their way through the undergrowth. It was always boggy up here, and more so after the recent rain. The cold and dampness seeped in through Elise's deer-hide moccasins as she squelched through the mud.

As their paths separated she hugged Nancy and

thanked her for her help. She meant, of course, for her friendship and her willingness to listen without judgement, as well as her assistance with the business. 'I couldn't manage without you.'

She kissed her friend's cheek then pulled her own woollen cloak tight and continued up the hill. The haunting call of the loon – a sound that always made her feel melancholy – filled the darkening air. Her thoughts veered towards Thomas who needed her but no longer loved her. Such was her fate, it seemed. Weighed down by her heavy thoughts, as well as her lantern and the old valise that bumped against her leg as it rattled with her money pouch and ledger, she trudged the well-worn path as it headed down towards the lake and home.

Thomas was in one of his better moods and a weight lifted from her shoulders a little. 'How did your remedies go today?' he asked.

'Busy, but good.' She changed out of her muddy moccasins and hung her cloak on its nail then set to and put the soup she'd made that morning over the fire to warm through.

Half an hour later they sat to eat.

'Elise?'

His voice startled her.

'I asked was there any news from home.'

'Oh. Yes, sorry, I forgot.' She reached into her pocket. The small bundle held a letter from Thomas's mother, which she handed to him, and a letter from her own mother. She smiled with pleasure and anticipation.

Thomas moved closer to the candle and they each broke the seals on their respective letters. As she read, her smile dissolved. She cried out and jumped to her feet sending her soup bowl crashing to the floor.

'What in God's name?' Thomas picked up the letter and read it. 'Oh, Elise. Oh my dear, what can I say?'

'Père!' she cried. 'No, no, no. Not Père!' She sank to the floor, unable to catch her breath. 'Damn to hell the black hearts of all ravens,' she cried. Thomas held her, rocking her as though she were a child, and cried along with her.

CHAPTER 22

The days shortened and the air turned sharp. It was dusk as Elise finished her stocktaking and locked up her storeroom. Thomas was back inside his bubble of misery and she had another winter to face. She reluctantly turned towards home when a hullabaloo caught her attention.

'The war is over!' came a cry.

'What? Really?'

'Over?'

'Signed, sealed and delivered.'

'Peace treaty. Signed in Paris. October.'

'Eight years of war over. Eight years!'

'Does that mean the United States is an independent nation now?'

'Suppose so.'

By this time most people were too tired of the whole thing to care about who won what or when. It would be well into the following spring before Elise was able to take any peace for granted. After all, treaties had been signed and broken before. Many times. By then she had another sort of war to contend with; the return of her night terrors.

Raven swoops. Screams above the lake. No longer a lake of gold. A lake of blood. Purple-black raven effervescent in the dying light. Blood flows from the lake. Washes over her. Drives her into the darkness of the backwoods. Thomas. Thomas, where are you? Help me. She calls and calls into the blackness, the forest, the mountains, the sky. Across the immense lake and out to sea. The wind. Full of weeping. Mountains rise, block her way. The red lake moans. Its song is the cruel kra kra kra of the raven. Thomas does not come.

Still in the grip of her pernicious nightmare, each morning she lay awake yet not awake, caught between her hallucinating and wakeful mind. If she could fathom the meaning... But what good would that do? Would it make Thomas become her husband again? Would it give her children?

Each morning she cast aside her feelings of dread and set to work at the trading post. Most afternoons she became engrossed in her herb garden or making her remedies, or she collected ingredients from the woods or the shore. Three or more days a week she and Nancy worked at her booth where they were kept busy with local folk and ships' crews, all eager to exchange their money for her curatives. She and Nancy came to know a large number of the seamen whose ships stopped in the port. At the end of these busy days by the seashore Nancy returned to Jake and their children while Elise went back to Thomas. Some days – good days – he had tidied their cabin, brought in water and put it on to heat, shaved. Other days he'd barely moved from their bed. On days such as these he narrowed his seeing eye and silently warned her not to start nagging. Sometimes he thrust his distorted face and blind eye at her or waved his damaged arm like a sort of token, a badge of hurt. She should have pointed out that two eyes were not a prerequisite for getting all sorts of things done, and that one good arm could accomplish much. Nevertheless it was easier and less trouble to indulge him. She tried to remember the Thomas she'd married in order to endure the man he had become.

***

A pleasant afternoon in June sprawled ahead. Summer and long days. As was their custom when a flotilla arrived, Elise and Nancy set up the stall by the shore. During a lull Nancy asked if she'd heard that Charles Robin was back in the area and would be stopping by on his way north.

Charles Robin. The man who had abandoned her and Thomas and escaped to the safety of Jersey. Once the war was over he'd returned to successfully set up his fisheries all over again. He was a dishonourable man. Where was the justice?

Before Elise had time to respond to Nancy, another customer stood before her. It was the portly master of the brigantine, *Trois Amis*. 'Why, M'sieur Torode,' she said, swallowing the sour taste that had risen in her throat at the mention of Charles Robin. 'It's been some time since we had the pleasure of a visit from you, M'sieur. Your normal order?'

The ship's master, a long-standing visitor to her stall, was an intelligent, chirpy Guernseyman, always eager to pass on what news he had of their homeland. As gallant as ever, he took her hand and raised it to his lips. 'Madame Galliard, you get younger each time I see you and, if I may say so, you are as enchanting as ever. Yes I'll take my usual poultice if you please.'

She chuckled, comfortable in the knowledge that his flirtation was but playful gallantry. 'You are too kind, M'sieur Torode.' She took up two large pots of flaxseed and charcoal poultice.

He handed over his money. 'Your remedy is the only thing that eases my wretched gout.' He laughed and his chins wobbled their appreciation.

'How fares St Peter Port?' she asked.

'Very well indeed, dear lady. We now have the finest wine and spirit vaults in the whole of Europe.'

She smiled. 'So you told me last time,' she said, always delighted to hear how Guernsey thrived as a commercial centre.

'And did I also say how well the island does through privateering? As an enterprise it has a great and beneficial impact on the economy.'

Her mind flashed with hatred to a certain Captain

John Paul Jones. Pushing aside how she'd once glamorised her paternal grandfather's privateering activities, she now had little time for what she considered to be legalised piracy, and asked the master of the *Trois Amis* if he had leanings towards that custom.

He shook his head. 'Indeed no. Couldn't stand the excitement and I do well enough without.'

'And where has trade been taking you, M'sieur Torode?'

'Recently shipped a cargo of wheat from Norfolk to Barcelona. Returned to Guernsey laden with brandy and wine.'

'You're kept busy.'

'I am. But, between you and me,' Monsieur Torode lowered his voice before glancing over his shoulder, 'the future is in tobacco.'

'Is that so, M'sieur?'

'Indeed it is. Since the end of that pesky rebels' fracas, it's the trade with Virginia that keeps us seadogs and merchants in pocket.'

When it was, at last, time to go home, she put her hand to her back and stretched an ache away. Another busy day. It was then that she noticed a man waiting to be served. It was, she believed, the tall, lanky shipmaster Mr Nicholas Lambert of the brigantine, *Badger*, a regular visitor to Saint-Pierre but not to her stall till now. 'What can I do for you, sir?'

'It's Mrs Galliard, isn't it? I've been told you can help me.' He seemed a pleasant enough man of perhaps forty. 'I'm having trouble clearing up a chesty cold.'

'You suffer from congestion?'

'Indeed I do.'

Elise reached for a large Sarnia pot, explaining that it was a poultice of stripped maple bark, and advised him to apply it every morning and night.

'I shall take a pot then, thank you.'

Elise took his sixpence. 'You must persist. Don't give up as it may take a few weeks to clear.'

'But what's this pot?' He studied it with care.

She told him about her Sarnia pots. The seaman looked first at Elise then Nancy. He frowned for a moment then smiled a cockeyed smile. 'Not one, but two talented ladies. I shall not hesitate to call again whenever I'm in port.' He executed a graceful bow and whistled a jaunty tune as he walked away.

By the time the sun slid behind the mountains the two women had packed everything onto the handcart. As they made their way through the streets she remembered to ask Nancy about Charles Robin's visit.

Nancy, concentrating on sidestepping the ruts in the path and a small steaming heap of something unpleasant, said, 'He's expected any day now, so I've heard.'

'I don't want to see that man, and I don't want Thomas to have to see him either.' Nancy raised a questioning eyebrow, so Elise continued, 'It would humiliate Thomas to be reminded that Charles Robin left us to our fate and now wants nothing to do with him.

It's no thanks to Robin that we survived.'

They had locked away the cart and trestles and climbed half way up the hill before Elise added, 'This impending arrival of the great Mr Robin explains why Renee is in a tizzy of preparation in the house. You'd think Charles Robin to be royalty. But what is he to us? Did you know he keeps his fishermen in debt, and that he dismissed a fisherman because the man broke the rules and secretly married a Roman Catholic Acadian girl?'

'True, that is harsh. He's not a good man, that's for sure. But be honest, is your dislike as much to do with him being a Jerseyman?'

Elise couldn't help but smile. 'It's no secret that there are a few lively differences of opinion and rivalries between the two islands. Goes back a long way.'

'That's as maybe, but no matter what you think, you better be careful not to upset Charles Robin. He's powerful so you mustn't end up as his enemy, for your own sake, and Thomas's.'

Her mind flashed to whispered stories; shadowy rumours of the misuse of the poor little indentured lads and lasses. Such thoughts could have consequences and she kept those rumours locked away inside her head. 'To be in Charles Robin's bad books? I'm not sure I care,' she said with a dollop of bravado and an exaggerated toss of her head. She kissed Nancy goodnight and, with a grim look on her face, headed up the hill.

Mr Robin arrived the following day, and with him Marcel de Forêt. When Marcel called on her a few days later Elise was preparing dinner. Here was a friend to lighten the pervading mood and she invited him to join them.

'I rather hoped you'd ask,' he said with a grin.

'I rather thought you hoped I'd ask,' she responded.

'You know me too well.'

She smiled. 'I somehow doubt that.'

Thomas sat picking at his fingernails, paying no heed to either of them.

'It's fish I'm afraid. Again. I've been far too busy to think much on food. But I do have some wild garlic and fresh-picked tarragon and Thomas and I would be glad of your company.' She lowered her voice. 'I'm pleased you're here. You always have a good effect on him and he's been in such a black mood since Mr Robin's arrival.'

'Charles will be heading north in a couple of days, so hopefully Thomas's mood will improve.'

'And you? Do you go with him?'

He raised his voice for Thomas's ears. 'No. I'll stay on here a while for supplies before returning to Isle Madame. Meanwhile I can enjoy some more of your company, Thomas. And more of your cooking, I hope, Elise.'

Even Marcel's presence failed to lighten Thomas's brooding. Elise cringed inwardly as Marcel did his best, but nothing could break the web of self-pity Thomas had wrapped around himself. When Marcel asked about his family in Guernsey, Thomas ignored him. Only the rum bottle held his attention.

Giving up, Marcel turned to her. 'What do you miss most about your very small island?'

After a long moment she said, 'My mother, my brothers and sisters and their families.'

'And your father? Is he in trade?'

She felt a stab of pain. 'He died. Last year. He was an apothecary.'

'You must miss him.'

She nodded. He touched her arm in sympathy. 'So, that's where you learned about curatives.'

'I learned a lot from my father and I was lucky to go to a dame school, but my grandmother taught me so much as well.' Her spirits lightened just to be talking of her beloved gran'mère. 'We were especially close. She was a remarkable woman – self-taught. She'd somehow got hold of a rare herbalist's almanac, a treatise on herbs, written, Gran'mère insisted, by a French monk, and obtained by a learned doctor. It is said that the doctor brought it home from the Crusades, but no one knows how true that is.' She paused for a moment, then added, 'Gran'mère died the year before I left home.'

She went to her dowry chest and brought out the ancient book that she kept wrapped in the fine wool and oiled cloth she'd brought it in. She handed it to him and he studied it with care. When he turned to the back pages he looked up at her. 'Are these your notes?'

'Mostly Gran'mère's. Her own recipes and advice added over the years. The later ones are my own.'

'Precious.'

'Yes, most precious.'

'I'm sure your grandmother would have been very proud of you,' Marcel said.

'I like to think so. From my earliest days I always strove to please her.' She glanced at Thomas, who sat apparently engrossed in his unlit pipe. 'Though I fear she would be disappointed in me.'

'Nonsense. You cope with your burdens better than most I could name.'

She sat lost in her memories until he added, 'Your father had a shop? Tell me something of it.'

As she filled their plates she said with pride, 'Victor Machon & Son: Apothecary, St Peter Port. My father's father bought it with privateers' gold and the profits from supplying English smugglers with French brandy. At least, so the story goes.' She wiped her hands before taking the proffered almanac from him, wrapping it and returning it to her dowry chest.

As they ate the fish and onions, she shared some of her childhood memories with him. 'From an early age I was responsible for Père's window display. I loved the names on the pretty jars. And the shop had a special aroma of its own, a mix of herbs and other mysterious concoctions. I can almost smell it now.'

'The way you describe it, I can nearly see it. Smell it, too.' They ate in silence for a few minutes. Thomas kept his gaze lowered as he toyed with his food.

'As usual, an excellent meal.' Marcel sat back. 'Thank you.'

She decided to ignore Thomas's sulks and chatted with Marcel like the old friends they were. She talked more of St Peter Port and how her grandmother was an expert at preparing the Guernsey dish of slow-cooked ormers, and how Islanders loved the pearly ormer shells.

'I bought some shells with me, only they got…' Her voice faded as she remembered the loss of so much that day in September over five years back.

Marcel was looking at her quizzically and she made a concerted effort to quell the bleakness that touched her. 'Guernsey people were known for the quality of their knitting,' she told him. 'Apart from me, that is – much to my mother's despair. I could barely knit a lumpy row without making a mess. Gran'mère, on the other hand, was the best knitter I knew. Her stockings were in great demand.'

Marcel looked at Thomas. 'Do I remember you telling me that Elise knitted that Guernsey sweater you wear?'

Thomas managed another grunt.

'Don't look too closely,' she said. 'I made a terrible mess of it. My mother had to rescue my work many times. It's deeply flawed, I'm afraid.'

'Looks good to me,' Marcel said. He held a spill to the fire and lit his pipe then settled back down again to listen to her tales of home. For her part, it was wonderful to re-live those happy times with someone who seemed genuinely interested in the insignificant details of her childhood.

Marcel turned to Thomas and said, 'You, too, must have many good memories?'

Elise was embarrassed by Thomas's shrug.

She filled in the strained silence. 'My grandmother's cottage was tiny and, apart from Père's shop, was my favourite place on the whole island.'

Marcel chuckled. 'You paint a colourful picture of an ideal childhood. I can imagine you in that white apron, with your copper hair dishevelled, and emerald eyes all aglow. A handful, I bet.'

Elise stood up. 'That I was. But enough of me. It's getting late and you must be bored with my silly stories.'

'*Au contraire.*' He too got to his feet and glanced at Thomas. 'I've really enjoyed your reminiscences. Perhaps I can persuade Thomas to tell me something of his childhood next time. Meanwhile, I thank you again and bid you both goodnight.'

A few days after Mr Robin's departure Elise woke early. The bed beside her was empty. She dressed and went outside. Calling Thomas's name, she searched high and low in a grey cloud of trepidation that soon turned to fear, then panic. The day and night crept by and in desperation she went to Renee and Amos early the following morning.

'Don't you worry,' Amos said. 'Thomas is able to take care of himself. He'll be fine, you'll see.' His unexpected kindness surprised and comforted her. He seized his hat and made for the door, adding, 'Nevertheless, let's organise a search party. I'll get one sorted at once.'

Renee added her own reassurances. 'We'll manage the search from the trading post here,' she said. 'I'll get the ladies to prepare hot food for everyone. We'll all need to keep our strength up.'

'Oh, Renee, I don't know what to say. I'm so grateful.'

'I've a soft spot for Thomas, you know that. He's a survivor. Don't fret now. Amos and I are good at organising.'

Most Saint-Pierre folk had cause to go to Amos and Renee's trading post at some time or another; perhaps on a visit or in search of good fishing or hunting, or for Elise's remedies if she wasn't at her booth by the sea. Before she knew it a small bustle of people appeared, and Amos lead the men and his dog, Sampson, along the lake's shoreline. In Renee's kitchen a group of women put together the makings of a large kettle of rabbit stew and a mound of bread. All these emergency preparations made Elise feel panicky again. It was clear that this was a serious situation. Soon more neighbours turned up and with them Marcel.

'Thank God you're here.' She grasped his hands. 'I thought you'd left for Isle Madame.'

'They caught me in time and told me the news.'

'Something bad has happened,' she said. 'I can sense

it.'

He placed a hand on her shoulder but she barely noticed the gesture. Seeing the volunteers he said, 'I'll help Amos sort these folk into search parties.' They soon organised people to systematically cover the area. He advised Elise to remain at the store while the search went on. 'Look at you. You're in no state to be out there. When did you last get any sleep? When did you eat?'

She wouldn't be dissuaded. She needed to be active, to block out the thoughts that crushed her mind. 'I'll go with Nancy and Jake,' she said.

Renee filled water flasks and the various groups set out. Elise and her friends were allocated the area to the west of the steep portage route from the Bras D'Or to the sea. Another group covered the east. During a brief break at the port, under a fierce sun, Elise passed the water flask to Nancy, asking her in a voice hoarse with tiredness and fear, if she thought they had any chance of locating him.

'If he's within reach, we'll find him.'

After another four fruitless hours of calling and prodding the undergrowth for any clues they arrived back at the lake hot, tired and dejected. The search parties declared themselves ready for the food and drink laid on by Renee and her willing assistants. Elise, without appetite, sat alone nibbling at a piece of bread. A man sat down and squeezed her hand.

'How are you bearing up, Mrs Galliard?'

It took her a moment to recognise the tall, bony

master of the *Badger*. 'Mr Lambert – thank you for being here.'

'I've managed to organise some available mariners into search parties. All these people who care,' he gestured around him. 'Goes to show how esteemed you are, Mrs Galliard. Here, let me fetch you some fresh water from the barrel.'

She couldn't trust her voice, but smiled her thanks.

The day folded into another long sleepless night. Another dawn. Another day searching. Marcel recruited some Mi'kmaq volunteers and, employing their tracking abilities, set out with them to search further afield. Amos took over directing the searches.

'Thomas will have taken off,' Amos said later that day. 'Perhaps to hunt. I expect he's hurt himself and we'll find him hot and bothered from waiting for rescue.'

It was not openly spoken, but common knowledge that if a man was injured, speed was crucial if he was to be saved. By not giving up she was reaching out to him. Keeping him alive. He's out there, maybe hurt, but he'd know she was sending him the will to hang on until she found him.

On the edge of exhaustion, she was re-filling some water flasks when a fisherman came running up. 'A skiff's missing. That abandoned one by the old portage route where it diverts near the lake.'

A discussion followed, but no one knew if the missing skiff was significant. Elise said that Thomas could manage a skiff with his one good arm. 'He might have gone fishing.'

'Maybe he drifted off course?' someone ventured. *Or he's fallen in and drowned.*

'If he did drift off he'll be trying to get back.' Elise looked around her. 'Please, please don't give up. Please, you've all been so kind, but don't give up. He's out there somewhere, I know it.'

Chapter 23

'Sure, he's out there somewhere, what's left of him, poor devil.'

Elise couldn't tell who spoke the words but they were followed by a general nodding of heads and regretful glances in her direction. She would not, could not, accept what they were saying to be true, so pretended not to have heard. Inevitably, after four days with no progress, the search had to be abandoned as the need to work drew people back to their everyday lives.

Thomas was given up for dead.

Her heart was a heavy boulder within her chest, and her future was a blank. Was really he dead? Had she not sensed impending disaster? Hadn't the raven, in its cruelly unfathomable way, predicted as such?

With most of the community abandoning Thomas she became driven – compelled – to search for him herself. With little hope and less strategy she clambered along the shoreline and the lakeside as far as she could, rowed the perimeters and scrambled about in the forest. All this time she called his name until her throat hurt and her voice dried to a croak. Then it came to her: she was acting out her nightmare, it had become the reality of her days. She stopped hoping and stopped searching. Her nightmare did not return.

Not everyone abandoned her or Thomas. Marcel and his band of Mi'kmaq doggedly kept up their search. After three weeks Marcel knocked on her door. Her heart jumped with hope when she saw him. 'You've brought good news? You've found him?' she asked, though his face told her otherwise and her heart seemed to stop.

Marcel took her by the elbow and guided her towards a bench. 'Elise, you'd better sit.'

'For pity's sake tell me!' She shook his hand from her arm. He turned his face from her and any hope she'd clung to crumbled into bitter dust.

He took her hands in his. His face was kind, but resigned. He and his Mi'kmaq searchers had heard a rumour, he told her. Some debris on the lakeshore about a day's journey by canoe, up towards North Mountains. 'We found the wreckage of what had most likely been a skiff,' he said.

'You can't know for sure that it's anything to do with Thomas.'

He pulled a small dark heap from his bag. With trembling hands she took it, held it to her, smelled it. She rested her cheek on the rough, damp surface of a darned and patched fisherman's sweater; the sweater she had made with love and hope and mistakes, the sweater she had proudly brought with her from Guernsey in her dowry chest.

In the weeks that followed, she tried to accept Thomas's death and to remember the good they had shared. She endeavoured to come to terms with his anger and his inability for so long to be a husband in any true sense. Even when separated from him by the sea and later by his troubles, he had been her life. She did not know how to live it without him. She was a vacant shell, a husk of loneliness. Each night she lay sleepless, his absence a deep pit. She had never been alone in the world before. The empty space he left made it hard for her to breathe. Her life became a blank page, an emotional limbo. The cold, black nights were worse. Sometimes she'd cry her feelings into the thick solitude. 'Thomas, what happened? Why did you go?' Did he hate her and their life so much that death was preferable? Or was it some awful accident?

What could she do now? Go home to Guernsey? The feint echo of her homeland called to her, but she wasn't that girl anymore. She couldn't slip back into that role. The dependent sister, the widowed aunt? No. Her life was here. But to what purpose? Such unanswered and unanswerable questions plagued her as surely as if the raven itself clawed at her mind. Yet, paradoxically, even the raven had abandoned her. She would never know why Thomas left or what had happened to him, or if she could have done more to comfort him. That was her punishment.

The song of the sea had been silenced.

CHAPTER 24

'Choose,' Amos said bluntly. 'Do the job you're here for or leave the cabin I provide for you. This has gone on long enough.' He stood at her open door, his arms folded across his chest.

Elise felt like weeping as she looked around her at the remnants of her stunted life with Thomas. His fisherman's hat still hung from its nail by the window, his razor and shaving mug sat on the shelf by the water jug. His best boots were beside the door and his once-loved fisherman's sweater was still by the fire where she'd left it.

'This is my home,' she said to Amos. 'The home I shared with Thomas for near on six years.'

Amos shuffled. 'It's been seven months since he...'

'Nine. It's been nine months since he died.'

'There you are then. We have to get someone else in if you won't pull your weight. This cabin goes with the job, you know that.' He tipped his hat and strode off.

Elise stood outside in the sun and tried to clear her mind. With the arrival of spring and its verdant promise of new life she had started to feel a lifting of her spirits. Once again she'd begun to enjoy the company of others and the fulfilment of working on her remedies. Her many customers, and especially her friend Nancy, had brought warmth back into her heart. She had started to relish her own company. No one else to be answerable to. No one else to fret over and to fear displeasing. The guilty pleasure in living the life of a self-sufficient woman was a great consolation.

As for Amos, she couldn't really blame him for asking her to move out. Choosing between working for the Sebires at the trading post and running her own small but viable business wasn't difficult. After their initial kindness on her arrival and again at the time of Thomas's disappearance, they had soon reverted to their mean ways. Renee rarely exchanged a pleasant word, and Amos had yet again became aloof and stern. Neither did they have time nor patience with each other. It was as if they'd used up the last dregs of their humanity.

So be it. After her day's work making and selling remedies, she began to search for a cabin she could buy. Nancy said that she knew of one nearby. 'Really sound and in a fine position. Plenty of land with it. My Jake did some carpentry work on it.'

Elise called the following day and met a Madame Boudreau. 'My husband's a coaster,' Madame explained, as she poured Elise a strong coffee. 'We're moving to Isle Madame to set up in trade with my sister. Let me show you. It's nothing fancy, but I keep it clean.'

'I think it more than adequate for my needs, M'dame,' Elise told her after her look round. 'And you've cultivated yourself a good-sized garden. That would do well for my herbs.'

'If you're interested, we might make arrangements over some of the larger pieces of furniture. I've no use for them.'

They came to an agreement and all was settled. Elise would have a real home. She'd be a woman of property; a fact that terrified and delighted her. When it came to packing her belongings she found that she'd underestimated the accumulation squeezed into her cabin and herb patch. Help came from an unexpected source.

'I believe you're about to move,' Mr Lambert, master of the *Badger*, said to her as she and Nancy were laying out her stall one morning.

She handed him the tincture of iodine he'd asked for. 'That's right,' she confirmed. *How quickly, whether for good or ill, talk and tattle jump in all directions at once.*

'I'm in port for a few more days. Perhaps I can be of assistance?'

Unwilling to be in this stranger's debt she began to turn the offer down, but Nancy had other ideas and chipped in, 'That's kind of you. We've borrowed a decent-sized wagon, but I bet Elise could do with some extra help with the lifting.'

After this she could not turn down the offer without appearing churlish.

Her heart squeezed in her chest as she contemplated discarding Thomas's possessions, especially his raggedy fisherman's sweater. She felt as though she were throwing away his existence. His best boots she gave to Jake Pinet, but in the end she kept little – only his bundle of letters from home and the small inscribed bible his mother had sent him some years back. She didn't need to open the bible to know its inscription: *To my dear son, March 1st, 1781, God keep you safe.* She should have returned these to his mother long ago, and would do so at once. All else, mostly old clothes, she took outside and burned quickly before she could change her mind. The tattered remains of Thomas's Guernsey sweater flared for a moment of splendour then shrivelled to nothing. The flames danced through her tears.

***

It took a whole morning to move everything but, with the good-natured help of Nancy and Mr Lambert, the proceedings turned into a light-hearted occasion with grunts of effort mingling with quantities of laughter. The bulk of her effects consisted of the tools and accessories of her trade. Elise found no time for fears, memories or regrets and by some miracle the rain held off. Nancy turned down Elise's offer of a lunch of cold pork and potatoes but Mr Lambert accepted. During the meal, her first in her new home, he kept up a steady flow of chatter about his ship and his home in Portsmouth.

'You live with your family?' she asked, as she re-filled his glass with beer.

'With my mother and my two children. Unfortunately I was widowed four years back.'

'I'm so sorry to hear that. You have two children? You being away so much must be hard on them, and on you.'

'It's not ideal, but mother is good with them and I spend time with them as often as I can.'

After lunch Elise felt overwhelmingly tired and begged to be excused. She had a great deal of work to complete before dark, starting with a final sweep of the cabin at upper Saint-Pierre. He immediately offered to take her back and then to return the wagon on her behalf. Too tired to protest, she agreed.

***

It was daunting at first, lying in her strange new bed in her strange new home, with different sounds seeping in and old sounds absent. As a priority she created a secure hideaway for her savings, Gran'mère's priceless treatise, her journal and her letters from home. *Funny*, she thought, *how it will always be Gran'mère's treatise, never my own. Seems like she's here by my side.* Within days she was again tending her stall, and her regulars and their shillings and pence continued to roll in. The cold wet spring had made it difficult to re-plant her herbs and vegetables, and harvesting became a glutinous chore, but by the summer all was as it should be and she began to enjoy the many advantages of her new home. It was bigger, had a storeroom for her work and was less isolated. Nancy and Jake lived not far away. Getting home after a day's work was, as she told Nancy, a hop, a skip and a jump. She did not have to feel guilty about neglecting her duties to Renee or Amos, for now she had none. She did not have to put up with Renee's bad temper or Amos's watchful bullying. A weight had lifted from her shoulders. Despite the loss of Thomas, Elise now flourished in this wild land as she fulfilled the long ago dreams of a pioneering woman. Renee and Amos on the other hand had sadly shrunk into an unhappy, bitter world of their own.

She never looked back once she'd moved into her new home. Above all, Thomas's ghost did not haunt her there. She felt settled, free and light of heart. Surely, at last, Thomas, too, was at peace.

Mr Lambert joined the ranks of Marcel de Forêt and Nancy and Jake Pinet as a valued friend. She thought the man lonely and they spent time chatting whenever his ship lay at anchor. It was interesting to hear of all the places he'd been, and she realised how little she knew of the world, though more than most folk did, he'd told her. She suspected that he particularly meant female folk, which she supposed was true.

August was busy and her plants grew and thrived. The mosquitoes eventually abated, but the weeds did not. As she plucked and dug these from the soil she enjoyed the satisfaction of a growing weed pile. Some of the chickweed, nettles, plantain and dandelions she shook clean and saved for their culinary or medicinal qualities.

Then. *Nights of horror. Of terror. Black-beak snares of the purple-black raven. Wings smother. Talons pierce. Claws snatch. Drag her over grey sea, dark sky. Kra kra kra. Blood-lust. Heart-stopping plunge. Through icy air. Into greedy sea. Spinning. Dragging. Down. Lungs scream, beg for air. Choking. Dying lungs. Dying light. Dying.*

She woke up with a scream in her throat, choking. In dawn's glow she still felt the raven's beak, its claws, the crack of her bones, the miasma, the dreadful tug of the sea. Even in the clear morning light of summer she could not shake off the raven's malignant black spell. Tears of anger, fear, frustration coursed down her face. 'Damn and curse you!' she cried at the coming day and the absent raven.

Many an evening, as an antidote to the raven, she worked out of doors, weeding, trimming, cutting back some overenthusiastic brambles then stripping their leaves for future use. The air calmed her. She needed sleep but, lingering outside, was reluctant to seek it for fear that the raven would pursue her. She resolved to try some of her honey wine with lemon balm and mugwort. As she stretched some of the knots from her back, a movement in the gloom caught her attention.

'Who's there?' she demanded, reaching for her knife.

'Nicholas. Nicholas Lambert. Sorry, did I startle you?'

'A bit,' she admitted, relaxing. 'I didn't notice your ship earlier. When did you arrive?'

'Yesterday. I've come here to ask a favour of you.'

She gestured for him to sit on the wooden bench near her door. From here she often enjoyed the dying light after a busy day.

'Coffee?' she offered. He nodded and she went to the pot over the embers and filled two earthenware mugs. She sat beside him and asked what the favour might be.

He shuffled for a moment. 'It's a trifle awkward. A medical matter. Not mine, you understand. My first mate, Johnson.'

Elise smiled. 'Dear friend, I'm not unused to customers seeking cures for embarrassing ailments. If you could give me some idea?'

'I'd rather you saw the man, Mrs Galliard. He begged me to ask that you visit him on board.'

'I'm not sure it's appropriate...'

'I would be there, of course. I would not subject you to any danger. The poor man is in a bit of a state and cannot bear to confide in me.'

Nicholas Lambert had been kind to her on more than one occasion, so after a moment she decided no misfortune could come of such a trip in broad daylight and agreed to call on the first mate early the following day. Into her leather satchel that next morning she packed a pot of ground willow bark and one of dried leaves of Indian mallow, both reckoned to alleviate diseases of a sexual nature (if indeed that was the problem, as seemed most likely). Which one she dispensed would depend on the severity of his symptoms. Perhaps it was a digestive difficulty? She added her hot root and willow bark elixir, just in case.

'It's not far.' Mr Lambert helped her into a rowing boat. The port was quiet, the morning overcast and heavy. She wondered that he didn't get himself tangled in his own gangly legs, but his rowing was proficient and smooth. He turned south then rounded the small headland. In front of her the two-masted *Badger,* displaying its red ensign, lay at anchor close to the shore.

'Can you manage?' he asked, as they came alongside. She nodded but when she saw the rope ladder stretching above her head she hesitated. After an embarrassing scramble, with Mr Lambert close enough behind to shield her modesty, though too close for comfort, her feet found the welcome decking.

She checked around and felt a stab of apprehension. 'Is nobody about?' she asked.

'Oh, they're somewhere. Here and there. Not far.' He handed back the leather satchel he'd carried for her. Too late for second thoughts, she followed him below deck. The reek of vinegar, stagnant seawater, damp canvas and tar took her back to her own voyage a decade ago. Memories rose sharply and disrupted her equilibrium for a moment. They arrived at a cabin door where Mr Lambert smiled reassuringly, knocked, opened the door and indicated that she precede him. Despite the small space being dimly lit she could tell nobody was there. She swivelled round but he was inside with her, the door slammed shut.

'What is this? Kindly open that door, I wish to go home.'

'Don't be startled, Mrs Galliard. I mean you no harm. I need to speak with you in private, that's all.'

She swallowed down her panic and suggested that they had nothing to say to each other that could not be said elsewhere.

'But here is the best place.' He leant back against the door and smiled yet again. 'Humour me for a few moments. I promise not to detain you long.'

'You tricked me, Mr Lambert. You got me here under false pretences. Whatever you have to say, I will not listen.' Regardless of the anger and alarm growing within her she spoke softly, looked him in the eye.

'I admit deception. But, dear lady, it's the only way I can convince you of my sincerity. Be assured, I have no intention of compromising you.'

'Deception between friends is not the right way, and I already feel compromised just being here. Let me leave your ship and we'll remain friends. Keep me here and we must become enemies.'

A flicker of doubt crossed his face but was replaced with that now familiar, slightly disconcerting smile.

'Your modesty does you proud, Elise. I may call you Elise?'

She said nothing.

'Such a pretty name.' He stepped forward and snatched her hand. Grasped it tightly. Forced it to his lips. 'But widowhood doesn't suit you. We should wed, don't you agree?'

She tugged her hand away, then gave a sharp laugh. Did she hear correctly? Surely not. 'You really think you must kidnap me in order to persuade me to marry you? This is ludicrous.'

'But I know you love me.' His eyes were slightly bloodshot and shone unnaturally.

Her face flared with embarrassment. 'Mr Lambert, I do not love you. I never will.'

'Your modesty is commendable, but fails to convince me. The shy love in your face gives you away, dear Elise. I know you want to be my wife. You want us to spend the rest of our lives together as much as I do.' He touched her cheek, apparently unaware of her recoil. The situation had become so ridiculous that it was hard to take in the gravity of it until he put his arm round her waist and pulled her close. His breath, his skin, his clothes all smelled rank enough to make her retch.

'Stop that right now, Mr Lambert. I shall cry out and have you arrested.'

'You underestimate me,' he whispered into her ear. 'My crew are occupied in the port. We're alone.' He abruptly let her go and she fell against the wall. 'Come, admit it. You are frantic with love for me.' He gave a childlike giggle that sent waves of horror through her.

'Of course I don't love you,' she hissed, trying to keep the tremor from her voice. 'You're mad. I lost my husband barely a year ago. I have no desire to replace him.'

'I knew you'd be reticent. I value you for that. And have no fear, I won't lay a disrespectful or unwanted hand on you. You and I, we'll sail to Portsmouth together and we'll be married there.' He grabbed her wrists and pulled her to him once more. There was a gloss of dampness on his forehead and upper lip. 'I adore you, Elise,' he gasped, 'and I know in your heart you feel the same.'

'But that's—'

He laid a finger on her lips. 'Enough, my dear. Your modesty does you proud, but you are not, after all, unfamiliar with the woman's role in marriage. The flame you carry for me in your eyes is impossible to ignore.'

'Sir, I can never—'

'And think – you will no longer need to degrade yourself with trade. Your status will be much elevated. You can enjoy being the respectable wife of a respectable ship's master, and mother to my two darling girls.'

'But I love my work. I have no intention of ever —'

'Your protestations are sweet, but no more, my dear.' His voice took on a harsh edge. 'You understand how it is. I'll take good care of you from now on. No one will come between us.' His hand went to the back of her head and he drew her face close to his. He kissed her cheek, then tentatively pressed his flaccid lips to her rigid mouth, leaving smears of sweat and spittle.

'Now,' he beamed, 'I'll fetch a bottle and we'll drink to our future. We shall seal our bargain. As soon as my crew return we'll make sail.' He pulled her hands to his lips and kissed them with an alarming reverence. 'I want you so much my darling Elise. But I honour you. Hard as it will be on both of us, I intend to spend the nights in my day cabin. I have a hammock strung there, so you've no cause for concern on my behalf. I shall be perfectly comfortable, and my height no less accommodated in the hammock than in my regular bunkbed.' He now gestured to the bunk and giggled. 'I even put fresh linen on for you.'

Elise realised that, in his madness, he actually believed what he said. The implications of her captivity struck home. Her mind whirled as she sought a way to reason with this man who had lost his reason. 'Mr Lambert – Nicholas. We must talk about this.'

'And we will. I shall leave you for a few moments, but I'll be back presently with a good claret and we'll make a toast to our lives together. Meanwhile, make yourself at home.' Again he snatched at her hand, planted an enthusiastic, wet kiss, then drew a huge brass key from the lock and slipped through the door. She heard him put the key to use and she was alone and imprisoned.

Momentarily stupefied, Elise stood rooted to the floor of the small cabin. She turned to the porthole. It was ajar and she pushed against it. Peering beyond the too small opening, she could make out a smudge of land beyond a strip of sea. She turned back and stumbled against her leather satchel. Picking it up, she jammed it angrily on the bunk. What a fool she'd been. She'd not even told anyone where she was going. In a rage she sat on the bed, throwing the satchel to one side. It clunked as it hit the wall. A thought struck her and she grabbed the bag again. Trembling, she fumbled inside it then tipped out the contents. There it was, right at the bottom, long forgotten: the tincture of hemlock, belladonna and henbane she'd once given to Thomas when he was so in thrall to the pain of his injuries.

She slipped the vial into her pocket then scooped everything else back into the satchel. As the key turned in the lock she jumped up, automatically straightening her hair and her expression. He stood with a bottle in his hand and glasses protruding from his jacket pockets; that manic glint in his eyes, that idiotic smile on his misguided face – but not so misguided that he forgot to lock the door after himself and pocket the key.

'Now my dear, are you settled in?'

She managed what she hoped to be a demure smile.

'Excellent. This is the best claret you'll have tasted, I'll be bound.' He extracted the glasses, meticulously polished them with a clean handkerchief and poured the red liquid with a flourish. He handed her a glass and raised his own. 'To us. To our new life together.' He stared intensely, unblinkingly into her eyes.

'Us,' she whispered, lowering her gaze.

He gestured that she be seated then sat next to her, that unholy smile glued to his face.

'Tell me more of Portsmouth,' she said, frantic to distract him and to buy some time.

He did. With zeal. Then he went on to describe in detail his house, his mother and his two children. 'The girls are seven and eight. You'll love them. A step-mother is just what they need. Mama is getting on in years. I can't expect her to act as mother to the girls for much longer. She will so much appreciate your help. How happy we shall all be. And hopefully we'll soon add to our family. I have a mind for two boys. What do you think?'

Elise nodded and smiled and kept him talking – and drinking – while her own wine quietly soaked into his straw mattress. Not, God willing, a mess she need concern herself with. The bottle emptied, the mad shipmaster began to have trouble focussing. She slipped two drops of the tincture into his wineglass. *Highly poisonous*, the Mi'kmaq Nathaniel had said. *Only to be used with care.* She couldn't afford for it not to work so added two more drops. Within a short while Nicholas Lambert lay snoring. Loudly. Elise extracted the key from his pocket and grabbed her satchel. Should she, after all, make sure he didn't wake up? Did the madman deserve to die? Perhaps, if it saved some innocent woman from being carted off and made the object of his delusional passions; a minder for his mother and children. She had no intention of becoming the slave of a madman, but was she capable of taking his life? Yes, if need be. In some dark place within her, she even relished the idea, but then practicality rather than conscience prevailed. The consequences would be too risky and she let the fancy go. Surely he would be too ashamed to make a fuss once she got ashore? She edged open the door and listened. A clumping noise and raucous laughter had her retreating into the cabin and re-locking the door. She held her breath. The ship was coming to life.

She swallowed her alarm and tried to gather her wits. Grabbing a coat and breeches from the back of a chair she put them on. She rammed her skirt into the satchel then hesitated. If she locked Lambert in, some crew member might get suspicious. As it was, he appeared to be drunk and the empty bottle added to the illusion. She disposed of the extra glass through the porthole. Unlocking the door again she took the key and slid it down the front of the snoring man's breeches. 'There, my fine captain.' She patted his shoulder, found his hat and jammed it onto her head, stuffing her hair in tightly.

If caught, she would be taken for a thief or a whore. If the shipmaster died she would be taken for a murderess. *Serves you right for wanting to help someone, and for trusting a man who was little more than a stranger. Marriage, indeed! Portsmouth, indeed! Do I look that stupid and fragile?*

Focus, she told herself. The next few minutes stretched endlessly. She found the rope ladder easily enough but the dinghy had gone. What to do? There was nothing for it. She secured her satchel, scuttled down the ladder and dropped into the sea before she could have second thoughts. The cold was a shock of pain.

The swim ashore stretched less than a quarter of a mile but the land receded with every stroke. As a child, she'd been a keen swimmer, but apart from her disastrous plunge into the sea at Arichat to rescue little Guérin Therriau, she had barely swum since childhood. Had she lost the ability? The icy grasp of water stole her breath and her strength. Cramp grabbed at her thigh. Hampered by her clothes and satchel and unable to free herself of them, she was dragged under. Sea water filled her nose and mouth. She clawed and struggled until at last she broke the surface. Choking and flailing helplessly she was pulled down once again. Burning salt water forced its way into her lungs. The horror of her near-death by drowning at Arichat and the subsequent pain of birth and death replayed in her head, as did her recent nightmares. Once again, surely for the final time, her face broke the surface. Frantically she gulped at the life-giving air. Death was close and seemingly inevitable.

Elise, listen to me. Calm down. Let the tide take you. Gran'mère's voice. As soft and clear as a summer breeze. She took heart and obeyed. At once she felt calmer. In control. As instructed by her grandmother, she stopped struggling against the tide. Her clothing no longer dragged her down but ballooned out to aid her buoyancy. She forgot the drag of her satchel, she forgot the numbing cold of the sea and the remembered panic of Arichat. Her arms and legs did as her mind commanded. Somehow she edged ever-closer to the shore. 'Thank you, Gran'mère,' she sobbed as she clambered onto dry land.

An hour later she shivered and stumbled through her front door. Still shaking, she stripped, scrubbed herself vigorously with a length of rough canvas and changed into dry clothing. As she sipped a basil and sage tea sweetened with honey she finally stopped trembling. 'You stupid, gullible woman, Elise Galliard,' she shouted. 'Don't you know any better than that?'

Then she found herself laughing. She laughed at the ridiculousness of Nicholas Lambert. She laughed as she remembered slipping the key down his breeches. She laughed at the thought of the hangover and confusion he would wake to, if, indeed, he woke up at all. She laughed until her hysteria turned into hiccups, sobs and terror. Finally she cried herself into a black dreamless sleep.

CHAPTER 25

The seasons dissolved one into the other and the *Badger* continued to sail into Saint-Pierre, but with a different master these days. Nicholas Lambert had most likely tried to kidnap other naïve women. Maybe he had even succeeded in finding one to marry him? If asked later what she remembered of the three years following the fiasco with the delusional Mr Lambert, she would have said that nothing out of the ordinary had happened and that life remained calm and relatively prosperous. Just as she liked it.

That June of 1786 the sun shone in a clear sky. At last the wind had shed the remnants of winter's chill. Elise was sitting outside her home grinding bark and quietly singing an old Guernsey song to herself when a sound startled her.

'Hello, Elise.'

'Marcel! How do you fare?' Since Thomas's death Marcel had visited her from time to time, perhaps stopping by for a meal. It was always good to see him and to hear his news. Such a rare pleasure, to have a guest at her table.

'I'm fine, thanks,' he said.

She brushed residual bark from her hands. 'Coffee? There's some on the stove.'

They sat in the sun sipping from their mugs. 'You are well?' he said after a moment.

'Yes I am, thank you. This time of year suits me. Winter gone, spring flowers tumbling over themselves, mosquitoes not yet awake.'

He smiled.

'You, Marcel de Forêt, seem to thrive in all seasons,' she accused. And he did. The grey at his temples was more apparent, the lines around his eyes perhaps more deeply etched, but he stood as tall, energetic and swarthy as ever.

He sat back and chuckled. 'Am I imagining things or is Saint-Pierre more than ever overrun by Loyalists?'

'A couple of shiploads arrived recently. Some moved on but many stay to farm here. The soil's good and they fit in well. We're a growing town. It's good for business.'

She picked up the mugs and rinsed them in her tin bowl. 'I would ask where you've been, but I know you'll avoid giving me a straight answer.'

'As a matter of fact I've come from Arichat. Had some business with Charles. John doesn't come out these days. A manager runs the new place.'

'I heard. I'm told they've set up at a cove east of the harbour now.'

'Easier to cut and run from there. After the island raid it made sense. The water there is pretty deep so it worked out well and the fishery's thriving.'

'I'm glad.'

After a companionable silence he said, 'I have an errand to do across the lake on Île de la Sainte-Famille tomorrow. Would you like to come along for the trip?'

'Holy Family Island?'

'It's not far, a few hours or so by canoe.'

She hesitated.

'It makes a wonderful outing, especially this time of year.'

They set out early. She admired the way Marcel propelled the canoe with confidence and strength. She did offer to take up the spare paddle, but he insisted she sit back and relax. She'd rarely ventured out onto this lake, and then not far. Now she appreciated how many islands of all shapes and sizes adorned it. Most were small humps with a thick covering of evergreens growing down to a shingle or rocky shore. It was turning into one of those glorious early-summer days, with clouds little more than wisps against a luminous sky, and the deep green of the lake flecked with a sprinkle of indolent wave-tops. Amid the lazy call of a few birds, the lap of water and the warmth of a lustrous sun, she sat suspended from all things except the here and now. By the time the sun was high she started to wonder how far their destination was. Not that she minded. She was happy on this beautiful lake: this Lake of Gold. She trailed a finger in the chilly water as the birchbark canoe cut through the gentle surface. A heron stalked the waterline of a humpbacked island to their right.

'You're going to meet someone? An Indian?'

'I'm going to pick something up.'

As always she got no straight answer and her curiosity nagged like a mosquito bite. After a few moments she sat up. 'Pass me that paddle. I'm perfectly capable of a little work, and I'm getting hungry.' She turned her back on him and took a few strokes until he had synchronised with her, then she pulled hard against the drag of the water. They scooted forward at a crisp rate and she let the rhythm occupy her before she said over her shoulder, 'How long did you say the journey would take?'

'I said a couple of hours but I lied. It will be more like four altogether.'

'Four! Then heaven knows what time we'll be back tonight.'

'It'll be fine. We're near enough on the summer solstice. Plenty of daylight ahead of us and a full moon tonight.'

'But why didn't you say four in the first place? Did you think I wouldn't notice the difference?'

'I figured you wouldn't come if I said four.'

'You were right.' She glanced over her shoulder and his grin provoked her into missing a stroke and splashing him soundly.

Before noon they pulled the canoe up the narrow

shingle beach of Île de la Sainte-Famille.

'Shall we stretch our legs?' he said. She nodded. He took her hand and she allowed herself to be led a short way up the hill, where he pointed out the remains of a burned-out church and priest's house. He showed her what he called the holiest of all rocks – the boulder that was said to have been Abbé Maillard's original altar.

'From here the abbé celebrated his first mass about forty years ago,' Marcel said.

A cross was carved on the makeshift altar and Elise felt the hairs on her arms prickle as she ran her hand over the surface of this papist memorial. It was simple and beautiful, and held the warmth of the sun.

'This is a sacred place,' he told her.

'I feel it.'

'You do?'

'Yes.'

'How so?'

She considered for a moment before answering. 'It's difficult to describe. At home we have a town church, big and grand, ancient. Perhaps you noticed it when you visited? I sometimes sat in that church and let the past flow through me. I could sense... oh, I don't know. I imagined my guardian angel was nearby.' She turned away, feeling foolish. 'I've never told anyone that before. Not even Gran'mère. Certainly not Thomas. He never understood that side of me. Thomas had a fear of witches.'

'But your gifts are so much part of who you are.'

Flustered, she said quickly, 'Tell me more of the abbé.'

'When he preached here the Mi'kmaq gathered for their annual divine service, hundreds of them from all over. Picture it, Elise.' He leaned close to her and pointed into the distance. 'All those canoes crossing the water like geese in an autumn sky. Weddings, baptisms, blessings galore. Everyone in their best clothing.' His eyes shone, but then a frown darkened them and he turned away.

'What happened?'

'When the abbé left the mission ceased to operate. Then the English soldiers destroyed it.'

'Oh.'

'This, the abbé's altar, is all that remains. Abbé Maillard himself died some twenty years ago.'

'That's sad.'

He nodded and they stood side by side, each lost in their own thoughts until Marcel asked if she was hungry. As promised, he had taken care of their picnic and when they returned to the canoe he unloaded a large leather satchel and a rolled-up trade blanket. In a clearing among the wild cherry and beech trees he spread the blanket with pewter plates that he filled with ham, cheese, bread and apples. He produced a pot of honey and a skin of red wine. She was impressed. Between mouthfuls of bread she asked why the island was called Île de la Sainte-Famille.

He laughed. 'It used to be called Vachelouacadie, but

who wants to cope with that mouthful? The Mi'kmaq call it Mniku, which means island.'

She too laughed. 'That makes sense.'

He crouched down, selected a few flat pebbles and flicked them one by one so that they bounced across the water until they sank. After a while he said he had better attend to his errand. While he went off on his mysterious business she packed the remains of their picnic. A shadow caused her to glance skyward in alarm. A huge eagle glided overhead. It had something in its great claws – a rabbit maybe? Whatever it was, it seemed too big for the bird to hold. Sure enough the weight pulled the eagle down towards the lake and it dropped the unfortunate creature, which disappeared into the water. With an angry screech the bird veered back towards land in search of a replacement for its lost dinner. Nature was harsh.

She lay back on the blanket, arms beneath her head, letting herself be cosseted by the quivering sunlight and the dappled shade of a wild cherry tree. Haloed above her head, a golden cloud of butterflies played in the air. She closed her eyes and became aware of wavelets slip-slapping onto the beach, accompanied by the lazy back and forth tumble of the shingle. Verdant aromas clung to the air. The busy flutter of leaves told of the presence of unseen birds while a soothing buzz disclosed the activity of bees, or maybe wasps.

A fly tickled her face and she brushed it away. It landed again. She opened her eyes. Marcel knelt beside her, a stalk of grass in his hand. 'I thought you were a fly,' she said.

'You were fast asleep.'

'Was I? How long have you been there impersonating an insect?'

'I've been here about ten minutes, but I've only been doing my insect impression for a short while.'

She smiled. 'Did you meet your man?'

'No man, just a package.'

'But you said there would be people here?'

'No, you said that.'

'You didn't say otherwise. You mean nobody's here?'

'We are.' He leaned over and kissed her lips gently.

'Oh Marcel, this is not right.' But she didn't move away.

'It's inevitable.' His voice resonated with passion. 'You know I've always loved you,' he whispered.

'I didn't, but I do now.'

He sat up resting on his elbow and gazed into her eyes. 'You realise what a freelance wanderer I am and that I cannot ask any woman to marry me? That I leave in the morning for Halifax?'

'I didn't, but I do now.'

'Then shall I stop making love to you?'

A flicker of guilt whispered Thomas's name in her ear. But Thomas was dead. Gone. In any case, he hadn't loved her for so long. In answer to Marcel's question, she took his face between her hands and guided his lips to meet her own. The intensity of passion that broke free from its habitual retreat took her by surprise. Instantly she knew that this love had burned inside her for years, a flame she'd denied until now.

'I've always loved you,' he said again.

His fervour started tenderly, almost shyly. Then it rose to a peak that matched her own. New sensations joined long forgotten ones. Something so right could not be wrong. The air suffused with sweet, urgent passion. Afterwards they lay side by side as the sun started its slow descent towards the horizon. Darkness would not arrive for hours.

'Elise.' Marcel broke into her reverie. He reached for his leather waistcoat, pulled a folded piece of paper from an inside pocket and gave it to her. Puzzled, she frowned enquiringly. 'It's my cousin's address,' he said. 'Did I tell you I had a cousin in Halifax? Her name is Sylvie Maythorpe and she's a nice person. I met her late husband a few times – a Loyalist and a respected merchant captain, sadly lost at sea. I'm around so little and I worry about you being here on your own. It's a sort of bolt-hole. You understand?'

She took the paper without comment. They both lay back, side by side.

'Marcel?'

'Yes?'

'I don't regret what we did and I know you will never make a husband. No, don't say anything. I have you for this moment and that's what matters. But this is a sacred

Mi'kmaq place. Have we desecrated it?'

'On the contrary,' he smiled, as he stroked her cheek. 'The Mi'kmaq may be Catholic but they believe in all things of nature. Natural things are a gift from God. Love is a gift from God and they would not condemn us for celebrating such a gift.'

'Really? You're not just saying that to make me feel better?'

'Really.'

'Then, perhaps we should celebrate one more time.'

He gave a whoop and rolled over on top of her.

The journey back was long and peaceful. A silver moon rose as the sun eased towards the west. Island mounds transformed into black humpbacked sea-monsters guarding their passage. Elise held tight to the moments left to her. The conclusion of her dreams was pre-ordained but was of no consequence during that soft June night. They did not say goodbye, they did not even say goodnight. He kissed her hand. She kissed his. The spell that was theirs settled deep within each of them and stayed there.

'I've always loved you,' he'd said, and she knew this to be true.

Outwardly, at least, life went on as before, until the legacy of Île de la Saint-Famille came home to roost. She was pregnant.

She closed her mind to the obvious and got on with her daily life. Throughout the summer she hid her condition and carried on working despite an all-consuming nausea that peppermint infusion did little to alleviate. When not at her market-stall, she tended her plants and when not doing that she prepared her remedies. Better to be busy, fill the days, fill her head. When her pregnancy was revealed she would be ostracised, washed up, her reputation and her trade in shreds. She hugged Marcel's love within herself, and cherished her love for him, refusing to regret anything, least of all this late gift that grew by the day.

The arrival of Charles Robin felt like a bad omen. When he called on her she was taken aback. Had he guessed her condition? Had he come to disgrace her, expel her?

'Haven't seen you since Thomas died,' he said, hat in hand. 'Wanted to express my condolences. It must have been hard for you, these past four or five years.'

She studied him for a moment. 'Long before that. It's been ten years since the sacking of Jerseyman Island when Thomas was left for dead.'

'Yes, I suppose it has. Most unfortunate.' Robin's gaze shifted about the room making Elise feel increasingly discomfited. 'Still doing your medicines, I hear,' he continued. 'A great success I'm led to believe.'

'I manage well enough, thank you.'

'I recall how you used to dose us up on Jerseyman Island. Keep us healthy through the winter. All sorts of remedies for scurvy and coughs and toothache.' He cleared his throat. 'The truth is Mrs Galliard... see here, do you mind if I sit?'

Puzzled and wary, she said, 'Of course. Can I offer you some coffee?'

'Thank you, but no.'

Elise sat opposite him and waited. Mr Robin had always been blunt and to the point, and was never discomforted. She didn't have to wait long before his ice-blue eyes focussed on her. 'You know of my fishery to the north of here?'

'Chéticamp? Yes.'

'The place is thriving. Growing rapidly. It's open all year round now. A great little community with plenty of passing trade.'

Elise still could not fathom the man's intentions and his next words astonished her.

'I have a business proposition, Mrs Galliard. Move to Chéticamp. Set up with your remedies.'

'But... but why?'

'Opportunity. You are an ambitious and capable woman. You have fire and mettle. More so than many men I could name. I have a growing business and think the fishery and the community would benefit from your remedies. In turn you can profit from the expanding trade.' He sat back, satisfaction on his face and a rare brightness to his eyes.

Such compliments! What was happening? 'Mr Robin, I cannot afford to give up my business and home here and go traipsing off to some backwater fishing outpost.'

Annoyance crossed his face before he changed it to a

smile. 'You misunderstand me. You can supply your assistant here, Mrs Pinet, with products and she can run this, your Saint-Pierre branch. Your business will double. I'll give you passage on a ship and provide you with a home and space at Chéticamp from which you can work. I want you to go promptly in order to take advantage of the rest of the season there. In return, you must also undertake to keep my ledgers in order, and I get ten percent of your Chéticamp takings. We both benefit.'

Elise sat trying to take in Mr Robin's proposition. *Your Saint-Pierre branch.* The words had quite a ring to them. He was fanning the fires of her ambitions, and he knew it.

'Let me think about it.' Even as she said this she knew that, despite her reluctance, it was a solution to her problems. She would start over again.

PART FOUR

Chéticamp

CHAPTER 26

'Been expecting you,' the manager, Caleb Therriau, said a few weeks later, as Elise disembarked at the little cove where the fishery in Chéticamp was based. This man, if she remembered rightly, was the son of Rhiné Therriau, the Acadian foreman on Jerseyman Island. A dull drizzle saturated the air and she was concerned that her belongings would suffer. She had little time to take in her surroundings, except to note a cluster of cabins, all simple constructions of sawn logs, set up the side of a steep hill. Her possessions were put ashore and a team of men handcarted and carried them up that same hill. Caleb Therriau led the way. Her mouth was dry, her hands shook. What was she doing in this strange place that felt so hostile? She followed the procession, keeping a close eye on her worldly goods. Fishermen stared with open curiosity.

They stopped at the outer edge of the settlement by a shingle-roofed cabin much the same as the others. Her things were taken inside and left in a small pile in the centre of the one and only room. She saw a floor of axe-squared wood, nails that served as hanging pegs, and a small fireplace. It needed a thorough clean but wasn't in a bad condition. The furniture, such as had been left, was basic: a plank table, two stools, some shelves, a straw mattress, a wooden sleeping couch with boards nailed to it forming a partition wall. A ladder led to a low attic space. It would do.

'Used to belong to a fisherman now gone home to Jersey,' Caleb Therriau said. 'You'll find a brook out the back. I've to clear a room for your use at the store. I'm going back now. You want help, say so.' She nodded her thanks, then she was alone.

From the doorway she had a misty view down to the harbour basin and the many schooners coming and going – good trade potential. When she walked round behind the cabin she found the brook and some terraced ground suitable for cultivation. The hill continued to rise behind her. She missed her cabin in Saint-Pierre, she missed her well-tended garden, and she missed Nancy and the friendly faces she'd got used to. Self-pity was no answer, but was hard to shake off. Sighing into the emptiness, she set to. After she'd settled into some sort of order, she spent a few days getting to know something of the fishermen and their work gangs. These and the townsfolk plus, hopefully, some individuals from the Mi'kmaq community, would be her main customers. Much of the trade would be year round.

A stout, bald Jerseyman called Mr Guilbert, was the beach-master. When she approached him, his eyes narrowed. 'What can I do for you?'

She introduced herself and he nodded. 'I know who you are.'

'I'd be grateful if you could show me around.'

'I dunno…'

'Caleb Therriau said you'd be willing to act as my guide.'

'Well if Caleb said so, then I must.' He led her to some tables on the stages and called a woman over. 'Evangeline, show Mrs Galliard the ropes.' He stalked off, muttering under his breath something about timewasters.

Evangeline shyly demonstrated how she cut off the heads and tails of the codfish, and split them before removing the bones and entrails. 'Fish tongues and livers go in these barrels. Nothing gets wasted here.'

The work of these dressers, as they were called, was pretty much as it had been at Arichat and Elise found the Acadian women pleasant enough. Determined to make the best of things she prepared her herb garden and began collecting such plants, bark and vraic as she could, adding these to the supply she'd brought with her. By the end of the month she'd set herself up in the room allocated to her at the back of the store. A decent enough space, it had a small window and its own door. Folk started to trickle in. As agreed, she oversaw the fishery's accounts and, not surprisingly, the main entries related to the Truck System – the method of credit the company operated.

Soon the money for the sale of her Saint-Pierre cabin arrived, and with it Nancy's accounts and payments and a list of orders. Nancy wrote that business was flourishing, but she and the customers missed her. Elise, for her part, pined deeply for Nancy, and sorely missed some of her favourite customers. She missed belonging. Here she did not belong. She couldn't say why but she feared she never would.

She secreted the money Nancy sent with her other savings in a concealed hole in the floor of her cabin and attended to the orders from Nancy. Already having a full workload she decided it would be better if Nancy made some of the remedies herself, so as well as shipping out a quantity of prepared curatives Elise sent her a selection of recipes and the go-ahead to work under her own steam. Nevertheless, there seemed to be few spare moments in each day, which suited her well enough. Keeping busy helped ease the lonely centre of her being and distracted her from too much introspection of her own life and the life that grew stealthily within her.

She let it be known that she was recently widowed, gambling on Charles Robin not having enough interest in her to reveal her true status. God willing, she would then raise the child as Thomas's with no one being any the wiser.

Taking time out to explore her new home, she soon found this tight-knit, remote community to be much smaller than Mr Robin had led her to believe, but the local inhabitants seemed confident it would expand rapidly now the fishing outfit was established. Maybe it was no bad thing to be here at the start of its prosperity.

Caleb Therriau, in one of his more amiable moods, told her that at one time, before the fall of Louisbourg during the war with the French in '45, the French built boats here in Chéticamp. Of the two or three dozen Acadian families who lived here now, most seemed to be related in some way and they combined working their own farms with working for the company, with many of the women employed as processors.

Those who worked in the fishing outfit or at the store, including Elise, lived on l'Île de Chéticamp where the fishery was located. She soon learned that this was not an island as such but a peninsula attached to Cape Breton by a causeway. She took about one hour to walk west to east and two hours south to north. The land was fairly hilly in places and at sea level in others. The fishery itself was in a deep cove at La Pointe on the southwest tip of the island, and there the usual landing-stages and flakes were to be found. The cove was pretty and the shoreline of great rocky slabs was wild and impressive. The manager's house sat at sea level near the warehouses, store, sheds and the like. The dwellings – simple wooden constructions – ranged around and above La Pointe. Chéticamp was no better and no worse than any of its ilk.

The settlers, whose numbers grew month on month, were creative folk. Aside from saws, knives, axe heads, cooking pots and kettles, almost everything was made from wood: spades, hinge-pins for the doors, buckets, even nails, and of course furniture. A smithy and a carpenter were established near the store and, along with her remedies, enhanced the slowly developing community.

To add to her solitude, news from home took even longer to reach her at Chéticamp than it had at Saint-Pierre, but arrive it eventually did. So it was that on a hot day in August a boat came in with a packet of letters for her. She waited until she got home before allowing herself the luxury of opening it. The news, which she scanned quickly in her excitement, then re-read slowly, both cheered and saddened her. Marie and Edward had a new babe – a girl at last – named after her far-away aunt! How proud she felt, and how sad that she could neither hold baby Elise nor share this news with anyone who cared.

Her mother described the new quays in St Peter Port that, she said, prevented the seas from running up to and between the houses and through the lanes and steps. *That must make things considerably easier.* Elise was already composing a reply in her head. She tried to imagine St Peter Port thriving and growing. Mère's description of High Street with its tiny crammed-in dwellings made her smile. Imagine being able to sit at your table and tell what your neighbour eats for supper! Reading further she discovered that St Peter Port had a plethora of new shops. How she envied her family those shops. She dreamt of shops where she could buy fancy goods and white bread and silks. The gentry, Mère wrote, were moving to fine villas on the hillsides above the town with splendid open views. *And no harbour smells I'll be sworn.* Père's shop was still thriving in William's hands and Berthelot Street remained unchanged. It sometimes seemed that Guernsey was not real but a fantasy world of which she often dreamed.

Maybe she could go back? Perhaps invent a husband then dispose of him? Could she spend the rest of her life living that sort of a lie? No, she could not. A distant sinner is easier for her family to conceal, than a daughter bringing her shame and sin back to the family nest.

CHAPTER 27

'Rain!' The beach-master's call came just as Elise was about to eat her meal of cod and potatoes. Caught unprepared, she muttered a curse and joined the dressers as they rushed to the fish drying platforms. Protecting the fish was not part of her job, but she could hardly stand by, or in this case sit by, and eat cod while she watched the women battle with the elements unaided. Everyone scurried about, turning the codfish skin-uppermost and covering it with canvas sails in a well-rehearsed procedure. The flesh must be kept dry at all costs. Unlike the women. They were wet through by the time they returned to their now cold meal. That cloudburst was only the beginning. Unbeknown to them a greater threat was imminent.

The immense power of an unseasonably late summer hurricane took the community by surprise. Les suêtes, the infamous southeast winds, beat against the coast for hours. When the wind hit it was unforgiving; a pounding pit-of-the-stomach rumble coming from the direction of the distant mountains. Furious gusts swept the sea, whipping it into a raging foam and then a heaving leviathan.

'Save the fish,' came the inevitable call.

This time canvas sails would not be sufficient – the fish must be removed to the storeroom. Elise, hindered by her skirt, with the breath driven from her, joined the other women to form a chain. She helped to pass loaded baskets of fish from flake to store, then pass the emptied baskets back to be re-filled. Looking around her, Elise saw the men battle against the force of the wind as they tried to salvage whatever gear they could. Fighting to keep her balance, she almost bumped into a fisherman struggling towards the cookhouse with a mass of nets spilling from his arms. Any stray object became a spinning missile. Wooden fragments of flake turned into deadly airborne weapons. A sharp splinter flew at her face. Instinctively, she raised an arm in front of her eyes and the splinter did no more than scrape the skin from her hand.

'Enough. Inside everyone,' called Caleb Therriau. The cacophony of noise snatched his voice away, but his gestures were clear enough. A woman in front tripped and Elise grabbed at her but in the effort nearly fell, too. A fisherman grasped her and her companion and the three of them staggered to join the others in the sturdy warehouse. Hessian sacks were shared round and utilised as makeshift towels and blankets, but the following cold, damp and deafening hours were unavoidable.

'Is it always this bad?' Elise shouted to a bedraggled woman, as she shuffled along to make room for her on a bench.

'The cove gives good shelter from all but les suêtes,' the woman hollered back. 'They are the very devil when they strike. The only thing to do is to sit it out here and hope your home will still be there when they've done their darndest.'

'Worst for the farmers,' someone piped up. 'They got no shelter for their barns nor crops nor critters.'

At about seven that evening Elise joined the others as they assessed the damage. Several fishing boats had dragged their anchors and suffered severe harm, a few more were swept out to sea and lost altogether. Luckily most of the fishermen, after securing what they could, had taken hasty shelter just in time. Elise found no real damage to her home. Some herbs had been uprooted and a hoe and wooden bucket were missing from the doorstep, but it could have been worse. As for the farmers: crops were crushed, barns shattered, roofs gone and livestock lost. Stoically, the community set to and did what they could to put things right.

One victim of the storm was a small, quivering, skeletal ball of damp red fur with a broken front paw. Elise spotted the squirrel as she returned from the stream on the evening after the storm. 'Oh, you poor little thing,' she cried, as she gathered him in her apron and took him back to the cabin. Avoiding his sharp teeth and claws she strapped the paw as best she could, found a box to keep him safe, and fed him on black bread, wild mushrooms and the seeds of trees, along with plenty of comfrey – the herb her grandmother had called knitbone. She built a cage for him from a small keg and an iron grid and she named him Harum-Scarum because she decided he must be a reckless creature to have been caught in the storm. His screeching was disconcerting but amusing. 'So much noise from such a tiny creature,' she scolded as he ran in circles within the confines of his cage. But he soon settled in and chattered and scuttled about, demanding attention whenever she came near. He was good company – her only company. By September his paw had recovered and with both relief and sadness Elise released him. If he managed to make it in the wild he would have to prepare for the winter ahead. For her part, she returned empty-handed to an empty cabin.

As the month progressed the delight of autumn colours were also a reminder of the inevitability of pending winter. Rising above the cove and its fishing outfit was a steep hill on top of which Elise discovered an escape from the noisy bustle and the smell of fish that made up her daylight hours. The climb was strenuous but worth it. The views were spectacular, the place an oasis of calm, solitude and solace. It was from here that she gathered wild herbs or snatched moments to sit and view the vista. From here she daydreamed as she gazed out to sea and to the shadows of land far beyond. From here she drew the strength to face her advancing pregnancy.

Thoughts of Marcel were never far away. Sometimes she wished she'd contacted him, told him he was to be a father. If he knew of this baby would he be willing to give up his wandering life and legitimise the child? Yet, as much as she yearned to have him by her side, she did not want him under sufferance and pity. She raised her head in defiance. *I will never stoop so low as to trap him. My cloak of widowhood will protect me and my child.*

CHAPTER 28

When she could conceal her pregnancy no longer, Elise nervously confided in the women on the work gangs and she received much kindly fussing and commiseration at her widowed status. They suggested she speak to Phoebe, wife of the Acadian, Mathias Le Blanc. Phoebe was experienced in midwifery. The Le Blancs farmed at Point Cross on mainland Chéticamp opposite the fishing outfit. They had arrived some years ago with their two sons, along with some dozen others – mostly farmers. So Elise called on Phoebe Le Blanc.

'Of course, my dear. It will be a pleasure,' Phoebe said when Elise asked for her help. The farmer's wife put aside the dough she'd been kneading. 'Stay for a cup of tea and let's have a little chat.'

A small sweet-natured woman of forty or so, she had wisps of grey hair evading the confines of her lace-trimmed cap, and a toothy smile that lit her weathered nut-brown face. Sipping tea and chatting to this kindly woman, Elise learned of Phoebe's early months at Chéticamp and began to realise how brave these first pioneers were. On arrival in this remote part of Cape Breton Island, they had only themselves and each other to clear land, build houses and develop farms.

As Elise prepared to take her leave, Phoebe's husband Mathias arrived home from his farming. 'I won't stop you ladies talking. I only popped in to fetch my hat.' Nevertheless, when Phoebe waved the teapot in his direction, he grinned. 'Just to be neighbourly.' They all settled down and Phoebe filled cups with the fresh-made brew.

Mathias was a jolly fellow, his build evidence to his love of the fat from his pig, the cream and butter from his cow, and the potatoes from his field. He told Elise he was a survivor from the deportation of years ago.

'I've heard some talk of deportation, but couldn't make sense of it,' she said.

He explained that the Acadian people were descended from the French settlers of long ago before the Canadas became a British colony. 'Before then this part was called Acadia,' he said, then added sadly, 'England and France are at war more times than not, so the English took the Acadians' lands and shipped the people off to foreign places.'

'Some of us hid in the forest to escape expulsion,' Phoebe added, laying a gentle hand on her husband's shoulder. Elise could see that this wound was still raw.

'Our people had a bad time back then. Many died, many more scattered to the four winds,' Mathias said. 'But those days are gone now.'

A deep sadness filed the cabin. Wars – always wars.

After a few moments, Elise asked, 'Is Mathias an Acadian name?'

He screwed up his eyes in amusement and nodded towards his wife. 'Go on, you tell Mrs Galliard.'

'Acadian?' Phoebe laughed. 'Lord no. What happened was this: his two grandfathers almost came to blows over naming him.'

'I was the first grandson on either side,' Mathias broke in.

'So what happened?'

'In the end Mathias's father decided he would settle it by opening the bible. The first male name they came across would be the baby's name. That soothed 'm all.'

The farmer chuckled. 'So Mathias it was.'

'Wasn't he Judas Iscariot's replacement?'

'Yes,' Phoebe nodded enthusiastically. 'Mathias says he's pleased they didn't light on Judas first!'

'Or Jonah,' Elise added. 'Or Titus. Or Hymeneus.'

Elise took her leave, promising to return in a week's time. How good it felt to laugh and gossip. Thereafter, despite their busy lives, she met with Phoebe whenever they could both manage it. During these visits Phoebe brewed tea before the needles, the loom and the spinning wheel were put to use, and they exchanged gossip in the dying light of the day.

***

The season turned and as the October days shortened, the workload eased. Soon the seasonal workers would go home and those remaining would prepare themselves for the imminent winter. However all was not gloom. Her pregnancy had become common knowledge and the community of Chéticamp seemed to defrost, responding instead with warmth and compassion. Maybe this would be the start of a new life after all?

Her quilted petticoat and flannel skirt and bodice, topped with a canvas apron were enough to keep her warm even beyond sundown, especially with knitted stockings and hide boots to protect her legs and feet. Wooden clogs were useful when it was dry and the mud didn't suck them from her feet.

At night she tried to settle down, but missed the chatter of the little red squirrel. She smiled as she pictured how, when offered his freedom, he'd dashed up the nearest tree then stopped to snatch a glance back. *He's saying goodbye*, she'd said to herself, until she corrected the sentiment. *He's saying good riddance*, she admitted.

Elise turned over in bed. The life within her fluttered and her mind drifted to Baby Thomas, so cold and alone in the ground on Jerseyman Island. She often dreamt of Baby Thomas; not one of her nightmares but happy dreams in which he told her he existed in a beautiful place and that he was glad about the new baby. Elise felt that Baby Thomas was close by and watching over this little one. He knew it would never take his place in her heart – this baby made in true but hopeless love.

By November, with the fishing done and the harvest safe, Elise had more time to spare, as did Phoebe. Elise sat by her friend's generous fire while Phoebe showed her how to make a traditional Acadian hooked rug. Elise learnt how difficult it was to keep the correct tension.

'To my dear mother's sorrow and deep disappointment, I never did have any skill with a needle of any sort, never mind this pesky hook!' she cried, as she tried to tug her twisted offering into a proximity of Phoebe's fine examples. She had hoped that one day she could produce a rug to go by her bedside. This was proving to be an impossibility.

'But you make a good cough linctus.' Phoebe indicated the pot of horseradish and horehound compound that was a gift from Elise. 'You think I learned this overnight any more than your herbs and tinctures happened by themselves?' She somehow managed to regard Elise yet keep her foot working the treadle of her spinning wheel and her hands busy with a life of their own.

Elise smiled. 'As I said before, I owe much to my dear gran'mère.'

Phoebe poured them each a cup of mountain shrub tea and put out a plate of oatmeal biscuit. 'What a tangle you've made. Here, give it to me. You are correct to say you have two left hands and only thumbs for fingers.'

Shamefaced, Elise handed her effort to Phoebe who suggested she work on the spinning wheel and she gratefully took over at the treadle. The wool came from Phoebe and Mathias's own sheep and was of the finest quality. This particular wool was the colour of russet leaves. 'Phoebe, you must tell me what dyes you use.'

'Traditionally, you know, we used our dyes for decorating clothing with designs but we soon learned that they work as well on wool.'

'It is certainly lovely.' Elise ran her thumb over the rich red fibre. 'What is this dye?'

'The red sap of the bloodroot.'

'How strange. I use bloodroot to cure ringworm.'

Phoebe smiled her toothy smile. 'Depending on the colour we want, we use leaves, flowers, alder and spruce bark, roots, mosses, the peel of onion, and gulls' eggs.' She picked up some knitting abandoned by Elise. A shawl for the baby. Soft and thick. And tangled. With a muttered, 'Dear me,' she put her magic fingers to work unsnarling the snags.

Lulled by the rhythm of her work, the glow and crackle of the fire and the effects of her tea, Elise stopped spinning for a moment, yawned, and stretched, then sat upright and hugged her growing belly.

'Phoebe—' she started, then pulled herself up. As on so many other occasions, she was overcome by the need to confess the truth of her baby's conception, but she was fearful of losing the respect and friendship of this kind woman. Better a lie than that, though such deceptions did not sit comfortably with her.

Phoebe, misunderstanding the hesitation, patted

Elise's knee. 'Let go of your fears. This baby will come into the world strong and blessed,' she told her. 'You conceived when the sun sat highest in the sky. The sun is the giver of life. He will protect you and your child.'

Phoebe knew this was not her first child, and such reassurances were welcome. The spinning wheel once more clacked under Elise's coaxing whilst Phoebe's rug evolved stitch by hooked stitch. Today she worked on a geometric design but sometimes favoured the traditional floral one. As Elise fought the mesmeric pull to close her eyes she watched Phoebe in whose work-worn hands she would be entrusting her own life and the life that grew within her. As usual her thoughts turned to Marcel. On bad days she told herself that he probably had bastards in every port and certainly wouldn't care about one more, but most of the time she knew this to be untrue. She often felt a strong connection with him. He spoke to her soul, and that was a comfort.

***

Elise, huge and smug, checked over her remedies and made a note of those needing to be replenished. Some she could do this winter, some would have to wait until next year. It had been a bad year for herbs as there'd been little time to grow many of her own or collect them from shore or forest. But she'd gathered some moss and eel grass and some seaweed – mostly rockweed, knotted wrack and dulse. Bark and roots were still available when they could be found under the snow. At least Nancy had sent a good stock of Sarnia pots. Most important of all, Elise had reserved a supply of blue cohosh root for herself.

Through trade and the exchange of remedies and recipes she had come to know some of the Mi'kmaq community. In particular, she had been befriended by Modeste, a handsome, wise lady skilled in weaving and remedy-making. She and Elise sat for many a happy hour comparing and exchanging knowledge. The men and boys of the family hunted, fished and traded. Modeste's daughter, Isi, made the best porcupine stew Elise had ever tasted. Her granddaughter, Dorothy, gave Elise a dreamcatcher of beads, quills and feathers reminiscent of the beautifully decorated circle of willow given to her by Laurel long ago. Where was Laurel now? Safe and happily married with a brood of children of her own, Elise hoped. Maybe Laurel occasionally remembered her Guernsey friend and her stories of a land far away. Sometimes Modeste invited Elise to a gathering of storytelling and music. It felt good, this sense of belonging, and she missed her nomadic friends when they left for their winter camp before the snows set in. She would not see them again until spring, after the arrival of her child.

***

The February days were short and sharp. Beneath a

purple sky, snow often piled itself high against the walls of her cabin. Those fishermen who overwintered surprised her with their thoughtfulness. Each morning someone came to dig her out, bringing firewood, a bucket of snow to melt by the fire, a skinned offering for her pot. Despite these kindnesses, she found the season hung dark, heavy, oppressive. She longed to taste a lemon, but luckily she managed to fend off scurvy with her tincture of spoonwort and some infusion of white cedar fronds she had stockpiled. As a thank-you she gave some of this mixture to the kind fishermen. She also relished her pots of cranberries that, along with the juice made from wild blueberries, stayed frozen until brought in to sit by the fire. The only thing in short supply year round was wheat. That had to be imported, making it too expensive. Elise fantasised about large chunks of griddle cake smothered in rich yellow Guernsey butter and piquant Guernsey goat's cheese.

There was no trace now of her earlier pregnancy smugness as she hauled her bulk about the confines of her cabin. After a month without venturing more than a few steps beyond her door, Elise felt restless and desperate to expend some of her unused energy. She decided to clean the window and brush down the walls. The exercise would do her good. Next year she hoped to paint the walls with lime as other householders had done. It made everything so much brighter even in winter.

Halfway through her work a pain shot through her.

And again. She caught her breath, dragged on her coat and boots, opened her door to an icy blast and made a fraught and painful journey to her nearest neighbour.

By the time the puffing and panting Phoebe appeared, a terrified Elise was crying for her mother. Less than three hours later, pale, exhausted, sore but self-satisfied, she held Colette Elizabeth in her arms.

CHAPTER 29

The Goldthread was plentiful and this pleased Elise, for a compound restorative she was working on required a large quantity. With enough of the plant to satisfy her needs she sat back and enjoyed the effect of the sun on the calm sea. Right from the beginning, when she'd arrived at Chéticamp three years before, she'd loved to escape the hubbub of the fishing outfit by climbing this steep hill above La Pointe. Collecting herbs was justification enough as far as she was concerned.

The startling flash of a dragonfly circled twice then disappeared. Phoebe had envied the dragonfly its gaudy colour. She'd said if she could but capture that particular turquoise in her dye she would be a rich woman. Elise had once collected Goldthread for Phoebe because the underground stem made an excellent yellow dye.

A familiar pain stabbed at her heart. She so missed her friend since the influenza had taken her the winter before. Elise had few enough friends in her life not to feel the loss deeply. On top of that, any death in the community reminded folk of how small and vulnerable they were in this untamed land. Poor Mathias had crumbled into impenetrable desolation and she rarely saw him these days.

Her gaze wandered to where the little cemetery assigned to Robin's men was sited. Most years it expanded by a grave or two, each topped with a wooden cross. The saddest little marker of all identified the last resting place of an apprentice boy. So young and so far from home. Whenever Elise climbed this hill she searched out some green or blue or yellow plant to place on the boy's grave. Maybe someone did the same for Baby Thomas who rested so far away?

To banish thoughts of death she focused on the living. Below her the fishing outfit bustled and prospered. Lazy woodsmoke curled from chimneys and squatted in the still air. A ship, newly arrived, added to the activity. She couldn't distinguish its wilting flag from here and wondered where it came from and where it might be heading. Across the water lay Chéticamp village. It had grown since her arrival, spreading now from the farms at Point Cross and La Prairie. This expansion provided a ready and eager market for her increasing range of curatives. She had an eclectic mix of customers: settlers, fishermen, passing sailors, Acadians, Mi'kmaq. Her savings increased almost daily.

'Maman, see big fish.'

Colette's cry brought her back to her surroundings. 'Careful Colette, stay from the edge.' She pulled at the rope harness that kept the child from wandering.

Her daughter stamped her foot. 'No Maman, want to see the fish!'

'Then I must hold you.' Elise grasped her daughter's hand firmly as they both tiptoed as close to the brink as could be safely managed. 'No big fish now, poppet.'

Colette complained in frustration as she pointed down beyond the fishing outfit and towards the open sea.

'I'm afraid it's gone away now, perhaps another day—' Then the sea erupted and a huge black monster broke the surface a hundred yards offshore.

'Oh my goodness Colette you were right! A whale, an enormous whale.'

'Canoe,' the child shrieked, jumping up and down.

'With that big hump it is like a giant canoe isn't it? The sort the Indians take out on the sea.'

This "canoe" blew a spout of water from its back. Sun-glinted daggers sparkled on the fountain as it reached towards the sky. Then the creature arched and slid back down into the water, raising its huge butterfly tail. In an illusion of slow-time it slid into the deep. Mother and daughter remained enthralled until Colette's cry of, 'More!' broke the spell.

'No more for now poppet but maybe the big fish will come to visit another day.'

The child's lower lip trembled in complaint at life's injustices. She removed her cap and thrust it at her mother in protest.

'You have to keep your cap on or your face will burn. Now be a good girl and let Maman put it back.' The toddler obliged even though the glint that turned her eyes deep emerald and the pursing of her stubborn mouth showed that in her opinion bonnets were her mother's invention designed specifically to blight her life.

'Oh dear, those freckles,' Elise said, as her own mother had said to her so long ago. 'How will you ever become a fine young lady with so many freckles?' Colette's fiery hair was as rebellious as the child herself, refusing to be tamed under any cap, but Elise did the best she could. She planted a kiss on Colette's cheek. No trace of Marcel returned her gaze. Colette was all Gran'mère and herself.

'That will have to do. Now, shall I tell you a story?'

The suggestion caused Colette's eyes to shine. 'Dragon story.'

'Again?'

She nodded.

'Very well. Let's sit here on the grass.' Colette snuggled up close and her thumb found its way into her mouth.

'This, as you know, is the story as told to me by my beloved gran'mère, who heard it from her own gran'mère, so it must be true.

'Once upon a time, long, long ago on the island of Herm, which is the little sister of my own island of Guernsey, there lived a colony of dragons. Herm is a

268

tiny island, so the dragons were also tiny.'

'How tiny?' the child asked.

'No higher than the top of your head.'

Colette looked up, her eyes widening and her mouth a perfect O.

'Or so my gran'mère told me her gran'mère had told her.'

'Say about the ratcreeps.'

'Those wicked ratcreeps crossed the sea from the mysterious island with no name.'

'And say how they killed all the little dragons,' Colette demanded.

'Not all the dragons. What happened? Can you remember?'

'They magicked into dragonflies and flew away.'

Elise laughed. 'So they did. And they lived happy lives for ever and ever.'

Colette wriggled with pleasure. She had an endless thirst for legends from Guernsey and Elise never tired of telling them, for they helped to keep her home island alive.

'But that's enough stories,' she told her daughter. 'How about helping Maman make a daisy-chain?'

Colette fetched the longest stemmed daisies she could manage and Elise threaded them one on the other until the garland reached twice around Colette's cap. 'Now you're a real lady,' she told her. 'And now we must go home and make supper.'

Colette frowned but allowed herself to be picked up

and carried past the burying-ground and the stagnant pond, and on down the hill.

A man, short, fair and purposeful, was striding towards them. He was vaguely familiar. Few people came this way except for a burial. A premonition of trouble seeped into her heart.

The man stopped and, hands on hips, waited for her to approach.

'Mrs Galliard,' Charles Robin said.

She stood rigid with shock.

'Well, well, what have we here?' He studied Colette with ice in his eyes. 'She's yours?'

'Of course. This is Colette. Colette, say hello to Mr Robin.'

The child wriggled and buried her face into her mother's skirt.

'Mr Robin is a friend of Maman's,' she reassured, without taking her gaze from his.

Colette studied the man who stood before her.

He crouched down. 'Hello, Colette.'

The little girl kept her mouth shut tight and her eyes did not waver.

'How old are you my dear?' he asked.

In a firm voice, Elise said, 'Three next February.'

The long silence that followed said it all.

'She's like you,' he said eventually.

Elise became aware of the bustle drifting from the flakes and wharfs below. 'You came on that ship?' she asked, though clearly he had.

He nodded. 'I've been in Arichat. The manager is a fellow Jerseyman.' He indicated towards where the ship was berthed. 'I'm here to check the books then I'm off north. New Brunswick. You were on your way down the hill?'

She nodded.

Mr Robin turned to Colette. 'May I walk back down with you?'

The child checked with her mother who gave a small nod. 'Yes,' Colette whispered, 'if you are Maman's friend.'

I doubt that, thought Elise as she lifted Colette to her hip. Mr Robin picked up Elise's basket and waited for her to lead the way.

'How did you know where to find me?' she asked, her eyes fixed on the path.

'I asked Caleb Therriau. He told me you'd likely be up here, but didn't mention the child.'

'Down now, Maman.' Elise set her down and, holding the end of the harness, allowed the little girl to trot on ahead. Colette stopped to pick a weed, sing a hymn, chat to any bird that caught her eye, and concentrate on a large yellow and black butterfly as it darted about a clump of purple-topped milkweed. A boastful rooster announced his presence to his family of clucking, waddling hens as they foraged in the dirt. Colette clapped her hands and cock-a-doodled back. All the while Elise's mind struggled to cope with the end of her secret.

271

Before they reached her home Mr Robin stopped. He turned to her. 'The father?'

She raised her chin and met his gaze. 'Why, Thomas of course. Everyone knows that. Whoever else could it be?'

***

She knew the blatant pretence would not be accepted. Not from such a strict, upright, Protestant man as Charles Robin (upright if one didn't count the women he'd entertained in his cabin on Jerseyman Island, or his infamous Truck System. Or the dark deeds concerning young apprentices she'd heard whispers of). Such an "upright" man would be conscience-bound to expose Elise for what she was and ask her to leave. She was not going to give him the satisfaction of a confession, or beg for some sort of mercy. Let him think what he wanted. Besides, he would be unable to forgive her duplicity in coming here under false pretences. Let what will be, be.

Charles Robin did not expel her. He had no need to put himself to that trouble. He knew the community would deal with her. A few words in the right ears was all it took. Red-hot gossip smouldered and the settlers and fishermen were morally outraged. Widowed five years and a child not yet three.

Shunned, she quickly became a figure of much speculation and debate. Not even little Colette's smile softened their hearts. The sweet child they had all petted became "that bastard brat" overnight. There were nods, winks, talk of the trouble women brought with them. Grumblings about why a fallen woman had been fobbed off onto their clean, God-fearing community. Saying she had been widowed shortly before she arrived! So brazen! Elise knew that speculative and aggressive eyes followed her wherever she went, as did the lewd stares and suggestive gestures – even outright propositions. Her customers shunned her. Yet again her life was spinning out of her control. Whenever she could, she took refuge up on the hill above the fishery where she could be alone with Colette. The child sensed the changes and became clingy and tearful.

Now her only customers were the Mi'kmaq friends she had made; Modeste and her family and others she had come to know. When she crossed the causeway to the settlements at Point Cross and La Prairie the Mi'kmaq welcomed her and didn't judge. They continued to show Colette kindness. Modeste's granddaughter Dorothy loved to play with Colette and she taught her how to make things with cones, feathers and bark. She took great pleasure in showing Colette how to blow rude noises through a blade of grass, an activity that had them both giggling uncontrollably.

Early in August as she weeded her herb garden, she had a visitor.

'Modeste, how lovely. I don't often bump into you here on the island.' She fetched a jug of cranberry juice and two cups and sat outside with her friend.

Modeste looked around. 'Where is your little one?' she asked.

'Having her afternoon nap,' Elise explained, pouring the sweet red juice.

The Mi'kmaq woman lit her clay pipe and they talked of family and herbs and skills. Modeste's granddaughter Dorothy, barely seven, showed great promise in beadwork, Modeste said proudly. Elise told her something of her marriage to Thomas, and its bitter end. She was deliberately vague about Colette's father and Modest asked no questions. Elise knew Modeste's visit was more than a friendly chat. She also knew that her visitor would say what she had come to say in her own time, which she did. 'We are leaving in a week.'

It took Elise a moment to take in the implications of Modeste's words. 'But why? All of you? Where are you going?' she cried.

'Not all of us. Me and Solomon and Solomon's brother Dominic, and my Isi, her husband Kingdom and their children, Dorothy and James. The seven of us are going to Sackville where Solomon has family business and a land issue to settle.'

Elise's throat was so tight she was unable to say anything so sat staring at her hands in her lap.

'You are in trouble here, I think?' Modeste laid a hand on Elise's arm. Elise nodded, unable to meet her friend's eye. 'I have a suggestion,' Modeste said. 'To get to Sackville we go by way of Halifax Harbour before we carry on up the river.'

274

'I don't understand.' Elise, distracted by her own misery, couldn't follow her friend's meaning.

'Come with us. You can make a life for yourself and your little girl in Halifax. Your chance to get away from Charles Robin and his kind.'

Elise regarded her friend blankly. 'But I can't go to Halifax. What would I do there? I'm not brave enough.'

Modeste stood up. 'You? Not brave enough! You who are brave every day? You who came so far to be with the man you loved? You who built so much from nothing? Who settled in this remote outpost rather than have yourself and your child disgraced? Elise, you are the bravest woman I know.' Then she sat down again and added with a twinkle in her eyes, 'For a European.'

Elise smiled. She sat thinking while Modeste applied herself to her tobacco pouch and pipe. Modeste's words were kind, and much of what she said had some truth to it. But Elise had already re-started her life three times. Could she do it all over again? At the age of thirty six? She had a two-year old child who meant more to her than anything or anyone else in this world. She felt a rush of anger that Marcel had left her to fend for herself, which was illogical, she knew. She had loved him of her own free will knowing that he had nothing to offer her. He was gone and was not part of her life. That was the truth of it. Thoughts of Marcel were as dry ashes in the wind.

Then a long ago conversation came to her mind: *it's my cousin's address. Her name's Sylvie Maythorpe and she's a nice person. A sort of bolt-hole.*

Did she still have that scrap of paper after all this time? Yes, she knew exactly where to find it. She looked again at Modeste who was puffing serenely at her pipe.

'I'll go,' Elise said.

CHAPTER 30

Anxious but resolute, Elise made her arrangements in secret. Time was short, allowing little space for reflection or second thoughts. Sorting her possessions proved to be easier than she imagined. Not a single unnecessary item would come with her. She put aside basic clothing in an oilcloth bundle. In her valise she stored her savings and day-to-day requirements, her letters from home and her journals. She stashed Gran'mère's well-wrapped almanac into her shabby dowry chest along with whatever remedies and ingredients would fit. She packed the remainder of her remedies and sent these to Nancy along with some recipes and a letter explaining that she gave her, Nancy, the Saint-Pierre business, lock, stock and barrel.

Before dawn of August 17th, almost three years to the day since she'd arrived in Chéticamp, Solomon and his brother Dominic called at her door. She and a bemused Colette clutching her rag doll, were ready. An adventure, she told the child. And so it would be, Elise decided.

The men carried Elise's baggage while Elise carried Colette and her valise. Silently they set out for La Pointe. There Modeste and Isi and Isi's husband Kingdom were securing their own luggage. Colette ran to join the game of kick-ball being played by Dorothy and James. Dorothy, at seven, relished her role as little mother to the two younger ones. They, in turn, adored her.

Two tethered canoes wallowed in the calm water, each ready to receive the six adults and three children who would be travelling. She was about to make a journey that would change her life – and Colette's – forever. A small group of Mi'kmaq well-wishers stood gossiping and smoking. Kingdom smiled a greeting and stowed Elise's luggage. She regarded the seemingly fragile bark canoes with trepidation. They were of the traditional style. Wide bottomed with ends and sides curving elegantly upwards, they were designed to prevent the taking on of too much water in rough seas. Rough seas, she fervently hoped, would not be part of their long journey.

Soon a small scattering of fishermen gathered. When they saw the preparations some of the men, especially those whose advances Elise had recently rejected, became unpleasant. 'So she's running off with her bastard and a group of savages, is she?'

'Which one fathered the child?'

'Go on woman, good riddance to you.'

'You always made like you were better than us. Be

278

on your way.'

Others showed more decency. 'Keep it civil, Jim.'

'No need for that language in front of the little ones.'

A few bad tempered nudges and curses were exchanged.

Elise refused to react but could not prevent her face from burning. Colette, thank goodness, didn't comprehend the words but the animosity and spite came across loud and clear and the child stood wide-eyed and rigid. Elise hugged her. Within minutes she and Colette were installed on the wooden plank seats, their baggage and supplies stashed in every available space. Dominic, as navigator, sat at the front and Kingdom, the helmsman, was behind.

Ahead of them Solomon, Modeste, Isi, James and Dorothy led the way. Before Elise could think, she was at sea. No turning back. They set out at a fair pace, leaving behind the harbour and the fishing outfit with its shadowy, dawn-lit landing-stages and flakes, and heading south down the coast of Cape Breton Island.

Trying to forget the angry scene, Elise gazed at the land from this new, sea-level perspective. With an unexpected lightness of heart and no regrets, she turned to her daughter. 'Goodbye Chéticamp, hello adventure,' she whispered.

Colette giggled, sat up straight and waved heartily. 'Bye-bye Chét'camp, 'llo 'venture.'

With a favourable northerly breeze catching at them, Kingdom taught Elise how to raise the small hide sail onto its central mast. At once it was as though an unseen hand pushed at the canoe, and Chéticamp evaporated into the morning mists.

As the shore disappeared she became aware of the weight that had crushed down on her since Charles Robin's visit. The fishermen, the visiting ships' crews, the Acadians, even the Mi'kmaq; all had been happy to buy her remedies and lotions. They sought her advice, talked of private things, and trusted her. Then came Charles Robin and his malicious tongue, sparking a wall of hurtful rejection from the community. She had been unveiled as a sinner and was scorned. She hadn't realised how bitter she felt until that bitterness began to lift from her shoulders on this glorious summer morning. She found herself breathing freely for the first time in weeks. The air was fresh and pure, her thoughts light and free. Her Mi'kmaq friends were true, and Colette was her dearest treasure.

They skimmed along and Colette, who had not been beyond the confines of Chéticamp during her short life, watched the land slide by with open-eyed curiosity, but she soon lost interest and became restless. At first she took to giggling and waving to the occupants of the lead canoe some few yards ahead. Finally, as this game paled, Elise sang to her. Her small repertoire, sadly stretched, was on its second round before the child, thumb firmly in her mouth and rag doll under her cheek, finally slept. Elise struggled to keep her own eyes open and was relieved when, at about noon, the lead canoe pulled into a pretty bay. They beached alongside on the shallow sandy shore, in a bay fed by a wide lazy river and backed by low round hills.

'How far did we travel this morning?' Elise asked Dominic.

'Maybe twenty miles, maybe less,' he said before turning away. Was he shy? Or perhaps he didn't approve of her being with them? Perhaps, like the fishermen, he condemned her for Colette's existence. Elise was not about to let him intimidate her.

Their meal became a glorious family picnic, and before long the youngsters tore about imitating the gulls, and the adults lay full out on a grassy bank stretching their backs. Humour was high and stories exchanged. Only Dominic kept himself apart, barely glancing at her. Before long it was time to round up the youngsters and clamber back into the canoes.

Elise noticed Isi working hard in the other canoe. 'Let me paddle for a while. It's been a long time, but I used to be quite good.'

Dominic stared at her, then without a word handed her a paddle. It was strenuous work. She was strong, but nowhere near as strong as the two men, and the effort stretched her unprepared muscles. The wind calmed and no longer aided their progress. Elise, glad to contribute and avoid being a deadweight, was determined not to give in. A brief stop two hours later provided a welcome break and gave her the opportunity to bind her blistered hands.

Back on the sea, she began to lose the rhythm. She had to admit defeat and put down her paddle, but she and Colette trailed a line together and she felt proud when, to much approbation, she caught two good sized mackerel and later a further two. Dusk was falling before they made their next stop.

'We'll camp here tonight. We've made good progress today,' Solomon said.

Fires soon spread their welcome light and they agreed that the aroma of the mackerel was mouth-watering. As starlight arrowed down from the vast indigo blanket above, pipes were smoked and canvas sails laid across the canoes for shelter.

Nourished and content and with Colette curled up beside her, Elise slept in the lee of the canoe for all the world as though she lay on her wool-stuffed mattress in Guernsey.

Before the sun broke through the early mist they were back at sea. Again the wind was their friend and they made a fine pace. She became aware of the gradual change in the landscape. Now she saw a succession of shallow sloping cliffs and low mountains, sometimes covered with sparse vegetation, other times with a forest of pine growing to the sea's edge. The rocky shore varied from copper-red to ochre-brown and from small sandy beach to discoid rocks tumbled seaward.

By noon, in the shelter of a small pebbly inlet they again enjoyed a hearty meal. Isi harvested blueberries from the surrounding woods and later the children climbed and chased beside the leaf-heavy aspen, balsam and poplar.

A scream from the woods had Elise on her feet in an instant. Where were the children? Her heart raced. Running towards the trees, she shouted for Colette. Then she saw James skipping towards her, followed by Colette and in the rear, Dorothy.

'Oh my goodness, Colette.' She picked the child up. 'Don't run off into the woods like that. What if you meet a bear?'

Solomon laughed, and said kindly, 'I don't think that's likely.'

'But Maman did got eated by a bear,' Colette said proudly, as she wriggled free from her mother's grasp.

Elise laughed and spread her arms wide. 'As you can see, Colette is mistaken. I did not get eated by a bear.'

'Cos M'sieur de Forêt banged his gun and made the bear dead.'

With everyone, even Dominic, regarding her expectantly, Elise felt the blood rise in her cheeks and she explained her encounter and rescue on Isle Madame. 'You perhaps know M'sieur de Forêt?' she added casually, her blush spreading without mercy.

'Of course,' Isi said. 'We all know Marcel.'

'He's in Halifax right now,' Modeste said. Elise's heart jumped.

'No,' Solomon said. 'He went to England – doing whatever it is he does in England.'

Elise couldn't decide if she was sad or relieved and

settled for feeling both at the same time.

That night they camped in a cove by a sparklingly clear river; The Place Where Two Rivers Meet, Kingdom told her.

By the afternoon of the following day the terrain had become flatter, with fewer coves and inlets. A network of creeks trickled into the sea. Then the sky darkened and the wind changed. The shallow water lacked the pull of the current and progress became slow and arduous. The canoes bounced angrily and the wind tried to blow them back on themselves. Spume-topped waves thrashed in a grey sea. Elise lowered the sail and settled Colette under a canvas. She then paddled with all her heart. When the rain came it took them an age to cross a wide bay and head for the shore but finally the rain stopped as the group, wet, stiff and sore, disembarked.

'Tomorrow, if all is well, we go through the Gut,' Modeste said later as she cleared away tin plates and cups.

'The Gut?' Elise asked, helping her.

'The Gut of Canso.'

'I remember Charles Robin mentioning the Gut of Canso.' Elise tried hard to recall his words. 'Didn't he call it the thoroughfare of all trade to and from the Gulf of St. Lawrence?'

'An accurate description,' Dominic agreed, then went on to explain that it ran fifteen miles in length and measured a mile or so wide. 'It separates the Island of Cape Breton from the peninsula of Nova Scotia. But there's a strong current and the tide seldom runs less than four or five miles an hour.'

'Is that bad? Surely with the tides in our favour we could whisk through this strait inside two or three hours?'

'This is a dangerous and deep waterway with swift-running tides,' Modeste told her. 'Winds can blow fiercely down through the strait.'

Solomon stood up and held a wetted finger to the evening air. 'A southerly gale quickens the ebb of the St. Lawrence. I'll check it tomorrow. For now, we sleep.'

In the event, they lost only one day waiting for a favourable wind and tide. Elise, enjoying her adventure, was happy enough to rest for that day and postpone the black hole of her future. *So much to go wrong*, her mind nagged. *Halifax: a huge town, a garrison, a port. Part of the dark side of human nature. What are the chances of Marcel's cousin still living at that address? What if she doesn't want anything to do with me? How will I live? What about Colette? How will I keep her safe?*

'Stop it!' she cried out loud. 'Just listen to you, scaring yourself half to death.' She grabbed a satchel and set out to collect berries. 'Do something useful and stop mithering,' she muttered.

Her satchel was half full when she became aware of the rhythmic impact of axe on wood. Seeking out the source, she found Dominic preparing branches for their fire. Though never impolite, and always kind to Colette, he clearly found her company onerous so she made to retrace her steps. He turned and smiled so she asked if she could help.

'If you want to carry some of this back it would be useful.'

She shouldered her satchel of berries and scooped up an armful of firewood.

'Elise.' He put down the axe and walked up to her. 'You think me unwelcoming?'

'Maybe,' she admitted. 'A bit.'

'You're right. I've been like a moose with a sore head. I'm sorry.'

Taken aback by his honesty she waited for him to continue.

'I admit I objected to taking a European woman and young child on this trip. Such journeys can be dangerous and I was afraid you would be a liability. I was wrong. I've come to admire your courage and resolve.'

She glowed inside. 'Thank you Dominic, it's kind of you to say so. I try to pull my weight.'

'You do pull your weight, really you do. You paddle long and hard and don't give up, though I read the pain in you sometimes.'

She blushed. 'Then we can be friends, Dominic?'

'We can be friends.'

The next morning both wind and tide satisfied Solomon. As Dominic had suggested, they flew through the Gut like eagles. Ultimately, it took them under three hours to reach Chedabucto Bay and, beyond that, the

Atlantic Ocean. Through the following days they paddled round the headland of Cape Canso and a further hundred and fifty miles down towards Halifax Harbour. The coast became tamer, softer, with a more generous scattering of settlements. Each night they enjoyed good food, a camp fire, stories and songs. Elise knew that whatever fate held in store for her, she would remember these days – this interlude – as special. She would have been happy if they could have gone on forever. On their last night Dominic approached her as she checked her rabbit snares, and asked if he could talk with her. 'We are now good friends are we not?'

She agreed that, yes, they were now good friends.

'Elise, you and Colette shouldn't be in a bad place such as Halifax. You need a protector. A husband.'

'It's nice of you to be concerned, Dominic, but, as I explained, I have Marcel's cousin to go to.'

'But if you had a husband?'

'I don't. And I don't want one. I can manage well enough, just me and Colette.'

'You know nothing of Halifax. It can be harsher than the wilderness. Full of drunken men and wanton women.' He took her hand. 'Elise, let me be that husband.'

She stared at him as she tried to take in what he said. Unless she mistook his words, Dominic had made a proposal of marriage. Could these past days become her future after all? Such mixed marriages were not unknown, though the white-skinned population frowned on them and tended to bar the miscreants from their society. Likewise the children of such a union.

He studied her face before adding, 'We could have a good life together. You are like one of us and I would be a true and strong husband. I have come to love your bravery and skills, your strength and resolve. And Elise, I have come to love you.'

She hadn't noticed before how his long silk lashes beautifully framed his amber-flecked eyes. She now saw the kindness of his face, how broad his shoulders were, how smooth his skin. He kissed her with tender passion. Her arms encircled his neck and her blood coursed wildly. It had been so long. So very long. Her heart spoke and she imagined leading the life of a Mi'kmaq woman. Many things about their ways attracted her. She was fit and strong so the hardships did not daunt her. Colette would thrive. Elise could forgo the life she headed for with its dirt, drunkenness, squalor and the other unavoidable and unpleasant elements found in any port. She didn't have to live that life or the chasm of loneliness that lay ahead of her. Then a series of pictures flashed into her mind: her mother, her whole family, full of anger and shock that she should fall so low and bring such disgrace upon them all. They would never understand and never forgive. Her name, once carefully written on the front page of the precious family bible, now ruled through. Expunged. Her grandmother looking down upon her and shaking her head in sorrow, tears escaping unchecked. And Colette would be beyond redemption and forever expelled from her own people.

'Elise?'

His voice broke through her nightmarish thoughts. 'Oh Dominic. You don't know how tempted I was for a moment. But I can't. You must see that. And though I love you as a friend and a brother, it can never be more than that. I'm deeply flattered, but so sorry.'

He nodded and hung his head. She touched his cheek. 'But we are still good friends, aren't we?' she asked.

'If friendship is all you are able to offer, then it is a gift I'm honoured to accept.'

By mid-afternoon the following day, eighteen days after they had left Chéticamp, they entered Halifax Harbour.

PART FIVE

Halifax

CHAPTER 31

It was a great wrench for Elise to say goodbye to her new Mi'kmaq family. Before they continued on to Sackville they helped her and Colette to a respectable inn. Colette cried pitifully and wanted to go with them. For Elise's part, a great doubt sat on her shoulders as she thought about the life she could have had as Dominic's wife.

With her pulse thumping fit to break her ribcage (could no one hear it but herself?) she and Colette found Creighton Street and Mrs Maythorpe's house. It felt threatening to be in such a large town after seventeen years spent in the backwaters of this colony, and Halifax was a town larger than she had ever experienced. As overwhelmed as she was, it was nothing compared with Colette's apprehension. How the poor child clung to her mother's skirts.

'Maman. Don't like it,' Colette whimpered, her eyes full of tears. 'Nasty people, bad smell. Don't like all the horses and them carts with people in them. Want to go home. Want Dorothy and James.'

It took Elise ten minutes to calm her down with hugs and promises that it would be all right, though she had trouble believing her own platitudes as she took a deep breath and knocked at the door of number seventeen Creighton Street. She had no idea how she would be received by Mrs Maythorpe. A promise given by Marcel all that time ago carried little weight. Maybe his cousin had moved or even died? If she was still there, maybe she would turn her away? She had prepared a note of explanation to present at Mrs Maythorpe's door. Elise and Colette had washed and changed into fresh, if crumpled, clothing at the inn but Elise soon appreciated how like paupers they appeared.

Suspicion was written all over the maid's face when Elise gave her the note. 'Wait here,' she commanded, before shutting the door sharply in their faces.

A pale woman with golden hair, who bore no resemblance to Marcel, opened the door. 'Mrs Galliard,' she said in a warm, gentle voice. 'Come in, please. I'm Sylvie Maythorpe. I'll get us some tea, and perhaps a glass of apple juice for your little girl?'

Elise, feeling grubbier than ever and aware of her rough, dirt-encrusted hands, sat in the luxurious parlour opposite Marcel's cousin. Putting Elise at ease with her ready smile, she chatted easily and asked her about her journey. Mrs Maythorpe's gentle yet vibrant spirit filled the room. She was about Elise's age and Elise felt sure she would like her. Even Colette, sitting on Elise's lap and clinging tightly to her mother's skirts, started to relax. When Mrs Maythorpe's little boy, Jerome, slid shyly into the room Colette forgot her fears and joined him at the table where he shared a picture book with her. Jerome was more like Marcel in complexion – dark as his mother was fair. He had his mother's warm smile, except that his childish grin displayed the central gap where once a baby tooth had been.

'Marcel did mention you some time ago,' Mrs Maythorpe said. 'I could tell he was concerned. I hope you don't mind but he told me something of your background and your family in the Channel Islands. I got the impression that he was fond of you, though he did not mention that you had a child.'

Elise blushed and glanced at her daughter who sat wide-eyed at the table with Jerome, spellbound by everything she saw. 'He's been a good friend,' she replied carefully. 'He didn't know about Colette. I'm so sorry. I'm probably being a terrible nuisance.'

'Not at all.' She topped up the teapot with hot water, then said she would be delighted to invite Elise and Colette into her home because Elise was exactly what she needed. She could offer accommodation and food in return for help in the school. 'I've run my home as a girls' school for the past half year and am now anxious to spend more time with Jerome,' she explained. 'And as they are getting on like brother and sister, I'd be delighted to take care of Colette while you're teaching. If things work out,' she added, 'when Colette's older she could join the other young girls at their lessons. Why don't we give it a three-month trial?'

Elise couldn't believe her luck. She saw the possibility of a new life, a new venture opening up before her. She was thrilled.

Sylvie and Jerome occupied the ground level, while Elise and Colette and the schoolroom shared the upper level. There was even a good-sized attic where Sylvie said she could set up a workroom for her remedies once she was settled in provided they were safe and didn't smell bad.

To Elise's joy Mrs Maythorpe, who said to call her Sylvie, had a real garden, one bigger than Elise had ever known. It boasted flowers and shrubs, an excellent vegetable plot, some currant bushes and two apple trees. Sylvie showed a keen interest in Elise's work and she had no objection to Elise planting culinary and medicinal herbs.

Magically, despite Elise's previous hardships and heartbreaks, she was now a respectable teacher living a respectable life at a respectable address. What, she wondered, would her dearest Père have said to that? Furthermore, she delighted in her teaching duties. Mostly she instructed the girls in numbers, nature, reading and writing. And Sylvie had a good library.

What a pleasure that was. Her nature studies class included botany, health and exercise. As a believer that girls needed fresh air and exercise as much as did boys, when the weather permitted she took the class out into the garden where they played outdoor games, and studied and drew plants. At other times she organised the girls into a neat line in pairs holding hands, and, like the tail of a cat, they snaked towards Point Pleasant, observing nature along the way. As for dancing and needlecraft, while she pretended to assist Sylvie in these subjects, she was as much a pupil as the girls – and a not particularly good pupil at that. Sylvie and Jerome assured her that they liked the arrangement a good deal. Colette settled in and got used to things and soon became delighted with her new life. Elise's days were full and she knew more contentment than she'd felt for years.

CHAPTER 32

'Elise, I think you need to set yourself up in a proper shop.'

Word had spread. Townsfolk, soldiers and mariners came to Creighton Street in ever-increasing numbers but as trade grew it became apparent that it was undesirable for so many strangers to be knocking on Sylvie's door. The set-up did not endear her to Magda, Sylvie's German maid.

'I'm sorry, Sylvie. I had no idea my remedies would be so popular. And I know I've neglected my teaching duties recently. But I don't want to abandon you,' Elise protested. 'And I love it here. You've been so good to us and I think of you as my friend. Creighton Street feels like home.' She had a sudden thought and added, 'Unless we've outstayed our welcome?' Had they? Had she and Colette taken advantage of Sylvie's kind nature?

Sylvie hugged Elise and smiled warmly, assuring her that it was only the business that needed to move out. 'You and Colette are more than welcome to stay. Jerome and I love having you here.'

'But what about the teaching?'

'True. It is a dilemma,' Sylvie admitted. 'But we'll find a way.'

A small lockup shop, no more than one pokey room with a store cupboard to the rear, became vacant on Grafton Street, a street as old as Halifax itself. Near the poorhouse and its adjacent cemetery, the street's north end was close to a church and the town burial ground. The premises were slotted between the printing press – home of the *Halifax Gazette* – and a livery stable, so would benefit from a good passing trade.

On a wet October day, some three years after her bedraggled arrival in town, and after much wall and floor scrubbing and the applying of a lime wash and arranging the fitting of shelves and a counter, she finally opened her shop. *Her* shop: two words to make her heart swell with pride. 'Thank you Gran'mère, you taught me so much,' Elise whispered, as she unlocked the door for her first day of business.

She traded each morning bar Sundays, and taught every weekday afternoon for Sylvie. Spare moments were given over to the production of her remedies. Colette, full of the adventure and novelty of the situation, settled in with glee as Maman's little helper. In a wistful echo of her own childhood in Père's shop, she made her daughter a white apron. Trade was slow at first, but soon picked up. She was content.

The malodourous raven. Shrieks it's delight. Kra Kra.
Each shriek pierces her soul. Elise burns. Inside.
Outside. Crushed. Mangled. She sobs. Her heart breaks.
A thousand pieces. A final kra of victory. Retreat into
the gathering dawn.

As she lay in the half-light, her head on the damp
pillow, she racked her brain in an effort to decipher the
message, but concluded that the only message was her
own anxiety. She remembered Nancy's belief that she
had these dreams, not to change things, for it would be
wrong to try to change the future, but to prepare her for
what will be. She consoled herself with the thought that
once her shop became properly established and she
stopped worrying, she would see the last of the creature.

In December, as the frost began to nip fingers and
toes, a package arrived from her sister Marie. Elise and
Sylvie sat on either side of the fire relishing its warmth
as Elise opened her mail, anticipation making her eyes
glow. Inside she found one letter and a bulky package
tied with a blue ribbon. She settled down to read but
cried out and jumped to her feet. Sylvie put aside her
crochet work and rushed to her side. 'Why, Elise,
whatever is it?'

Elise clamped her hand across her mouth as though
to keep the words from being said, but nothing could
hold back the truth. 'Mère,' she gasped. 'Gone.
Typhus.'

'Oh Elise, my dear, I'm so sorry.' Sylvie fetched the brandy bottle and poured a generous quantity. She led Elise to the sofa, put the glass in her hand and sat with an arm round her.

The liquid coursed down her throat and washed her stomach with its heat. Eventually she murmured, 'Even though she was sixty-seven, the letters she sent were full of life and hope. Apart from when Père died, and when we lost William and his family to cholera, she always found the good in everything.'

Tears welled and fell unnoticed by her. She held the package close. 'All my letters home. So many. Nearly seventeen years, most of my adult life, a thread joining us across each and every mile. She never knew the adult me except though these letters. Mère was my bastion.' Elise gave a cry of pain and sobbed into Sylvie's shoulder.

The raven. What good the taunting raven? No guardian angel, this malevolent messenger of death. When the sobs eased Sylvie passed her a handkerchief and left the room to make an infusion of chamomile. She then sat with Elise until late into the evening, encouraging her to talk and recall her memories of Guernsey and her family there.

'Mère often wrote of the comfort she found in her Methodist religion. My own beliefs are less clear, but she will join Père and William and his family in my prayers. I'll miss her letters so much.'

'You mentioned typhus. An epidemic?'

Elise nodded. 'Marie says it struck with no warning but that many others have since died. I hope and pray that the rest of my family remain in good health.'

Eventually Elise allowed herself to be put to bed. There, in the absence of the tormenting raven, she at last fell into an exhausted, empty sleep.

Still in deep mourning, she turned to her work for consolation. Trade was brisk. She had trouble concentrating on her customers and replenishing her stock, but she kept going. Tending to her herbs was different, she found it soothing and restorative. For Colette's sake she learned to show an untroubled face to the world, and only when unobserved did she slide down a slope of sorrow almost too much to bear.

Eventually, under the weight of necessity, her peace of mind and spirit won through and her listlessness decreased. She made plans. One day soon she was going to be a respectable trader with her own property in a smart part of town, she confided to Sylvie.

'Your ambitions are admirable. Does nothing daunt you?'

Her thoughts flashed to the raven, but she quashed them and said brightly, 'Not in the long run.'

***

The purple-black raven returned, conjured from her very thoughts. No attacks, no scenes of death. Worse, much worse. Stifling panic and dread. Overwhelming, malignant, foul: a deep, dark evil.

That spring the raven would not leave her nights. Worn down, she had cause to doubt her courage. At the end of one working day she was helping Colette gather up some glass marbles the child had been playing with, when the shop door opened and a chill, damp air swept in. She turned. 'You just caught me. What can I do for you?'

A thickset man closed the door behind him. His wide-brimmed hat sat low on his brow, his neck linen high to his ears. Small, watery eyes stared at her. 'It's what I can do for you,' the man growled.

'How so?' She said warily.

'I've a message from a friend of mine. He says you're to clear out. Stop all this.' His beefy arm gestured at the rows of vials and bottles on display. A stack of Sarnia pots fell victim to his spite and tumbled over the countertop.

'What are you doing?' Elise cried. Anger vied with fear, and helplessness vied with anger.

'Like I said, stop selling this poxy crap. If you don't, you'll be stopped in a not nice way.' The aggressor pushed Elise against the wall, causing several glass bottles to fall and shatter. Their contents splashed her skirt and spilt over the floor. Colette screamed, dropped her bag of marbles and ran to her mother's side. The man, snarling at the child, added, 'Pity if the brat gets hurt, ain't it?'

Elise looked up at this bull of a man as she tried to

comfort Colette. She found the courage to return his glare. 'What it is you want?'

'Let's say that this particular friend of mine is a bit irritated by you setting yourself up here. This is his territory. He's the medic an' he don't like to be irritated. You're stealing his living. An' stealing's not polite, is it?' He yanked open the door, and as a parting shot, added, 'You got till the end of the month, missus.'

Elise knew of the garrison surgeon, Doctor Boggs, and of the Loyalist Doctor Halliburton who had come up from New York and was attached to His Majesty's Naval Hospital. Both were respectable practitioners. However, a customer had once mentioned a small faction of quack doctors in Halifax. Elise had been told that people trusted her because she made no bold claims, yet her remedies gave real relief. One customer told her that townsfolk were abandoning the quacks and charlatans with their gallstone remedies of burnt eggshells, soap and snails, their "magnetic thrones" and their incantations. 'You offer traditional medicine and great knowledge,' Elise was told, much to her satisfaction. Until now.

She paid a visit to Doctor Halliburton. The man did not try to hide his antagonism. 'Now see here, Mrs Galliard,' he bristled, 'I've heard about you and your medicine shop. What cause have I to believe you are any better than the others? Let me tell you this, madam. Halifax has become a haven for you pseudo-medics. Registration for the practice of medicine and surgery –

301

that's what's needed. That would put a halt to the likes of you coming from wherever you're from and setting up your quackery.' He turned from her and stared at the street beyond his window. 'If others are inclined to be shot of you, who am I to object?'

As she left she remembered to slam his door fit to break it.

Elise got a kinder reception from Doctor Boggs, but no advice other than to shut shop and leave the doctoring to the doctors.

Within the week she again saw what was most likely the same man beneath his cloak, hat and red neck-linen. He was leaning against the wall opposite her shop. Every time she glanced up there he stood. He lounged, drew on his pipe, picked at his fingernails and his nose, and he stared. Customers kept their heads down and hurried past. Disturbed and annoyed, she called on a magistrate, seeking the protection of the law. The portly, unimposing man smothered a yawn while assuring her he would instruct a town constable to call by on occasion.

***

On a wet and gusty Tuesday, the first day of May, Elise arrived with Colette for her morning's work and saw the splintered wood of the shop door. She stiffened and glanced about her. For once, there was no loiterer. Unsurprisingly, no constable either. She instructed

Colette to wait outside.

Blood pounded in her temples as she edged the door open and peered inside. There was no one there, but a trapped moose could not have made more mess. Jars and their contents had been smashed up the walls. The wooden table that served as a counter was upended. Creams had been smeared over the floor, and their containers ground into the mess. Worst of all was what she took to be human excrement rubbed into the whole hellish concoction. Backing out and quelling the urge to vomit, she rushed home with Colette clasped tightly by the hand.

Just the same, she would not be bullied. She had come too far and endured too much to buckle beneath the threats of a lout working for a gaggle of quack doctors. Reluctant to alarm Sylvie, she left Colette at home on the vague pretext that the child harboured a cold. She arranged for the door to be repaired then hired a lad from next door's livery stable, along with his brushes and mops. Her fury gave her the drive she needed to face it and together they cleaned up the horrific mess. With the shop re-stocked and up and running again, and Colette once more chatting to her mother's many customers, life returned to normal. There was no further sign of the burly man. The raven continued to fill her nights with alarm, but the man must by now have understood that she would not be intimidated.

***

Business grew, as did her savings. At closing time towards the end of the month, with the spring weather creeping towards summer, she locked the store cupboard as usual and called to Colette. But the child wasn't in the shop. Neither could she find her outside. Elise's mouth went dry. She hoarsely screamed her daughter's name. She raced up Grafton Street then down. She searched the church and the burial ground. She tried the printers and the livery stable, all the time calling out until she gasped and sobbed with fear and frustration and self-recriminations. She rushed back to the shop again, hoping, praying that this was simply one of Colette's silly games. Inside she collided with the burly man. 'Lost something?' he said.

'Where is she? What have you done with my baby?'

'She's safe. For now.'

'What do you want?'

'You know what I want.'

With no thought for her own safety she sprang at the man but, laughing, he thrust her to one side, a fly to be swatted. Again she lunged. He gripped her wrists and held her at arm's length, amused by her frenzy.

'I asked you nicely, didn't I? Then, though I've more than enough to do, I hung about so's to remind you. Then I got a bit cross, right? And still you ignored me. What's a man to do? So I got the brat...'

She moaned. She could no longer hear the man's

304

words, could make no sense of anything except that this brute had taken her baby and she wanted to kill him. He shook her so hard her head snapped back with a vicious jolt. 'Listen to me, silly cunt. Stop that noise and listen.'

She took a deep shuddering breath and glared at him.

'Better. What a great fuss. Like I said, only you wasn't listening properly, you pack up here and get out of Halifax. Then you get the brat back all safe and sound. Got me?'

Beaten, she nodded.

'You got one week.'

'Please, give me back Colette. I will go, I promise. But she's only a baby. She'll be frightened. Let me have her and I'll go at once.'

'Should of thought of that earlier when I give you the chance to do things nicely.'

'Please, I beg you!'

The man hesitated and Elise held her breath. 'No. Told you once. Not saying it again. You caused me a lot of fuss, so now you do as I say. There's a ship Boston-bound in one week. Be on it and I'll have the brat on board waiting for you.' He turned on his heel and was gone in a moment.

Somehow she found her way home.

Sylvie, glowing with excitement, rushed to meet her. 'Elise, at last. My dear, we have a visitor. Just back from England. Come and see.' Full of smiles and laughter Sylvie dragged her into the front parlour. In the middle of the room stood Marcel de Forêt.

305

'See,' declared Sylvie triumphantly. 'What a surprise!' She stopped in her tracks. 'Why Elise, whatever's the matter? Where's Colette?'

Both Marcel and Sylvie helped her to a chair where she shook uncontrollably. Sylvie produced smelling salts while Marcel put a glass of brandy into her hand. Barely taking in the man's presence, she stuttered out the whole story.

'By God, Elise,' he said, his eyes bright with anger. 'What mess are you involved in?'

She sprung to her feet ready to attack him, to claw his face. How dare he criticise her when she'd only been doing her best to scrape a living for herself and his – yes, *his* daughter! If he hadn't deserted her in the first place...

She found words only heard in the tavern or the dockside and used them with relish; words she hadn't realised she knew, and in her right mind would never have uttered. Sylvie came between them and took Elise into her arms. 'Marcel,' she shouted. 'I don't think you're helping.'

He put his hands over his face for a moment, then touched Elise's shoulder. 'That was crass of me,' he said. 'Forgive me. Let me help.'

'I don't know what to do,' Elise cried. 'What can we do? I must go. Do as they demand.'

'Don't be too hasty. Let me think.' He stared into the fire for a short while before turning to them, a harsh, resolute expression filling his face. 'I know people,' he said. 'I'm no stranger to Halifax's shady underworld. I will not balk at using shady methods of my own, if need be.'

'But what will you do?' Sylvie asked.

'I intend to pull in every favour I've got going.'

He sat Elise down and gently but thoroughly guided her through the events leading to Colette's kidnapping.

'Don't do anything until you hear from me,' he said. 'Leave it to me.' With that he was gone.

The next day, and the next were a torture. Life became suspended, a waking nightmare filled with the shadow of a gloating, purple-black raven. Every time she closed her eyes she heard Colette sobbing for her; saw the fear in her child's face, not understanding why her maman had deserted her, left her in this strange place with these bad people. And those were the better images. What kind of mother was she, to let this happen to her baby? She had never felt so inadequate. Even during the invasion of Jerseymans Island she'd put up a fight. She'd got used to coping. Now she knew only helplessness. And rage.

At last Marcel returned, arriving on the doorstep dishevelled and offering hope.

'Colette can be found in the room of a dockside whore,' he told her. Her eyes widened and Sylvie took her hand and squeezed it. 'That brute who took her,' he continued, 'He's a pimp. A man for hire. No job too dirty.'

Elise made for the door. 'We'll go now.'

Detaining her, he said, 'We'll go tomorrow mid-morning when it's likely to be quiet.'

'But—'

'It's the only way.'

She took a deep breath then nodded. 'But you won't go without me?'

He hesitated. 'Very well, but you must hold back, be there for your little girl. Leave the rest to me.'

Sylvie, with Jerome to care for, reluctantly agreed to stand by at home. The hours stretched on. They all tried to rest, for a clear head would be vital. But rest was an elusive beast, uncatchable, untameable.

The next morning Elise and Marcel walked in silence to the house in Lower Water Street, one of the many crowded hovels filled with filth and despair. Her breathlessness was more to do with fear and anticipation than to the three rickety flights of stairs they climbed. Marcel knocked and Elise hung back. A tired woman answered the door. In the dingy light she could have been anywhere between fifteen and fifty.

Marcel waved a purse at her. 'Jake said you'd be available,' he told her. The woman eyed the purse and stood aside. Marcel strode in, Elise followed close behind him.

'What in blessed hell?' the whore cussed as Marcel pushed her against the wall.

Colette lay on a tussled bed. Elise, ashen-faced, checked for signs of life. The child's eyes flickered open, a smile lit up her face at the sight of her mother and then her lids drooped once more.

'Take her home,' Marcel said. 'I'll finish up here.' Elise nodded and with little more than a backward glance, picked up Colette and left the room.

Later Marcel told Elise and Sylvie that the contents of his wallet bought him everything he needed to know. The name of the quack doctors who were behind the scheme, the pimp who had done their dirty work and where they could be found. Marcel dealt with the whole squalid business, but would give no details. He did tell her later that week that she could safely re-open her shop and that there would be no more trouble. Sylvie suggested to Marcel that he must have friends in high places. Elise added that it was more likely that he had friends in low ones. He laughed, but deftly sidestepped any awkward questions – something Elise knew of old was one of his talents.

He said that he felt inclined to believe the woman when she swore she had been kind to Colette. She admitted to keeping her drugged, but said she had fed her and even kept her amused. Certainly the child showed no worrying after-effects, and sometimes talked of the nice lady who'd played with her and made her a baby out of a wooden clothespin.

As normality returned to their lives, Elise began to wonder at Marcel's sudden and fortuitous appearance. She also became aware that many years had passed since they'd last met; three of those spent surviving the hardships of Chéticamp. She was nearly forty years old.

How disappointing she must appear. She avoided examining her feelings for him. He was a man who could not be tied down, could not remain in one place for more than a season. She wouldn't give her heart to him again. That belonged in the past.

He called on her early one evening shortly after Colette's rescue. He didn't settle with his usual panache but paced awkwardly about Sylvie's parlour. 'It's good to see you. I hope you and Colette have fully recovered.' His voice was husky. Did he harbour a cold?

'Yes, thank you,' she said. 'We're both well.' They stood in silence until she added, 'Sylvie made a pot of fresh coffee. Can I pour you some?'

When she passed his cup, their hands touched and she caught her breath.

'I was in London,' he said at last.

'So I heard.'

'I arrived in Halifax a short while ago. I had no idea you were here. I'd been in England for some time and when I arrived here I dropped a note to Sylvie. She wrote back that you lived here with her. I confess, I was amazed. She asked me to call by. I got here of course just as all that hoo-ha exploded. I'm glad I was here. Glad I could help.'

'And I never thanked you properly.'

'No need.' He stirred his coffee. 'Tell me about the child.'

'Nothing to—'

'But she is mine, isn't she?'

She looked him straight in the eye. 'Who else's would she be?'

There followed another long pause. To fill it she crossed to the table and put down her cup, the coffee still untouched. She asked him when he planned to leave.

'I don't. At least only for brief periods. Halifax is my home now.'

Stunned, she stared at him; at this man, the father of her child, the source of the niggling desire locked within her. His hair may have collected a little more grey, the sun-carved creases around his eyes may have deepened, but to her he was as strong and striking as ever. How she found herself in his arms never became clear to her. Maybe the soft touch of his hand on her cheek, maybe the way he lifted a lock of her hair and tucked it gently back from her face. Maybe she scrutinised his coal-dark eyes and saw the light of love there. Whatever the trigger, the sensation melted the ice shard that had existed for so long in her body, mind and heart.

They stood in an oasis of their own making for long moments before reality caught at her and she pulled away. 'This is because of Colette, isn't it? It's not necessary. We've done well enough without you. You have no obligation. As far as Halifax is concerned I'm a respectable widow with a young child, a role that suits me well. I will not be your obligation or the target of your resurrected conscience. I never wanted that before and I don't want it now.'

'No. This is not about our daughter.' *Our daughter.*

He took her arms and held her tightly. 'It's about you then and you now; what I've always, *always* felt for you. It's about me then and me now. The life I led. A life not fit for a wife. You knew that when we parted.'

'I knew you well enough to understand that no matter what your feelings may have been you had no room in your life for me. When I discovered I was pregnant I knew that to be even truer.'

He told her that he was now a different man leading a different life, and pleaded that he be allowed to meet his child and be a part of their lives.

How much weight could she give to his words? What if he won Colette's heart, then let her down? Truth be told, she wasn't sure she was ready to share Colette. They talked, debated, argued. In the end Elise agreed that he could meet Colette properly, but not as her father. As far as the child and society knew, Thomas had been her father, so she introduced Marcel to Colette as Sylvie's cousin who now lived in town. This was, in any case, the truth. Colette took a great fancy to him.

Elise owed Sylvie the truth and sought her out. Sylvie laid aside her needlepoint and sat back. Elise had a speech planned but instead she blurted out, 'Colette. She's Marcel's!' Would Sylvie draw back in horror? Would she politely suggest that Elise take her daughter and leave?

Instead she smiled gently. 'Do you think I didn't guess?'

'But aren't you shocked? Don't you despise me?'

Sylvie hugged Elise. 'Why don't you tell me all about it?'

***

Elise was grateful that her shop was re-opening, yet despite Marcel's assurances she was nervous each time she opened the shop door in the morning, and each time someone came in. Nevertheless, her business thrived and bigger premises were called for. At last she found what she wanted: a shop in Bedford Row. It couldn't have been better. The move went smoothly. It did her good to escape the bad memories that clung to the little shop in Grafton Street. Bedford Row was in a respectable area of town and in a good position for trade. It managed to avoid the coal company and the timber yard and the twin evils of the garrison and its rowdy goings-on, and Water Street, with its wharves, taverns and houses of disrepute. Bedford Row housed respectable tradesmen and labourers and their families, seamen, longshoremen and shop assistants. Among the cobbler's, fish monger's, milliner's, the coffee house and one of the best bakers and pie shops in town, sat Elise's new shop, and above it her new home. She would be sorry to leave Sylvie's but felt the time was right to do so. Besides, they'd only be a few streets apart.

Meanwhile Marcel courted Elise in a way that both embarrassed and touched her. He proposed to her every full moon. She dithered and dissembled until, some twelve moons after his return, she happily capitulated.

CHAPTER 33

The wedding party was a great success. Elise thought that Marcel had never looked more handsome. For her part, she floated in a daze of happiness and disbelief at the existence of such joy. How did she get to deserve so much?

Colette was beside herself with excitement and young Jerome volunteered to keep an eye on her for the duration. Sylvie's boy was small for a nine year old and Colette, two years his junior, almost matched his height, but he was sensible and reliable for his age, and Colette adored him. Jerome took Colette's hand and, like brother and sister, they perched side by side on the window seat where he let her show off her reading skills.

Once Colette was settled with Jerome, Marcel led Elise to a table by the window. She fanned her face and eased her stiff new shoes from her feet, poking the abandoned footwear with her sore toes. How lovely these shoes were. The latest fashion – embroidered silk brocade, jewelled buckles and a high curved heel.

Lovely, fashionable, expensive. And painful. She remembered how, in Saint-Pierre, she had made her own shoes from animal hides. Not the height of fashion, but truly the pinnacle of comfort.

'Madame de Forêt,' Marcel said. 'Mine at last. About time, too.'

Elise smiled. 'A woman mustn't be rushed into these things.'

'Rushed! I fell in love with you eighteen years ago and I've begged you for the past year to marry me.'

'You did not fall in love with me eighteen years ago. I'd only just met you.' She raised her glass, peered at him over the rim as she sipped.

'Well, in lust, at least. You must give me that.'

'I'll give you that. But, sir, tell me, when did the love arrive?'

'It was the second time I set eyes on you; the day you attacked that poor defenceless bear to attract my attention and sympathy. I held your supine body and my heart ignored my head.'

'So, you saw through my ploy?'

'Your ploy worked. What a pity we waited so long.'

'I've given in now, so no more waiting. If you weren't always off here, there and everywhere you might have won me over sooner.'

'Ah,' he groaned theatrically. 'Business.'

'Business, business, business! I only agreed to marry you because it would be just a matter of time before you noticed I'd become an old woman.'

'Who else would marry an old man?'

She tossed a flower from the table decoration at him. It landed in an abandoned wine glass.

'Truce?' He held up both hands in submission. He was thoughtful for a moment then said, 'I should never have deserted you all those years ago. I should have settled down and cherished you. When I think how brave you've been bringing up Colette all alone, and how you must have hated me...'

'I never hated you! Well, maybe once or twice. Briefly. But we had a deal. I understood that. And it wasn't all bad. I had Colette.'

He stroked her face and smiled, then grasped her hands. 'Now, it would be rude to ignore old Henry's fiddling, so will you have another gavotte with me?' He leaned forward and kissed the tip of her nose.

'I'm exhausted. I've danced more tonight that ever before in my life.' She grinned at her husband then nodded to where a sticky-faced Colette was digging pudgy fingers into a cupcake. 'Why not ask Colette?'

He got to his feet but then hesitated and bent to whisper, 'Doesn't she have the right to know she's mine?'

Without hesitation Elise shook her head. 'She must never know. How could we tell her she's... you know?'

She saw a flicker of regret in his eyes. 'I understand,' he said, and after a moment he rested a hand on her shoulder before making his way to his daughter, whom he could never acknowledge as his daughter, to ask her to dance with him. Colette had, without prompting, chosen to call Marcel "Papa", so she hoped this would compensate him.

As she sipped cranberry juice made from her own grown fruit, she watched Marcel lead the giggling child onto the space that, earlier, had been cleared in Sylvie's parlour. Elise smiled as her husband and their daughter gave their best to a lively tune. Her fingers tapped along to the music. Her old silver wedding band had long worn away and as her fingers danced she couldn't help but admire the shiny gold glint of her new ring beneath exquisitely crocheted white gloves. These gloves were a wedding gift from Sylvie, and more than welcome, hiding as they did the roughness of her reddened hands. She could barely remember a time when her hands had been soft and white. If she could but find the secret of youthful skin she would be the richest woman on both sides of the great Atlantic Ocean. Nowadays she was kept so busy with her remedies that she hired a man for a few hours a week to tackle the heavy work in the garden but she was reluctant to give up all contact with the soil.

On a practical level, things couldn't have worked out better. Elise and Sylvie continued to share teaching duties and between them, organised things so that each of them could be involved in the classroom as well as with their own children, yet giving them the freedom to follow their individual dreams. Sylvie, in remembrance of her late husband, became a tireless committee member for the Charity for Destitute Loyalists, while Elise worked on her remedies and carried on running her shop.

Amongst the townsfolk her reputation as a skilled herbalist and healer grew steadily and her healthy savings, nowadays deposited in the Halifax Bank, grew likewise. Most of her customers paid in cash, although she still accepted barter from those with limited means. Fortunately there'd been no more trouble from the few remaining quack doctors, or from the town's physicians.

She had at last joined the respectable bourgeoisie, Marcel had teased. She'd retorted that she'd never left it.

As soon as one dance ended another began and half a dozen or so people, including Marcel and a tireless Colette, made use of the improvised dance floor. Sylvie, a wonderful hostess, organised guests and hired staff so smoothly and with such a radiant smile that the day was a triumph. The sound of laughter, the dancing, the smiles of friends, the delicious canapés and fine wine. Marcel so handsome and finally hers. Her happiness welled up until she felt she would burst.

Her gaze was drawn to the corner of the room where the fiddler, Henry, resplendent in powdered wig and fine-woven coat, smiled his huge smile. The man winked at her as he played a jaunty jig, clearly enjoying himself enormously. Elise had become accustomed to the many negroes living in town and as she regarded this man with his ebony skin, his huge sooty eyes, his fine cheekbones, broad nose and hair like the coat of a black lamb, she speculated over his sad and turbulent past. Despite his outward show of cheerfulness she sensed his heavy sorrow. Today, her wedding day, he grinned and played his fiddle as though the devil pursued him. Perhaps it did.

'Maman, now you must dance.' Colette dumped her red-faced self next to Elise so she reluctantly squeezed her feet back into her shoes.

As people started to go home, Sylvie gathered up Colette and Jerome. Colette would sleep at Sylvie's tonight.

Back in Bedford Row, in the bedroom Elise would now be sharing with Marcel, panic made it difficult for her to catch her breath. There had been little opportunity to be intimately alone with Marcel this past year. When they first celebrated their love she had been a fine enough looking woman in her early thirties. Now she was ashamed and shy of her body.

'You are as beautiful as ever,' he whispered. She self-consciously submitted as he slowly undressed her. He knelt, his arms clasped about her. 'Madame de Forêt, I love you. I'll love you forever, and forever started a lifetime ago and continues to the edge of time.'

Her blood rose. She forgot to fuss about her worn body and remembered only the passion this man – now her husband – roused within her.

CHAPTER 34

That New Year's Eve, in Halifax, Nova Scotia, as the eighteenth century sat on the cusp of the nineteenth; Elise, Marcel and Colette joined the throng that gathered outside Government House. Squibs and firecrackers exploded, lighting up the beautiful façade of St Paul's Church, and on Citadel Hill a bonfire blazed. The air was thick and acrid.

Elise snatched glances at Marcel and Colette's radiant faces, enjoying their pleasure, and she gave yet another silent prayer of thanks for her family. Marcel ducked and laughed as a rogue squib whizzed past his ear. Clearly the revellers were determined to make the most of the occasion.

She'd had a few qualms about allowing Colette to stay up for this free-for-all. The child was not yet thirteen, but Marcel had given in to her pleading and overruled Elise's fears. She still wasn't convinced about the wisdom of that decision, and things were definitely set to get livelier. Around them people sang songs, both decent and indecent in equal measure. Yellow-gold lanterns bobbed in the air while the night throbbed with excitement and celebration. Respectable citizens mingled with disreputable ones – whores with churchmen, drunk with sober, the homeless with those who would later sleep in mansions. Public houses did a grand trade, pickpockets and brothels likewise.

In the frosted air her breath hovered inches from her pinched nose as she watched Colette boot-skating with the other youngsters. Marcel had been right. All the young people had been allowed to greet the new millennium. Their skidding turned Barrington Street into a rink. Snow underfoot ranged from grey, unpleasant slush to solid compacted ice. The frozen harbour had been idle for weeks.

Marcel, alongside her, nuzzled his icy face into her cheek.

'Hey, that's damp.' She shivered and he briskly rubbed his gloved hands up and down her arms to warm her. 'Nice,' she said.

As she watched the heaving throng her thoughts turned to Sylvie's garden, which she continued to make use of, and the good-sized allotment near the common she'd acquired last year. Both now lay dormant and snow-thick. Most houses in Bedford Row, including their own, contained shops at street level, with homes above. At least she could open the shop in the morning without putting a foot beyond the threshold. Whether there would be customers was another matter. She shouted in Marcel's ear, 'I certainly don't intend to venture out tomorrow if I can help it. In fact I think I'll put my feet up by the fire.'

'Put your feet up? When did you ever sit around when you could be downstairs in that shop of yours, or in the workroom out the back using a mortar and pestle to crush merry you-know-what out of some poor defenceless piece of bark or other?'

Her answering nudge was none too gentle and he nearly lost his footing. Before he could retaliate Colette came skidding up, face aglow, her eyelashes like frosted pelmets against the green sparkle of her eyes.

Elise regarded the scene around her with approval. The regeneration work undertaken during Prince Edward's term as commander had made quite a difference and the town was a far cry from the crumbling, shabby place it had been. And on top of that the prince had taken a stern line against drunkenness and gambling.

'Much nicer nowadays, isn't it?' she said. 'Especially now we've got all those New England puritans here. They come into the shop and are positively respectable.'

'It's true, they do tend to buckle down and quietly get on with their own lives,' he said, before whispering out of Colette's earshot, 'And they have no truck with all those wild goings-on at Government House or the depraved orgies in the dives of Barrack Street.'

As though to prove that nothing had really changed beneath the shiny new surface of Halifax, an inflamed fracas started a short distance away. Marcel drew Colette closer and put protective arms around his family.

Elise, staring in the direction of the argument, said, 'In the end, folk are folk and we still live in a port and garrison town with all its thievery, brothels and drinking dens that thrive on the vices of the troops and fleet.'

Marcel frowned as the drunken brawl escalated. 'Half the population getting rich selling rum to the other half.'

They both took a keen interest in current affairs and often enjoyed late night debates on the comings and goings of Government House or church edicts or the state of the military. Colette, however, had other ideas. 'No more gloom and politics,' she demanded. 'Let's get some chestnuts. Jerome told me there's a vendor by the market.'

They wound their way to the marketplace. The aroma was mouth-watering and Marcel bought three paper wraps of the steaming nuts. They'd barely finished them when the cannon announced the new century. Great cheers echoed through the town. Everyone hugged everyone else, and hands encased in thick gloves grasped the hands of those about them. Marcel turned to Elise. In the muted lantern-glow she saw the love that warmed his eyes and, her heart full to overflowing, she swallowed as a familiar passion gripped the pit of her stomach. This man was her mainstay. How had she survived so long without him? He kissed her, then drew Colette into their circle of love.

***

With the rigours of winter now a world away and the June days full of flowers rather than firecrackers, the town once again filled with a happy crowd – though on this occasion it was considerably less rowdy and more decorous. Elise stood with Colette amongst the throng in Barrington Street as they waited to see Prince Edward, now Duke of Kent, lay the Masonic Hall cornerstone. His Royal Highness, as Grand Master of the Masons of Lower Canada, would lead the celebrations. A masonic procession had formed and the band of the prince's own regiment, the 7th Fusiliers, played with gusto in a civic display to outshine even last New Year's festivities.

'Look at that!' Colette shouted, pointing out the officers and members of the Halifax lodges who were marching by, bedecked in their aprons, jewels and regalia, contributing a great pomp, formality and colour to the occasion.

The warmth of the day added to the holiday atmosphere. Wherever Elise turned rich ladies paraded in their best satin-lined Dunstable bonnets trimmed with all manner of bows or silk flowers. She would have loved one of those bonnets, preferably one decorated with ribbons and lined with sky-blue satin. Then there were the delicate shawls of camel hair worn over cashmere or silk dresses. And how handsome the gentlemen were in their beaver hats.

'What do you think of those fine silver buckles adorning the gentlemen's shoes and the knees of their breeches? Should I get Papa some, do you think?' she asked Colette.

'Do you suppose he'd find them rather too fancy?'

'Perhaps.'

'But,' Colette said, 'he'd love some of those.' She pointed to a pair of brown, calfskin boots.

'They're called Wellington, but don't ask me why,' Elise said. These boots fitted snugly to the leg and had a small built up heel. She and Colette agreed that they were indeed smart. They also admired the dazzling silk and the richly embellished brocade waistcoats of crimson or indigo, and corduroy breeches of spruce green, plum or cinnamon that were *à la mode*.

Other folk, Elise and Colette included, made do with their Sunday best. Others still were not put off enjoying the occasion by shabbiness and poverty.

Elise had never seen hunger like that which haunted the poorest of the poor here in Halifax. Members of the fishing communities where she'd once lived and worked rarely had much money but there was always food for their tables. They could fish, hunt, trap and gather. They could barter. Even the weakest did not starve unless they let winter catch them out. Here, for some there was only begging.

'How impressive the Duke of Kent is,' Colette said. 'So tall and dignified.'

Elise pointed out the governor and his beautiful wife and several other dignitaries she recognised.

Colette stretched up on her tiptoes to enjoy a better view. 'Oh, how grand everyone is. What a pity Papa is away; he'd have enjoyed this.'

Marcel had branched out from marine insurance to house insurance and he was at present in Windsor, due home any day. He preferred not to travel in summer when the roads could be a torment of dust, but alas this was not always feasible. Like most people, out of choice he'd travel by sea, but if that wasn't an option, then in winter a horse and sleigh was the easiest mode of transport; easier, at any rate, than travelling in spring and autumn when the roads became impassable quagmires. He tended to be kept from home two or three times a month. All but a few buildings were of wood, so fire insurance was a necessity for the astute property owner, and a profitable living for Marcel.

The stone now duly laid, carriages collected the dignitaries, no doubt heading for some feast or reception at Government House. The crowds began to disperse and Elise and Colette, arm in arm, turned towards Bedford Row.

'That's a distracted smile,' Colette said, as they enjoyed the walk home.

'I was thinking how much your gran'père Victor and your uncle William would have enjoyed this morning.

They were both ardent freemasons, you know.'

Colette squeezed her mother's arm.

The journey down Salter Street and along Hollis Street to the shop in Bedford Row took no time at all, despite the dallying townsfolk reluctant to end their holiday mood. Thank goodness the rain had stayed away as getting about would have been like wading through molasses – more fitting for hob-nailed boots than fancy footwear – and the plethora of outfits and bonnets she saw today would have made a sad display. As they neared the waterfront the wooden, shingled houses were less grand and more tightly packed together. Nevertheless, she felt a familiar shiver of pride, disbelief and delight when she read the sign: *Halifax Herbal Remedies, Prop. Mme de Forêt.* Inevitably the memory of her father's apothecary shop in Rue Berthelot came to mind. A man from England owned it now. After William died fifteen years back, Mère had sold the business. What else could she have done?

Turning to Colette she said, 'Poppet, we need honey. Would you be a dear and fetch some from Widow Jeffries?'

Elise fumbled in her beaded reticule until she found the keys. Any likeness to her father's shop existed more in her mind than in fact. It was true she had a polished wooden counter and a display of many sorts and a variety of pots, jars and bottles, and she and Colette wore white aprons. Likewise, their home was above the shop, only bigger and quieter than her childhood home, but her little shop was not nearly as smart as her father's had been. The glass containers were plain, the window to the street small. But this successful business was her own creation, and *Halifax Herbal Remedies* did echo a long remembered aroma, evocative and appealing. Unless, of course, she was preparing seaweed in the back workroom.

She changed into her workaday skirt and blouse and checked her stock. Once Colette returned with the honey they shared a light lunch. Elise was delighted that Colette, already well versed in preparing many of the remedies, loved the art as much as did she. She certainly had the feel for it and even at thirteen she appreciated the need to keep trade secrets. Colette too changed into her everyday clothes and donned her white apron. She disappeared into the workroom and set about grinding dried St John's Wort and lemon balm into a paste.

Elise smiled to hear Colette's sweet voice singing a popular song as she worked. Behind the shop counter she made a note to stock up on slippery elm elixir. Dinner was somewhat later than planned but they enjoyed a walk towards Pleasant Point in the fresh warmth of the early evening air. The song of the sea was part of her life once more.

CHAPTER 35

By the time Colette had turned sixteen she was more than capable of taking care of the shop, and the customers inevitably fell for her charm. This left Elise free to spend more time experimenting in the workroom and selecting the choicest herbs; the side of the business she loved most.

On a balmy afternoon in spring, Elise, on her way home from her allotment carrying a basket of fresh-picked lemon balm, stopped to look about her. The trees were in bud, yellow crocuses nodded under the soft rain that washed the frost from the ground, the highways were mud-bound but at least passable, the harbour and wharfs bustled, the town prospered and so too did her shop. Life for her and her loved ones sparked like the sun on the sea. *You've become smug my girl*, she warned herself with a smile.

The shop bell welcomed her as she opened the door. Inside, Colette was tidying up in readiness for the end of the trading day. The sight of her daughter broadened that smile. Before her stood a young version of herself, only more graceful and more confident than she had ever been at that age. As Elise took off her coat and bonnet she asked if Abby had finished cleaning upstairs.

'Yes,' said Colette, adding that Abby, their young daily maid, was now on an errand to the butcher's shop.

'Good. Is your father in? Are his visitors here yet?'

'Papa got home earlier, and two men arrived not long ago. They're upstairs.'

Automatically straightening her hair, she said, 'Oh dear. I meant to be here to greet them. Be an angel and lock up then prepare some tea while I make myself respectable, will you? Not the Bohea leaves, the Souchong. And the sugar loaf.'

In a new dove-grey cotton bodice and skirt, with her hair scooped into a fresh, lace-edged cap, Elise arrived in the parlour just after Colette had delivered the tea.

'Sweetheart,' Marcel sprung to his feet, 'let me introduce two old and dear friends of mine, Mr Richard Uniacke and Colonel Jonathan Eddy.'

Mr Uniacke, Elise guessed as she shook his hand, was a little younger than her husband. He was tall, wiry and had a brisk, dry handshake. 'My dear Madame de Forêt, how pleased I am to meet you at last.' His voice held an Irish lilt.

Colonel Eddy, perhaps twenty or so years older than Marcel, had greying hair and was shorter, rotund and ruddy-cheeked. His well-tended hand was damp, his handshake lacked firmness, but his smile was genuine and his eyes sparkled as he executed a little bow. 'I am charmed, ma'am,' Colonel Eddy drawled in an unmistakable Yankee accent. 'I've heard so much about you. I cannot think why it's taken so long for us to meet.'

'You know Marcel,' she said with a meaningful glance at her husband. 'He prefers to keep business matters close to his chest. Tea gentlemen?' She busied herself pouring the fresh brew into her best porcelain cups. She always enjoyed the excuse to show off her fine rose-patterned tea set. She, too, was wondering why she hadn't met these men before.

After a polite amount of small-talk Marcel checked his pocket watch against the mantle clock. 'If you'll excuse us, my love, we've arranged to go to Gallagher's.'

The food was congealing on the stove before Marcel and his visitors returned. She dragged Marcel out of earshot. 'You didn't say you'd be gone so long,' she whispered furiously. 'The food is spoilt.'

'But my dear, we dined at Gallagher's.' His lopsided grin confirmed what the reek of brandy already told her.

She exhaled heavily. 'Then I shall get you strong coffee.'

As she returned with a laden tray, raised voices made her pause outside the door.

'Spy. Double agent. Traitor. Do I care what term you use?' Marcel's voice exuded bravado, and drink.

The Yankee, Colonel Eddy, slurred in return, 'It's a fact that if a man has a reputation to keep up, such things could ruin him.'

'Such things,' the Irishman hissed, 'still lead to the gallows.'

'Nonsense,' the Yankee said. 'Not if you keep that big mouth of yours shut. We weren't alone in our rebellion 'gainst London rule. Y'know that.'

'Look, my friends,' Marcel placated, 'we're talking of twenty-five, thirty years ago. Nobody remembers anymore. Nobody cares.'

'When it comes to reputation, people care, believe me.' There was petulance in Colonel Eddy's words.

'De Forêt's right,' the Irishman said. 'All that business is in the past. Keep buttoned-up and there won't be a problem.'

The Yankee fumed. 'Always do. Hope you do too, Uniacke. And you, de Forêt.'

She stood frozen to the spot, the tray forgotten in her hands. Traitor? Spy? Who was a spy? Her mind couldn't make sense of what was being said, but she recognised trouble when she heard it.

'Maman, whatever is the matter?'

'Colette! Don't sneak up on a person like that.' She thrust the tray at her daughter. 'I've just remembered something important. Take this in for me.'

Evening had fallen before she was alone with Marcel and could demand an explanation. Taken aback for a moment, he regained his composure and said coolly, 'It was nothing. You must have misheard.' He picked up the *Gazette* from the parlour table and gave the inside pages his detailed attention.

She was not going to be put off by his casual dismissal. 'Come on, Marcel, you're an expert at evasion but a bad liar.'

He glanced up then frowned and put the newspaper down. 'It was something Eddy, Uniacke and I got up to ages ago. Of no interest to anyone else.'

'If that's the case I think you should tell me. Otherwise I'll worry a great deal for no reason.'

He got to his feet and paced a moment. With no outward sign of his earlier inebriation he turned to her. 'You won't like it.'

Her stomach muscles contracted. 'Try me.'

'All right.' He cleared his throat then reached for the port wine, hesitated, put the decanter down and went to stand by the fire. 'Early in '75 the American rebels recruited agents to investigate the state of local defences. I was young then and hungry for adventure. I became one of those agents, as did Eddy and Uniacke.' He ignored her gasp and continued. 'Our job involved sounding out the feelings of the Nova Scotians, estimating who they supported – crown or rebels. We unearthed a strong wish to hoist the rebel flag. A wish badly hampered by a lack of arms and ammunition.'

'You mean...?' It felt blasphemous to even say the word. Her fingers twisted unconsciously at the fringe of the silk cushion she clutched.

'If you're asking whether I became a spy for the rebels, then yes I suppose I did.'

She sat rigidly, staring at him. The fire crackled noisily in the hearth, the tick of the clock filled the room, rain started to tap against the windowpane. Could this treacherous stranger be her husband?

He cleared his throat. 'Later on I... um... I was employed to incite the Indians to insurgency and supply them with arms. My work took me all over, including Saint-Pierre and Arichat. In the end the Mi'kmaq had second thoughts. Anyway, by then the moment had passed. Things quietened down hereabouts so I did more work for the Robin brothers instead.'

'And what of this Colonel Eddy? And Mr Uniacke?'

'Such a long time ago. Such a different world.'

The rain had become a loud drumming. She got up and tugged the drapes against the black night. She wished she could do the same to her mind.

'I don't blame you for being angry, but—'

She spun round to face him. 'Angry! I'm a British citizen. You betrayed my country. Of course I'm angry!'

'But I'm not British. I had no real allegiance other than Acadian, and maybe Mi'kmaq. At that time – Yankee, British, French – it mattered little to me. In any case, I soon redressed the balance.'

'What do you mean?'

He ran his hand through his hair and sat at the table. 'By the winter of '76 there were harsh trade restrictions. Vessels lay idle. I needed to find a new source of revenue. An officer in the Royal Navy approached me.

He asked if I could get together some pilots with a sound knowledge of the coast thereabouts, and a few good sailors. He wanted me to help out with coastal expeditions to supply the king's navy with provisions.'

'So you swapped sides?'

'Let's say we agreed terms and I got together what they wanted.'

The conversation she'd overheard earlier started to fall into place. 'You were, by your own admission, a double agent. Isn't spying a hanging offence?'

He looked away but said nothing. Unable to be still a moment longer she went to the sideboard and helped herself to a glass of wine. The decanter rattled against the glass as she tried to make sense of what he told her. She remembered how he'd teased her whenever she'd asked what business he was about. He joked that being a man of mystery gave him an edge on any rivals he might have to her affections. At other times he insisted that his business was too boring to discuss. And now she remembered: didn't he and Charles Robin have secret meetings? And didn't her trip with Marcel to Île de la Sainte-Famille involve some papers for Mr Robin? Thinking of that magical day made her feel used. Her anger grew. Yet, it hadn't been like that, had it? She sunk onto a chair by the door. 'And Île de la Sainte-Famille?' she asked.

'Some negotiations to secure a trade deal with the United States. Nothing bad. Sensitive, yes. Secret, yes. But not bad.'

She didn't believe him. 'How did you supply the British navy with provisions?'

'We called on hamlets and farms and negotiated for corn, vegetables, chickens, cattle – anything we could.'

'Negotiated?'

'We tried to. But that winter was cruel. Local goods became scarce. People started hiding produce from us.'

'And?'

'I admit it, we had to be a bit hard on them sometimes.'

'Oh this is intolerable.' Unable to stomach the sight of him, she turned away.

He slammed his hand on the table, making her jump. 'Make up your mind, Elise. I'm castigated for not supporting the British then castigated for helping them. You can't have it both ways.'

'But that's exactly what you did. Had it both ways.'

After a tense silence he continued in a quieter vein. 'Then the Hessians arrived.'

'Hessians?'

'King George's infamous mercenaries, though not mercenaries in the true sense of the word because they didn't get paid. A rough lot. Conscripts, debtors, petty (and not so petty) criminals, sold to the British as fighting men by a gaggle of greedy princes of the German states.' He glanced at her, his voice full of irony. 'Most enterprising of them, don't you think?'

He gave a lopsided smile. 'I felt sorry for the poor wretches, but they were fierce as hell, with looks to chill your blood. Emaciated faces, heavy black moustaches, hard mouths, voices thick as a Cape Breton fog.'

He sat looking at her but she would not meet his gaze. Her head was full of black clouds, her heart as heavy as iron. 'Let me get this right. Way back in '75 when we first met, you were a spy for the enemies of Great Britain?'

'Yes. But you have to realise I belong to a nation previously expelled by the British. I lived in an occupied country.'

'That's a matter of opinion,' she snapped.

'It's a matter of fact, Elise. There is no black or white in this story. It depends where you happened to be born. Occupation, revolution, reclamation, transgression, aggression – it's all a matter of perspective.' He crossed the room and touched her shoulder. She flinched. 'Let's not argue, Elise.'

'The shouting earlier on? You and your fellow-conspirators. Simply drunken nonsense?'

'Exactly. We got a bit heated, that's all. Scouting like I did for the Yankee rebels was wrong, I know that now. But it didn't seem so at the time. I didn't know you then. I had no allegiances but my own.'

'And the rebellion you tried to incite? The weapons you supplied to the Mi'kmaq?'

'The rebellion failed. No weapons were involved. It all dissolved into history.'

'What about when you were an agent for Mr Robin? That's what you told me you were when I met you. Were you spying then?'

'I was an agent. No more, no less.'

'Agent, spy, what's the difference?' she shouted.

'I don't know!' he shouted back. 'I acted as agent for anyone who paid me. It was my job.'

In the silence that followed, Elise became aware of Colette's footsteps above. She thought of Marcel's mysterious trips to Chéticamp, Halifax, Arichat, Windsor, New Brunswick and God knew where else. Only a bit of business. Only another secret. Only one more untruth. And between these expeditions, he'd come and share her table. After a moment she said, 'And the marine insurance? I suppose that was a lie too.'

'No, that at least is true.'

She turned from him. 'I need to think about this. About your deception, your lies.'

He crossed the room and took up the decanter again, this time filling a glass to the brim. He drank deeply then cleared his throat. 'I must tell you something else. Something bad.'

She waited, her mind whirring. Could there be worse? The simple answer was, yes.

He said, in a voice so quiet that she could hardly make out his words, that in '75 he met an American by the name of Lieutenant Grinnell. 'We shared a few drinks, got on well enough—'

'Wait, I know that name. Are you talking about the Lieutenant Grinnell who invaded Jerseyman Island? The man who worked with that filthy pirate John Paul

339

Jones? The coward who put a knife to my face?'

'Yes.'

She dreaded what was coming. 'And?'

'And nothing… at the time. But I happened upon him again in the summer of '76. I…' His voice broke and he turned away as he continued. 'I may have casually mentioned Petit dé Grat and Jerseyman Island. About the British fishing outfits there.'

'You did what?'

'It was just talk over a few drinks.'

'We were on the brink of war, for pity's sake!'

'Grinnell said they had no interest other than to know where the British might be in that area.' He examined his empty glass before putting it on the table. 'He told me that they had no intention of doing anything.'

'So you supplied him with enough knowledge for him to invade us. I hope you were well paid.'

Marcel's hands scrubbed at his face. 'Yes.'

'What? What did you say?'

He eventually made eye contact. 'I said yes. I got paid well.'

She stood up, her wineglass falling to the floor unheeded. Seeking escape, she backed towards the door.

'Don't run from me, Elise.' His voice trembled. 'We have to talk.'

She told him they had nothing further to say to each other.

'For God's sake,' he mumbled, trying to take her hand, 'I hardly knew you when I did that deal.'

'So that's all right, is it?' She drew away from him. 'I can still remember the lieutenant boasting about buying the information that allowed him to destroy everything. I thought at the time, what kind of person could do such a despicable thing? Now I know. I married him.'

Marcel said nothing.

'Don't you understand?' She closed in on him, her fists clenched. 'You flushed out my life. You, and only you, were responsible for what happened that day and for all that happened after. For what they did to Thomas.' She wanted to hit him, to really hurt him. 'You sold our lives for a few—'

'I know that!' he roared.

'I'm going to bed,' she said quietly.

CHAPTER 36

Elise boarded the ferry to Dartmouth Cove. It was a glorious May morning and the seabirds celebrated the early spring with raucous cries. While the ferry edged across the open water she recalled the few times she'd previously undertaken this crossing from Halifax Harbour. The first occasion had been to deliver a supply of hot root and willow bark in brandy to ease the stomach of a wealthy merchant who lived in one of the splendid houses over there. She'd been paid well for that trip and had gone in the company of Colette, Sylvie and Jerome. They'd hired a pony and trap and enjoyed escaping the midsummer humidity of the town. They'd spent some time exploring a little of the fine countryside thereabouts. Jerome had been allowed to take the reins and had beamed with excitement and importance. Later the cove became an occasional place of assignation with Marcel; somewhere they could enjoy each other's company away from the tutting classes.

Now, a few weeks after Marcel had left their home in Bedford Row at her insistence, she was convinced that her love had been stretched to the point of no return, that her marriage tottered on the brink of extinction. Then Marcel wrote, begging that she meet with him. They needed to discuss their future, he said.

Did they have a future?

He asked that she take the ferry to Dartmouth Cove and he would have a pony and trap at the ready. If the weather was fine maybe they could take a trip out to the lake, away from the eyes of Halifax?

His words were full of regret and sorrow but her heart remained icy.

Now she felt the need for a dose of her own stomach remedy to quell the butterflies that flipped about inside her as she approached their rendezvous. So much hung on it. Impulsively she rose to her feet.

'Stay seated ma'am. The wind can pick up all of a sudden,' the ferryman warned.

'Sorry, I was trying to listen to the sea.' She blushed at his stare. There was no song today, just the flap of the sail and the steady slap, slap of the oars. As they approached the beach her heart, perhaps not ice after all, pounded frighteningly. She both longed and dreaded to see him.

She caught sight of the pony and buggy first then saw him pacing near the landing-stage. After the ferryman wished her a pleasant day Marcel solemnly took her hand and helped her from the boat. For a brief moment she caught his eye then she let him assist her up the shingle beach to where the pony waited. No words were exchanged, neither as he helped her into the buggy, nor when he flicked the whip above the pony's ear and they headed away from the shore. Feeling awkward and on edge, she concentrated on the road. The trot of hooves, the crunch of the wheels, the call of the gulls; these were the only sounds until she felt she had to break the stark silence between them. 'A fine pony. Yours?'

'A friend's. It's a bit long in the tooth but a gentle beast. I've packed a picnic. I hope that's all right?'

She avoided his eyes but nodded her agreement, then turned her attention to the countryside. Red spruce lined the pitted road and the undergrowth was thick with alder and rhododendron.

'Our coastline may seem a barren landscape to some,' he said, clearly attempting nonchalance as the pony made a fine pace, 'but the interior is a real Garden of Eden, don't you find? Here we are so close to home yet corn and potatoes, cabbages and beans, even the most delicate fruits, all ripen successfully.'

She smiled, finding his inept ramblings endearing.

Eventually he tried again. 'Where's Colette today?'

'When she's finished at the shop she's going to visit Sylvie and Jerome.'

'Good boy, that Jerome. He's attracting notice in his work at the bank, so Sylvie tells me. I'm really glad things have worked out well for Sylvie.'

She nodded again. Since Sylvie's recent marriage to the charming and eccentric Mr Longfellow, a retired newspaper proprietor, she and Jerome lived in Mr

344

Longfellow's grand house in Buckingham Street.

She noted his sideways glance and how he fumbled at the pony's rein. She still felt angry with him but his contrition and nervousness were winning her over, though she didn't think he deserved to know that right now. She said at last, 'I'd forgotten how good it is to get away from the hustle, the noise, the stink of Halifax.'

He smiled. 'We should do this more often.'

When they reached the shore of a small lake he reined in the pony. 'Walk?' He picked up the bulky hamper and a folded blanket and they set off along the lake's shore side by side, drawn together yet not quite touching, the gap between them more in her mind than her body. The sun played on the calm water. Dragonflies danced, birds called and fussed. The occasional plop followed by perfect rings on the lake's surface announced the presence of fish while the twangs of invisible Green Frogs imitated an orchestra of banjos. All these sensations melded with the rich earthy smells that filled the air.

He stopped and stared across the water. A few white cauliflower clouds sat in the dense blue of the sky. Two grey herons, unfazed by the presence of these quiet intruders, stood sentinel at the water's edge.

'What are you thinking?' she asked.

'That other picnic. On Île de la Sainte-Famille,' he admitted with a shrug. 'Our Holy Family Island. That day in June so long ago. The day that we made our darling Colette.'

She was irritated by his reminder of her previous naïvety. 'That day in June when I allowed my longing for you to overcome my good sense. When you were most likely on one or another of your secret missions. I suppose I was a mere diversion, a side-line to your important business?'

'Yes, I had business, but you knew that. And no, you were never a "side-line" as you put it.'

'I was a fool.' The pain in her throat made it hard for her to swallow.

'You don't mean that.'

'Don't I?'

He stood looking down at the grass. After a moment he grasped her hand. 'Come on, I've a bottle of wine and quite a spread in this hamper.'

She watched, grateful for the distraction as he unfolded the rug. Once they were settled comfortably he produced a meat pie, a wedge of cheese, a small jar of blueberry preserve, some tomatoes, apples, a loaf of pumpkin bread and a bottle of wine. He even extracted cutlery, a linen cloth and fine crystal goblets.

She was hungry and tucked in. 'This pie's good. Where did you get it?'

He grinned. 'New pie shop in Albemarle Street.' All at once he drew in a sharp breath.

'What?' She froze.

'Can't you hear it?'

She sat bolt upright and stared around. 'What? What is it?'

'Bears.'

'Sorry?'

'Bears. There was a noise just then and I thought of bears. One bear in particular. A bear that nearly had you for its supper and left you sobbing beautifully onto my manly chest.'

'You'll never let me forget that, will you?' She threw a piecrust in his direction, laughing despite herself. The day drifted on and she began to relax as they concentrated on the carefully chosen fare.

Picking up a small knife and a choice apple, he expertly produced a single thread of red peel. 'Is Colette well?'

'Missing you.'

'I miss her, too.'

As she ate the proffered apple he shook their emptied glasses and bottle onto the grass and packed them back into the hamper. 'How's that new remedy of hers coming along? The Echinacea.'

'So far her customers are reporting back extremely favourably.'

'Do I detect the deadly sin of pride?' he teased.

'You do. Clever, isn't she?'

'Like her mother.'

She glanced at him through a prism of tears. 'And her father.'

He swallowed. 'My dear love, I don't blame you for how you feel but what happened is in the past. I realise it impacted on your life and caused you great pain, but I couldn't have known that at the time. Please, can't we put it aside?'

'I want to, but… how?'

His answer was a kiss – a kiss that held all the love they shared; the same love that now battled with her cautious self. Was this the answer? Did this resolve their differences? Could she really forgive him? His breathing became heavier and she chose to ignore her mental conflict, letting her breath match his. He placed his hand on her back, drawing her down onto the rug. She returned his kisses again and again. The blood hammered through her veins and reached the pit of her stomach when he entered her. All rational thought evaporated as he cried out her name.

Later, lying beside him, she became aware of the soft lap of the water, the rustle of branches, the call of a cuckoo and the gradual slowing of her pulse. When she turned to him she saw his silent tears. 'Oh my love,' she murmured, as she drew his head to her bosom and stroked his hair.

The sun, past its zenith, had barely begun its slow descent into the horizon and the last ferry didn't leave till five. Still a few hours left. He fed her titbits of maple cookies until she begged for mercy and the salvation of her waistline.

'There is one thing.' She sat up with resolve. 'Those two men – the Yankee and the Irishman. Please, tell me you won't see them again.'

He looked crestfallen. 'But they're old buddies.'

'They remind me of your past; of all those bad things. It must be the same for you. Surely what you have now, what *we* have, is enough?'

He paused then breathed a self-pitying sigh. 'You're right. And there's always the insurance business. You've no idea how exciting that can get.' He ducked but not in time to prevent her from ramming his hat down hard on his head.

'I love you Marcel de Forêt.'

'Please can I come home now?'

CHAPTER 37

'Maman, guess what's happened?'

'Colette, a young lady does not barge in and upset her mother's busy shop.'

'Sorry Maman. I was so excited I forgot myself. Sorry Mrs Abbott, Mrs Robinson.'

The customers smiled.

'Madame de Forêt, how can you say your lovely daughter is not a young lady?' Mrs Abbott chirped up. 'Why, look at her. Two ounces of your sarsaparilla mixture if you please. Mr Abbott has a most tiresome cough.'

'It's the season for coughs,' agreed Elise. 'Colette, please stop jumping from foot to foot and serve Mrs Robinson.'

Colette supplied Mrs Robinson with a wrap of the dried chamomile she was so fond of making into tea, and a small glass bottle of the ever-popular elixir of echinacea. The cruelty of the March winds and the ensuing colds and snuffles meant that the supply of echinacea was often at risk of running out.

'I believe your kind parents gave you a big reception at the Assembly Rooms for your coming-of-age.'

'They did indeed, Mrs Robinson. I had a wonderful time. Will there be anything else?'

Eventually the customers left.

'Colette, what's got into you? I think you must have swallowed a pound of jumping beans, or maybe you need a good dousing of our flea remedy?'

'Maman!'

'Then calm down and tell me what the matter is.'

'I've met a young man.'

Elise stopped gathering up clay pots and looked at her daughter. 'Indeed?'

'Not in that way!' A hot blush spread to the roots of Colette's hair before she casually said, 'I've asked him to call. I knew you'd want to meet him.'

'Colette, that's most forward of you. You spoke with him? What young man is this?'

'Wait till I tell you.'

'I wish you would. You're startling me.'

'His name is Alain Brehaut and—'

'Brehaut!' Elise interrupted. 'Well I never. That's a real Guernsey name.'

'Maman, stop talking and listen.' She took the pile of pots from Elise and placed them back on the counter. 'He *is* from Guernsey. He was born there.'

'Is that so? We don't see many Guernseymen here. How did you meet him? Does he live in Halifax?'

'I met him through Jerome. And yes, Mr Brehaut

does now live here. He lodges near the harbour in Water Street.'

'But what's this Guernseyman doing here?'

'He came over as an indentured blacksmith. You'll never guess who he worked for.'

'Why don't you tell me?'

'Robin and Company.'

'He worked for the Robins? Are you sure?'

'That's what he told me, but why don't you invite him to dinner then you can ask him yourself?'

Elise frowned and stood thinking for a moment. To gain time she picked up a dusting cloth and applied it to the countertop with vigour. A blacksmith? Who knew what sort of boy this was? She was reluctant to invite a stranger into her home. Yet, how fine it would be to chat to a Guernseyman, especially one with relatively recent knowledge of Guernsey and Isle Madame. She turned to Colette. 'Is he presentable, this Mr Brehaut?'

Colette's face again flushed. 'I don't know. I haven't given it a moment's consideration. But if you're asking will he know how to use a knife and fork and will he get drunk, then I'm sure the answers are yes and no in that order.'

'Then we'd better invite this Guernseyman of yours so he can tell us all his news from home and all the goings-on from Mr Robin's company.'

'Maman! He is not *my* Guernseyman.'

A message was sent and when Alain Brehaut arrived for dinner later that week Elise noted his cleft chin, fine clean-shaven cheekbones, chiselled nose and expressive mouth. It took her only moments to see how handsome he was. He appeared to be in his mid-twenties and was tall for a Guernseyman. His eyes were the same sandstone-brown as his hair, his clothes hugged his broad shoulders, his scrubbed hands were those of a working man. Fresh washed hair curled to the collar of his old yet well brushed coat. He wore a clean but inexpertly pressed shirt. In short, he was extremely presentable. No wonder Colette was a little overwhelmed.

Marcel joined them and after pleasantries they all sat at the dining table. Once settled Elise said, 'My daughter tells me you're a blacksmith by trade.'

'That's right. I work for John Makin at his forge near the harbour. Do you know it?'

Elise did not, but Marcel looked up from carving the steaming beef joint and said, 'I know the one. Between the rope-makers and the livery stables.'

'Maman is dying to have news of Guernsey.' Colette offered Mr Brehaut some bread.

He smiled and took a white crusty roll. 'These look good.'

Colette blushed. 'I made them this morning.'

'Colette,' Marcel cut in, 'pass Mr Brehaut this plate.'

Alain Brehaut turned to Elise as she handed him the tureen of carrots. 'Do you have family at home?' he asked her.

'Three sisters, one brother surviving. I lose count of

how many nieces and nephews, even great nieces and nephews. Sadly, since my mother passed away we don't correspond so often.'

Plates were filled and the gravy boat did the rounds before Mr Brehaut said, 'You'll know, perhaps, that the toffs now live on the outskirts of St Peter Port? Got too smelly for them near the harbour so they upped sticks and built their mansions above the town. High Street and Le Pollet are now left to the shopkeepers and artisans.'

'I knew the trend went that way. And are they still enlarging St Peter Port by hacking their way through the granite cliff at the back of town?'

They talked much of Guernsey and Elise gleaned what she could from Mr Brehaut's memories of her former home.

'But, tell me, when did you leave home?' she asked. 'I couldn't help noticing that you retain a strong hint of Guernsey patois in your speech. It's so evocative. I haven't heard that accent for I can't remember how long.'

'I left in 1794. I was twelve.'

A quick calculation told her that, as she'd guessed, he was in his mid-twenties.

'But that's so young,' Colette said. 'How brave for a boy to come all this way alone.'

'I don't know about brave. A youngest son without prospects, more like. I didn't fancy a life at sea so when I got the chance to come here as an indentured apprentice I jumped at it.'

'Do you have fond memories of Guernsey?' Colette asked. 'Maman is always telling us how beautiful it is.'

'Yes, it's lovely. I remember our farm clearly though I never had much to do with life outside my parish of Torteval. My mother died when I was six but we were always a busy, crowded home. My sisters took over the household duties and dairy work, chickens and the like. My brothers and I had our farm chores. I'd fish when I could, and poach conies for the pot. I remember getting into a great scrape over those conies.' He gave a small laugh, then added, 'The fur made good mittens.'

His plate now empty, Mr Brehaut laid down his knife and fork. 'Madam de Forêt that dinner was a real treat. Thank you. I can't remember the last time I had such a feast.'

After enjoying preserved plums covered in rich yellow cream – not, Elise insisted, as thick and yellow as the cream from Guernsey cows (and Mr Brehaut could attest to that) – they retired to the parlour for coffee. Elise saw Mr Brehaut's interest in the spinet that stood in the corner of the room. 'You play?' she asked.

'I have a guitar. It's in a rather shabby state and I'm self-taught, but I enjoy it.'

The fire had burned down and Marcel fed it with logs. He turned to Mr Brehaut. 'I don't think I've heard of a guitar.'

'I have,' Colette said. 'My music master showed me one. It's like a lute with strings you pluck with the fingers of one hand while the other hand changes the note. It makes a pretty sound.'

'I like it because I can sing at the same time.'

'You must play for us some day,' Elise said. 'As for myself, I'm most unmusical. It's Colette who plays the spinet.'

As they drank their coffee, Elise spoke a little of her own experiences of Jerseyman Island, before asking him about being an apprentice. She was enjoying this sharing of memories and hadn't realised how much she'd missed it till now.

'When my father signed me on,' Alain Brehaut continued, 'I went to Arichat – that's where the fishery is these days. There I worked at the forge under a Jerseyman.'

'What was involved in learning to be a blacksmith?' Colette asked.

'Like many young indentured apprentices, I was signed up for a term of six years.'

'Six years? That's a long time for a young boy so far from home,' Colette cried.

'I was released from my indenture when I reached eighteen. Now I have a valuable trade and can earn my way in the world. And I learned a fair hand, as well as how to calculate weights and measurements. But the company's a harsh one and no mistake.'

Elise poured their guest another coffee as he told them something of the life he led. 'It was tough, right enough, when I had to rise at five each morning. After prayers, off we went to our various jobs, a motley crew of fledgling clerks, coopers, a carpenter and me – the would-be smithy.'

'Did you like the work?' Colette asked.

'It suited me. Mind, you should have seen my blisters those first months. And my muscles ached so badly. How I envied the clerks at first. But it was a good life and after I repaid my indenture I stayed on for another three years. By then I'd saved enough to make my own way in the world.'

Marcel began looking pointedly at the mantle clock, checking it with his pocket watch.

Alain Brehaut, taking the hint, jumped to his feet. 'But for heaven's sake, is that the time? I've kept you good people so late.'

'I fear it is we who have kept you. We've been enthralled with your stories.' Elise got to her feet. 'You must come again and tell us more, mustn't he Marcel?'

Marcel nodded. Elise knew that nod – polite but lacking enthusiasm. As Marcel saw the young Guernseyman to the door, his protective, fatherly reservations shone bright enough to light the room.

CHAPTER 38

Alain Brehaut became a regular visitor to the house in Bedford Row that summer and as the somnolence of the season took its hold, the young man often accompanied Colette and Elise (or, as it seemed to Elise, it was she who accompanied them) when they enjoyed their after-dinner strolls to Pleasant Point and back. Sometimes Marcel hired a pony and trap and Alain joined the family on outings into the fertile sleepiness of the countryside or along the coast as it meandered from the busy harbour.

Marcel began to warm to Alain, but still insisted that Colette was too young to be courted. Was twenty-one too young to fall in love, she wondered? Who was she to say? When she saw how besotted Colette and Alain were with each other she reflected on the bitter-sweetness of young love; on how it filled the world with unbearable longing and self-doubt, yet at the same time made you feel invincible.

After only fourteen months the latest treaty halting the conflict between England and Bonaparte's France had come to a not unexpected end. Halifax was again swamped in chaos, the town all but given over to the Royal Navy. After dark the streets became more unsafe than ever for any self-respecting citizen. His Majesty's navy was in part populated by convicts who ran riot, assaulted women and even committed murder, apparently with impunity. Worse still was the presence of the press gangs. Law abiding fishermen were taken from their own vessels, merchant ships were robbed of their crewmen, coasters were afraid to come to town.

Marcel was furious. 'They've reached new heights of impudence. Townsmen are arming themselves against the navy, and who can blame them?'

'Thank the Lord you're too old and Colette's not a lad,' Elise said. 'Poor Mrs Kent down the road lost her husband to a press gang last month, and her expecting their second child. I feel wretched for her.'

'My dear, you do what you can with your food parcels. The council granted a warrant to the admiral on the understanding that impressment only applied to vagabonds,' Marcel said. 'All fine and good, but how many vagabonds do you see about when the press gangs swoop?

'Vagabonds know full well which backstreet crevice to disappear into. It's the law-abiding men and boys who are pressed.' She put a hand on Marcel's arm, seeking the assurance of his presence. 'Oh, Marcel, I fear for Alain. Colette and I constantly warn him to have his wits about him at all times.'

'That he should. Life aboard a naval ship is a short and terrible thing.'

During this period of urban unrest Marcel suggested they purchase a handsome house that had caught his eye in Barrington Street. It was a most attractive dwelling. The rooms above Elise's shop could provide useful extra storage or maybe be rented out to a respectable family. Barrington Street itself was impressive, boasting as it did the presence of St Paul's Church and Government House, and all the gardens were extensive. Marcel had a valid point; with the town in such turmoil it was preferable to live in a better quarter. And Elise was not so tied to the shop now that she employed an apprentice. Young Davie Birch was a reliable lad coming on fifteen and keen to learn. In a year or two he would make a good assistant. For all that, if they moved she would miss her present home in many ways; the first real home she'd had since leaving Guernsey. Indeed, there was plenty to consider. Once the heat of the day had abated she intended to do just that whilst she harvested more pennyroyal.

***

Soon after Colette turned twenty-two, much to Elise's delight and with Marcel's reticent permission, she and Alain became betrothed. Happily for the celebrations, the harsh winter gave way to an early spring that took the town by surprise. Although snow and ice still clung to the shadows and gardens, the streets cleared and the weak sun was greeted with hungry appreciation. As Elise pointed out to Marcel, now that Colette was twenty-two, he could no longer complain that she was too young. She knew he struggled with the idea of losing his daughter, but he was a fair man and would come round to the idea in his own time. They held the party in their magnificent new house in Barrington Street. She had immediately loved the house and took great pride in furnishing it to her satisfaction. To be prosperous was a wonderful thing.

She continued to oversee the shop accounts, run the household and manage the allotment and garden, but these days her gardener did the hard work. Her hands had begun to look almost respectable, or as respectable as they ever would. As for the shop, Colette, with the assistance of Davie Birch, prepared the remedies and served the customers. Elise now considered herself to be a lady of retirement with all the fun and none of the mundane chores of life – a good state to be in.

At least it was until, after many years of blessed absence, the purple-black ravens once again invade her nights, bringing a faceless, unspeakable evil. They force her from the light into the shadows.

Soulless eyes. Vile worms. Putrefaction. Stench. She gags. Is helpless, defiled, trapped. They gloat. Smother her with a hate greater than any she's known. Kra kra kra.

After one such black night she went downstairs to

make a cup of camomile tea and wait for her heart and mind to quieten. The spring morning was dark and cold. It was as though winter had returned and the whine of a rain-heavy wind formed a backdrop to the silent house. Deep in thoughts of ravens, she cried out when the door to the kitchen leapt open and a flood of lamplight scattered the gloom.

'Marcel! You scared me half to death.'

'Sorry. You all right?' He sat by her side at the table and laid a hand on hers. 'Bad dream?'

'Mmm. Couldn't sleep. Sorry, did I wake you? Cup of tea? There's some in the pot.'

'I was already awake. My mind won't stop running over the new insurance company. Such a big step, competing with the established British companies.'

She busied herself with the teapot. 'Have you set a date to go public yet?'

'We make the official announcement in April, so there'll be no going back after that.'

'The Halifax Fire Insurance Company. That sounds grand. I'm sure most people will prefer a local enterprise where they don't have to rely on British corporations. You'll have them queuing at the door.'

'I hope so.' He sipped his tea. 'My major concern is all this talk of unrest between the United States and Upper Canada and how it might affect the new business.'

'It's hard to say what'll happen, don't you think? It seems to me that most Americans believe that Canada should've been subjugated during the rebellion and become part of the United States at that time.'

'Thank goodness that didn't happen,' he said.

'Always wars or talk of wars,' she moaned. 'Pity about Admiral Nelson. And still the French conflict rages on.'

'It's a tough truth, but it's war that gives Halifax its prosperity.'

Elise got to her feet and placed a hand on Marcel's shoulder. 'And it's the threat of war that will alert folk to the services offered by The Halifax Fire Insurance Company. Things are going to work out fine, you'll see.'

CHAPTER 39

That May, Elise began to feel that she was being watched. The rain had remained persistent for weeks and her folding waxed umbrella along with the heavy showers meant that the impression of someone hovering nearby was only vague, an intuition. Perhaps it was just an echo of disquiet brought about by her nightmares? Yet her skin crawled.

Then she saw him.

Closing the drapes against the growing darkness one evening she'd hesitated, trying to judge the weather. The glow of a pipe caught her attention. The clouds parted and the grey light disclosed a shadowy figure hunched in the gloom. For a moment, seeing that red glow set in a dark silhouette, she thought it was the raven. She gasped, drew back before nerving herself to peer round the curtain's edge. The shady figure, if indeed a shady figure ever existed, had disappeared.

In the shop the following day, as she inspected the order book she casually asked Colette if by any chance she'd noticed any loitering stranger.

'No. Why do you ask?'

She parried the question and returned to her bookwork. She must have imagined it. By the end of the month she convinced herself she was mistaken and she relaxed.

In early June she paid a visit to Sylvie. Since Mr Longfellow's sad death the winter before, Elise made a point of dropping in on her friend at least once a week. That evening they enjoyed a good gossip and Elise was relieved that Sylvie was in better spirits than previously. As she hurried homewards, windows spilled their light onto the pavement. She had allowed herself to be taken by surprise with the arrival of dusk. How unwise she'd been to let time slip by; no self-respecting woman wanted to be out alone after dark. Still, it wasn't far. At the corner of Duke Street and Barrington there was a scuffle. She stopped, held her breath, listened. A dog, some sort of rangy black mongrel, ran past. Feeling foolish, she relaxed. In a flash she was slammed face first against a wall, the breath knocked from her. Red terror flooded her mind.

'Stay still, silly bitch, or I'll hurt you.'

Was he after money? Please God nothing more. She kept as still as her trembling legs allowed.

'Better.' Using the weight of his body, the man pinned her tight to the wall. 'Not a sound or it'll be your last.' His breath stroked her cheek.

Her assailant released his pressure and in one sharp movement turned her to face him. A miasma of stale tobacco and rankness hit her. She couldn't make out the face beneath the greasy broad-brimmed hat but when he pulled the hat off she cried out. Her heart jolted then seemed to stop. She could not breathe and then her breath came in a ragged gasp.

'So, you know me.'

'Thomas?'

As thin, haggard and old-looking as he was, she couldn't have failed to recognise his battered face, his blind eye, that limp arm. She peered at him through the waning light and, despite the filth of unkind years, she thought she could distinguish the shadow of the man she had wed. For a split second she saw the once sparkling blue of his eyes, the soft brown of his hair, and the shy, dear smile that used to play on his lips. But the moment was gone almost before it flashed into her mind.

'But you died. You died in the water.' Even to her own ears her voice sounded thin and unsteady. Fear paralysed her wits and she could make no sense of what was happening.

'Alas for you, I did not.' He leaned so close that the reek of him threatened to overwhelm her. She forced down the bile in her throat and made herself look at his face.

In the deepening dusk the state of him repulsed her: his filthy old clothes, straggling greasy hair receding to a deep M, his mean tight face with days of beard growth. She didn't bother to hide her revulsion. Should she have felt pity? If so, she found none in her heart.

366

'This way.' He shoved her round the corner into the shadows of Duke Street.

She didn't know what to say. What to think. 'Thomas, is it you? Is it you alive?'

'I'm no ghost, me, if that's what you mean.'

'But where have you been? What have you been doing? All this time. Twenty-five years!'

'Twenty-seven, I think you'll find.' He stuffed the hat into his pocket. 'Been having adventures, that's what. Better 'n being stuck with you and your nagging ways. My useless arm never got in the way of what I wanted. I learned to cope without it. Done all sorts, me.' He threw her a defiant look, waiting for… what? Admiration? God forbid.

Then he added, 'After a bit of this and that I got a job on a fox farm.'

'You killed foxes?'

Looking ridiculously pleased with himself he nodded. 'Course, you couldn't shoot 'em. The pelts, you see. So I'd poison them. How those vixen screamed.' A smile flickered across his face as though the memory amused him. 'The pelts were shipped all the way to London. I was going to be a wealthy man, maybe go home to Guernsey. Maybe take you back with me, if you asked nicely enough. You an' me – rich and fancy, landing at St Peter Port, your folks and mine in awe of us.' His face changed abruptly as he added, 'Anyhows, foxes didn't suit me so I moved on.'

'You really thought you could turn up here and I'd

go back to Guernsey with you?'

His grip tightened. 'Be nice to me,' he muttered, then added cheerfully, 'Anyways, got me a passage to Boston. Now that's a place. Bigger 'n I ever imagined a town could be. Brick built houses so grand they took your breath away. Best of all, the place was full of well-to-do people who didn't deserve all that money. Course, it was no trouble to relieve them of some of it. Ever noticed how toffs can be so easily fooled?'

'But you never used to be a bad person, Thomas.'

'When bad things happen to a man how else is he supposed to survive? And wasn't I entitled to have my fun? Believe me, the whores of Boston clambered to take my money off me, any service I fancied. Sometimes I'd pretend they were you.' He looked hard into her face and added, 'You think I wasn't up to it?'

She said nothing.

'You do, don't you? Well, I was. It was you and your self-righteous frigid ways what castrated me.'

By now he was stabbing viciously at her chest with his finger. She stared at him. He was disgusting but she refused to react. Did he actually imagine she was impressed by his goings-on?

He laughed harshly, then said, 'Course, Boston jail ain't no picnic but things got better in New York. What a time I had of it. Drank, gambled and whored my way through a fortune. That's till the abolitionists started throwing their weight around, making things difficult for a man who wanted to earn a dishonest crust. So, it was time to move on. Still that's the way it goes, eh?'

'You really did sink low, didn't you?'

'Oh, you'd be surprised at how low a man can sink, dainty lady. And don't you set yourself above me. You and your bastard are no better 'n me.'

She chose to ignore the insult and desperately tried to reason with him. 'Thomas, it's getting dark. Why don't you let me go? This could get you into real trouble but I won't say anything to anyone, so you can leave Halifax a free man.'

'I ain't done with you yet, madam.'

He'd loosened his grip on her arm and she pulled away, but she'd forgotten about the dog. It shuffled forward, snarled, slavered, looked at Thomas, as though asking permission to bring her down.

'Thomas!'

He shoved the animal back with the toe of his shabby boot, then said, almost conversationally, 'I got King while I was bootlegging across the St Lawrence River. He and I see eye to eye. He likes a bit of rough, too, don't you King?'

The dog whined and gazed at its master with adoration.

'Some shit double-crossed me,' Thomas said after a moment. 'So when the American troops took me and gave me two years' hard labour, it cost me most of what I'd got to bribe my way out. I made the traitor pay for that, mark my words.' His lip curled and he glanced in her direction as though to assess her reaction. She concentrated on retaining a bland expression. 'Still, it all worked out for the best, 'cos that's how I ended up here. I couldn't believe my luck when I found out my wife was living here like a duchess.'

'But why did you pretend to drown?' Burning tears of shock, anger, bewilderment, escaped down her face. She half expected the raven to appear and *kra* with delight at this living nightmare.

'I never pretended to drown. Not my fault if that's what you thought. I just left, that's all. Went away when you stopped loving me.'

'But I never—'

'Shut your face. I'm saying how it was. I'd no plan. Wanted to get away from you, that was all. I saw you with the Acadian. Close and cosy. Ignoring me. How d'you think I felt. That bastard pretended to be my friend just so's he could have my wife. You thought I was dead and you were glad of it.'

'That's not how it was. Back then there was only you. Even when you scorned me and turned from me it was only ever you.'

His grip tightened until her arm throbbed. 'I may only have one eye, but I saw clear enough how things were. So I drank a skinful. Took a boat. Kept going till I hit a rock. That sobered me up a bit.' He sniggered, hawked with a horrible rattle, spat. 'Got rid of that fisherman's sweater you made for me. Thought, if I'm not a fisherman anymore, don't need that. Then thought, if I'm not a fisherman anymore, what am I? Decided to leave it all behind. Specially you.'

To her astonishment a tear trickled down his raddled cheek. As he angrily smeared it away, she took her chance, kicked out at him and twisted from his grasp. She'd taken but one step before the mongrel sprang. It showed its teeth in a drooling snarl. She screamed.

'Be still,' Thomas ordered the dog. 'And you madam, you be still an' all, or King here will have the throat out of you.'

'You wouldn't.' Her words were defiant, but she couldn't keep the tremor from her voice.

'You'd better believe me Madame de Forêt. Oh yes, I know you got what you wanted. I saw that fancy shop of yours, I've been asking round.'

'You were dead. I had the right.'

'Bit of a shock then, now your real husband's back.' Her stomach twisted; his face held such hate. 'That's right. You and de Forêt are adulterers and bigamists. Wonder if they'll let you share a cell?'

'Don't be ridiculous. We did no wrong. Marcel is my husband.' All the same, a small voice in her head wondered if there was any truth in his words.

'And then there's the girl to think about.'

'What?'

'Your bastard daughter. How's she going to take all this, what with her marriage plans and all?' She flinched. He stepped back, looked her up and down. 'See, there's lots I know.'

Taking her by surprise, his hand yanked aside her

coat and he squeezed her breast viciously as he leaned his whole weight against her. A scream rose in her throat but she refused to give vent to her disgust even when he tried to nuzzle her neck. He lunged his wet lips at her mouth. All she could do was turn her face aside. It took all her willpower to remain outwardly calm as she demanded that he get off her.

'Frigid as ever, Elise? To think I once believed you to be my one true love and I yours. I've known real women since then. Mind, you've kept well, I'll say that for you. Very tasty.' His tongue left a trail of spit on her cheek and lips.

Instinct told her that panic would arouse him further and so she kept her voice even. 'If you don't get off me I'll scream and damn the consequences.'

He grinned but moved back a little. Her mind, no longer paralysed by shock, began to race. She kept her gaze steady. 'Now I know why you deserted me, why don't you tell me why you've returned?' *Keep him talking. No harm can come to you if you keep him talking.*

'Curiosity? A sudden craving to see my wife? Finding myself at a loose end? Happened to be passing? You choose.'

Could he be mad enough to think she'd go back to him? He obviously detested her. Perhaps it was revenge he had in mind. Hard to believe after all this time. Money? Did he want money? She could afford to buy him off. Judging by the state of him, his demands wouldn't be too high. 'How much?' she said.

'That might have been what I wanted first off. Now I want more.'

'More?'

'You.'

She stared at him. 'What?'

'You are legally my wife.'

'You are legally dead.'

He nodded towards St Paul's. 'Not in the eyes of the church. Nor the law. You're still mine, I checked. I've only to contact the crown prosecutor and all this will blow up in your face.'

'What are you saying?' This could not be true. It could not.

'It's your bad luck that fate cast me up in Halifax, but here I am and that's my good luck. You've done nice for yourself and I've got rights, me. What you have is mine. That's the law. Anyways, you owe me, you whore.'

She opened her mouth to speak. His slap made her ears hum, her eyes water.

She lost the strength to argue with him and scanned the streets hoping for salvation. She jumped as he snapped his fingers. The dog edged closer, never taking its eyes from her. A deep rumble echoed in its chest.

'Thomas, I'll pay you money, but please go away. Leave us alone.'

'I want what he's got. I want you in my bed where you belong. I want that man gone and he can take the girl with him. I want your nice cosy life. I've decided I want to be respectable. You're mine. I have the right.'

Revulsion and hopelessness threatened to crush her. 'You can't mean that.'

'But I do.' He smirked at some sudden thought. 'And to prove it I'll have you here and now. A reminder of what's mine by rights. And a sample of the delights to come. Who'd blame me?'

She was transfixed with fright and disgust as he lifted her skirt bit by slow bit, eking out his pleasure, and her terror. She was only too aware of the low growl of the dog awaiting permission to pounce. Thomas's rough hand pinched and prodded at her flesh, forcing itself into her body as he panted and groaned. He was going to rape her and there was nothing she could do. Her mind shut down.

'Tell you what, though.' He abruptly drew back. 'I don't mind waiting a bit longer. We'll have plenty of time for that later. No more backstreet pleasures for me. You and me in a nice big cosy bed. Lovely.' His grin was crooked. With his good eye fixed on her face he let go of her skirt. He licked at his fingers with sick relish. She closed her eyes and gagged.

'Now. You go back to that man you live with and tell him to get out of my house. If he's still around in three days' time, I'll kill him. Maybe I'll kill you all.'

'No!'

'You all right, ma'am?' The voice came from the direction of Barrington Street.

Thomas cursed and stepped away. 'Do as I say or you'll be sorry, damn you.' He spat and a wad of tobacco-slime smeared down her skirt. Then he and the dog disappeared into the shadows.

CHAPTER 40

Elise's first instinct had been to tell her husband everything, to seek solace and strength from him. But what if Marcel wasn't her husband after all? What if Thomas had been right about that? She was tortured by this thought and its implications. And she wouldn't risk Colette finding out what a monster Thomas – the man she believed to be her father and believed to be dead – had become. Her heart froze at the thought of Colette discovering her mother's disgrace and her own illegitimacy. On top of all that, worrying Marcel would benefit no one. His new business was at a delicate phase and he didn't need the distraction, neither did he need to be chasing about after Thomas, pistol in hand.

As time went by with no sign of Thomas, his appearance took on the guise of a bad dream. Thomas had surely gone back to wherever he came from. He'd decided his threats weren't going to do him any good and could even rebound on him, leaving him the one on the wrong side of the law. She had been right, she decided, to let sleeping dogs lie and to keep this from

Marcel.

Unable to bear her inaction a moment longer and with the warm bright day enticing her out of doors, she decided it was safe to recover from her "severe chill". She took a cautious walk to the allotment to speak with her gardener. This she followed with a more optimistic trip to her shop.

'Maman, what a surprise,' Colette beamed, when the shop bell announced her mother's arrival. 'How well you look.'

'I believe I am,' Elise nodded, removing her gloves. 'Now, where's Davie Birch?'

'He's making a delivery. He shouldn't be more than a half hour.'

'Why don't you take the rest of the day off? I'll watch the shop until Davie returns then I'll work in the back. Show me what needs doing. It'll be good for me to be occupied.'

That day thoughts of Thomas did not haunt her at all and, despite the lingering echoes of her recurring nightmares, the whole episode became unreal. By the time she got home roses of health had returned to her cheeks.

'Now you've recovered,' Marcel said over breakfast early the following week, 'how do you feel about accepting an invitation to dinner from Emmett Hastings and his wife? It's not far. Argyle Street. All the directors of the Halifax Fire Insurance Company are invited. We decided it's time we got to know each other socially.

What do you think?'

'What an excellent idea. Those houses on Argyle Street are grand and I'd love to see inside one. Anyway, I haven't had an excuse to parade in my finery for weeks.'

It was one of those delightfully still June evenings filled with the soft gold of the sun and the glory of birdsong. Beyond the fetid reach of the harbour the deliciously ripe aroma of late spring perfumed the air. Colette, nursing a sore throat, opted to stay at home and treat herself with her own echinacea remedy. Alain had paid a short visit earlier and now she insisted she was content to finish her book then retire to bed.

'You and me then, Madame de Forêt.' Marcel held her at arm's length. 'You look extraordinarily beautiful tonight, if I may say so.'

She felt herself blush and raised a hand to her throat. 'Blame Colette if you think I show too much of myself.'

'On the contrary. How can a mature and attractive woman show too much?'

'Colette calls this an empire-line dress.'

'It suits you.' He let a finger trace the low line of the bodice then ran his hand over the moss-green silk. He lingered at a short puff sleeve then followed a path down to the high, gold-banded waist into which she'd tucked the corners of her cream lace shawl.

'I love your hair like that, all curls and coils and feathers. You're good enough to eat. But I'd better save that until we get home. I think we might be making our excuses rather early tonight, Madame de Forêt.'

She felt her blush spread downwards until it disappeared beneath the daring neckline of her dress. 'M'sieur!' Her reproach was half-hearted, unlike the warm tingle that filled her stomach. He held her cape and fan while she drew on her long gloves. An early night might indeed be a desirable thing. After all, he was pretty dashing himself.

He made a charming bow, enabling her to admire the still-fine shape of his calves. 'What do you think of the new jacket? Does this maroon meet with your approval?'

She adjusted the wide lapels and high-standing collar and stood back to admire the effect. 'You'll do.'

'Then shall we go?'

She took his arm and they stepped into the soft night.

Emmete Hastings and his wife were good hosts and the company was genial. The décor of the house in Argyle Street impressed Elise but she thought it no better than her own; a satisfying notion. She'd met two of her fellow guests previously when she was with Marcel, and another was a regular customer at her shop. The dinner was excellent: an extravagance of plump tender chicken served with a good supply of seasonal vegetables and mashed potatoes sweetened with sugar and sherry. She barely had room for the baked apple crisp with hot gingerbread but, glad that tight bodices were no longer *à la mode*, she made a commendable effort.

As the men joined the ladies in the drawing-room Marcel approached Elise at the card-table where she played a hand of piquet with her hostess. 'Your pardon, Mrs Hastings.' He turned to Elise. 'My dear I hope you don't mind but I left some papers at home. I won't be above fifteen minutes.' His lips were a warm caress on her hand. Her eyes lingered on him appreciatively before she smiled and turned back to her card game.

It was the last time she was to see him alive.

CHAPTER 41

It was only when Elise became aware of a commotion outside that the sound of the fire bell registered. Someone said, 'That fire's close by.' She looked around for Marcel. Could he still be out? Maybe he'd become distracted by the fire. After all, fire insurance was his business, and she was proud that he'd been instrumental in forming the town's Volunteer Fire Company. The dinner guests congregated at the front door. Surely it's Barrington Street, someone suggested, and Elise joined them as they headed round the corner where flames and black smoke gathered and swelled with bitter menace.

'Stand clear,' the fireward demanded. The crowd pulled back to allow the firefighters to manoeuvre ladders, leather buckets and pumps. Two of the firefighters, sweating in their leather capes, faced each other as they pumped alternately up, down, up, down. A thin jet of water gushed into waiting buckets.

Now she saw the conflagration. 'No! Dear Lord, no!' she cried. Her house was awash with a light and heat that pulsed from within. She'd known other houses lost to the flames. Who had not? And who had not felt pity? Now she knew the indescribable shock of seeing your own home being devoured by a red and orange monster that spewed smoke and stench into the night.

And what of Colette and Marcel?

She sprang to life, shoving with elbows and fists to get through the assembled crowds. 'Let me by! Let me pass, I say.'

Colette, hunched on a chair produced from somewhere, had a blanket wrapped over her nightdress. Her dishevelled hair hung loose to her waist, her face blanched and bewildered beneath smears of black soot. Awash with relief, Elise's arms enfolded her daughter and together they sobbed their shock and disbelief. Eventually she noticed an unkempt figure sitting on the pavement with his head on his knees. 'Marcel?' The man raised his head.

'Thomas! What are you doing here? Where's Marcel?' Overcome with fear and fury she struck out at him. 'What's happened to Marcel?'

'Steady lady,' a man said. 'You don't want to be hitting this fellow. He's a hero. Saved this young woman here. Dragged her from that burning house at great risk to his self. Says he's called Thomas Galliard.'

She stared from Thomas to Colette and back again. Thomas coughed and someone produced an old trade blanket to put round his shoulders. What was his part in this dreadful thing? His presence was no coincidence. There was much she needed to ask him. Instead she turned her back on him and knelt beside Colette. 'There, baby. It's all right, you're safe now.' Her voice trembled as she crooned; a mantra chanted as much for herself as for her daughter.

With the fire at last under control the smudge-faced fireward decided, much to everyone's relief, that adjoining properties would not need to be torn down to create a fire-break.

'Likely, we're not needed tonight lads,' said a lieutenant from the garrison. His men exchanged glances and retired a little way down the road just in case, lit their pipes and settled in for a gossip and a throw of dice.

Thomas shivered. 'I thought it was you.'

She turned to where he sat on the pavement. 'What?'

'I thought the girl was you. Upstairs. Then she called out and I knew it was her so I had to save her.'

'You were in my house?'

He squirmed.

'You were in my house.'

Thick air caught at her lungs and she coughed as she surveyed the sodden, smouldering wreck of her home. Where was Marcel? She needed him. Where was he? She clung to her daughter, unheeding of the tramping feet of firefighters as they stacked away equipment and dragged ruined furniture into the street. The fireward approached them. 'That lady in the green coat, she's your neighbour, right?'

She looked up in confusion before nodding. 'Mrs

Greenway? Yes.'

'She said to get you inside her house and she'll find you a hot toddy. Medicinal like.'

Elise, Colette, Thomas, and the fireward sat in Mrs Greenway's parlour nursing hot sweetened whisky and water. Colette shivered and stared at Thomas, bewilderment on her face. Elise, unable to control her own violent trembling, uttered meaningless clichés in an attempt to comfort her daughter. At the same time, she too stared at Thomas. Thomas looked at the floor. All she could think of was Marcel. What had happened to him? Was he hurt? Her heart thumped so hard in her chest that she thought both heart and ribs would burst.

The fireward cleared his throat. 'You, mister. You pulled that young lady from the burning house?'

'I did, but… I never meant for anyone to get hurt. It was an—'

Elise jumped to her feet. 'What have you done to Marcel? Where is he, damn you?' she cried.

Thomas stared sullenly at the floor. The fireward scratched his head and took a book from his pocket. 'Report,' he muttered, as he scribbled something down.

Comings and goings from the street, the pen dipping into the ink stand then scratching on paper, the muttering of the fireward's concentration, the repetitive tick-tock of a grandmother clock, Elise pacing – all these sounds scurried about the room.

'Papa?'

Elise froze. Thomas watched Colette and a feeble

smile gathered itself on his lips.

'Papa, who's dead?'

'I ain't—'

'Yes, Colette, that person is your papa.'

Thomas glanced from Elise to Colette and back again. His eyes narrowed. 'Yeh, why not? I got no one else. But ain't so dead after all, it seems.'

Colette rose from the chair but clearly didn't know how to react to this man – this so-called father who'd supposedly died before she was born. She looked at her mother.

'Yes, Colette, this is the man we all presumed to be dead, only he wasn't.'

'But why? Where?' Colette's legs lost their strength and, waxen-faced, she sank back onto her chair, breathing hard. Elise sat by her, holding her hand. Marcel would sort things out.

The lieutenant, last seen outside with his men, entered the room. He removed his hat, scanned the room, whispered to the fireward.

'You sure?' the fireward said. He glanced at Elise, as did the lieutenant who looked away before nodding.

'The lieutenant's told me something distressing, ma'am.'

She stood up. Her hand went to her mouth and she gasped, swamped by the certainty of what had not yet been said.

'We can't be sure. A… person's been found in your house. No ma'am, you can't go there, it's not safe.'

Fuelled by fear and madness she broke free and ran outside to the half open, black-singed door of her home. A soldier barred her entrance. 'Marcel!' she screamed, as though she could undo what had been done. She stood moaning and pulling at her hair until someone guided her to where the others now stood on the pavement. Colette, supported by the lieutenant, sobbed without restraint.

'Don't take on so,' Thomas said to Elise. 'I saved this one, didn't I?' He tried to take Colette's hand.

Elise put herself between him and her daughter. 'What were you doing in my house?'

'I wanted to speak to you.'

The lieutenant turned to Thomas. 'Do I understand right? You were in this house when the fire started?'

'So what if I was? It weren't my fault. That man she lived with – it was him.'

Elise stared at this dissolute, scarred man. Marcel was dead. Dead. With a scream she lunged at him, her nails scraping furrows down his face. In the confusion she rushed back to her front door and shoved past the soldier. She staggered into her smouldering front hallway where a few bleak lanterns shed dull light on the devastation.

Black walls, black ceiling, ravaged drapes and furniture, cracked windows. She saw none of this. Nor was she aware of the suffocating smoke.

The blackened, twisted shape on the floor was all she saw.

She was in a strange bed. Colette slept in a large chair by her side. For a split second she felt comfortable, as though waking after a long illness. Then the sharp blow of reality struck. She cried out from its impact and struggled to sit up.

'Maman, no, lie back.'

'Where is this?'

'Our neighbour, Mrs Greenway, gave us use of her house for as long as we have need. She's been kind and assures me it's no imposition.'

'What is the day?'

When Colette told her, Elise thrust the bedclothes aside and stood. Dizziness threatened, but she ignored it. 'Do I have clothes?'

Colette, the pallor of her face accentuated by her tired, reddened eyes, pointed to a pile on a chest under the window. 'The fire didn't destroy everything, especially upstairs, but they smell of smoke I'm afraid.'

'No matter. But my fingers shake.'

Colette helped her. Her fingers, too, trembled as did her voice. 'Mama, Alain is downstairs. He's been waiting since first light. He wants to help.'

The world lacked focus and she didn't take in Colette's words. She needed to be with Marcel. 'Where have they taken him?'

'The surgeon took charge and the coroner will make

a report to the Chief Justice.' Colette's eyes spilled more tears. 'Mama, we need to bury him.'

'And him? What of him who did this?'

'Thomas? He's held in the jail.'

'I will go to Marcel, then him.'

'No, Mama. They won't let you.'

'They won't stop me.'

Colette proved right about the coroner. He remained sympathetic but firm. He could not allow a frail widow to experience such a heart-breaking sight.

Widow. The term slapped her in the face so hard she actually brought her hand to her cheek. Widow. It now defined what she was. It was her reality. It was the rest of her life. Her pleading and weeping merely entrenched the coroner's decision. Colette and Alain persuaded her to leave, maybe try again when she felt stronger.

Although the jail wasn't far from her home, she'd never given the building or its stout wooden door more than a passing glance. However, one was never far from justice and retribution in this town. To see a guilty man or woman in the stocks or being whipped through the streets was not unusual. Neither was it unusual to witness a public hanging, though Elise never had. The sounds of some unfortunate miscreant soldier or sailor being cruelly flogged existed as part of life and loss. Nevertheless these things made her shudder. She avoided the waterfront when mutinous seamen were hanged at the yardarm to the knell of rolling drums. She averted her eyes from the rotting bodies of the ill-fated men left dangling from the gibbet on Mauger's Beach, a warning to like-minded others. As always, life and death were close companions. Elise was nauseated by the bloodlust of her fellow citizens, both in their crimes and their punishments. Yet now she stood before the county jail, one husband dead, one facing a murder charge and the end of a rope.

The sharp-faced jailer's wife admitted her into the building, Colette and Alain close by her side. Elise insisted she would see Thomas alone and left them waiting in the front room. She followed the jailer. Once through the iron-barred door at the top of the stairs the world shrank to a small space of five doors, each with an iron grid. Three doors stood open, their cramped interiors a smudge of brown-grey staleness. Through the grid of a locked cell a thin arm stretched towards her. 'Pretty lady, got any rum? Give an old woman a sup of rum, there's a dear.'

The jailer rapped on the door with his wooden club. 'Now then, Molly,' he said, not unkindly, 'behave yourself and leave the lady alone, you hear me?'

He turned a large key in the last door and paused. 'You sure, Missus? This one's a vicious killer, y'know.'

What was she doing here? This man was a murderer. He had killed Marcel and so put an end to her own life. He had assaulted her, threatened to rape her. He was evil. She wanted to turn and run. Instead, she nodded her head and the jailer added, 'If you say so, but I ain't gonna lock you in wiv 'im. I'll be right out 'ere.' He tapped his wooden club against his palm as if to emphasise his words and his power.

She entered a small dismal rectangle of space. The barred window let in but little light. Taking up one wall was a truckle-bed roughly covered with a grubby trade blanket. Through the fog of her mind she was aware of the pungency of vinegar that partly overlaid the stench of dirt and stale sweat, poverty, slops and despair.

His voice, when it came, startled her. 'No palace, eh? Still, I've known worse, me. If you don't mind the lice you can sit on the bed.'

She backed away from him, shaking her head. Now she was here, she didn't have anything to say. Her head was empty, her mind blank. He stood in the corner by the window, his face in shadow. 'If you won't, I will.' He sat, knees to his chin, his dirty bare feet drawn up on a straw-spewed mattress. His back rested against the lime-washed wall, his gaze directed at his feet. His face bore not only the old scars, barely diminished after all these years, but fresh, red scorings. She had a vague memory of lashing out at him after... after what happened. The sour animal smell of him hit the back of her throat. This pathetic mockery of a man, once the love of her life, repulsed her. She should have brought a knife. She had an overwhelming desire to plunge one into him over and over again. To obliterate him – but not before she found out why. Only now she knew there were no answers. Just hate. And rage. And death.

'Why are you here?' he said. 'To gloat?'

Gloat? Was he mad? She stared at him.

He turned from her. 'You only wanted him because you stopped loving me.'

Why was he talking this nonsense? He'd disappeared long before she gave her love to Marcel. What did all this matter now, anyway?

He stared hard at her then slumped back. The bed creaked a protest. 'I meant to go away, y'know. But instead I went to that fancy house of yours. I don't know why. Maybe to catch a last glimpse of you. I saw lamplight in an upstairs room, but no other sign of life. Didn't know what to do, wait another day or just leave. Then I saw him arrive in a hurry and all prettied-up.'

A picture of Marcel flashed into her mind. He was so handsome in his new maroon jacket with its wide lapels and high-standing collar. His lips had gently caressed her hand. I won't be above fifteen minutes, he'd said. Then the image of a blackened corpse pierced her mind. She moaned in pain. Her hands clamped to her mouth as though to hold it back.

Thomas's voice broke through her anguish. 'I pictured him climbing the stairs,' he said. 'Going into your room, making love to you – you who belonged to me!'

He took a deep breath then went on, 'He'd left the front door ajar. Don't know what I was gonna do. I'd no plans, but I think I wanted to have a go at him, shake him out of his self-satisfied world. Make you both hurt.'

'That's one success in your life then.' The acid in her

voice made it sound alien, even to her own ears.

He stared at her, opened his mouth then shut it again. She said nothing more.

'When I sneaked in he must of heard me. I was full of rum. I stood in the hall, saw a light and there he was. He shouted out, then recognised me. I'm not hard to spot am I?' Thomas gave a harsh laugh. 'He sort of drew back, gasped, asked me what I was doing, what I wanted.'

'What did you say?'

'Rage took over. There he was, unmarked, dressed up like some gentleman, living with my wife in what should've been my house.'

'I'm not your—'

'That's what you say, but you are before God.' He ignored her protests and continued. 'Where is she?' I asked him. 'She's not here,' he said. But I knew he was lying. I'd seen that light upstairs, that flicker as someone moved against the drapes. I told him I'd come to take my wife back and he laughed. Laughed in my face. I hit him. Hard.'

Elise drew a sharp breath.

'He shouldn't of laughed. He had everything of mine, yet he laughed at me. Anyway, his mouth was bleeding and we tussled and… and he got the better of me. That's not surprising seeing as how I've only got one good arm and wasn't so well fed.'

Elise tried to blot out the pictures in her head. Her mouth was dry, her heart thumped. She waited. After a moment he said with a sneer that Marcel was a fool. 'He got all preachy and went on about giving me a few guineas to make a new life. Then the fool turned his back. He shouldn't of turned away. What was I supposed to do? Take a pat on the head and a handout, then go away, my tail between my legs like some dumb cur? I picked up something, I don't know what, and hit him hard as I could. He went down without a sound.'

I made this happen, the voice in her head shouted. *Instead of trying to spare him the worry of Thomas, I should have warned him. He should never have been taken by surprise like that. It's all my fault. My fault, God help me.*

The silent scream went on ceaselessly and her torment filled the small space between them.

'Why did you set fire to my home?'

'Accident. Wasn't supposed to happen. Lamp got knocked over. Not my fault, see?'

How dared he deny responsibility? Hatred rose within her like a fountain of blood. Her head filled with angry bees. She hadn't intended to cross to the bed and strike him, but the blow she landed on his face gave her a split-second of relief. He drew his tongue across a trickle of blood seeping from his lip.

Sickened, she turned from this man for whom the sea had once sung, and whose existence now filled her with abhorrence; an abhorrence that fuelled her with enough energy to keep breathing. Her eyes narrowed, her words were slow, deliberate. 'Go to hell.'

He caught his breath and the colour drained from his face. 'And I will, won't I?' he whispered. 'I will go to hell, me.' Before she could snap an answer back at him his bravado dissolved and a sob exploded through his thin body. Tears and snot ran down his twisted face. 'What I said before, when I... when we spoke in the street. About having adventures and a high old time. It was all lies. Yes, I did those things, sometimes dreadful things, but none of it was what I wanted. I wanted to be Thomas again. What I used to be. I wanted to be fit and strong and loved by you. What happened, I couldn't help it, none of it.'

She stared at him. Did this fiend want pity?

'They'll hang me.' He fell to his knees. 'Help me, Elise. Don't let them hang me. For the sake of what we had, help me.'

'You strangled what we had, whatever that might have been; something that died so long ago I can't even remember it. And now you've killed my future. You've killed me.' Long suppressed tears at last coursed down her cheeks.

'Elise. Don't. I'd do anything for it not to of happened. Please, tell me what I can do to make it better.'

'You can hang, Thomas Galliard. You can hang long and slow, that's what you can do. And I'll be there to watch.'

CHAPTER 42

Long before the clock at the bottom of Citadel Hill sounded three, townsfolk began to congregate around Market Place and along the route. Courting couples, shop-keepers, fathers with youngsters riding high on their shoulders. The festive scene was made all the merrier by laughing jongleurs who tossed and twirled lighted torches, bakers peddling fresh-made bread, youngsters playing catch-me. Nothing like a hanging on a summer's afternoon to bring out the crowds. After an hour or so of entertainment the throng would go home for their suppers with good appetite.

The whole thing felt unreal. One of her nightmares. The air was still and stifling. The sky sat low and heavy over the town. A black mongrel whined and sidled about, sniffing at the heels of the crowd. Elise stood alone, well to one side. A numb dread clenched her heart. *For you Marcel. I'm here for you so that maybe we can both rest in peace.*

People gave her a wide berth, some crossing themselves as though to ward off the bad luck of her.

Their whispers filtered into her brain. She kept her head down, avoided people's eyes, held a tight rein on her thoughts and emotions.

A hush fell. Then came the sound of tramping feet and the measured thud of a drum; a sound that echoed the pounding in her head. The sheriff, along with a brawny thickset man and a priest, led the pathetic procession. Four soldiers next, and between them Thomas, hands bound behind his back. The black dog whined. One of the soldiers aimed a vicious kick at the skulking animal and it cowered away.

For a moment Elise lost the ability to breathe as the truth of the situation caught in her throat. Such a long and lonely last walk. From somewhere he'd got hold of a decent pair of breeches and a good shirt. Even so, he appeared pathetically small and contemptible. How could someone formerly so fine but now so insignificant, have ruined her life, not once but twice? Each day, each night over and over, she heard Marcel's tortured screams, watched him writhe in agony, saw the blackened shape that was all that had remained of him. She didn't need the raven to conjure up these images.

Two soldiers shuffled Thomas up the gallows' steps and the sheriff read out the charges and his confession. Hearing the words, so public, so raw, so final, made her feel physically sick.

The executioner placed the noose round his neck. Despite the oppressive heat of the August sun, she shivered. Thomas, his eye wide with terror, searched the crowd. When he saw her he trembled and a weak smiled lifted one corner of his mouth before he stared down at his bare feet. Where was the man she had once loved? Certainly not on that scaffold. She closed her eyes and there beside her stood Marcel. He smiled sadly and she gasped and reached out to him. Then she heard his words. 'Madame de Forêt, I love you. I'll love you forever, and forever started a lifetime ago and continues to the edge of time.' She opened her eyes, desperately looked about her. He had gone. 'Marcel, don't leave me.'

The priest chanted a few words then the world slowed as the executioner hauled on the rope. Thomas was laboriously dragged nearly as far as the crossbar to the raucous cheers of the onlookers. His legs flailed uselessly, frantically. His futile attempts to suck at the air pleased the onlookers further. From the crowd, ribald remarks and laugher accompanied his dance of death. Elise covered her ears against the noise but remained mesmerised by the horror. The seconds and the minutes passed. Thomas's face turned purple as he kicked his life out. After what seemed like an eternity his kicking slowed then stopped. The crowd lost interest and started to drift away. But he lived still, his bulging eyes seeking her out as slowly, oh so slowly, his choking body twirled in a limp, obscene ballet. Round and round, round and round and with each circuit his eye fixed on hers.

This was hideous, yet he deserved it. He had become a monster. This was what you did to monsters. Marcel must have justice; *she* must have justice. Red fog closed over her. Then she felt the support of strong arms.

'Ma'am, you shouldn't be here.' Davie Birch, her young shop assistant, his face a blur.

'How long does it take?'

'Half hour maybe. Depends how lightweight. Do you want me to pay the executioner to end it?'

'Can you do that? Here take this. Make it end. Enough is enough.'

CHAPTER 43

They laid Marcel to rest in the churchyard. Elise planted love-in-the-mist and a wild rose bush. The inscription on his slate headstone was indelibly carved into her heart: *Marcel André de Forêt 1747 to 1809. Beloved husband of Elise, adored father to Colette. Rest with God.*

Being with him in that churchyard gave her a scrap of solace and she sat by him for hours at a time; a thread of contact that she believed kept insanity at bay. Perhaps he sensed her there? She remembered keeping company with Gran'mère in St Martin's churchyard. She remembered Baby Thomas's tiny grave on Jerseyman Island. She imagined the graves she would never know – those of her mother and father, her sisters, brother, a niece, her two nephews.

At Sylvie's insistence she and Colette had moved to Sylvie's house in Buckingham Street. Sylvie gave them shelter and a place of calm at a time when they were unable to make decisions or plans for themselves. Sylvie was adamant that since the loss of Mr Longfellow she pined for company and they were welcome to stay as long as they needed to. She was kind and unassuming and didn't expect conversation. In the evening she read to them and Elise felt free to listen or no. In any case, the distraction was welcome. Colette said she felt the same, though Colette had Alain to give her comfort, for which Elise was both grateful and, to her shame, a bit envious. Sometimes Elise could pass a whole hour, maybe longer, immersed in the perusal of her grandmother's herbal treatise or her collection of letters, all kept safe in her old valise, luckily stored in the shop. She had also saved her old journals, but these were too painful to open. Perhaps one day. So much had been lost, but not, thank God, Colette and not these few things.

Ten months after that terrible day in Market Square, Colette and Alain were married. On the eve of the wedding Elise came upon Colette weeping in her room.

'What's troubling you, dear?' She put a comforting arm around her.

Colette took out her handkerchief and dabbed at her eyes. 'Oh, Mama, I was thinking of Papa.'

Elise stiffened and Colette said, 'No, I mean Marcel. My real father. I was wishing he was here to walk me to the church.'

'How on earth did you—?'

'I've always known who my real father was – for as long as can I remember. It felt so right. But I couldn't ever say so.'

Elise had fled to Chéticamp and later to Halifax to avoid the stigma of her daughter's illegitimate birth. And now it seemed she knew after all; knew the truth of her mother's wrongdoing. 'But why didn't you say?' she asked.

'I did. To Papa. He didn't want me to speak to you of this because he thought you would feel shame.'

Open-mouthed, Elise stared at her daughter.

Colette hugged her. 'Mama, you did no wrong in my eyes. I never wanted any man other than Marcel de Forêt as my father, least of all that fiend who took him from us. I mourn Marcel with all my heart.'

Elise closed her eyes and held her daughter tight. *Marcel, forgive me. I should have trusted Colette with this precious gift of the truth.* She felt relief. No more lies. No more pretence. Marcel's daughter had known and had shared this knowledge with him. That would have made him happy, which is what mattered.

***

Colette's marriage that year brought Elise real pleasure. Alain was a good man. Still in mourning, the couple chose to have a quiet affair with a simple service. Sylvie took care of everything and Elise was pleased that young Jerome, who now lived in the township of Windsor with his new wife, had taken the trouble to come. Colette was an angel in a gown of a soft-green satin that brought out the emerald of her eyes.

For Elise, this wedding was inevitably filled with mixed emotions, carrying as it did the remembrance of her own wedding to Marcel. That day had been such a long time coming – the best day of her life. Now it was a bitter-sweet memory of love and grief, of holding and losing, of a pain still so raw and sharp that she sometimes felt she would die from it. Colette remained her mainstay, the reason she rose from her bed in the mornings.

As for Thomas, on the few occasions his ghost broke into her thoughts she felt only bitterness and saw only the enduring image of his slow painful end. She never spoke of him or his hellish death. She needed to keep that terror locked away inside herself or she would surely lose her reason.

Shortly after Colette's wedding Sylvie moved to Windsor to join Jerome and his wife. Elise had been at a loss, not knowing what to do or where to go. Barrington Street, now sold, renovated and occupied by a whiskered merchant with a large family, had never been an option. With Alain's approval, Colette suggested the three of them live above the shop in Bedford Row. The generous sum paid out by Marcel's fire insurance sat untouched in the bank. Death money.

The living arrangement worked well. Alain prospered at his blacksmithing and was talking of setting himself up in business. Elise, unable to stand her own unhappy company for long, now worked side by side with Colette in the shop downstairs. Colette ensured that her mother ate enough to stay healthy.

Elise tried to take an interest in public affairs again. She so missed the wrangles and discussions of local and world events she used to have with Marcel. They had always enjoyed pouring over the *Gazette* then spent many an evening in discussion.

These days her letters home were few and far between, exchanging as they did, morsels of news with her sister, Marie. Her little sister now a grandmother, imagine that. This made Elise a great aunt, but she felt neither great nor an aunt. Sadly, she struggled to write more than a few banal lines, finding that Guernsey, an integral part of her, had faded into a place she no longer had a meaningful connection with. She was, however, pleased to have some fresh news to share, asking Marie if she remembered a family called Brock, who'd lived in High Street, and possibly still did.

His family must be proud of him, she had written, *for he had been promoted to major-general and was a man of great importance. Recently he was appointed administrator and military commander of Upper Canada. To think that such a small island in the English Channel could produce a national hero!*

The *Halifax Gazette* covered the appointment in detail, even remarking that Brock was a Channel Islander – a Guernseyman. She enclosed a cutting in her letter. The *Gazette* stated that, as head of both civil and military affairs, Major-General Isaac Brock could more efficiently and rapidly mobilise the colony's defences.

Did the colony's defences need to be rapidly mobilised?

***

As much as Elise appreciated Colette and Alain's company, she remained mindful that the young couple needed time for themselves, so most evenings after a light supper she picked up her book and a lamp and headed for her bedroom, leaving Colette and Alain some privacy.

One bleak December night eighteen months after the wedding, Alain detained her as, book in hand, she made for her room. He said he had something he wanted to discuss. She sat back and waited. His gaze fell on her then on Colette. His hesitation caused a small knot to settle in her stomach. Something bad was coming though she couldn't guess what.

He cleared his throat. 'My dears, I'm sure you're aware that America will be declaring war on Britain and her colonies any day now.'

Colette stood up and clasped her hands. 'You cannot be sure of that.'

Elise knew the truth of his words and the situation had been worrying her for some time. She turned to Colette. 'They've been heading towards conflict for an age, poppet. You know as well as I that ever since they won that last war all those years ago, the Americans have regretted not helping themselves to the British

North American colonies. They've said so themselves enough times.'

'Your mother's right, I'm afraid.' Alain picked up the *Gazette* and waved it in the air like a banner. 'It says in here that the American Congress calls for the conquest of British Canada.'

Elise took the proffered *Gazette* and read the article aloud. The *Gazette* warned that the Twelfth Congress, ominously known as the War Hawk, claimed that Great Britain had violated America's honour once too often. These American warmongers denounced what they said was the detested impressment and violations of American neutrality on the high seas. Her mind went to Jerseyman Island. Violation! She could write an article or two on violation. She flung the *Gazette* on the table in disgust, but couldn't resist retrieving it and reading further. These War Hawks, it seemed, declared openly that conquering British North America would clear the way for American domination of the northern fur trade. Men, the article stated, had gone to war for less and it warned that armed conflict was increasingly likely.

'No!' Colette cried, her face ashen. 'This isn't possible. The *Gazette*'s rabble-rousing.'

Alain shrugged his broad, blacksmith's shoulders and a deep frown signalled his concern.

Elise wasn't worried for herself. She was fifty-eight years old and had lived a full life and known a great love, but Colette and Alain – it didn't bear thinking about. She'd never forget or forgive how the American rebels had turned her own life inside out but she wouldn't think about that. Again she tossed the newspaper aside and this time left it where it fell.

'They put fifteen stars on their flag back then,' she said bitterly. 'Now they've a mind to make it sixteen. You know as well as I do that they've had their eyes on our trading companies, our homes, our lands for years.'

Alain went to Colette and held her hands. 'It's not a one-sided animosity, my dear. Plenty of Canadians are crying out for a chance to put the American upstarts in their place. Whatever the rights and wrongs, if there's an invasion it could mean burning and pillaging, the violation of our women. The murder of us all.'

'Alain!' Colette cried out, as she pulled her hands from his clasp and clamped them to her ears.

'Is there a purpose to all this talk?' Elise didn't think that frightening Colette was necessary or helpful.

'I'm trying to be realistic.' He scrubbed his hands across his face. 'You read the *Gazette*. I'm worried for our future and I don't think we can ignore the facts any longer. Border and sea skirmishes are already going on and will get much worse come the spring.'

'What do you suggest?' Elise asked.

He paused before reaching into his pocket. 'I picked up a letter today.'

Colette looked up. 'Bad news?'

'No. But it made me think.'

'What about, dearest?'

'About us not having to go through another war.'

406

Elise was intrigued. 'Alain, why don't we all sit and you can explain.'

Once they were seated Alain held up the letter. 'This correspondence is from my mother's cousin, Jean Le Lacheur. I think I remember him slightly. He writes that he remembers me. Second Cousin Jean is now settled in the British colony of Prince Edward Island with his wife and children.'

'Prince Edward Island?' Colette said. 'That's a bit north of Nova Scotia, isn't it?'

He nodded.

'But that's only a few days' journey from here. Why didn't you say?'

'I didn't know until I got this letter. He's only just got in touch, via my father.'

'But why has he written?' Colette asked. 'What does he say?'

'He starts by saying Guernsey suffered bad times after the harsh restrictions on the sale of tobacco and spirits.' Alain adjusted the lamp by his side then studied the thick letter. 'Jean says how, with times so hard, he and a group of his neighbours and kinfolk moved to Prince Edward Island about five and a half years ago.'

'Why Prince Edward Island of all the places in this wide world?' Colette asked.

Alain turned his attention back to his letter. 'They had the opportunity to buy some prime land there at a good price.'

Colette frowned. 'I know neither good nor bad about

this place,' she said.

Elise got slowly to her feet and added a fresh log and a shovel of coal to the fire. She had a worrisome feeling as to where this conversation was leading. Was he going to take Colette away from her? Surely not.

Alain said into the silence, 'He writes that he'd always wanted to be a farmer, have his own farm.' He looked up from his letter. 'I know all too well the smallness of most Guernsey farms, and how hard they can be to get.'

Colette asked how many of them went to Prince Edward Island.

Alain ran his eyes over the letter. 'Seventy three members of eight families – men, women and children, including Cousin Jean, his wife Elizabeth and their two children.'

'A whole community,' Colette said.

'Indeed. They sailed to a place called, um, yes, here it is, Murray Harbour.' Alain read from the letter, ' *"Some stayed on there and a few, including us Le Lacheurs, settled further south at a small cove half a day's sail round Cape Bear. We were well pleased with the deal. The density and size of the forests astounded us and by our reckoning, soil that could produce such immense trees must assuredly be rich and good. In the summer we farm and fish, in the winter we fashion barrels, kegs, household utensils and the like from wood. Come spring we send our products to Charlotte Town by schooner"*. Cousin Jean writes that they all thrive and live in peace and prosperity. He describes it as *"an insignificant and lovely island over which no nation would bother to spill blood"*.'

Alain looked up from the pages in his hand, and said, 'He writes that the place is rich in energy and optimism.'

Elise sat down and stared into the flickering fire, listening to Alain's words but not wanting to hear. She thought her life empty now, but if he took away the one good thing left to her...

'But why has this cousin written to you?' Colette asked.

'He says there is still plenty of land going at a good price and that they have need of more settlers at Cape Bear and – now here's the thing – he writes that a smithy would be a most welcome addition to their community.'

There followed a long pause as they each explored their own thoughts. Elise's heart danced in her chest and her throat went dry. So, she was right. She stared at Alain. Unable to control the tremble in her voice, she said, 'Are you suggesting you might take Colette to live there?'

'I'm suggesting we all go.'

The only sound was the crackle of the fire, until she said, 'Oh no, not me.' Elise was on her feet in a moment. 'I've shuffled from place to place, from home to home too many times. This is where my Marcel is laid to rest, and where I intend to join him in time. I'm here now and I'm not going to start all over again. Not at my time of life. No. Never again.'

PART SIX

Guernsey Cove, Prince Edward Island

CHAPTER 44

Fourteen years on and Elise could still recall, with some irony, how rebellious she had been at the idea of moving from Halifax.

'This is where my Marcel is laid to rest, and where I intend to join him in time. I'm here now and I'm not going to start all over again,' she'd pronounced loud and clear. 'Not at my time of life. No. Never again.'

Yet here she was settled in this lovely cove and barely a moment's regret since she'd first arrived.

Poor Alain and poor Colette. She'd caused them such trouble. It hadn't been her intention to be awkward, to behave like a spoilt child. It was fear of change that had gripped her. Worse still had been the fear that Colette would leave her all alone in Halifax. And what if Colette had refused to go out of love for her? What if something

410

bad had come of her selfishness? How could she have lived with herself? She'd had no choice but to quell her own concerns and to cut and run.

Her first view of Prince Edward Island was on a bright day in May just weeks before the war between America and Great Britain and her colonies officially began. She knew at once that here they had found a haven of peace and beauty in a time of war.

The arrangements had proved surprisingly simple: a few letters between Alain and the unknown branch of his family, a few to the landowner who sold them one hundred and fifty acres of prime land, which they undertook to clear and plant, and all at once their futures lay in the hands of strangers, the toil of their bodies, and the courage in their hearts.

Oh, but it was devastating to leave; to sell her shop, to say goodbye to Halifax and their friends. Most of all to bid adieu to Marcel.

Meeting them at Charlotte Town on Prince Edward Island had been Cousin Jean Le Lacheur, a dear man they took to at once. That first night she'd sat for many hours at the window of her bedroom in the tavern staring at a sliver of moon, letting the cold air play on her face. As she breathed the rich sea smells and listened to the night sounds, her initial euphoria dissolved. She was a million miles from all she knew. The sky was so huge and she so small. She felt lost, alone, empty and afraid.

The four of them sailed from Charlotte Town as a lush red sun seeped into a dawn sky. She remembered the weather as being unseasonably mild, even for that time of the morning. The schooner turned south out of the wide harbour, then east towards the wakening sun. They then rounded a headland before following a shore that stretched to the north-east. Red cliffs lined the cove-dotted shoreline and the luxurious greens and browns of the forest were set against the deep blue of the sky. The mood of the previous night faded with the morning mist. Hope was a butterfly in her heart. The beautiful little bay where they were to make their home had filled her with delight. Before them stood low, russet, sloping cliffs topped with lavish green vegetation. The cove had a tranquil, inviting air about it. *It's fine here,* her heart told her.

'This place is still in want of a proper name, you know,' said Jean.

'How so?' she asked.

He told them that no one had got round to registering it. To her there was only one name this perfect little cove could be blessed with. She asked Jean if she might make a suggestion. He drew on his pipe and said slowly, 'I don't see why not, dear lady.'

That was when they all agreed that this little bay should be called Guernsey Cove. Inspired by her new home, she had taken up her neglected journal and wrote: *I am happy because I feel that I have brought a little bit of my own Guernsey with me from the other side of the ocean and planted it in this delightful spot. I feel the warm approval of dear Gran'mère, of Mère and Père –*

of all my Guernsey family.

She, Colette and Alain had so much to learn when they first arrived. A demanding, frightening and rewarding path lay before them. They hired help and toiled alongside them clearing the beech, sugar maple, yellow birch and hemlock. Back-breaking work. Their new neighbours were welcoming and full of good advice and their home rose slowly from the ashes of the forest floor. *My task*, she wrote in her journal, *is to organise the kitchen and herb gardens and tend the goat and chickens. I am in my natural element.*

One of many lessons to be learnt, Cousin Jean had announced, was how to make mussel mud fertiliser. There has been a long pause before Elise said, 'Mussel mud?'

Jean had delighted in explaining the joys of this process to them. 'You'll have seen how all our barns have manure sheds out back of 'em,' he said. 'That's for storing the vraic – the seaweed,' he'd explained. 'What we do is, we throw in the used straw from the shed and from the threshing, along with chicken manure, and mussel mud that's hauled from the mussel banks in the winter.'

If he'd noticed his listeners' apprehension he made no comment, continuing on blithely. 'You cut a hole in the ice and set a digger up over it. The sea mud is thick with the remains of rotting mussels and such like.'

Again there was a long silence as the newcomers tried to understand Jean. Their blank looks caused him to chuckle. 'The digger,' he explained, 'uses a team of horses to raise shovels full of mud and you load it onto your waiting sleigh. This material stinks like the devil but it's right good for the soil.' He'd drawn on his pipe with satisfaction. 'Can't do better, believe me.'

Colette and Alain glanced at each other wide-eyed. Elise tried hard not to flinch.

Alain broke the silence. 'Is that the manure ready?' he'd asked, an element of hope in his voice.

They were unprepared for Jean's bizarre answer.

'Not by a long shot,' he'd said. 'It's not ready till the old sow's been in there with it.'

Again they'd looked at him blankly until Alain finally asked, 'Why in heaven's name would a sow be put in with the manure?'

Jean gave another mighty chuckle followed by a good cough before he'd said, 'To mix it all up of course. Sows love to do a fine jig in mussel mud.' He'd rubbed his hands together with relish. 'Come the spring,' he added, 'out on the fields the mixture goes. A right hard-packed mass it is too.'

'Oh good,' Alain said, with a watery smile.

They had their hard times – their mussel-mud times and their bad weather times – but their chosen home had more than enough to commend it. She truly loved the clear air, the hot sunny days of liquid golds and greens, and the lavishly vivid nights when the sky was jewelled and infinite.

Marcel had, after all, accompanied them to this

lovely place, for Elise and Colette often shared their memories of him and this gave them comfort and pleasure. Elise wondered how he would have fared here. She was sure he would have relished the adventure; an adventure they should have been sharing together.

Her biggest joy was her grandchildren. First came Victor, now a strapping and able twelve year old. Then two years later came James, a bright, self-taught lobster-spearing expert. Both boys took after their father while nine-year old Louise, with her emerald eyes, wilful freckles and even more wilful hair the colour of chestnuts on an autumn day, was an adorable miniature of her mama. *I am rather inclined to spoil Louise*, she confessed to her journal. *She so reminds me of my Colette. The three of us are like the line of dancing paper dolls I cut out for Louise. It thrills me that she shows a real curiosity and a natural talent for working with remedies.*

Dear little Samuel – was there a shade of Marcel in his dark, handsome looks? – enjoyed his status as the baby of the family and was mollycoddled by each of them.

She often talked to them of Gran'père Marcel. *They will know you*, she promised him.

Here I have found peace, she wrote. *And here Colette and the children are in Alain's safe hands, and that is as it should be.*

At last she had come to terms with the purple-black raven. Twice since their arrival it had visited her, and each time its warning was clear. Because of the raven she had stopped Victor from eating poison ivy, and she had warned Louise (most severely and just in time), about staying away from the boiling kettle. Having agreed a truce with the raven, she was no longer tortured by it.

Perhaps the raven is, after all, my guardian angel, she confided to her journal.

***

One September night she awoke full of energy and decided, despite the dark, to get some fresh air. She put on her coat, lit a lantern and went outside. As was her habit when the night was overly long, she was drawn to the seashore. She had witnessed many a sunrise in her lifetime but none as spectacular as those enjoyed from their small sandy cove. Her secret pleasure.

From there she could gaze at the endless extravagance of sky; a sky pierced that night with a million pinpricks of stars. The Milky Way tracked a silver path into infinity. Moths, some tiny and some the size of Victor's fist, flirted with her lantern. The tremulous rhythm of a whip-poor-will's song broke the air. Her hair was ruffled by a gentle breeze as she sat on a large flat rock and leant against the cliff face. The lazy waves caressed the sand with a languid tickle, the fiery red of the pre-dawn sun began to seep out of the sea in an ethereal glow. How beautiful it was. Beautiful in all weathers and all conditions – but none more so than early on a September morning with the red of the sandstone alive under the rising sun's embrace. A great peace enveloped her as she sat back and watched the sun climb from the horizon. She closed her eyes. The corners of her mouth softened as she listened to the sea.

Through the early morning mist a small, grey-haired lady emerged.

'Gran'mère?' She was so happy to see her. Then she had a shock. 'I look just like you,' she told her. 'That is, you look like me. How strange.'

Gran'mère chuckled and nodded. 'Peas in a pod, beans in a jar.'

Elise laughed. 'You always made the best bean-jar in Guernsey,' she told her.

'I'm proud of you my dear.'

'Thank you Gran'mère. I have missed you, though.'

'I know. But you managed without me perfectly well.'

'Did I?'

'You did, my dear.'

'I love you Gran'mère.'

'I love you too, Elise.'

Elise opened her eyes with a start. It had been years since she'd had such a vivid dream. She looked about her. Of course, no one was there. Again she sat back, pleasantly sleepy. The song of the sea was soft and gentle.

'Do you still hear it?' Thomas asked. His presence

neither frightened nor surprised her.

'Yes, the sea still speaks to me,' she told him.

'The song was never ours.'

'Wasn't it?'

'No. The sea is tenacious, constant in its strength. You have the tenacity and constancy that I never had. You were always stronger than me. The song of the sea is rightfully yours – yours and Marcel's.'

'Yes. I'm so sorry, Thomas.'

'I had your love and I threw it away. My own fault. And what I did was unforgivable. Justice was done.'

'I think it was. Goodbye, Thomas.'

She heard an echo from the past. 'Madame de Forêt, I love you. I'll love you forever, and forever started a lifetime ago and continues to the edge of time.'

'Oh, there you are.'

'Are you coming now, Elise?'

'Yes, I'm very tired.'

'Shall we go then?'

'Yes Marcel, I'm ready.'

BIBLIOGRAPHY

An Account of Two Voyages to New England Made During the Years 1638, 1663. John Josselyn, 1865

A People of the Sea. The Maritime History of the Channel Islands. Edited by A.G Jamieson, 1986

A Series of letters, Descriptive of Prince Edward Island. Walter Johnstone, circa 1820, ed. D.C. Harvey

A short account of Prince Edward Island. S.S. Hill, 1839

A Social History of Canada, George Woodcock, 1988

Buildings In The Town And Parish Of St Peter Port. C.E.B Brett, 1975

Canadian Frontier. Ed Brian Antonson, 1976

Channel Island Plant Lore. Brian Bonnard, 1993

Daily Life in the Great Age of Sail. Dorothy Denneen Volo & James M. Volo, 2002

Domestic Life In Early Halifax. Nova Scotia Museum, 1976

Evangeline. Henry Wadsworth Longfellow, 1847

Fisherman Knitting. Michael Harvey & Rae Compton, 1978

From Outpost to Outport: The Jersey Merchant Triangle in the 19th Century. Rosemary E Ommer. 1978

Journal of Charles Robin. Charles Robin, 1767-1774

Halifax Street Names. Edited by Shelagh Mackenzie with Scott Robson, 2002

Halifax, Warden of the North. Thomas H Raddall, 1971

Intimate Fragments, An Irreverent Chronicle of Early Halifax. Edited by Robert E. Kroll, 1985

Isle Madame Stories. Don Boudrot, 2006

Landscape of the Channel Islands. Nigel Jee, 1982

Letter from Captain John Paul Jones to the Marine Committee: Account of his cruise since the 7th current. American Archives

Mi'kmaq Medicines. Laurie Lacey, 1993

More of Peter Girard's Guernsey. Peter J. Girard, 1990

Nova Scotia. Stephan Poole & Colleen Abdullah, 2004

Prince Edward Island/Guernsey Families. Elizabeth and Thane Le Lacheur, 2008

St Martin, Guernsey, Channel Islands. A Parish History from 1204. Richard Strappini, 2004

Storied Shores. A.J.B. Johnstone, 2004

St Peter Port 1680-1830, The History of an International Entrepôt. Gregory Stevens Cox, 1999

St Pierre du Bois, The story of a Guernsey parish and its people. Marie De Garris, 1995

The Canadians. George Woodcock, 1979

The Great Migration – Crossing the Atlantic Under Sail. Basil Greenhil, 1968

The Guernsey Merchants & Their World in the Georgian era. Gregory Stevens Cox, 2009

The History of Guernsey. James Marr, 2001

The Journey of the Mi'kmaq, Wagmatcook Culture & Heritage Centre

The Last Pilgrimage of a Jerseyman to the Gaspé Coast. George Francis Le Feuvre, 1983

The Papers of B G Hawkins. PEI, by kind permission of his daughter Michelle Graham

The Quiet Adventurers of Canada. Marion Turk, 1993

The Richmond Map. 1787

The Seaflower Venture. Phyllis Gertrude Ross, 1979

The Sea was their Fortune, a Maritime History of the Channel Islands. Roy McLoughlin, 1997

Times Past in Guernsey, Alderney, Sark and Herm. Carel Toms, 1985

ACKNOWLEDGMENTS

Guernsey: Gillian Lenfestey, without whom I would have strayed from the path of accuracy. The Priaulx Library, for their unfailingly helpfulness and patience. Janet Rolfe, Pippa McCathie & Guernsey Writers for believing in me.

Jersey: Anna Baghiani, Librarian, The Société Jersiaise; home of all things Jersey.

Isle Madame: The Isle Madame Historical Society for making us so welcome. Louis Boudreau, for taking us to Jerseyman's Island. John MacLeod Langley for taking us out to Île de la Saint-Famille, now Chapel Island.

Chéticamp: Jean Chaisson, Chéticamp Fishing Museum for our own private viewing. La Société St Pierre and Charles D Roach based at Les Trois Pignons Museum. Mathias Poirier, Chéticamp Camp Ground for letting me use his name and explaining how he got it.

Saint-Pierre: Judy Madden at the Nicolas Denys Museum whose assistance was so willingly given.

Halifax: Garry Schutlak, archivist, Archive Centre, Halifax. Craig Pierro, Cultural co-ordinator, Wagmatcook Culture and Heritage Centre, who put me straight on Mi'kmaq culture. Ken Hiltz, Old time Halifax Maps, for his generosity.

Prince Edward Island: Thane & Elizabeth Le Lacheur, who have become valued friends. Wade Hawkins, for introducing me to Thane and Elizabeth. David Hume, a fount of local knowledge.

I am especially grateful to the amazing team at my Publishers, Cranthorpe Millner, for their faith in me and their support.

And above all: Ian Larby; supporter, critic, sounding-board, proof-reader, road manager, laptop carrier, friend and husband.